T0365095

THE LEADER *of the* WORLD

The Last Messenger

E. Mann

Balboa Press books may be ordered through booksellers or by contacting:

Balboa Press
A Division of Hay House
1663 Liberty Drive
Bloomington, IN 47403
www.balboapress.com.au
1 (877) 407-4847

Printed in the United States of America.

ISBN: 978-1-4525-1237-2 (sc)
ISBN: 978-1-4525-1238-9 (e)

Balboa Press rev. date: 12/05/2013

PROLOGUE

Blackness overtook Daniel, and he found himself hurtling through a black void and heading out somewhere in space, out amongst the brilliance of the never-ending universe. Approaching him in the distance was a round light with a streaking tail. It headed straight for another larger, brighter sphere, which appeared familiar to him; he recognised it—the moon. A comet was on a collision course with Earth's moon.

He watched as the two hit, and he saw the surface of the moon and the comet become one in a blaze of shattered debris. The entangled mass went out of orbit like a ball being pitched in a baseball game, and his heart sank as he saw the direction it headed. The blue ball of Earth was the target. He saw the jumbled mass hit Earth, and the whole agglomerate headed out through space towards a bright fireball thousands of times bigger than the orb heading towards it.

CHAPTER 1

Previously—January 1, 2025

Flinders Ranges, South Australia

"I am the leader. I am the leader."

"Look, mate, calm down. Just calm down. Relax. Take a sip of water. Slowly now. That's the boy. Have another sip. Good. Now, just take it easy, okay, mate?"

Close by, behind a bush, black hands cautiously parted the thick shrub, and peering eyes keenly surveyed the scene before them.

Two white men were on a small bush track. One was completely naked and lying on his back, while the other, in khaki shorts and shirt, knelt next to him and propped up his head to help him sip water from a well-used army water bottle. The man with the bottle eventually stood up and revealed a full shock of blonde hair as he took off his bushman's hat and wiped down his sweaty brow with his handkerchief.

In the dry and glaring midday heat, the young man sat down on a rock beside the track, under the shade of a leafy eucalyptus tree. He looked at the strange man stretched out on the ground in front of him. He was curious as to how this naked man had ended up in this isolated place.

This day was turning out to be a lot more eventful than he had envisioned. The outback police officer, Peter Brand, had never encountered anything like this during his career with the force.

It was the first day of the new year, and if it was an indication of how the rest of the year was going to shape up, then it was going to be a year to remember.

He had been stationed in Port Augusta in the state of South Australia for nearly five years, ever since graduating from the police academy in Adelaide. Patrolling the local area of approximately ten thousand square kilometres was his primary duty. This was a country for men—harsh but beautiful.

Brand loved travelling from town to town, helping the local forest rangers. He particularly liked the Flinders Ranges; these ranges extended for over 430 kilometres and contained three national parks. There, he could lose himself among the rugged beauty of the purple mountains. His youth and his bronzed good looks attracted many a young lady, but he still preferred his own company somewhere out in the bush, away from the human race.

The local Aborigines were his main concern, and they kept him busy. Peter considered them a lost cause with no real prospect of a future in their own land. Most of them coped with the white man's rule by drinking alcohol. The invading whites, with their superior attitude, considered the blacks not much better than animals. They stripped them of their humanity and their rights as the indigenous people of the land. The Aboriginals had no concept of ownership. They were simply the caretakers of the land and were thankful for the bounty it provided.

That day, Brand had made his way to Wilpena Pound in the Flinders Ranges National Park, approximately 250 kilometres from his base at Port Augusta. This reserve lay just over 400 kilometres north of Adelaide, and the Pound was one of the most extraordinary geological formations in Australia. It was a vast natural amphitheatre ringed with sheer cliffs and jagged rocks. The Pound floor was flat and covered with trees and grass. To Peter, it appeared as if the land and been formed by a meteor that had fallen to Earth millions of years ago.

He was investigating a complaint from German hikers camping in the area. The young couple claimed that four young Aboriginals had attacked and robbed them. Brand surmised that the German tourists had probably just been intimidated by the sight of the youths and fled, leaving their belongings behind.

He had driven his four-wheel drive as far as he could along the main track to the Pound. He set up his one-man tent on a hilly outcrop and took off on foot through the smaller tracks towards the hikers' campground.

The refreshing breeze blew gently on this torrid day. It helped alleviate his hopelessness in finding the young men. They were undoubtedly watching him. He would only find them if their curiosity got the better of them and they showed themselves.

Peter stopped to look intently at a haze glittering through the trees in front of him. It was a strange yet beautifully coloured sight. The haze started to concentrate at one spot on the track ahead and thickened downward and inwards, changing shape as it whirled around. Even with his attention focused on the phenomena before him, Peter noticed that the breeze had stopped. All was unusually and absolutely still. Yet something made the thick mist move. He could not hear a sound, not even the familiar cawing of the many crows that inhabited the area.

It took him a few moments to comprehend that the haze was no longer there. Something else had taken its place among the trees—a solid and pale object, not an animal.

The apparition started to move unsteadily, and as it staggered through the shrub and headed towards him, he stood his ground and waited.

Brand soon saw a man completely naked, reeling from side to side, coming slowly closer. Staring ahead with glazed eyes—seemingly unaware that Peter was there—the man mumbled, "I am the leader. I am the leader," as he walked past the astonished onlooker.

"Who in fucking hell are you?" Peter yelled in a frightened and quivering voice.

The naked man stopped, unsteady on his feet, turned around, and, for the first time, appeared to notice Peter standing on the track. When the man opened his mouth to speak, his eyes rolled back into his head, and he collapsed to the ground.

Peter bent over the man and began reviving him with sips of water.

"What's your name, and what happened to you? Where are your clothes?" Peter asked. "How long have you been out here?"

The man looked up at him in a vague and puzzled trance. Peter noticed the man's eyes were the biggest and the most vivid blue he had ever seen. It seemed as if two chunks of the clear sky had broken off and imbedded themselves in his face.

In that region, afternoons in January were stifling, while the nights could be freezing. "Were you out here last night?" Peter queried.

Receiving no reply from the hapless man, he decided to stop any further interrogation for now. The stranger had a serene look about him, with long, wavy dark hair and a long beard. Odder still, his hair and beard were perfectly washed and combed. His pale body was proportionate—not overly big, but muscular. There was not one grain of dirt on him. He looked as though he had just stepped out of a bath. Peter found it difficult to estimate how old the man was, but he figured he was roughly his own age: twenty-nine, maybe a bit older.

This is weird, he thought. Peter felt uneasy about admiring this seemingly perfect man. "Come on, mate. I'd better get you to the car and get a helicopter out here. You look physically okay, but I'm no doctor. You may need to be in a hospital."

He helped the man to his feet, and they started trekking back to Peter's camp, which was three kilometres away. With the naked man walking in front, Peter swatted at the endless annoying flies. "How come these bastards aren't pestering you?" he called up to the man. The little pests buzzed all around Peter, but the mystery man was free from them.

No answer came—not that Peter had really expected one anyway. Seemingly unaware of what was happening around him, the man walked on, still mumbling about being the leader.

A skinny black hand reached out from behind a tree and shoved the back of Peter just as he stepped clumsily over a log lying across the path. Peter tripped and fell heavily. His head slammed into a low-hanging branch, and as he struggled to stand up, blackness overtook him, and he fell unconscious to the ground.

Within what seemed seconds, the light returned, and he struggled to his feet, using the closest support. It took awhile to realise he had used a car fender to help him stand. He was back at the camp, next to his gold-coloured four-wheel drive.

Peter quickly looked around and couldn't see anyone. *Did I dream up that strange man?*

He staggered around the back and then to the side of the vehicle, where he discovered the dream had indeed been real. The man was still there, gazing into the side driving mirror. Intrigued, Peter quietly watched him for a couple minutes. The stranger had adjusted the mirror to get a better view of his own image, and with a disbelieving expression, he continued to peer intently at his face. Next, the fingers of his left hand became the focus of his attention as he opened and closed them several times.

Impatiently, Peter Brand interrupted the man's fascination with himself. "How the hell did I get back here—did you carry me?"

The man slowly turned around and smiled, revealing a set of pure white and perfect teeth.

"No, Peter, you walked here." The reply came from a calm and soft-spoken man.

"Walked? I can't remember walking," said Peter, puzzled. "And how do you know my name—did you go through my pockets?"

The man gave an answer that confused Peter even more: "You were thinking of your mother, and she called your name." He stopped, and an intense look came over him. "Please don't bother getting any help for me; I just want a lift to the nearest town."

Reaching into the console of his car, Peter drew out a packet of cigarettes and a lighter, but as he tried to light the flame, he found that the cigarette in his mouth would not light. He tried several times to no avail; he swapped the cigarette for a fresh one, but that too would not light.

"That is a dreadful habit—bad for you and all those around you, as well as the environment. I don't like you smoking," the mysterious man admonished Peter, who glared angrily at him, but he mellowed almost instantly and turned his thoughts to the present dilemma.

Peter abandoned the search for the Aboriginal youths, and after clothing the man with a spare pair of old, frayed khaki shorts and a soiled white T-shirt, he packed his gear and decided to head back to Port Augusta. *There is a good hospital there, and although the poor guy appears quite well physically, he probably needs psychiatric help.*

He settled himself behind the wheel and started the engine, and then, remembering the blow he had suffered on his forehead when he had fallen, he looked down onto the top of his shirt and saw it was covered in blood. Turning the rear-vision mirror towards his face, he grimaced at the thought of what damage he had sustained; but what he saw was far from what he had expected. He peered at his reflection in disbelief; not a scratch showed on his face, there was no blood, and he couldn't even feel the slightest bump.

On their way, Peter ran many questions through his mind that he wanted to ask his passenger, and as if he knew, the stranger began answering some of his thoughts.

"This may sound strange, but I know very little of what happened to me. I can't seem to remember my name, and the one thing that keeps going through my mind is that I am the leader."

"What do you mean by 'the leader'?"

"I'm in charge; I am the leader."

"Okay! For now, your name is Leader." Peter conceded that this man was definitely demented. "Okay! Leader, how did you end up at Wilpena Pound, and where is your car?"

"Peter, please believe me—I really don't know much more, except I think that I have an important job."

"You are on a job?" Peter repeated Leader's words sarcastically. "What sort of important job?"

The dazed man gazed out in front of him and seemed to be waiting for another instalment of his story to enter his mind. "I am not sure what is happening to me, but I believe there is a task I must complete." He hesitated and slowly turned to face Peter. "First, I am going to become rich and powerful and then save you all."

"You don't have a cent on you, and you didn't even have a shirt on your back until I gave you one—and you are going to be rich and powerful?" Peter couldn't help laughing out loud.

The bearded man's blue eyes opened wide, as if he had become aware of a new revelation. "You finding me was no accident. You're meant to help me."

"Me! Help you? The best help I can give you is to introduce you to a psychiatrist," Peter mocked. "And another thing: Did you push me, or did I just fall back there on the track? I could have sworn that I felt somebody push me in the back, but it couldn't have been you; you were in front of me. Look, just answer this one question and I'll be happy for now: How did I get to my car? You did say I walked?"

"Yes, you walked," he replied in a quiet and humble tone.

"But how could I have walked? I was unconscious, wasn't I?"

"I made you walk."

"You made me?"

"Yes," insisted the man.

"Let's give up on that one too." An agitated Peter surrendered.

Darkness approached and quickly overtook the light of day. Anxious to get to town, Peter sped down a windy descent, ignoring the signs warning "Beware of Kangaroos next five kilometres" on the side of the road.

"Stop the car—*now*!" screamed the passenger.

The last urgent word reverberated through Peter's ears, giving him such a fright that he automatically slammed his foot onto the brake pedal, bringing the car to a halt at a bend in the road.

"What the fuck are you trying to do—kill us?" Peter screamed at Leader, who calmly pointed his finger towards the front. Peter looked back to the road and saw a mob of about twenty kangaroos; the car's headlights dazzled them as they casually hopped across the road.

"Shit!" exclaimed Peter. "We would have ploughed straight into them if you hadn't seen them—good call."

Maybe he isn't as nutty as he makes out, mused Peter. *My God, he must have fantastic eyesight. Shit, come to think of it, he must see around corners.*

"Peter, I need to ask you a stupid question—a question that I am frightened to ask because I don't think I am going to believe the answer that you will give me."

But then again, maybe I'm wrong, thought Peter. *He's starting to sound nutty again.*

"What date is it"? the man asked hesitantly.

"January first. Most people get a holiday today, but not me—duty calls," Peter answered as he reached over to turn off the car's air conditioning.

"The year—I meant the year," the scared individual clarified.

"It's 2025, of course." Peter rolled his eyes upward and started driving again.

After about ten minutes of silence, Leader began muttering again, and Peter could make out some of the things he said.

"Daniel. Daniel—that's my name. I have been gone for sixteen years, and that makes me fifty-six; it only seems like yesterday. It has to be a dream; it has to be."

The distraught man would mutter a few words and then fall into complete silence, only to start his muttering again as they travelled over two hundred kilometres to reach Port Augusta.

Peter realised that he should take Leader to the lock-up or the hospital. But he couldn't be bothered; with the headache he had developed from the lack of nicotine, he figured he wouldn't be able to cope with all the paperwork this situation would entail—not that night anyway. He decided to stop at a local hotel for a well-earned beer and a meal. It dawned on him that he had not eaten since breakfast, and God knew the last time his passenger had eaten.

Peter bought himself a fresh packet of cigarettes, immediately opened it, and popped a cigarette into his mouth. Daniel waited as Peter headed for the glassed-in corner room specially set up to cater to the outcast smokers. To his frustration, he still could not light his cigarette. Peter approached one of the smokers and politely asked him for a light. The man obliged and tried unsuccessfully to light Peter's new cigarette. As the agitated Peter walked back towards Leader, he heard screams coming from the smokers' room he had just left. Water from the ceiling's fire extinguishers was spraying down on the smokers.

Surprisingly, Leader ate little; he just nibbled at his pasta dish.

Maybe he wasn't out there for very long after all, thought Peter. Although weary of him, he couldn't help admiring Leader; he exuded confidence and trust.

"My name is Daniel." He reached out and shook Peter's hand. "And I thank you for believing me trustworthy."

The young constable felt that his privacy had just been invaded.

"Okay, that's a good start. Daniel is a nice name, and what's your surname?" asked Peter.

"I can't recall. A lot of things are coming back to me now—things that I don't understand."

"Okay, it's now Daniel Leader," Peter said with a little laugh.

A glazed look came over Daniel. "Strange—that seems so familiar."

Musical sounds coming from the next room aroused Daniel's curiosity. Peter explained that the hotel was a licensed poker-machine venue.

"Do you mind if I play?" Daniel asked.

"Gambling on those is for fools—much better on the horses," Peter advised.

"Lend me a dollar, and I will give you back a hundred."

Peter laughed as he watched Daniel enter the pokies room, but within minutes, he returned and placed a hundred-dollar bill in front of him.

"How much did you win?" the surprised Peter asked.

"Oh, about seven hundred dollars. Well, that's a start."

Taking a stranger to his house was not the usual trend for Peter, but he made an exception that night. His rented house had plenty of room, and in reality, this guy wasn't a prisoner, just a lost soul. To his dismay, at his own home and even after discarding the lighter for matches, Peter still couldn't light his cigarette.

Parkes Observatory in the State of New South Wales, Australia

A young woman, barely twenty years of age, excitedly ran along a corridor and into an office with a sign marked "Director" displayed on the door.

The elderly goateed man sitting at his desk with his head buried in some documents looked up at her from the top of his reading glasses, sarcastically shook his head, and calmly said, "Clara, have you heard of knocking?"

"Sorry! Sorry, Professor Morey, but I think you should come and see this," the young lady requested insistently. She ran back to her post at the radio telescope and cocked her eye onto the small eyepiece that abutted the massive telescope pointing to the heavens. The grin on her face widened as she found what she was looking for. With its sixty-four-metre dish outside, which was the largest individual instrument in this telescope, and working in conjunction with another two radio dishes at two other sites across the state, this massive radio telescope had been used to track space probes, besides its use for astronomical discoveries. As soon as she heard the elderly man approaching, she called out, "There! It's still there, Professor—have a look." Clara's face reflected her obvious excitement.

The professor took the young woman's seat and looked up at the night sky, and within seconds, he too started to get keyed up.

"Clara, you beauty, I think you have made a new discovery. There are no known comets due in that area at this time of the year." He thought for a moment and then eagerly continued. "Clara, let's start getting some coordinates; maybe we are the first to see it."

Sergeant Roberts was not too impressed with Peter. "You should have brought him here last night; my God, man, you know nothing about this bloke. For all you know, he could be a mass murderer."

Roberts only had two years to go before his retirement, and he resented having to work his last years in a country town. He disliked the young man, mainly for his contentment in working in a town like Port Augusta, and he didn't hide it from Peter.

"Just get the paperwork done, and after that, take him over to the hospital for a check-up," Roberts ordered.

There wasn't much personal detail Peter could write down about Daniel, and the sergeant was again unimpressed.

"You are telling me that you don't even know your name?" He snorted at Daniel.

"It's Leader, I think—it's Daniel Leader," the bearded man replied.

"Daniel Leader—now, there is a familiar name," Roberts muttered, almost to himself. "Did you ever live in Adelaide?"

"Can't recall," he replied.

"Constable Brand, run the name Daniel and with the surname spelled L-e-e-d-e-r through the system, and concentrate on South Australia and particularly the Adelaide area. When I was stationed there, I remember a fellow by that name just disappeared without a trace. The only problem is that I'm talking of over fifteen years ago, so I would have imagined he would be much older than this joker. But who knows? If it isn't him, maybe he knows something about his disappearance."

To Peter's surprise, the sergeant was right; there had been a missing person by that name. Daniel Leeder had been a wealthy man, aged forty, who ran an engineering empire with employees Australia wide. He was a wanted felon—wanted for the murder of his wife.

One item on the report stirred Peter's imagination: the wanted man's abandoned car had been found at Wilpena Pound. A photo attached with the report showed a dark-haired, clean-shaven man, and with some imagination, taking away the thick beard and long hair, he did have an uncanny resemblance to the man at the station. The eyes of the man in the photo were blue, but they were certainly not as large and vivid as the ones of this Daniel Leader.

Roberts was pleased with himself. A discovery like this would be the pinnacle of his career. Solving a cold murder case and the mystery of Daniel Leeder's disappearance would make those bastards in Adelaide take notice.

"Right, first we keep this to ourselves until we can come up with some answers. Although this fellow only looks around thirty, he does resemble that photo somewhat; you never know—he may be related. Maybe he had plastic surgery and it's actually him." The sergeant pondered his next move for a few moments.

"Peter, get him fingerprinted, and then take him to the hospital, get him checked out, and get a blood sample for DNA testing." As an afterthought, he added, "And two more things: take him to the dental clinic for teeth X-rays, and after that, take him to that psychiatrist, Henry Cohen, at the medical clinic. See if he can get a bit more info out of him."

Daniel had no need to be admitted at the hospital. The check-up proved him to be in excellent health; his blood pressure and his pulse rate were those of an athlete. The physician repudiated the thought that this man could be a fifty-six-year-old man.

The dentist was also amazed at the condition of his teeth. In his twenty-seven years of practicing dental care, he had not seen a person with such perfectly formed and healthy teeth.

The psychiatrist had to determine his mental condition, and the hospital arranged an appointment for that afternoon with Mr. Cohen. They assured Peter that they would urgently test the blood samples they had taken and were hoping to have the results of the tests by the next day.

With some time to kill, Peter took Daniel to lunch. No sooner had they sat down outside the cafe, when Peter leered at Daniel and asked him a question he needed to ask: "You insist that you are Daniel Leeder, so if you are, did you kill your wife?"

"Peter, I can't even recall ever having one."

Daniel entertained himself by watching the crowd going by. He appeared to be perturbed by the drunkard Aboriginals who were either sitting on the footpath or on the grass in the park across the street. They seemed to fight and argue amongst each other and, at the same time, completely ignore the white people who walked past them.

Daniel turned his attention to the newspaper Peter was reading and asked if he could have the sports section.

"You're getting more normal by the minute," Peter said.

After a quick perusal of the racing guide, Daniel said, "Peter, please take all this money I won on the pokies and put a bet on a horse for me."

"Look, Daniel, you were just lucky last night. You'll lose it all."

"Please trust my judgement, and it is my money, so I insist. Please put it all on race two, horse four, just for a win only."

Peter looked up the race guide and laughed. "You want to bet on a twenty-to-one shot just for a win."

"Yes, please, Peter—I insist."

"Okay, Daniel—after all, it is your money."

On the way to the psychiatrist, Peter placed Daniel's bet at the local betting shop.

In the waiting room, Peter pretended to read an outdated *TIME* magazine as he watched Daniel staring at a tall, skinny black youth sitting across the room. The young man had become agitated when they had first entered the room. His wide nostrils were fluttering in and out with every breath he took, but quickly, he settled and became calm. He sat there entranced, as if bewitched by Daniel, and to the amazement of Peter, the two seemed to be silently communicating. As he watched the two staring at each other, the serene atmosphere that now engulfed the room overtook Peter's senses; the stillness made the rest of the world seem to no longer exist.

The large, gentle smile on the youth's face degenerated into a sullen look as the door to the doctor's room opened, breaking the silence, and an older, big-bellied black man emerged. The stench of alcohol filled the room, and with a sneer, the big man looked towards the two white men; when his gaze locked onto Daniel's eyes, without saying a word, the unshaven man sat next to the black youth. Together they stared at Daniel, and the three appeared to be transfixed in a silent conversation.

From the open door, a short, balding man in his mid thirties, wearing thick eyeglasses and rubbing the tip of his hooked nose, observed the people in his waiting room. A few minutes passed before the man, in a tight-fitting blue suit, interrupted the serenity by asking Peter to come into his office.

The eyes of the two Aboriginals lost contact with Daniel's, and they quickly stood and walked towards the exit. Without speaking a word, they opened the door and disappeared into the hallway.

After Peter explained the situation, Mr. Cohen advised Peter to leave him alone with Daniel, as he needed to assess whether the doctor/patient confidentiality applied in this case. The psychiatrist stretched out his right hand and shook hands with his new patient. A pleasant tingle went through his body that made him quiver all over; he opened and closed his eyes several times, which made him blush and feel uncomfortable.

Peter headed for the door, but Daniel insisted that the constable should stay at the interview. Mr. Cohen conveniently forgot the instructions he had given Peter earlier and now had no objection to him staying. He felt intimidated by this new patient.

"Daniel, before we start, can you tell me what went on in the waiting room?" Mr. Cohen enquired rather nervously. "I couldn't help noticing you and the other two men somehow made quite an impression on each other."

Daniel's explanation baffled the two listeners. "Jimmy was telling me about his father; his abuse of alcohol has ruined their whole family. They have been through a lot of suffering, especially his mother, by his hands. I reassured them that there is a solution to every problem and told them that they need to take control of their life and work together to resolve their troubles."

"And you said all that without saying a word?" a wide-eyed Peter butted in.

"Well, it's a common problem with some of the Aboriginals, and that's why a lot of them come to see me under the directions of the courts," Cohen explained. "But you are saying they told you all that without a word being uttered between you?"

"Yes!" Daniel replied.

The bemused psychiatrist changed the subject. "Now let's get on with the problem at hand—namely you, Daniel." He looked down at the notes he had scribbled on a writing pad after his brief conversation with Peter.

"You can't remember what has happened to you and how you ended up at Wilpena Pound."

The uncertain man hesitated with his reply. "If you had asked me that question yesterday, I would not have hesitated in my reply to you, but today I have a strange notion of what may have happened to me—but I am not willing to divulge it to you right at this minute."

"Why wouldn't you want to divulge it?" enquired Cohen. "Did you do something that might incriminate you or something that you are ashamed of?"

"No! Absolutely not—or at least I don't believe so." Daniel shook his head and appeared to be deep in thought as he persisted with his answer. "The reason I won't tell you what I believe happened to me is that you will not believe me. I would like you to find out by probing my subconscious; in that way, not only might you believe me, but more importantly, I may believe it too."

"You want to be hypnotised?"

"Yes! As a matter of fact, I insist on it."

Henry was having difficulty focusing as he scribbled notes on his writing pad. He took his glasses off and cleaned them as he listened; putting them back to his face, he found that the clean glasses made no difference, so he took them off and put them on his desk. To his surprise, he could see more clearly with them off.

"Peter, seeing I am going to use hypnotism, I think I have to reconsider you staying; it would not be prudent in case my patient incriminates himself."

Peter was reluctant to leave the room; he did not want to abandon Daniel or be left out of something he had started, but he understood.

An hour passed, and as Peter reached for money in his pocket to pay the waitress at the coffee shop, he came across the ticket for the bet he had placed for Daniel. At the same time, he pulled out a cigarette to light, but with one look at it, he couldn't be bothered anymore; it was a filthy habit anyway. Leaving his packet of cigarettes and his lighter on the table, he strolled down to the betting office.

Henry Cohen asked Daniel to sit in the waiting room while he talked to Peter, who had already taken a seat in the doctor's office.

"I really don't know where to start with all this," the puzzled man began. "If you or your office is expecting a quick written report on Daniel's condition, forget it. I would have no idea what to say; even if I could, I wouldn't dare. I don't even know what to make of it all myself, let alone make out a report. How can I even have the slightest inkling inside me that I should believe him? Am I stupid or something?" He talked to himself more so than to Peter. He walked to a mirror hanging on one of the walls and looked long and hard at himself, especially his eyes, and on noticing the reflection of the bemused young officer sitting on a chair looking up at him, he turned abruptly away from the mirror and faced Peter.

"Look at my face; this is the first time I haven't worn glasses in over twenty-five years. My eyesight is back to normal." He walked around the room restlessly. "I shook hands with him, and I felt the strangest sensation go through my whole body, and now I have perfect eyesight." Henry threw his hands into the air as if to say, *I don't understand.* He stopped abruptly in front of Peter and flopped down in the chair beside him.

"Peter, do you have any idea what he told me?" Henry asked.

"Doc, at the moment, I am likely to believe anything you may say about him. I can tell you one thing for certain: he is no ordinary man." Peter shook his head and laughed nervously. "There sure is a lot of head shaking going on in this room, and there is only just the two of us." Peter laughed once more, but when he spoke again, he had a serious tone in his voice. "There is something there"—Peter pointed to the waiting room—"that is beyond explanation," Peter confided. "What has he told you that has you in such a flap, Doc?"

Cohen continued, "Under hypnosis, he told me a story, and although it wasn't fully coherent, I understood the gist of it. He said that about sixteen years ago, he drove up to the Flinders Ranges and went walkabout in the Wilpena Pound Crater. He intended to disappear and never be found again, as he felt he had nothing to live for, and for what seemed weeks, he wandered through the bush, completely lost. He had no food, water, or camping gear, so he had to endure the sweltering heat of the day and the freezing cold of the nights."

The doctor hesitated, gathering his thoughts, which gave Peter a chance to pass a comment. "Well, the guy we suspect him to be left his car at the Pound."

Peter hadn't mentioned the murdered wife to Cohen, but he couldn't resist asking, "Did he mention a wife?"

"That was one of the questions I asked him, but no, he couldn't remember anything about a wife."

With a quizzical look at Peter, he went on with his story. "Daniel claims that his body—or maybe his soul—just melded into and became part of the very natural environment that surrounded him. He became part of the elements—the very air itself—and a part of a natural energy that is beyond description or within the realm of human understanding. He likened it to a drop of water falling into the ocean; it automatically becomes part of that ocean. You can't distinguish that one drop from the rest of the water; he knew he was there, but he couldn't separate himself from his surroundings. Time did not exist for him as he travelled wherever the rushing air went and watched the ever-changing world go by. Even watching the grass grow was exciting; he could see the blades of grass growing, the minute details of leaves in the trees being formed. Throughout the years, he traversed the entire planet many times, all the while being completely re-educated by some power. This power or energy, although we know it and we live with it every moment of our life, is still beyond our comprehension. Although he can't describe it, he says that it is what we know as nature. He says it's the creator of the human race and it is interconnected with the natural energies of all the millions of worlds throughout the universe."

Peter had been listening intently and leaning forward with his hands clasped together; he held them over his mouth and chin. He wanted to ask questions, but Henry was so engrossed in his retelling of Daniel's story that Peter decided to wait until he had finished.

"Daniel claims that he is the newest of all the many messengers our Creator has sent us throughout our evolution. These messengers have altered our lives dramatically, but not always in the directions the Creator wanted. We either misunderstood or corrupted its intentions. Daniel's mission is to mould the world into one and bring it back into line with the Creator's original intention; how he achieves this is up to him." He paused and looked at Peter, almost pleading for help.

"There is a word that comes close to describing what he is saying, and that is *animism*, which is a belief that all natural objects and the universe itself possess a soul." Henry again stopped. He flung his arms out to his side and clapped his hands together as if to say *What the hell?* and went on with his summation. "He told me all this while under hypnosis, so he has to be both completely insane and living in a world of fantasy, or he is telling the truth. Peter, how can I, as an educated man, believe all this? It's as if I am being compelled to believe it and, worse, to help him."

The door opened, and Daniel appeared in the doorway. He stood there, and the three stared at each other until Daniel lifted his arms out to his side in a pleading position. "I need your help. I believe I am Daniel Leeder, but there is no positive way I can prove it. And as I can't prove my identity; I am a man who does not exist."

He looked at the two puzzled men, and in a reassuring voice, he continued with his tale. "You and more like you will help me. I am the only solution to this messed-up, complicated world. It needs one advisor, one ruler, a fair and just one, who must take control and make decisions for the good of all on this planet. The world needs to be put back into some sort of order, and it's my mission to do this. This planet is in peril; it is being destroyed by the human inhabitants, and the time we have to reverse this tide is quickly running out."

There was no reaction from the two listeners; they were too stunned to retort to what they were hearing.

"We have a limited time to do this. What the actual time frame is, I do not know, but I do know that the Creator has lost all patience with this speck of dust we call Earth, and I believe we do not have time to waste." He paused momentarily, and a look of concentration came over him. "Peter, I know your doubts about me are abating, and I will reinforce them further. You collected the winnings on that horse I asked you to back, and you have a cheque for twelve thousand six hundred and six dollars in your shirt pocket, showing you as the payee. Please bank it into your account."

"How did you know I had picked up the winnings?" asked an astonished Peter as he gazed at the cheque, which showed the exact amount Daniel had quoted.

Ignoring the question, Daniel unrelentingly continued. "Henry, I want you to go and buy a lottery ticket. If we win, will you both believe me and help me?"

"Help you!" the astounded and almost speechless Henry uttered.

"To save our world." An enthusiastic Daniel raised his closed-fisted right arm as a sign of triumph.

Peter, caught up in Daniel's excitement, called out, "There is a major lotto draw tonight. It's actually telecast on TV. Tell you what, mate—you pick tonight's lottery numbers, and I am yours. We'll get a system-eight quick-pick ticket; that way, the numbers are picked at random, and we only have to get six out of eight numbers to win. That will make it easier for you." A cynical Peter rolled his eyes towards the ceiling.

Henry glanced at Peter and acrimoniously turned to Daniel. "Just as a matter of interest, why are you picking Peter and me to help you?"

"The answer is quite simple: you both are good people, and you, Henry, being Jewish, might come in handy."

Henry was too intrigued with the whole conversation to get Daniel to clarify what being Jewish had to do with anything.

They had agreed to meet that night for a barbecue at Peter's place, and a grinning Peter welcomed Henry to his humble abode. "Well, mate, did you bring our winning ticket?" He snickered sarcastically.

"It's right here." Henry reached inside his shirt pocket and pulled the ticket out. As he went to pass it over to Peter, a gust of wind blew through the open front door and carried the ticket from Henry's hand onto Daniel's lap.

Daniel rose from the couch he was sitting on in the corner of the lounge room, casually looked at the numbers, and walked over to the two perplexed men and handed the ticket back to Henry.

The three of them were sitting on the back veranda, sipping on beers, when they heard a noise coming from the rear of the backyard. It sounded as if someone had scaled the back paling fence and jumped down onto the lawn.

"Who's there?" Peter called out apprehensively.

"I want to see Daniel," a quiet, frightened voice said from the dark.

At first, they saw a set of large white teeth, and as the intruder emerged closer to the veranda, the figure of a black man took shape under the light.

"Jimmy!" called Henry. "What are you doing here?"

"Jimmy? Who is Jimmy?" Peter demanded.

"The Aboriginal boy, Jimmy Wirra—the boy from my clinic you saw today."

"Ah, Jimmy," Daniel said. "Come up here; glad you came, my friend."

The thin, lanky young man, in a wrinkled black shirt and grey shorts, reluctantly made his way onto the veranda and nervously shook hands with Peter when introduced to him.

"I invited Jimmy here," Daniel assured the others. "He is to be my third helper."

"You're telling us that he knows what you're about?" queried the doubting Henry.

"Yes, his mind is so open and fresh, not corrupted by greed or by material gain. He and his people are more attuned with nature than probably any other ethnic race in this world. He will follow what he deems to be true, without question, and will make an excellent leader to his people," Daniel commented.

The three sat around the television set, waiting for the 8:30 draw. Jimmy, uncomfortable inside, took his can of Coke and plateful of lamb chops outside and sat on the steps leading up to the veranda. Henry and Peter were edgy as they sat on the three-seater couch with their feet stretched out on the coffee table in front of them; they kept glancing at the single seat to their left, where Daniel sat. He was motionless, in a state of meditation.

How can I be so anxious about all this stupidity? What the hell am I doing here? I'm off like lightning as soon as the draw is complete, Henry thought to himself as he looked down at the ticket in his hand. The draw started, and Peter called out the numbers as they were drawn, to ensure Henry wrote them down correctly.

Henry slowly stood up and turned pale; with his mouth wide open, he collapsed onto his knees. Without even a thought for Henry, Peter reached down and snatched the ticket from his hand, and with a slow and deliberate perusal of the numbers, he walked towards Daniel and said in a whimper, "We won—we got all eight numbers."

They sat gathered together in the lounge room, looking at Daniel with incredulous stares. "This is getting a bit too far-fetched," Peter said, interrupting the peace. "There has to be a logical explanation for all this."

"Peter, I understand your confusion," Daniel agreed. "I too am confused; I am aware that I have been given an enormous responsibility. There is a power building up inside me, and with this power, there is also a powerful compulsion to do what I have to do. I have no doubt that if I don't succeed in my mission, it will be the end."

An agitated Henry jumped to his fee. "All this is now getting me a bit worried. What do you mean by 'the end'?" he yelled at Daniel.

"Henry, please let me try to explain what I comprehend," Daniel persisted as a dejected Henry sat back down next to Peter. "My mind is becoming clearer with each moment that passes." Daniel stood up and stared down at the two restless men.

"Please keep your minds open. I'll keep it as simple as possible, because that is one of the main problems of this world: everything has become so complex. Imagine, if you can, the most powerful energy possible, unfathomable to our minds—an energy source that created itself into what we call the universe. This energy is very similar to what most people believe in anyway. I mean the God or the Allah that so many follow is inexplicable and incomprehensible, and the majority of the world believes that there is something out there—some power or being that created everything imaginable. Now, this energy force could be said to be nature—Mother Nature—as we know it. It has a mind of its own, and it changes our lives and surroundings every moment of the day. Nature is, for the most part, very good to us, and it provides for all our needs." Daniel stressed this point. "This power created many different creatures; there is no reasoning why it did, but it did. Maybe it was testing the potential of these creations. Perhaps the planets, like Earth, are nothing but evolutional testing grounds for the Creator. The creatures evolved to suit the temperament and the nature of the particular planet they inhabited. Humans, as we call ourselves, and every other living thing, including plants, are made of a substance, which suits our planet. There are many forms of living beings, even intelligent lives, on many of the worlds of this never-ending universe, and there were many more that no longer exist. There were creatures on some of the planets in our own solar system, but we are the only ones left. Unfortunately, these creatures were not evolving to the Creator's desires, and they were destroyed, making future room for new evolving creatures. The humans on this planet were and still are the new creatures the Creator saw as being the inhabitants of not just this small planet but also our part of the universe. It wants us to spread to our neighbouring worlds. We now have sent and landed many exploration satellites on a number of the outer planets, and we have landed astronauts on Mars to explore it more thoroughly with a view of starting a settlement there. This is what nature intended for us to do, but it does not want us to spread our war-mongering ways like a cancer throughout the universe. Some of the other planets in our neighbouring galaxies still have beings on them. Some are still at an infancy phase; maybe the Creator will see these as having more potential in inhabiting their part of the universe as well as our own world. There is an array of beings on the countless planets in the millions of galaxies, and some of these beings are just as advanced as humans." Daniel paused and looked deeply at the others.

An intrigued Peter said "I am still trying to understand why this Creator would destroy the creatures it created in the first place."

"Peter, you can relate the destruction of these creatures to the dinosaurs that ruled Earth; they vanished after a time, and we, the *Homo sapiens*, took over. All these beings on these planets, including our dinosaurs, evolved in a direction that the Creator, or nature, did not approve of, or they did not reach the standard that was expected, so they were eventually destroyed. You have to imagine, just as it is written in the Bible, man is made in the image of God. This image is not in appearance but in our physical make-up—atoms. The whole universe is made up of atoms, and the Creator is the universe, so we are part of the Creator's own body. If we humans develop a cancer on our body, we have it cut out, and that is exactly what the Creator has done in the past and is contemplating doing with us now. The human race has become a cancer on the Creator's body, and we are starting to spread. I am the doctor who has been sent to evaluate and maybe cure this illness in order to avoid radical surgery."

Although his audience members were fidgeting, Daniel continued his explanation. "The Creator has put many forms of creatures here that suited the nature of this planet. Slowly, these creatures were guided to develop in a certain direction. We humans slowly evolved from the combination of the cells of the many different creatures, and nature considered us the best creation to rule and further develop this world. The Creator has guided us in the past and is still doing so to this day. By a quirk of nature, some of us are born to develop ideas that will help us grow to the next phase it wants us to achieve. Sometimes the Creator does what it did to me: takes us away, educates, and returns us to pass on this knowledge. A few are given extra powers to achieve the Creator's will, and these people are known as the messengers of God.

"Over the centuries, the Creator has educated many humans to mould our future. We had Buddha, the Indian philosopher who chose to lead his people to peace through suffering and meditation. When the Creator was displeased with the direction our world was taking, It gave Noah the ability to destroy most living things by using the power of nature and then to start afresh. There was Abraham, David, Moses, and many more. Jesus Christ—definitely a very notable messenger. He chose to be gentle; although he had the power to destroy or alter situations at will, Jesus decided to change humans by example and by preaching kindness to the masses, telling them to love each other and to love thy neighbour. Well, that got him a long way—they killed him. But the movement he had started pleased the Creator, and it did not destroy the world. Jesus took a gamble in allowing his own killing to happen. Before he died, he made sure that his followers would continue spreading his teachings, and as we know, from this, the Christian movement started. At first, the Christians were persecuted, but when Christendom took hold, many of them became fanatical about their religion, and they became the persecutors. From there on, wars broke out between different factions of this new religion and the older religions, such as paganism.

"The last well-known prophet or educated human who started a massive following was probably Muhammad, and through his teachings, we have the Koran. In this, he advocated social and economic justice. Unfortunately, for all the good he did, another religion, which also encompassed some of the Christian Bible, began. This new religion took a long time to develop, and when it did, many of the followers also became fanatics about this new belief. This was not the intention of the Creator. It wanted us to live in peace and to develop for the good of the entire world. The Creator doesn't give a damn about what or whom we worship as long as we don't persecute each other or the rest of the world's inhabitants. Over the centuries, It has seen many wars, slavery, starvation, genocide, and much more. In the last couple centuries, we humans have been destroying the balance the Creator fashioned for our planet. It took billions of years to create everything needed by the residents of our world, and it has taken us a few hundred years to destroy it. It is bad enough when different countries are at war, but when even the closest of neighbours or families are at odds with each other, then surely this spells the beginning of the end for the human race. Think of the many wars we have had over our history and how much more proficient we are getting at the mass destruction of our brothers. This has to stop." Daniel thumped the wall in anger. He took a few deep breaths before he composed himself enough to continue.

"The Creator wants this to end, or It will simply destroy the world." Words kept flowing out of a man who genuinely felt disgusted and disturbed with the history of the human race. "I am this new messenger, and I seem to have powers within me that I suspect will grow stronger and stronger as we get closer to the end of our world."

Daniel paused, and a strange and powerful inner strength came over him. "I have chosen to do whatever it takes to save our planet. The Creator chose me to be the new saviour of the world. Why he chose me, I do not know, and it doesn't matter. It is the way it is. If within the short time we have our objectives are not accomplished to the satisfaction of the Creator, I believe that my power, in some way, will be instrumental in the destruction of all." He stopped again, and then in a sad whisper, he continued. "Then the human race will no longer exist anywhere in the universe."

Peter interrupted Daniel's profound speech. "You keep mentioning this short time we have; can you be more specific about this time frame? You say that the Creator has no concept of time, so could this ending of the world not be hundreds of years from now?"

Daniel pondered the question for a moment before replying. "That is a good question, Peter—one that has also come to my mind—and you are right. It could be a hundred years from now, or maybe it could be five minutes from now. I believe the Creator does not want us to know the exact time; if we knew we had a long time, we may not be concerned about changing our ways too soon. And again, if the time was too short, we may not even bother starting any changes and simply wait for death."

Daniel, unrelenting in his tirade, continued. "This latest threat to peace is basically the last straw for our Creator—the threat of a religious war between the Muslims and the non-Muslims, especially Muslims against the Christians and the Jews. If this happens, this world is finished once and for all. The Creator is giving us a last chance." Daniel pointed to himself and, in a cutting voice, continued. "I am that last chance."

For the first time, they noticed Jimmy sitting on the floor, listening; they had been so engrossed in what they were hearing that they had been oblivious to their surroundings. Daniel smiled as Jimmy's dark eyes told him that he understood.

"The first step of our endeavour is to become completely independent, and independence in this world means money. We will achieve this aim by any means possible. Many, like you, will be my helpers—helpers who must do as I bid, as there is no time to waste in arguing with my reasoning. We must change the world to a level acceptable to the Creator."

The exhausted expressions on the faces of his audience made Daniel realise it was time for him to stop and allow them to rest.

Almost in unison, the three new apostles woke up the next morning. They were lying in the lounge room, in the same spots they had been in the night before. They woke from an abnormally deep sleep and with a feeling of having been completely reborn. They went about their business without speaking or even looking at each other; Peter showered and brushed his teeth while Henry sat on the toilet, and as for Jimmy, he went out the back and sat under the veranda to welcome the new day.

Peter and Henry left the house without even saying farewell to Daniel or each other. Their minds were focused on a mission they had dreamed about—a dream so vivid that nothing could deter them from completing it.

Sergeant Roberts was his bombastic self when Peter walked into the station. "Well, what did you do with that character you found?" were his first bitter words.

"I left him at my house," replied Peter meekly as he sat in front of his computer.

"Well, you can keep him; he's not Daniel Leeder," an obviously disappointed man told him. "They had no records of his fingerprints, and the DNA samples were in a complete shambles; they can't figure it out. They reckon the blood sample was contaminated. Also, the dental X-ray was completely different. The weirdest thing, though, is that he has got the most perfect teeth imaginable—never had a filling or anything. Another thing: if you read further through the report, you'll see that the Daniel Leeder we're after had three fingers missing from his left hand."

Peter nodded as he mused over this new information, and then he began typing.

"The pricks in Adelaide don't want us to pursue this any further, so take him over to the welfare group and let them take care of him; just get rid of the bastard," he added.

Peter stopped any further conversation by handing the sergeant the note he had typed. "No, I decided to keep him, so I want to hand in my notice, and there is no need to waste your time trying to talk me out of it. I am finished as from now." And with that, Peter walked out of his chosen career.

Henry was even more abrupt. He simply left a baffling note on the door to his clinic: "My apologies, but I have gone out of business. The world needs saving, so please seek an alternate doctor."

A hesitant young man sat next to Daniel on the steps leading down from the back veranda of Peter's house.

"Daniel, I am sorry for what happened back there in the bush." He was visibly upset as he talked. "I didn't mean to push your friend; I really didn't even know he was a policeman. The two of you made an odd couple—very strange seeing a naked white man out there in the bush—and my mates and I were just trying to scare you for some fun. I didn't really push him that hard, but he suddenly fell very heavily. My friends and I got frightened when we saw all the blood, and that's why we ran away. We didn't rob anyone; the campers ran away when they saw us black fellas. All their stuff is still where they left it, if they go and have a look."

"Jimmy, I know all that; you are a good person, and you are going to make a fine leader for your people to follow," Daniel assured him.

"Me! Leader for my people? I am not leader quality, Daniel. My people will not take notice of me."

"My young friend, if we succeed, you will go down in history as one of the greatest Australian Aboriginals who ever lived, and your people will sing your praises for many centuries. I am expecting a lot from you, Jimmy; you are going to be the one to start our mission, so I am placing a lot of responsibility on you."

Daniel walked with his hand across the nervous youth's back as they talked. "Jimmy, you have to realise that the way of your people has been over for a long time. I hate saying these things to you, but these things must be said, and you know that I speak to you from the heart. We need to set an example for the rest of the world, and the Aboriginal problem, especially alcoholism, is our starting point."

A smile crept over Jimmy's face as he saw his mother sitting with his father, holding his hand on the front steps leading to the small veranda of their run-down shack. This was the first time he'd ever seen his parents smiling and appearing happy with each other, and more importantly, he noticed for the first time they didn't have beer cans in their hands. With teary eyes, Jimmy turned to Daniel, but he was nowhere to be seen. Jimmy walked over to his parents and sat down beside them. No words were spoken.

Within a few minutes, people started to come out of their hovels and sat in the dust in front of the three. Jimmy had always been a quiet person; he was lean and tall, with shining, curly jet-black hair and skin so dark that it glistened in the morning sun. He stood up and faced the small crowd, and the words flowed from his mouth in an easy and soft tone.

"We were a proud race, tall and lean. We wanted for nothing, hunting when we needed food and walking our land at will. We were a free people that owned no land; if anything, the land owned us—it was our mother. Then the whites came, and we welcomed them. We were a race with no concept of land ownership, and they took advantage of this and took possession of our land. They enslaved us and made us work, because they thought we were lazy and that we should be like them. They killed us, and we died by the thousands from their diseases, and they introduced us to their bad habits. They took away our people's pride, and we need to get it back. I look around me at my people and see a race with many drunkards and unhygienic and obese people in dirty and torn clothing. The death rate for our newborns is one of the worst in the world. Although this country once belonged to us, we now only represent a very small proportion of it. We are depending on our conquerors' charity to survive."

The people listened, and most of them drank their cans of beer as they did so.

"Only a few of us have made it in the white man's world. We have had some leaders in politics and the arts and have had many other successful brothers and sisters, mainly in the sporting world. These blacks made it even though the land had become hostile to its own people."

An obese young man stood up from the dirt and offered Jimmy a can of beer. With a sullen look, he shook his head in refusal and went on with his talk.

"Understand this: I am not forgiving or forgetting what the whites did to us. But we cannot turn back the hands of time. We must gather together and grow in the very white man's society that we hate. We must ensure that our children have as much opportunity as the white Australian kids. We need to look to the future. Yes, we must look ahead and put the past behind. This is the only way our future generations will survive in our own land. We will and we must learn from our conquerors, for this is the only way we can reconquer our land and our pride. We will mix with them until they accept us as their equals, as Australians."

Jimmy's father, sensing that his son was done, looked at his wife, and they both stood up almost simultaneously. They walked into their modest home and re-emerged in a few minutes with their arms full of alcoholic drinks. In silence, the people outside watched as they threw their load in the rubbish bins close to the house. The bins were nearly empty, but debris all around them proved the lack of self-respect that had engulfed the settlement.

Jimmy's parents were not finished with simply throwing away their alcohol; they now started to pick up the rubbish and put it into the bins. Jimmy watched with tears in his eyes as the rest of his audience struggled to stand and wandered back to their shacks to emerge again carrying bottles of alcoholic beverages, soft drinks, and packaged junk food. They filled the garbage bins and emptied the drinks onto the grassy areas of the reserve.

An atmosphere of hope filled the air as a lone wedge-tail eagle, as if their ancestors had sent it from the Dreamtime, soared overhead, casting a giant shadow over the people below. Jimmy was pleased with his people, for he knew that this was the beginning.

Two days later, Henry arranged to have his lottery win of over a million dollars credited to his bank account, and afterwards, he met up with Daniel, Jimmy, and Peter. Dark, heavy clouds hung low over the town as they sat together in the park near the shopping centre and planned their next move. They needed to establish their headquarters in a bigger city, where they would be inconspicuous.

Henry and Peter agreed with Daniel that the city of Melbourne, in the state of Victoria, would be the best place for them, but Jimmy had to remain in Port Augusta and work amongst his own people.

"Henry, give me some money, please," Daniel said. "I think I might need to buy some clothing; I am sick of going around in these hand-me-downs from Peter."

"The strange thing about those clothes I gave you," exclaimed Peter, "is that they seem as new as the day I originally bought them. I am sure the shorts had a small tear near the right pocket, but I can't see it now."

Daniel and his three followers entered the local clothes store across the street from the park. The two salesmen welcomed the three white men, and one attended to them while the other devoted his time to watching Jimmy's every move. Daniel was dismayed at this but was proud that the young man had not lost his smile.

They emerged half an hour later with Daniel spotlessly dressed in a white shirt under a white coat, with white shoes below his immaculate white trousers. His long, flowing beard made it difficult to tell if he had an opened-necked shirt or if he had a tie around the collar.

The salesmen were pleased that they had finally sold the ghastly white suit; it had been in the shop for over two years. They couldn't believe how perfectly it had fit the customer; it was as if it had been tailor made for him and he had just picked it up.

The four headed for Peter's place, and as they walked under the shop awnings, the grey skies burst, and the rain poured down in torrents. They waited for some time, but the rain did not relent, and an impatient Peter decided to run the two blocks to his house and bring back his car; he didn't want Daniel to ruin his new suit.

"Come on, Peter," called Henry, taking the initiative and challenging Peter as he sprinted across the road. "I'll race you!"

Peter ran after the chubbier man. The fitter Peter passed Henry by a fair distance and waited for him next to the four-wheel drive under the carport at the side of his house. Henry joined Peter, and together they gasped for breath as the water poured off their heads and clothing. Reaching for his car keys in his pocket, Peter was surprised to see Daniel and Jimmy walking down the driveway towards them. The Aboriginal youth, unperturbed that he was soaked to the skin, had his usual smile as he looked at Daniel, who had not been touched by one raindrop.

Peter was again awestruck by this man—and not just because he remained dry in the teeming rain but also because his eyes were no longer the vivid blue he had got used to; they were now grey. Daniel's eyes matched the mood of the sky.

A week later, Peter and Henry packed whatever could be carried in the four-wheel drive while Daniel spent the last few hours with Jimmy, reiterating the importance of his task.

"Make them understand that they have not been forgotten by their Maker. They are the indigenous people of this land, and their old beliefs, the Dreamtime, and the way they respected the land pleased the Creator."

Daniel reached out and embraced the humble youth as he said his last words to him: "Tell them all about me, Jimmy, but don't panic them by telling them that the world will end if our mission fails."

A concerned Professor Morey stroked his goatee beard as he walked up to his young assistant, but before he could say anything, she spoke first. "What's the problem—the world ending?"

"You might be closer to the truth than you think." He nodded and added, "You guessed it in one. Those calculations you and I worked out about Comet Clara are not as accurate as we thought; if that thing keeps going on the same course and speed, it could wipe us out in a matter of a few years."

"Wow!" the young woman said.

"Clara, your namesake is on a collision course with Earth."

CHAPTER 2

Peter, Henry, and Daniel had left Port Augusta before dawn, and they made the arduous but trouble-free trip in good time and reached Melbourne, the Garden City, before darkness set in. They had booked themselves a room at a cheap hotel near the city centre, where they would spend the next few days. They wasted no time in looking for a suitable building to use as their headquarters. With the lottery win, the three men were able to put up a reasonable deposit on a large warehouse on a main street in the inner suburb of Collingwood. They had to purchase the building in Henry's and Peter's names, and they had ninety days to settle the rest of the purchase price. Henry and Peter were reluctant to enter into a contract with a nine-million-dollar debt. How were they going to raise the other nine million required for settlement? Daniel's confidence eased their fears somewhat.

A lottery of over fifteen million was being drawn the following Saturday, and Peter took his turn in buying a ticket in his name. Daniel could not be involved in any winnings or any ownership of assets, as legally, he did not exist. The only transactions he could be involved in were those using cash. To avoid any suspicion, this would be the last lottery win they could chance until they enlisted new disciples.

After another systems entry and another win, they paid off the property and replenished their diminished finances.

Within two weeks, the warehouse had three new occupants. Alterations to their headquarters were paramount, and accommodations to cater to more people would be the first step. They needed to furnish the warehouse and install the latest computer system available.

The rest of the winnings were credited into Peter's account, and a few days later, he transferred some of the money into the reduced bank balances in Henry's and Jimmy's names. Henry opened share-trading facilities with several no-advice stock brokers as well as an online broker.

Daniel insisted on attending company general meetings and interacting with any members of the board or chief executive officers of the bigger corporations. He appeared to have a knack for picking the appropriate shares to purchase at the right time.

After meeting a CEO from a mining company called Gold Search, Daniel advised Henry to purchase shares in the company.

Even the no-advice broker tried his hardest to talk Henry out of placing a hundred thousand dollars into this penny company.

"Gold Search? You are throwing your money away," he told Henry. But they made the purchase, and Henry ended up with ten million shares, making him one of the largest shareholders in the small company.

In a short time, Daniel became proficient in gathering investment information from the appropriate people, and he would look through the stock-market reports and instruct Henry on the investments to make. The day after their first computer was installed, Henry started share trading on the Internet. Daniel would instruct him to invest in companies that were takeover targets or had a special dividend to be paid—companies on the verge of making announcements of discoveries, increases in profits, or medical breakthroughs. Henry never doubted Daniel's capabilities, and within days, he had transacted millions of dollars, and each transaction made them a handsome profit.

A few days later, the broker who had tried to talk him out of the Gold Search company investment rang. The excited broker screamed over the phone, "Have you heard the news about Gold Search? I can't believe you invested so much in it! You are a multimillionaire! They discovered the richest gold deposit ever in their tenements, and very close to the surface, too—over twenty grams per tonne. Do you understand what I am saying to you?" He finally drew a breath and allowed Henry to say something.

"What are the shares worth now?" Henry asked.

"They have suspended trading on them for now and probably won't come back on the market until tomorrow. They could open at anything from one to two dollars." The broker hesitated before continuing. "Eh, Henry, please don't be offended with what I am about to ask you, but I am a bit concerned about insider trading—as you know, it is highly illegal in this country."

Henry put the broker at ease. "With all the trading I have done in the last few days with you and the other brokers, it won't be hard to prove that I am a genius stock picker."

Peter, sitting at the next computer, listening, raised his eyes and muttered, "A genius stock picker—God give me strength."

The next day, Henry arranged to start selling his shares at best starting at two dollars onwards. After taxation, they would end up with well over twenty million dollars on that one investment.

At noon on a sizzling February day, a large black sedan, with the two front doors wide open, had parked in the middle of a laneway. The narrow street divided the backyards of the old terrace houses and allowed access to the rear of the blocks of land. The open car doors hid an opening in the old timber fence adjacent to the car. A gate in the fence had been kicked off its hinges and lay on the lawn in the backyard of the old building. A muffled scream could be heard, and a scantily dressed young blonde woman with grey masking tape over her mouth was pushed through the opening and into the laneway. Two sinister-looking men quickly followed behind her, and one of them grabbed her by the hair and shoved her towards the car. While one held her, the other opened the back door closest to them, and they proceeded to push the struggling, bruised, and terrified woman inside.

"Let her be!" a soft yet stern voice from the driver's side of the car commanded. The startled men looked up to see a lone bearded man in a white suit daring to challenge them.

The smaller of the two men smugly walked over to Daniel. "This is none of your business, mate—get lost."

"I asked you to let the girl go," Daniel repeated, still in a quiet tone.

The thug swung his closed-fisted right hand at Daniel's head; inexplicably, the punch veered to the right and smashed into the wooden fence wall. The man fell to his knees, screaming and clutching his bloodied, broken hand. The second, much-bigger man, who was still holding the girl, pushed her aside and pulled a knife out of his jacket pocket as he ran towards Daniel; he flicked his right hand in the air, and a blade instantly appeared. He brought the knife down towards the chest of the unassuming man, who simply stood his ground. The knife-wielding arm missed its target and lodged the knife in the assailant's own left hand.

Both wide-eyed and terrified men leapt into the car, one holding his right hand, while the other had a knife protruding out of his left hand. The man with the knife in his hand hastily started the vehicle while the other screamed out at him, "Run the bastard over! Get him!" Daniel was still in front of the driver's side of the vehicle. The thug planted his foot on the accelerator, and smoke came from the tyres as he steered the car towards the man in front of them. The vehicle swerved past its quarry and straight into a brick pillar that divided two backyards. A hissing noise and a spray of steam emanated from under the bonnet as the two bewildered men clambered out of the sedan; they took a quick glance at Daniel, whose glare sent them scampering as fast as they could down the laneway.

Daniel helped the young woman to her feet and assisted her back to the opening in the fence to her yard. He pulled the tape off her mouth, and with a smile, he turned around and started to walk away.

"Please, please don't leave me here!" she cried. "They'll come back for me, and they will kill me this time. They will kill me for sure after what you did to them. Please don't go."

Daniel turned towards her and, with another smile, motioned to her, and as she followed him down the lane, he removed his jacket and placed it over her shoulders.

Nothing surprised Peter and Henry anymore, so when Daniel came back from his walk with the girl, they looked at each other and continued with whatever they were doing, pretending that they had hardly noticed her. Without any introductions, Daniel took the young woman to his bedroom and told her to have a bath and clean herself up.

Later that evening, while they were eating the roast Peter had cooked, the woman walked into the dining room, and seeing an extra setting laid out on the table, she pulled the chair back and joined them. She wore Daniel's summer white satin bathrobe, which she had found hanging on the back of the bathroom door, and although it was much too large for her, she wore it well. It wasn't hard to notice she had a magnificent body with perfectly shaped, long legs. The beauty of her face was not overly affected by the bruising on it. Her long, shiny blonde hair hung down over her shoulders, and her long eyelashes enhanced her blue eyes. The heavy bruising all over her arms became visible as she sat down and the large sleeves of the robe rolled back, exposing her injuries. She wasn't in a talkative mood, and the only information Peter gleaned from her was her name: Caris. But after eating a few mouthfuls, she freely divulged her age: twenty-three.

They ate the rest of the meal in silence, and when she'd had enough, Caris stood up, thanked them for their hospitality, and walked back to

Daniel's room. A few minutes later, Daniel followed her and closed the door behind him.

She lay on the bed, still wearing the bathrobe, which had opened up in the middle, revealing her long and slender legs. He sat down on the end of the bed and just looked at her; a stirring in his body reminded him of how good it felt to want a woman. Caris looked at Daniel and felt a sense of calmness; she had been through a traumatic day, but being with him gave her a feeling of belonging. Sadness appeared on her face as she sat up next to him. "I owe you my life, and there is nothing that I wouldn't do for you to repay that debt. I know that you want me, and I want you to have me, but you need to know why I can't let you."

"There is nothing that I don't already know about you," Daniel said. "I need you to trust me completely; I may be able to help you, and maybe you will be able to help me."

A puzzled look came over her as she sat there listening to a complete stranger stating that he knew everything about her. Not even her parents or her best friends knew much about her current life.

"Your full name is Caris Marie Garvey, and you are a drug addict. You have prostituted yourself to pay for your habit, and those men who attacked you were henchmen working for your pimp. You have been trying to break away from him, but he won't let you go. I can tell you are a good person; not many in your situation would care enough not to go with men when you found out you had AIDS."

She looked at him in astonishment. "You must have guessed all that—I mean, how hard is it to see the bruises and needle marks on my arms? A lot of addicts have AIDS, but how did you find out my full name?"

Ignoring her question, in an adamant voice, Daniel surprised her even more when he made an unexpected request: "I want you to have unprotected sex with me!"

"For an obviously smart person, you are quite stupid to want unprotected sex with me." She flicked the robe and covered the parts of her upper legs that were showing. "You were right; I do have AIDS, and I will die from it. You are willing to catch it just to have sex with me? That's stupid—don't you think? Look! I'll have sex with you as many times as you want as long as you use a condom. God! You're no different, and here I thought you were someone special."

Daniel stood up in front of her, looking deeply into her beautiful eyes. "I asked you to trust me, and I only want to have sex with you once—once only."

"No! Please no," she moaned, seemingly losing any will to fight off another man. Daniel slowly reached over and took off her robe, revealing her full, firm breasts; her long, beautifully shaped legs; and the waxed pubic hairs that left her with just a small strip of fine curls.

Daniel removed his clothes and lay over her; his heart beat faster, and his body trembled as he gently thrust himself into her. When he had finally finished, he started ejaculating and kept doing so for an abnormally long time. Caris had been with many men but had never experienced anything like this. Her insides seemed to burn, but it was a pleasing burning that seemed to envelop her whole being. Her orgasmic thrust stiffened her entire body, and she too felt an ejaculation that had never happened to her before. Daniel lifted himself off her, put on the robe Caris had been wearing, and walked out of the room. She lay in bed for a long time, reliving the pleasure she had felt—a pleasure that would remain in her memory forever.

She awoke the next morning feeling the most invigorated she could ever recall. Naked, she went to the bathroom, and glimpsing herself in the mirror, she admired how well she looked. It took her a few seconds to realise the changes that were staring back at her; her eyes and mouth opened wide at what she saw. The bruises on her face and the massive ones on her arms were gone; they had vanished. Even more amazing, the needle marks had also disappeared.

She heard a knock on the door, and a smile came over her face as Daniel walked in. He appeared shy at seeing her naked sitting up in his bed. He looked at her, and Caris felt the attraction between them, but the feeling disappeared when he said in a quiet yet firm voice, "Caris, I want you to have an AIDS test, and when you get the results, we will talk some more."

She wanted to say so much, but Daniel walked out of the room, and with tears streaming down her face, she shouted at him as he closed the door, "I have AIDS! I have AIDS! What is wrong with you? Don't you believe me? Why would I lie about something like that?"

The next few days proved fruitful for the group. The share trading had netted them well over thirty million dollars, and Peter had been picking up many thousands of dollars at the racetrack and the Melbourne casino. Daniel only had to look at the racing guide to enable him to pick the winners for Peter, who had to take care to vary his bookies as well as the tracks, although he preferred the telephone betting.

Caris had now shifted into the warehouse and had claimed a small room for herself. The men had gone to her house and brought back some of her belongings, and she took great pride in decorating her little room with her own things.

For several days, Caris quietly sat in a corner and watched Peter and Henry going about their business, but she preferred her long, admiring glances over at Daniel. He was normally reading newspapers or news magazines, and he read them from cover to cover. He seemed to be getting more and more obsessed with them, and he read with such speed that Caris surmised he must only look at the pictures; with each passing day, he flicked through the pages at a faster rate.

Putting down the magazine she was reading, she hesitantly walked up to Daniel. "I need to talk to you; I can't follow what is happening here." She pointed towards the passageway in an insistent matter and said, "Can we talk in your room?"

"Talk here; there is nothing to hide from my friends," Daniel told her calmly.

"Okay, I guess you are three peas in a pod; the boys tell me that you won the lottery twice and that you are never wrong with the share market or the races. I would love to know how you do that, but that's not what I want to talk to you about; I need to know what you did to me."

"I did what I needed to do," said Daniel.

"You knew I had AIDS, yet you still had unprotected sex with me, and you didn't do it just for your own pleasure, did you? I had new blood tests—twice now—and I am completely cured. There is no sign that I ever even had AIDS. My teeth are completely perfect again; I went to my dentist to check them out, and the fillings are gone. And one more thing: the scar from an appendectomy I had years ago has vanished. I need to know what is happening here, please," she pleaded.

"Sit down and listen." Daniel began his story.

An hour seemed only a few minutes to Caris as she listened. She believed everything he told her. How could she not after what she had seen occurring in the last few days? She thought about the whole issue for a few minutes and then began asking questions.

The others were intrigued by her quick acceptance of the situation. "What happens when we die? Is it completely the end for us? No more—just kaput?" She gestured with both hands.

Daniel replied in his usual quiet manner. "Nothing and nobody on this earth—or in the entire universe, for that matter—can ever be utterly destroyed. Things can only be changed from one state to another. In a matter of time, a mountain can change its state to that of mere sand. Species of fauna and flora survive by spreading their genes from the old to the new generation so that there is always some part of the creatures still living on. When any creature, including a human, dies, does it not always end up back as part of the earth or the air itself? All living things must breathe and must eat. They inhale the air or gases of the dead, and they eat the vegetation that has grown from the earth. Carnivores, in turn, also eat the creatures that have eaten the vegetation. It's a never-ending cycle; with every breath we take and with every mouthful we eat, we are recycling the dead into the living creatures' new regenerated cells. So we are literally reincarnated back into the cells of the many different species of living things that are indigenous to this planet."

Daniel smiled at his attentive audience and simply returned to his reading. It was at least an hour before Caris came back to reality from the profound thoughts that were reeling through her mind. She had been sitting across the room from where Daniel sat, and she began to have her first real close look at her benefactor. How could she have missed those beautiful blue eyes on that well-formed face or that perfect body? *If a god were to be reincarnated into a man, surely he would have to look like him,* she thought.

She admired his long hair and beard and wondered what he used to keep them in such good condition. "Daniel, I think that your hair and beard need to have a good cut and maybe be styled, and I am the girl who can do it. Believe it or not, I was a hairdresser not so long ago." She gave him a smile that oozed affection.

The amount of hair she clipped from Daniel's head made Henry green with envy. When Caris had finished, the three of them were amazed at the final result. She had used a number-one clipper on the sides and a number three on the top; now they could see his ears, and his clean-shaven face made his blue eyes stand out even more. There in front of them stood a handsome man.

The computers were finally installed, but now a new problem arose: they needed an operator compatible with their new state-of-the-art system. To set up the multitude of spreadsheets to cover all their current investments and the many more expected in the future was beyond Henry.

"Things have a peculiar way of working out," Daniel told him.

Inside an hour, Peter walked into the warehouse, guiding a peculiar-looking young boy; he was thinly built, had unkempt hair and protruding front teeth, and was of Asian appearance. He wore Coke-bottle glasses, and he certainly didn't need his dark suit and yellow bow tie to make him stand out in a crowd. "I found him fumbling his way around out front. He tells me he is legally blind and is lost. I'll give him a drink and then take him home."

"I am so sorry for any trouble." His Aussie twang surprised them, as they had expected an Asian accent. "This is the first time I have ever been lost; I was trying to ring my mum, when someone snatched my mobile, and the bastard took my walking cane too."

Having a shortage of chairs, Peter led him to a seat in front of one of the new computers. The young man thrust his face to within an inch of the computer screen, and his fingers ran over the keyboard. He picked up the new manual lying on the desk and put his face so close to it that his glasses almost touched it.

"Oh my God, this is the greatest; it's the very latest. What I could do if I had this at home." He sighed as if in a dream.

Henry, thinking how cruel nature could be to deal this young boy such a miserable hand, suddenly took a greater interest in him. "You are computer literate, are you?" he eagerly asked.

"Computers are my life; without them, I have nothing and might as well be dead," he replied sadly.

Henry stretched out his hand to introduce himself. "I'm Henry. What's your name?"

"David Chan," he replied without reaching out to shake the outstretched hand.

Although embarrassed, Henry understood. "I gather you have a sight problem, so how do you manage on the computers?"

"I can see if I am within about ten centimetres of anything. It limits me greatly, but I have patience—something I inherited from my ancestors, I guess."

"Do you work for anyone?"

"Who would want to employ me? I've tried, but nobody wants me; I just spend my time at home with my mum and my old computer."

Daniel stopped his reading and stood up from his usual spot on the table. "Henry, why not offer this lad a position helping you?" he said as he approached the two and just as Caris and Peter came into the room with cups of tea for them. David was getting excited about the prospect of a job.

"I'll work for you for nothing until I can prove myself," he said eagerly. "I just have to convince my mother about it—that's all."

Daniel took it on himself to ring David's mother's mobile phone. She answered on the first ring, and after introducing himself, Daniel mentioned the boy's name, and immediately, he heard a frantic voice calling out, "David—is he all right? Is he all right?"

Daniel explained the situation, and she gave a sigh of relief when he told her that David was safe. She had been frantically looking for him, driving around the streets, and as it turned out, she wasn't far from the warehouse. Within minutes, she rang the doorbell.

"I'm Paula Chan, David's mother," she uttered eagerly as soon as the door opened.

She was an unusual-looking woman of Eurasian appearance but not as Asian looking as her son. Without the old-fashioned hairstyle towering above her head, she would barely have been five feet tall; Paula wore large-framed glasses, and her old-fashioned clothes accentuated her maternal build. On seeing David, she charged inside, and the embrace she gave him quickly turned to a berating.

Over a cup of tea, they talked at length about the prospect of David working there. Mrs. Chan turned out to be an interesting person; her father was Italian, her mother was from the Philippines, and she had married a Chinese man, and that was how she had ended up being a Chan. Paula had been a widow for over five years, and she spent her life looking after her son and being the locally elected member of the People's Party.

Paula Chan took an instant liking to Daniel and the others. She explained David was an exceptional boy who had been born with an eye defect and that nothing could be done to help him with his problem.

"Mrs. Chan," Daniel said in a slow and deliberate manner, "we have a need for someone such as David to help us run our computer system, and more importantly, we need your help."

"Well, you are my constituents, so my job compels me to look after your interests," interrupted Mrs. Chan.

"It won't be that kind of help, Paula. It will be far more important help than that." Daniel continued, "I am going to try to do something here that will hopefully make the story I am going to divulge to you more believable."

Holding the worried woman's hands, Daniel looked deeply into her eyes, and with a begging quiver in his voice, he murmured, "Please trust me with what I am about to do to David."

The intrigued woman nodded in consented trust and sat quietly as Daniel walked up to her son, took him by the hand, and made him rise to his feet. He took the glasses from David's face and placed both his thumbs on each of the boy's eyes. Stress appeared on Daniel's face as he went into a deep sense of meditation.

Paula was terrified and apprehensive as David's body rose slightly off the floor and started to tremble violently. Daniel gently lowered the boy until his feet touched the floor, and instantly, David stopped shaking. Coming out of the trance, Daniel took his hands away from the boy and picked up his glasses. To the horror of all around him, he dropped them to the floor and stood on them, breaking them into many pieces.

Paula, completely shocked by such a hideous act, stood up in a rage. "How could you be so callous as to do that to my son? You're nothing but an animal! You disgust every fibre in my body." She had tears of hate and disappointment flowing from her eyes. Wasn't her son's plight bad enough without someone being this cruel?

She rushed at Daniel and, with her handbag, took a wild swing at him. Her swing veered off to the side, making her lose her balance; she dropped her bag and started to topple to the floor. Daniel's hands reached out, grasped her, and stopped her fall.

"Mum, Mum." David was in front of his mother, holding her by the shoulders. "Mum, I can see—I really can see." He stooped over, picked up the handbag, and handed it to her. She looked at his face and saw the clarity in his eyes. He was looking at her for the first time in his life.

"Mum, I see the tears in your eyes; I see the colour of your dress. I can see that far wall over there and the bright green colour it's painted. Mum, I can see." His tears fell in unison with his mother's.

She turned to Daniel, embraced him, and sobbed, "He found my bag; he found my bag, and he picked it up." From that moment, she believed whatever Daniel had to tell her.

They sat around the table, sipping cups of tea, but soon the cups changed to glasses filled with sherry as Daniel explained his mission.

"Is this one of those religious sects?" was the first thing that ran through Paula's mind.

Looking into her eyes, Daniel shook his head.

She sat in silence, looking down at her clasped hands in front of her for what seemed an eternity, deliberating in her mind what she had seen and the story she had just heard. Finally, she jerked her head up swiftly and looked at Daniel.

"Okay! Okay! Let's say I believe you. Where do I fit in this picture? How would I be able to help?" Her voice sounded almost hysterical.

Daniel reached out and held her hands from across the table; he inhaled deeply. "You are to be an integral part of this whole movement. Arguably, you will be the most important helper in initiating the massive changes needed to turn this world around. Paula, you are currently a backbencher for the People's Party. I can assure you this will change; you will become a frontbencher and, eventually, the leader of the party. Your ultimate goal is to become the prime minister of Australia."

Paula gave out a muffled laugh. "I'm to become the prime minister? Me—the prime minister? The only reason I was elected as a member of Parliament is because most of my constituents are of Asian and foreign origin. Since the clash between the Islamic and Christian religions over the past years, the majority of Australians are wary of the Asians, and you only have to look at me to see my origin." She pointed at her eyes.

"My father was Italian, and my maiden name, Petrosanto, got me the Italian vote in the area. Any Asian living in this country, even if they were born here, will tell you that we are not the most accepted people in this community. Do you really believe that the people of Australia would elect me as prime minister?"

"Yes! Paula, the whole world needs a complete change in its thinking. We need someone and someplace to start the ball rolling, and with Australia's multicultural population, it is the ideal place to start from, and you, with your mixed heritage and position, are the ideal person." Daniel stood up as he persisted. "For example, your election platform would be based on many issues that are highly controversial. Illicit drugs are and will always be a problem as long as massive amounts of money can be made from them. The addicted need to get other vulnerable kids addicted in order to sell drugs to them, and in turn, this helps to support their own habit. The new addicted kids then do exactly the same thing, and we now have a vicious circle happening, and so it just keeps going on and on. The only way to stop this cycle is to legalise drugs and enable addicts to get their supplies free from health centres set up especially for them. It will give the authorities a chance to help them in many ways. Maybe over time, they can be weaned off this bad habit, but in the meantime, they won't need the large amounts of funds to buy the illicit drugs. The reason, I believe, it hasn't been legalised to date is because the drug barons are very influential in our political system. They would lose their multibillion-dollar industry if illicit drugs were legalised."

The excitement showed in Daniel's eyes; in his mind, the prospect of this woman being elected as the prime minister of Australia was feasible.

"Most of the young voters are well educated in conservation, so we go for the Greenies' vote." Daniel suddenly became sullen for a few seconds. "Believe me, Paula, the Creator is not very happy with the way we have devastated our rain forests; they need to be saved.

"All newly constructed houses should have frames made of aluminium or steel. This alone will reduce the need of timber by thirty percent. Paedophiles are another scourge on our society; they must be stopped from ruining the lives of our young. Repeat offenders should be castrated and even have their genitals severed off completely."

Daniel looked into Paula's eyes, and she immediately understood that he was not happy with what he had to say next.

"Australia has an aging population. Grey power rules our country, and without their vote, we wouldn't stand an iota of a chance of getting you elected. You will promise them a substantial increase in their pension entitlements."

Paula, although not an economic expert, realised that that would be one promise that would be difficult to keep, but before she could raise that issue with Daniel, he answered her thoughts.

"Paula, sometimes we have to tell a little white lie, and this is only a little white lie when you compare it to the ultimate total destruction of our world if we do not succeed. I need you to be controversial—very controversial—to stand out amongst all politicians, not just in this country but also in the whole world. We need the imagination of the Australian people to run wild with new ideas. Frankly, Paula, I need you to be head of this country no matter what it takes to get you there. There are many other issues that need changing, and the majority of people would agree as long as the right person presented these new concepts to them."

With her mind working overtime and David in tow, Paula left the warehouse. She had agreed to let David start work the next day, and she would consider all that had happened that day. Daniel smiled as he heard David say to his mother, "Mum, you don't have to hold my hand; I can see, remember?"

Caris sidled up to Daniel and, with a smirk on her face, coyly asked him, "How come you could heal David with just a touch, but in my case, you had to have sex with me? Eh?"

Daniel's red face showed his embarrassment as he tried to explain. "My powers are still at their infancy, and I wanted to ensure that I fought microbes with microbes. I did what I thought was best at the time. Anyway, that's my story, and I'm sticking to it," he concluded with a smile.

The next day, a worried Daniel confided to Peter, "I need you to recruit security guards; in a few weeks, Paula will need to have protection twenty-four hours a day. The drug barons may try to silence her as soon as the legalisation-of-drugs debate starts to take off."

The wealth of the group had, within a few short weeks, exceeded two hundred million dollars and was growing fast. Henry was still in charge of the share trading, but now he had a willing apprentice in young David Chan.

Peter still raised money through gambling with Daniel's help, especially at the casino, where he was always at Peter's side.

Caris now had her own share-trading account as well as telephone betting, and she too won the lottery, bagging over eleven million in another of the draws.

They needed to diversify into different forms of investing and gambling in order to avoid suspicion and notoriety. They started dealing with investment fund managers in Australia as well as trading derivatives, such as options, warrants, and the currency markets.

David was proving to be more than just a computer whiz. His quest to learn and his ability to grasp new knowledge in this new world Daniel had opened up to him made him an invaluable part of the team. With his help, they started share trading worldwide; they now were able to accelerate their wealth at a much faster rate. With the many spreadsheets he created, he supervised and monitored the growth of their fortune by the minute.

Articles about his mother's revolutionary views filtered into the local paper, and slowly, the major newspapers took an interest. Although she was ridiculed by many critics, she became a much-sought-after celebrity for radio stations. Soon her appearance as a guest on many of the talk shows on the local television networks became a regular occurrence. Paula was a natural for the many current-affairs shows. The media could not get enough of her controversial views. People rang in and wanted to see or hear more about her ideas. The movement for change had started.

The warehouse was a hive of activity, as alterations seemed never ending. The whole facility had now been altered to cater to a large number of people. There were many new bedrooms and bathrooms. The kitchen was large and in need of a chef, waiter, and cleaner.

Peter and Henry were quick to recruit a couple who owned a small restaurant where they often ate. Ang and Maria Deposa had been having difficulties managing their restaurant since her husband's accident whilst training his greyhounds. The small man had had too many dogs on the leads, which had been wrapped around his arms, when a cat had run out in front of the greyhounds. The dogs had given chase, dragging Ang several hundred metres before he was able to stop them.

The oversized Maria had insisted Ang sell the dogs, and when Peter offered them the catering and cleaning job at the warehouse, she accepted.

Paula had now become a household name amongst the people of Australia. Daniel insisted that she and David move into the warehouse, which now boasted four burly security guards living on-site. Two of these guards were dedicated to Paula.

One night, she and her son packed their essentials and secretly shifted into the warehouse. Paula kept her mailing address at her house, and not even her family and closest friends knew where she now lived; any communication was through her mobile phone. The public was under the impression she still lived at her house. The security guards were always close by, one inside her electoral office and the other parked in their car outside. They drove her to the ever-increasing functions or official duties she had to attend.

Peter had recruited the security guards from disillusioned police officers and, with their help, set up a sophisticated security system at the warehouse.

Caris spent a lot of time educating Paula on the world of the drug addict, and her knowledge of the drug dealers and the underworld surprised even Daniel. He kept inundating Paula with advice on more controversial topics to talk about to her adoring public.

"People in the world are starving, yet we cull kangaroos, rabbits, buffalo, pigs, and more and leave the carcasses to rot. We have the audacity to kill our livestock if world prices come down. What a waste of food. Why not refrigerate this fresh meat and ship it to the countries that need it?"

Some of the ideas were not really practical, and they were too costly, but to the average person, they made sense. Paula always declined to debate her ideas publicly with any of the so-called experts in the various fields she had touched on. She did not want to get sidetracked by details or red tape; her sole aim was to interact with the majority of the average voters.

The interest that the public took in Paula made it difficult for her political party to ignore her popularity. The People's Party had been in opposition for the last five years, and polling showed they would lose another election if it were held under their currently unpopular leadership. Her invitation to take an opposition ministry as shadow foreign minister came as no surprise to Daniel. His plan for her was well on its way.

Daniel's friends, at times, felt intimidated by the uncanny way he seemed to be able to guess what they were thinking. Sometimes they suspected he was actually reading their minds.

Their fortune overall now exceeded a billion dollars, but they were not wasteful with their accumulated wealth.

Daniel, still in his white suit, appeared more youthful and vibrant than ever as he and Peter boarded the aging Learjet at the Essendon Airport. Six months had elapsed since their arrival in Melbourne; they hired the jet to fly back to the beginning and to see Jimmy Wirra in Port Augusta.

The unusual-looking pilot, Garry Foster, was in his early fifties; was short, fat, and broad shouldered; and had a barrel chest that made him look shorter than he really was. His wavy ginger hair complemented the freckles over his face and body, and he was endowed with a large, hooked nose between two beady blue eyes.

Peter sniggered internally when he met the pilot, but when Garry smiled, his whole face lit up to such a degree that he suddenly wasn't so bad looking after all. Daniel took an immediate liking to him, and Garry had no objection to allowing him to sit in the co-pilot's seat for the trip. Daniel took a keen interest in the plane, and Garry took pleasure in answering his many questions.

The aging, well-looked-after Bombardier Learjet could seat up to eleven passengers, including the crew. Garry was having financial difficulties in keeping up the payment on the lease, and he had sunk all his money into its purchase. The business was no longer viable, and this would be his last flight.

By the end of the journey, Daniel had purchased the plane and hired a pilot. Garry Foster would be in charge of all their travel requirements.

Daniel and Peter felt there was something different about the town as they walked down the main shopping area. There were no barefoot, dusty Aboriginals reeling in the street with beer cans in their hands. The park in the middle of town was clear of any rubbish, especially the familiar beer cans and wine casks. A beautiful sight befell Daniel, and a renewed hope surged through his body; the children—black and white—were playing on the swings and running around together.

The town appeared cleaner and the people happier; both races intermingled in the streets and in restaurants, where black youths served alongside their white counterparts. New shops with Aboriginal motifs had opened in the main street, and they had black and white employees. The townspeople had become colour blind.

They travelled the short distance to the Aboriginal settlement in a hire car, and there Peter's face lit up with astonishment. The houses had all been repaired and painted in bright, happy colours. Gardens were blooming with flowers, and new lawns had been laid. These were the houses of proud owners.

Jimmy emerged from his parents' house to welcome them. The huge smile on his face showed the pride he felt, and he eagerly brought Daniel up to date on the achievements of his people—not just in Port Augusta but also in the many settlements around the district.

The forward-looking attitude had spread throughout the surrounding area. With the financial aid from Jimmy's ever-supplemented bank account and by amalgamating their meagre savings and earnings, Aboriginals bought houses in the white men's areas, and surprisingly, the whites were accepting and welcoming towards their new neighbours.

The pride this race was radiating affected the attitudes of the whites as well. The coloured children looked forward to attending school, and the education department had to employ more teachers for the district. Indigenous artists held many exhibitions all over the country, and their music was being heard in the streets and on the stage. They had a natural talent for athletics and sport in general, and with their new, disciplined attitude towards life, they became well sought after by many sporting clubs.

Jimmy, with the assistance of many recruits from different local settlements, had spread the new way effectively amongst his people in the area; now his word was spreading throughout the land. Daniel spent many hours motivating Jimmy's eager recruits, and a glow emanated from their faces upon conclusion of the meeting.

St. Bernadette's, the local Catholic church situated around the corner from the warehouse, on this typically cold Melbourne winter Sunday, had a first-time visitor sitting at the rear of the church. He had to laugh at the audacity of the white people; the statue of Jesus on the cross and of the Virgin Mary showed such overly whitish skin. Surely if they were from the Middle East, they would have been much darker, maybe even black, but heaven forbid; the whites would not pray to a dark Christ. On the other hand, blacks were expected to accept a white man and woman as their Saviour and his mother.

The lacklustre way the young priest presented the mass bored the parishioners, but they became more alert as the priest ascended the few steps of the pulpit to the right of the altar and began the day's sermon. Daniel, along with the other parishioners, felt the passion the young priest exuded in the sermon's delivery. The homeless youths and adults of this rich country were the theme of his talk and undoubtedly a favourite subject of his. He had his audience in tears and reaching deeply into their pockets to donate towards the upkeep of these unfortunates. The priest impressed Daniel in his dedication and passion to help the less fortunate of his parish.

With Mass over, the church slowly cleared, except for one individual sitting on his own at the rear of the church. Daniel waited for over half an hour before the priest, after seeing his parishioners depart, re-entered the cathedral. On spying Daniel, he walked up to him. "Can I be of any service to you, my son?" asked the priest, who had wavy dark hair and was slightly overweight. The young priest felt nervous and intimidated by Daniel. "I am Father Andrew Costa. I am sorry, but I can't recall seeing you before."

Daniel stood up and introduced himself. "I do want to talk to you about many things, Father, including your work with the homeless; we may be able to be of great help to each other." Father Costa immediately became interested at the mention of his favourite subject.

Daniel looked down on the shorter man. "Father Costa, firstly, I hope you won't mind me calling you Andrew, and secondly, I want to buy your interest in what I have to say. There will be a cheque delivered to you within a week for one million dollars to help your charity."

The priest was agog. "You will give me a cheque for one million dollars?" Andrew shook his head in bewilderment. "Look, you already have my interest without making ridiculous promises." Andrew tried to control his excitement, which quickly turned to annoyance; this had to be a prank made by a loony.

"You are thinking this is a prank and I am a loony," Daniel retorted, "but at the same time, you are thinking how much food a million dollars would buy for the homeless."

Andrew, surprised that Daniel had used the exact words he was thinking, persisted. "Look, I have no idea if you are genuine or not, but I can't ignore such an offer; I think you want more from me than I can imagine."

Daniel started slowly, as he had done on previous occasions when telling his story. This time, he had to convince a young Catholic priest.

"Andrew, you are a good man, and any god would be very proud and pleased to have you as a follower. Your kindness to mankind is why I must convince you of what I am about to tell you. Mankind needs men like you, now more than ever. The sacrifices you have made in your lifetime to help others will mean nothing unless you believe me and help me in my mission."

Two hours later, they were sitting in complete silence on a bench in the garden at the back of the cathedral, staring at the freshly mown lawn. Finally, Andrew broke the peace as he leaned forward with his elbows on his lap and clasped his hands together. "You have just asked me to destroy everything I have always believed in—my total faith—and believe your theories."

"No, Andrew, I haven't. Think for a moment; your faith teaches you that God is the creator of this world and the whole universe. That God created everything, provided everything we need, and is everywhere. He is in the air we breathe, in everything we can see, and in everything we cannot see." Daniel knew that this was the god that Andrew believed in.

"Think again, Andrew—think about Mother Nature. Everything on this world is natural. Sure, humans can create things that might seem unnatural, but they are always made from a natural source. Nature is everywhere, in every nook and cranny of the world. It provides for us; it is the air we take in and the water we drink. It is in the grass we walk on and in the sun that keeps us warm and makes things grow, in the moon and the stars that shine on us at night. Yes, yes, Andrew, God is with us, and if you can comprehend that God is nature, then very little has really changed in your faith. You believed in a higher power—a power much greater than us. Now just replace God or this higher being with Creator, or Mother Nature, and you are back to where you were yesterday."

Andréw nodded as if indicating that he concurred with Daniel. "I have always doubted the existence of a heaven and a hell and our concept of a God Almighty sitting somewhere up there in the sky on a throne. I've always known that to be a bit far-fetched, but I just followed blind faith, as we Christians have always been taught to do." He sighed and shook his head in abandonment.

Andrew looked at Daniel, pursed his lips, and spoke in a slow and quiet tone. "You are telling me that the world is near its end, and if I am to go along with what you are saying, what can I do to help?"

"In my mind, I have many phases that have to fall together, just like a jigsaw puzzle. You are another integral piece I desperately need. You are the man to start the peace movement between the Christians and the Muslims and also to cement the many religions. I want you to start recruiting other holy men from all the different religions: the Jews, Muslims, Buddhists, various Christian faiths, and any other religion. They, in turn, must recruit other followers from their own groups, and they must start integrating and spreading goodwill amongst all man, no matter what religion they are. They must start slowly introducing the common Creator that wants us to take care of the planet it has made our home. Andrew, you must achieve this task I am setting you, without telling anyone all that I have told you. At this early period, do not divulge that the end of the world is upon us if we are not successful. If the masses knew what lay ahead, there could be mass hysteria, and that alone would ensure the end of the world."

Andrew looked stunned. "And how do I do this without telling anyone everything?"

"You leave that to me for now," Daniel advised as he stood up from the garden bench. He put his hands on Andrew's shoulders. "Obviously, I don't expect you to believe me, but I will ask you to play along for a while; there is just too much to lose if there is the slightest chance that I am what I say I am."

Daniel smiled, turned, and walked out of the garden gate, leaving the young priest staring after him.

The next day, Andrew had a visit from a reporter with a photographer in tow. The local newsman had done his research on the priest and asked him all the relevant questions regarding his passion in aiding the homeless, including how he had used his inheritance to purchase a house for this worthy cause. Andrew refused to comment on the subject and, lying, told the reporter he had his facts wrong. The photographer snapped his picture before Andrew had time to close the door on them.

Two days later, Henry sat in the church residence's lounge room, and after bringing tea for them, Andrew looked down at the certified bank cheque on the glass coffee table. He stared at the zeros behind the number one and felt weak at the knees. He had doubted the promise of the cheque and all that Daniel had told him.

Henry handed the priest the local newspaper, which featured a story and picture of Andrew under the headline "The Good Samaritan."

"This is Daniel's way of helping you and me with the next phase of his plan. I have been instructed to help you with what he has already talked to you about."

"I guess I really have to go along with you; after all, Daniel has definitely paid for my time."

The next morning, Henry arranged a breakfast meeting at a modest local cafe with the rabbi he knew from the synagogue he had attended on a couple of occasions since his arrival in Melbourne. Henry recalled what Daniel had said to him the first day he met him: his "being Jewish may come in handy."

After Henry introduced Father Andrew to Rabbi Goldstein, they sat and chatted. The rabbi—a slim, tall, stooping man with a hooked nose—wore a yarmulke, mainly to hide his bald patch.

He had read about Andrew and had thought about ringing him, so when he'd received a call from Henry, he'd eagerly accepted a meeting with the young priest. Their main topic of conversation was, as expected, religion. Henry noticed their enthusiasm when the subject changed to helping the community at large. They agreed to meet again the following week, and they would endeavour to bring other ministers from other denominations.

The security guard opened the front door of the warehouse to let a distressed Paula in. On sighting Daniel, she headed straight to his comforting, outstretched arms. "My house! My house is gone—burned to the ground," she sobbed. "The police say the fire was deliberately lit sometime last night. I think someone tried to kill me. Oh! My God, if David and I were still sleeping there—oh my God."

Daniel didn't appear surprised. "I thought they would try something, but I didn't think the scum would act so quickly. Paula, make sure the guards are always with you. You hear me? At all times." He added, "David will be safe here."

But a mother's love needed more than just words of reassurance; she shook her head and sobbed, "I can't take a chance on David's life. I don't care what happens to me, but I don't want David hurt. I want out of this mess you got us into." She trembled in fear.

"Paula, I know that you don't mean that. You can't quit. You are a pivotal part of what we have to do." Daniel tried consoling her, but before he could say another word, one of the guards interrupted him. The solemn man motioned insistently for Daniel to follow him, and he led him into the security room.

On the monitors, Daniel saw two suspicious-looking men outside, parked across the road in a big black sedan. Another burly man, neatly dressed in a dark striped suit, had walked to the door in the laneway at the rear of the warehouse. He had a pistol clearly visible in his hand. The guard quickly explained the situation. "They followed Mrs. Chan here; we saw their car pull up just as she arrived. They made a U-turn and parked across the road, and if you look at the steam coming from the muffler, you will see they have left the engine running—probably for a quick getaway. What do you want us to do?" the excited guard eagerly asked.

"Nothing—you and the others stay here." Daniel's anger showed.

The guards watched him walk the long way over to the back door and were shocked to see him, without the slightest hesitation, open it. The thug standing in the laneway was taken aback as Daniel confronted him.

The surprised man raised his arm and pointed the gun directly at Daniel's head. The rage the man saw in Daniel's eyes petrified him. He tried to squeeze the trigger of his Browning automatic, but his finger wouldn't work. Sweat poured from his brow, and it became worse when his hand slowly turned towards his own head, and suddenly, he was looking at the barrel of his own gun.

The horrified man's eyes were protruding out of their sockets, and he became so frightened that he lost complete control of his body functions and emptied his bladder over his trousers and shoes. His eyes were now looking inwards at the nozzle of his gun, and his finger started squeezing the trigger. The hammer receded, and he closed his eyes and waited; he heard the click of the hammer hitting the chamber, but the expected loud bang didn't follow. The relieved man opened his eyes and realised that the gun had misfired, but the relief he felt was short lived. His finger started to squeeze the trigger again. The thug turned white, weakened at the knees, and fell to the ground in a dead faint.

The bewildered guards, watching on the security screens, were amazed at the sight before them. With Daniel out of camera range, they watched as the hooligan tried unsuccessfully to shoot himself.

Daniel hurried to the front door, and as he passed the guards, he asked them to carry the man at the back door into the warehouse and keep him under watch. Everyone in the warehouse was again amazed as he opened the door and stood in the doorway.

Daniel looked intently, not at the car parked across the road with the two men inside curiously watching him, but at something else. Daniel looked down the main road to his left.

Across the road, the puzzled passenger in the car turned around to look through the back window, wondering what the man from the warehouse was looking at. The driver looked through the rear-vision mirror. They could only see a ten-tonne tip truck heading in their direction. It seemed to veer out of control for a moment, and then it straightened and picked up speed as it neared their parking position.

Not till the last few seconds did they realise that it was bearing straight for them. The panicking driver quickly turned and jammed his foot down on the pedal. The screeching car accelerated and pulled out from the kerb, directly into the path of the truck, which hit them with a tremendous crunch. The vehicle was swept along the road for over a hundred metres before crashing into a light pole. Parts of the sedan were scattered all over the road, and the truck, with little damage sustained, ended up sitting on top of the crushed mess. Surprisingly, they were not killed, although their serious injures would be enough to keep them out of action for a long time.

The distraught truck driver wasn't quite sure what had happened. It was as if the truck had had a mind of its own; it had suddenly picked up speed and headed deliberately at the black sedan.

A man in a white suit came up to him and comforted him. "My friend, I saw it all. They pulled out in front of you; it was entirely their fault." The man gave him an envelope and told him not to ask any questions and to accept the gift as compensation for any financial loss. The driver had a quick look inside the large envelope, and his eyes widened when he saw the wad of notes protruding from it. He instantly shut the envelope and hesitantly looked around, but the man was gone.

Daniel held Paula's hand as she looked across the road at the carnage that had just taken place, and she realised that he, somehow, had caused it. She felt a new confidence in him; she knew that he would protect her and her son.

The shaking man in the guard's room had revived to find himself handcuffed to a chair. Daniel was staring at him. The man refused to answer any questions. The only thing he would divulge was his name: Hank.

He was frightened and intimidated by the man questioning him, but although scared of Daniel, he feared his employer more. He knew the danger he would be in if he divulged any information to his interrogator, and with every question asked, his head shook in defiance.

After a few minutes, Daniel thanked Hank for his cooperation and started to go through the answers that the puzzled man was supposed to have given him.

"You and the other two burned down Mrs. Chan's house, and when you realised she wasn't inside and dead, you watched her house and eventually followed our guard, who picked up her mail, here. You were under strict instructions to finish the job you were sent out to do. Your boss is Bill Konikos, a supposedly respected property developer. Your mates out there are Sal Coco and Tony Marino. There are another fourteen hoods like you working for Mr. Konikos, as well as two others in the police drug squad, Phil Connors and his partner, Barry Cole. Does that sound about right, Hank?" finished Daniel.

Sheer terror came over Hank's face. "I didn't say a thing—how did you get all those names? They will kill me; I am a dead man. I am a dead man! I don't have a chance." He trembled so violently that he vomited over himself.

"Oh, come on now, Hank—there is a chance for you; become a crown witness, and the police will protect you. One thing is for certain, mate, and we both know it: it's the only chance you have." Daniel knew full well that this was Hank's only option.

Peter took charge of the situation and, with the assistance of the security guards, arranged for police from the drug squad to come interview Hank at the warehouse.

After listening to his eyewitness accounts of numerous unsolved murders and the many drug deals his boss had been involved in, the elated members of the drug squad couldn't thank Peter enough for handing them such a prize. Peter made one stipulation before they whisked Hank away to a secret location: Peter and the warehouse had to be kept out of any reports. The reports were to show that the instigation of this investigation had been prompted by the attempted murder of the local member of Parliament, Paula Chan.

The police officers had no problem agreeing; the witness they had been handed on a platter would give them an airtight case against Konikos and his men. They certainly did not want to share the glory, and besides, for their own safety, it would be better if they were never mentioned.

In the next few days, the two crooked police officers were arrested, as well as Konikos and his gang; with all the murders Hank had witnessed, the magistrate had no option but to refuse bail to all the accused.

To put Hank in jail would mean certain death for him, so after he became a crown witness, he would eventually be given another identity through the witness protection programme.

The attempted murder of Paula Chan was big news, and the newspapers played up the story by giving her credit for the capture and closure of a huge drug ring. Now she was able to demonstrate to Parliament and to most Australians just how worried the drug lords were with the thought of legalising illicit drugs. Her popularity grew at an unprecedented rate, and rumours persisted that she should replace the leader of the opposition before the next election if they were to have the slightest chance of winning.

Within two weeks of the drug bust, there was a leadership challenge by the different factions of the People's Party. Paula, encouraged by her supporters, put her name forward amongst the other two challengers. To her surprise, a large majority elected her as the new leader, and with her increasing popularity, the ruling prime minister thought it prudent to call an early election.

Father Andrew's appearance in the paper endeared him to the public, and donations and offers of help towards his cause started arriving at the church. The archbishop in charge of the archdiocese was impressed by the good publicity one of his priests was receiving. These days, the Church needed all the goodwill it could get, and he saw an opportunity to exploit Father Andrew's popularity. Through the bishop in charge of the diocese that St. Bernadette came under, he invited Father Andrew to lunch.

Archbishop Bradley was an obese man with a head so large that his neck was not visible on his massive shoulders. His red face stood out in contrast to his black outfit and white collar, but it matched the red cap he wore.

Andrew was dwarfed by the archbishop as he followed the waddling man over to the well-adorned table in the dining room. The young priest was embarrassed by the volume and eloquence of the lunch they were being served by the two servants who indulged the archbishop's every whim.

The reason for the invitation became obvious to Andrew as his superior, with his small nose in the air, started the conversation.

"Young man, the Church needs you; we are currently going through another of those bad phases in our history." The archbishop hesitated as he gobbled down another large, peeled tiger prawn. "We want to enhance the fresh publicity you are getting to our advantage. My boy! Any ideas how we can keep the momentum of this hype going?"

"Your grace"—Andrew didn't hesitate in answering the big man, who was reaching for more food—"the Church, from Australia and all the way to the Vatican, needs to take drastic action if we are to turn the tide of bad publicity back in its favour. We need to be seen to be lowering our standard of living and helping the poor, especially in poorer countries." His statement was an intentional dig at that very luncheon—one that the archbishop chose to ignore. "We need to be seen as unifying all Christian religions and, in turn, have closer ties with the non-Christian religions. In the last few years, the fanatical Muslim countries have restricted their population to the Islamic faithful by forcing the followers of minority religions to flee to safer countries. They are a suspicious group and very devout in their beliefs. We have to try to assure them that their religion is respected by us, and therefore, hopefully, they will in turn learn to tolerate and respect ours. We have to try to stop terrorism that is committed in the name of religion. The pope has to be proactive in these changes, and it's a forward-thinking archbishop that has to make these points to His Holiness."

The stunned man stared at Andrew. *Is this young whippersnapper talking about me when he talks about reducing the standard of living? And those ideas—does he really expect me to pass them on to the pope himself? This man is crazy.*

"Well, Father Andrew, thank you for your input; maybe you could give me some finer details of your ideas," the big man suggested in a cutting voice.

"Your grace, all I know is that if we don't start changing, we, the Church, will have no future. The Catholic Church will have no further relevance in this world. We have to come of age and listen to what the people expect of us."

Silence followed, and the young priest took this as a sign that he had overstayed his welcome. Father Andrew made his excuses and left the archbishop sitting at the table, deep in thought but still eating.

The elections were held in November, and Paula proved to be a seasoned campaigner. The excitement she generated enveloped those around her, and her popularity grew stronger with each day she went out to meet the people. The voters wanted and needed a fresh approach to running their country. The "We are each other's keeper" slogan was paying off, especially amongst the middle class, the poor, and the aged.

The emigrants—or the New Australians, as they were called—loved Paula. They could relate to her, and the majority of them would vote in her favour. Women regarded the current prime minister as a chauvinist. They felt that a woman such as Paula running the country would bring a breath of fresh air.

Her party won the ballot with an eleven-seat majority—a wonderful result—and Australians had a new prime minister.

CHAPTER 3

The second year had begun with Daniel putting David in charge of running all the investments for the group, much to the delight of Henry.

The group now consisted of many members, but Daniel only confided in a few, and they were the only ones who knew the dark secret that drove Daniel.

The warehouse staff suspected strange happenings in their place of employment. But they were well paid and highly respected Daniel and the others.

David was so grateful for his new life that there wasn't anything he wouldn't do for his miracle worker. He held Daniel in awe, and he figured someone who had such knowledge of the investment markets had to be special.

When at the warehouse, Daniel instructed David on the day's investments, either verbally or via notes scribbled on any piece of paper Daniel could lay his hands on.

On the first occasion his mentor was not at their headquarters, the young man took it upon himself to make a substantial investment on the equities market after an inner sense urged him to do so. The success he had with this first transaction was the confidence he needed to ensure that he would always heed these feelings.

Their wealth grew at such a fast rate that their combined holdings in cash and investments exceeded the two-billion-dollar mark.

Daniel had grown moodier, and he spent most of his spare time in his room. A concerned Peter, with a cup of tea in hand, knocked on his door, and Daniel only opened it after Peter persisted for some time. Daniel tried hard to show a smile. Peter walked in without being invited and passed the cup over to his friend. He sat down in a chair in the corner of the room, while Daniel sat on the bed.

"Are you going to tell me what the problem is?" Peter enquired.

A frown appeared on Daniel's face as the dejected man shook his head and looked at Peter.

"Sixteen years of my life have been lost, and I still cannot recall all aspects of what I am missing. I keep getting flashes of a force—a very powerful energy all around me, inside my head, and inside my body. Most of the time, I am an ordinary man, but when I put my mind into gear, I automatically become something else. It's as if I make a wish and it comes true; there is a power within me that I don't fully understand. Worse still, I have a feeling that these powers are growing.

"The more I read and hear and see regarding the injustices of this world—the sadness and the cruelties men bestow upon other humans and on animals and the devastation they cause to the planet—the stronger I seem to get. I have a suspicion that this power will only stop growing when there is a significant turnaround in these bad deeds. The greatest worry of all is this power might be out of my control, and I feel it could grow so powerful that it could in some way be the cause of the destruction of Earth. Maybe that is the way the Creator will eventually destroy our planet; maybe I am a trigger for some great catastrophe." An agitated Daniel stood up and walked over to his sitting friend. "Peter, I am worried that the time we have may not be long enough; we have to work faster."

A mouse in the corner of the room caught Daniel's eye, and instantly, an unseen power picked it up, drew it through the air, and dropped it, dead, onto the bed.

"This is another power I now have; I can kill with just a look and a thought," Daniel told Peter. "Just shows you how human I am. I saw a mouse, and the first thought I had was to kill it."

A somewhat-calmer Daniel picked up the little rodent and grasped it in both hands; he concentrated for a moment and then put it back onto the bed. Peter felt a weakness within himself for feeling sadness for the little animal, but the sadness turned to astonishment as the mouse stirred, rolled back onto its legs, and scampered away. Peter had no need to say any more; he understood the urgency in what Daniel was saying.

Regular meetings were now taking place at different venues with all the various factions of the Christian faiths and some of the other religions. Together, as Andrew put it, they were the Religious League of Nations, with the Catholics, Protestants, Baptists, Lutherans, and Greek Orthodox making up the Christians, whilst Judaism, Hinduism, and Buddhism made up the other creeds.

Rabbi Goldstein still attended, and also, surprisingly, a small, quiet man with a shaven head and long red robe from the small number of Buddhist monks in Melbourne also became a regular at the meetings.

Peter had become a good friend to Father Andrew, who now frequently visited the warehouse, and he and Henry were the only two Laymen in attendance at these meetings.

The common theme was to unite the people of the world in the fight against poverty and injustice but mainly to find a solution to the ever-growing tension with Islam. Soon, Catholic Archbishop Bradley became actively involved in the movement, and he ensured that His Holiness, the pope, knew of his efforts. He had no hesitation in writing directly to the pontiff's personal cardinal, enclosing copies of articles from the various newspapers on the good publicity these meetings were generating. The big man had great ambitions.

Paula didn't mince her words at her inaugural speech to Parliament. Her views on legalising illicit drugs, aiding the hungry worldwide, and combating the AIDS problem brought the house to its feet for a standing ovation.

"The days of standing by the wayside must come to an end. Action is needed, and it's needed now. As from today, I am instructing our health minister as well as our foreign minister to enlist the help of as many countries as possible to help Australia in these quests.

"If all countries considered legalising drugs, our combined efforts should reduce the problem slowly, until eventually, in the median future, we reduce it to a low percentage of what it is today.

"This new and stronger AIDS virus must be stopped from spreading; this problem is mainly in the African countries. Swift and harsh action must be taken—and taken now.

"Yes, the actions that must be taken are hard actions. In the past, the soft approaches to world problems have not gotten us anywhere. The United Nations is currently next to useless. It must be strong and deal with major problems decidedly. I am calling on them to take the lead in these problems. They must prove to the world that they are a relevant body.

"Our culling of introduced animals to this country and some of our indigenous animals—why do we let their bodies rot and go to waste? They are edible, and all such animals killed are to be stored in the large refrigerated warehouses that are available on many of our wharfs. These quite often lay half full or empty. Unemployed people can be used in this project; they should be earning their keep. When there is enough food to fill a large tanker, the foreign minister is to arrange to export it to a country in need. Yes, this will cost Australians money, but in the long run, the costs will be overtaken by the benefits achieved to humanity."

That night, the world's television stations ran a feature story on Paula and her ideas, and the world's newspapers ran her speech in full. The majority of the people were agreeable with this new approach to old problems. But she also had many critics who insisted that she was insane and that none of her ideas would or could ever come to fruition. But whatever view people had, her ideas started them debating.

The secretary of the United Nations was the first to invite Paula to address the next meeting of the UN, to be held in New York in the next few weeks. The American president followed suit and invited her for a meeting and dinner at the White House prior to her commitment to the United Nations.

Spending most of her time in the Australian capital proved difficult for Paula, but she stayed in contact with her son and Daniel, who never missed an opportunity to reiterate her importance to the mission.

The jigsaw puzzle playing around in Daniel's overactive mind had many pieces, and so far he had managed to fit only a few of these together, but now another one had fallen into place; he wanted to be included in the American trip as one of the prime minister's advisers.

Peter was surprised when Daniel told him of his plan to meet the American president. "How are you going to get a passport? You don't exist, remember?"

"I'll borrow yours."

"You'll borrow mine?"

In the short time they had known each, Peter had gotten used to shaking his head in bewilderment, and this time was no exception. He looked over at Henry, who put down the paper and honed in on the conversation taking place.

Annoyed, Peter walked over to his room and returned a minute later with his passport in his raised hand; he opened it to the first page, which contained his photo, and passed it over to Daniel.

"How can you get away with using mine? I look nothing like you," he insisted.

Daniel handed the passport back, and a dazed look came over Peter's face. After peering at the photo in the passport, he immediately walked over to Henry, who was too intrigued with the whole conversation to interrupt. He handed Henry the passport and, at the same time, asked in a rather bewildered tone, "Whose passport is this?"

"Yours," answered a somewhat-puzzled Henry.

"Mine!" He rudely grabbed it back and looked at it again. "What do you mean *mine*? It's got Daniel's photo and details on it! It was mine, but now it's Daniel's. Am I going barmy, or are you mad?" he shouted at Henry.

Henry stood up, snatched the passport back from Peter, and looked at it again. "No, it's definitely your ugly face," he said sarcastically as he turned and raised the passport picture close to Peter's face.

For the first time since they had met, the two heard Daniel laugh out loud. "Don't you worry about who it belongs to—just let me borrow it for my trip, okay?" he insisted.

With over a billion Muslims worldwide, Daniel was well aware that they were to form a massive piece of his puzzle, and they became his next concern. Their Islamic beliefs were strong and biased. Daniel needed to recruit a respected member from this religion to join Father Andrew's group—and this task would be difficult.

Midmorning on Friday, the mosque close to the city had an unusual visitor. The paler Daniel, in his white suit, stood out amongst the congregation assembled in the prayer hall to perform the ritual Friday prayers. He admired the plain yet beautiful main arch of the mosque, which was covered by a light-filled dome.

Daniel acted no different from the other worshippers who faced and bowed in the direction of the holy city of Mecca. The mosque wall, the closest to the holy city, had a niche known as the mihrab built into it to show the direction of Mecca. He had read the Koran and found that, in a lot of ways, it had the teachings of the Christian Bible, and like the Bible, it was open to interpretation. One part of the Koran Daniel interpreted and liked was the idea that a wrong or a sin was really a state of mind; if a person's own conscience believed without doubt that he or she was in the right, then he or she was in the right. Individuals committed sin when they knew that something was wrong, but when they were absolutely sure that they were right, they were really not committing any sin. In other words, a person's conscience was his or her guide to right or wrong. Daniel, located at the back of the crowd, looked at the people in his immediate vicinity. They were a mixed lot, and their appearances ranged from simple people to professional graduates. Their attitude towards their religion greatly differed from that of the Christians; they seemed all in one mind and focused on their Koran.

Daniel sensed that their belief that all followers of other religions were infidels was strongly imbedded in their minds, and to change that attitude would be formidable. Even if he succeeded, how would the person he converted survive if he or she dared to preach against the Koran? He realised that he would have to be totally and personally involved with any convert or converts.

One man stood out in the crowd; he prayed at the back, not far from Daniel, kneeling on his mat and bowing with the rest of the congregation. He was a big man in a white robe, bearded like most of the other men, and Daniel noticed that he wasn't as enthusiastic with his prayers as the rest. He was restless, as if he needed to be elsewhere.

The big Muslim also observed the stranger looking at him, and when the prayers were over, he approached Daniel.

"I haven't seen you here before, brother. Where are you from?" He asked the question in Arabic, and Daniel was surprised that he understood every word.

"I am new to this mosque; I have only recently moved into the area," Daniel answered in English.

"Well, I am the mosque's doctor, and if you would like, I will introduce you to our mufti if you haven't met him yet."

"That won't be necessary just yet; I actually came to meet you," Daniel quietly replied.

"You know me?" the surprised man exclaimed.

"No, but it is essential that we talk," Daniel said as he looked at the puzzled man in front of him.

Two men standing in earshot and looking at them laughed out loud, and the doctor turned towards them and insisted on knowing what was so funny. The men stopped laughing, and one of them, although clearly intimidated by the doctor, shyly answered him, "Well, your conversation sounds very odd. You are talking to him in Arabic, and he is answering you back in English. It just sounds funny—that is all." The two men hurried away.

The doctor stared at Daniel for some time before he motioned for him to follow. The mosque had its own small hospital with a medical clinic attached to the doctor's private dwelling, and as they entered one of the rooms, the doctor gestured for Daniel to sit.

"Before we go any further, what did that person mean about you talking to me in English? All I am hearing is Arabic."

"My name is Daniel—Daniel Leeder. What is your name?"

"Doctor Tomas Adofo—I am in charge of this clinic for my people."

"Well," continued Daniel, "now that the formalities are over, I had better explain a few things to you. Yes, that man was right; I am talking to you in English because I don't speak one word of Arabic. Yet I can understand everything you say."

The confused Tomas remembered an important duty he had momentarily forgotten, and he now reverted to well-spoken English to interrupt their discussion. "Please excuse me—I must check up on my children and my mother."

He walked through the hallway and disappeared into a door running off it.

His two boys didn't even notice he had walked into the room; they were still where he had left them, engrossed in watching cartoons on the television. He smiled and left them as they were and entered another room off the same hallway. He gingerly walked towards the old woman lying on the single bed, and taking her arm, he felt for her pulse.

His eyes watered as he realised she had deteriorated further, and he doubted she would make it through another night. He was startled by a noise behind him, and turning, he saw Daniel in the room.

"She has had a hard life." Daniel's soothing voice calmed the annoyed doctor. "You love her very much, and she is needed by you and your sons.

I realise I am a stranger to you, but would you indulge me for one minute and let me stand over her? Trust me, Tomas."

The words "Trust me" rang in Tomas's ears, and at first, he didn't even notice Daniel slipping past him and taking his mother's hands into his own. Tomas watched as the stranger stood over his mother, staring at her, and although her eyes were closed and she lay motionless, the two appeared to be communicating.

Her body quivered slightly, and Tomas saw his mother opening her eyes. A smile appeared on her face. She looked at Daniel and, in a whisper, said to him in Arabic, "You are a very kind young man; thank you so much for your concern."

"You rest for a while, Mrs. Adofo; you must be starving. Tomas will call you when he has prepared some food for you." Daniel spoke in English.

"I am famished," the enthusiastic old woman replied in Arabic.

Turning to the stunned man beside him, Daniel smiled and said, "Tomas, you heard your mother—she is hungry."

Within half an hour, with the grinning mother sitting at the head of the table, Tomas, the boys, and Daniel enjoyed a delicious lunch together. Afterwards, back in Tomas's private room at the clinic, the two men faced each other across the large mahogany desk and sipped their coffee.

"My friend, you are an amazing man," Tomas said, breaking the peace. "I heard you talking to my mother in English, even though she does not understand one word of it, and yet she comprehended what you were saying. More importantly, my mother was close to death, and now she is back on her feet, better than she has been for years."

Tomas raised his large frame and muttered, "How is this possible?"

Daniel started to explain in a quiet, soothing voice. "Tomas, your name suggests you were born in Egypt, and it translates as 'fighter,' and I need a fighter to help me bring peace in that part of the world."

Tomas stared at Daniel. How could anyone make such a ridiculous statement about such a momentous problem?

"No worries. I will snap my fingers and—poof—the Jews will walk out of Israel, and the Palestinians will walk back in, and there will be peace," a laughing Tomas sarcastically replied.

"You are saying that that is the only way there could be peace in the Middle East?" Daniel asked.

"My friend, the land was home to the Palestinians for centuries, and then the British and United Nations decided to send the Jews back to the homeland they claimed was theirs thousands of years ago. If everybody claimed back the land of their ancestors, the world would not be what it is now. Here in Australia, the white people only go back just two hundred and fifty years. Would you give this country back to the Aboriginals? Of course not, but the Palestinians had no choice. They let the Jews into their country, and slowly, they took over completely. They kicked the people off their land—and most of them out of Palestine altogether. My homeland, Egypt, has many refugees from there, waiting to return to their own homeland. Only the elderly remember their motherland; the young only learn of it from their elders. What would you do if the Chinese invaded Australia and kicked you out of your own country? Would you love the Chinese or hate them? How far would you go to get your country back, and how long would you fight for the cause? Would you not pass on the hatred to your children? The Israelis took their land from them, and they want it back; it is as simple as that."

Tomas sipped his coffee. "The Palestinians fight the Jews with rocks, and the Jews fight them with tanks. They are willing to die to the last man for their land. The Palestinians' main weapon is what you people call terrorism. Their young people have nothing to live for, so they are willing to strap bombs onto their bodies and kill themselves in order to hurt their enemies. The Jews in America—and some even here in this country—are very wealthy. They control the wealth of America, and they supply their brothers in Israel with the tanks and planes that kill those poor bastards. Now these so-called terrorists are attacking the American people, and there is a world condemnation against the killing of innocent civilians. Well, how many thousands of Palestinian civilians has America's friend Israel killed? Besides the cursed oil, the only thing of importance we, the Arabs, including the Palestinians, have in our lives is our strong belief in our Koran and Muhammad. No, my friend, there can never be peace there." The Arab let out a long sigh, and immediately, Daniel continued the tirade in the same verve as Tomas.

"Now, you sit yourself down and listen to what I have to tell you. You are about to come to a pinnacle in your life that is going to affect the entire earth, and you will be playing a big part in whether humanity continues or dies."

Tomas's almond eyes narrowed as he digested what Daniel had to tell him.

As if right on cue, when Daniel finished his tale, the door to the clinic opened, and Tomas's mother brought in more coffee for them. Once she left, the conversation continued, starting with a sigh from Tomas.

"My friend, all my senses tell me that this is one big hoax or one big nightmare. But I look at my mother, and I have to say, this is not a hoax or a nightmare; this is reality, and I want to believe you are this powerful prophet here to save us. I must. I will believe you, Daniel."

"Please understand that I more than anybody else in this world wish this to be a hoax or just a nightmare that I will wake up from in fright at any moment." Daniel sounded desperate.

The impossibilities of the situation were hard for Tomas to grasp, but he knew he had to help in any way possible. "How do we start with this peace programme?"

"A small start for now is for you and your spiritual leader to attend meetings with a group of people from different religions, including Judaism. I know that your spiritual leader is the mufti for the Australian half a million or so Muslims. He happens to also be the holy man for this mosque, and he is a very controversial and outspoken member of your community. Now, if we could convince him to attend these meetings, that would be a forward move. Tomas, I want you to befriend one of my followers, my friend Henry, who is a Jew, and I want you to help each other try to come up with some ideas on this peace problem. Australia is to become an example to the rest of the world that there can be peace with the different religions and that they can coexist. We already have a head start here, as we have freedom of expression and of religion. But we need to bring these religions together to help fight the bigotry between them," Daniel concluded.

Tomas took Daniel to meet the mufti, and as they entered his quarters, Tomas closed the large solid-timber doors behind him. The white-bearded, thin man was dressed in his white robe and had his unkempt hair covered by a white fez.

Tomas introduced the two. "This is our mufti, Sheikh Abdul Farho, and Your Holiness, this is Daniel Leeder."

"Ah, Daniel—that is a very old biblical name," the old man commented, showing he had a reasonable grasp of the English language. He didn't make eye contact with his visitors, and immediately, Daniel felt the insincerity in him.

After Tomas explained the religious meetings being held in the community and the reason for them, Farho didn't appear too impressed. "I doubt if you will find any Muslim youth homeless and hungry in our community. We look after our youth, not like some of the other people of this country," he commented, almost with a sneer. "We like to keep to ourselves and stay apart from the people we consider infidels."

Daniel stared at the old man until his will not to look at Daniel was broken; Farho slowly raised his head, and their eyes locked onto each other. Farho saw the anger in Daniel's face, and at first, a feeling of intimidation came over him, but this feeling soon changed to pride as he realised that he had hit a nerve with this Christian.

Angrily, Daniel replied to his comments. "Firstly, I am not a Christian, nor am I a Muslim or, as a matter of fact, a member of any other faith that you can think of. But also understand this: I am not an atheist. Secondly, you are from Iran; how many Christian churches have you there? I believe that country is one of those that has recently outlawed all non-Muslim religions. Yet here, in this country, you can go about your business as you please. Here you have freedom of religion and of speech. In your old country, there is no freedom of religion or speech. Thirdly, there probably are more Muslims starving in this world than any other denomination—just take the African countries into consideration. The movement we are trying to get off the ground here is only the tip of the iceberg. Our ultimate aim is to spread this movement all over the world so that the needier are helped. In Australia, even the neediest of people are much better off than most of the third-world people. And last but not least, if you feel so strongly about staying separated from the rest of the community in this country, then, sir, may I suggest you go back to Iran. If you do not want to go back, then be man enough to embrace this country and help it develop in a way that it can be an example to the rest of the world."

An irate Daniel turned to exit the room, and as he approached the closed doors, they flung open with such force that they flew off their hinges and splintered into pieces against the wall. A frightened Farho watched as Daniel walked out of the room and disappeared into the courtyard.

A few days later, Henry let Daniel know he had met Tomas and the holy man Farho at their latest meeting and that they had agreed to be part of the group.

Daniel was a guest adviser to the new prime minister for her first meeting with the world's most powerful man, the president of the United States of America. Along with Daniel and Paula was a contingent of reporters and photographers as well as a number of office staff. Daniel had insisted on taking Con and Serge, two of the warehouse security guards, with them. Using Peter's passport, Daniel had no difficulty going through customs at their destination: Washington Dulles International Airport.

On their arrival, late in the afternoon, the secretary of state along with the Australian ambassador welcomed them. They were escorted from the airport to one of the most exclusive hotels in Washington, DC, and Paula was shown to the presidential suite on the thirty-third floor, while Daniel had a much smaller room across the hall, which was usually reserved for an assistant or servant to the special guest in the major suite.

A welcoming dinner at the White House had been arranged, and the prime minister would meet the president that night. Daniel stationed the two burly Australian guards at the front door of Paula's suite and asked them to be vigilant. Another two American security guards, one black and one white, were out in the foyer down at street level. They joked about the waste of time and effort in providing protection for an Australian prime minister. Most Americans wouldn't even know Australia's location, let alone want to harm its leader.

Paula had a shower, put on a robe, and took her time getting ready for this auspicious occasion. She reflected on her humble start in politics, the quick rise up the political ladder to become the prime minister of Australia, and the realisation that her name would live forever in the history of Australia. Now she was there to meet the president of the United States and hoped that she would not be overawed by John B. Rose.

Loud thudding noises suddenly interrupted her thoughts—somewhat like the sound of firecrackers going off in quick succession—and then she heard the definite sound of breaking glass. The noise came from the hall outside her room, and it got unbearably loud. She cautiously made her way to the door and slowly opened it. The noise was now deafening, and splinters of wood, chunks of plaster, and dust showered over her, blurring her vision.

Rubbing her eyes, Paula slipped her head out into the hallway, and what she saw through the haze sent a shiver through her spine that immediately made her let out a piercing scream.

The two guards were lying over each other, covered in blood, and Daniel stood over them with his back to Paula. He was completely naked. Without turning his head, he growled at her, "Get inside, and get under cover."

The quick glance she had taken showed three men with guns in their hands, facing and shooting at Daniel. She ran inside and hid in the bathroom, and although shivering from fright, she felt ashamed of herself; for a split second, she had forgotten the situation and could only think of the sight of Daniel's naked body.

Within seconds, all was quiet, and an anxious Paula gathered her courage, opened the bathroom door, and again headed for the front entrance. Her concern for Daniel was foremost on her mind as she slowly opened the front door and silently peered out into the hallway. The petrified woman was horrified at the carnage that lay in the hallway and in the alcove to the left of her room, where the lifts were. To her relief, she saw Daniel, who was still naked and the only person left standing. She wanted to call out to him but stopped herself from doing so; she was intrigued with what he was doing.

He had a gun in his hands and was placing it in a dead guard's hand. He knelt over the two men and put his hands over them. Paula saw him raise his head, his eyes closed, and a sudden stillness befell the area; her ears felt the tense quiet as loudly as if a bomb had gone off. She could feel the intensity emanating from Daniel's whole being, and it frightened her.

The floor in front of the lifts was covered with broken glass, and the three men who had been shooting at Daniel lay dead on top of it. Daniel opened his eyes, and on seeing Paula, he came up to her and, consoling her, led her into her room. "You saw nothing of what happened out there—just leave everything to me," he instructed her.

"Jesus, what the fuck happened here?" said the white American guard as the two US guards, with guns drawn, stepped out of the elevator. They stood in the doorway, looking at the naked man as he held the dazed and frightened woman.

"Are you okay?" the black guard asked.

"Yes, we are all right. Check on our guards, please; see if they are hurt," replied Daniel.

The black American checked the bodies of the attackers. He turned back and approached the other man, who knelt over their Australian counterparts.

"Weird—those three guys have been shot once right between the eyes," he said in a southern drawl. "They each had machine guns and let off hundreds of rounds, and they are dead." The tall black man shook his head in disbelief. "You two Aussies are riddled with bullet holes, and you are still alive."

The Australian guards helped each other to their feet and looked as puzzled as the Americans. They gazed at each other and could see and smell the fresh blood all over themselves; their clothes were littered with holes, which had to be bullet holes, but they were still alive.

The white American guard, looking at them in utter amazement, muttered, "I tell you, those bullet-proof vests you guys are wearing are something else."

"What the fuck happened?" the other excited American asked. "And where the fuck did those guys come from?" He pointed to the dead men.

Serge, still dazed and in shock, tried to explain. "Out of nowhere, we suddenly saw those three men outside the building, swinging from ropes and shooting at the glass panels in front of them. I remember glass splattering everywhere, and I reached for my gun; I am sure I got one shot off, but to be quite honest, I can't remember anything else after that." He stalled when he realised he was still holding the gun in his hand. After examining it, he continued his explanation. "But I must have got some shots off; my gun has four bullets missing." He handed the Browning over to the white American, who inspected it.

The second Australian guard could only say, "That's my recollections too, except that I didn't fire any shots."

Daniel wanted to end the inquisition. "Well, that explains it all, and we have a president to meet, so please excuse us while we get ready." Motioning to the Australian guards to follow, Daniel entered Paula's suite and then closed the door after them.

"You fellows did a good job out there, and I am sure it will be hard to get it out of your minds, but I am asking you to do just that; your prime minister needs you," Daniel said, trying to comfort them.

Serge was still perplexed, and his whole body was shaking as he spoke. "We will, Mr. Leeder, but what we can't understand is that we were shot at a number of times, and we are not wearing any bullet-proof vests, like the Yanks thought. They couldn't have missed us; look at all the bullet holes in our clothing. They definitely hit us—we should be dead."

"Just thank your lucky stars that they were bad shots and, more importantly, that you are both still alive." Daniel grinned. "Nothing else matters. Now go and change and meet us downstairs; the secretary of state should be down in the foyer right about now, so let's not keep him waiting too long."

Paula looked at Daniel with awe. "You shot those men, didn't you? Our men were dead, and now they are alive. What happened? I need to know."

"Paula, I am sorry for all of this. Now you know why I wanted to be close to you. I need to ensure that you are safe to complete the mission I have for you."

"But who were they? And to go to this length to kill me?" the distraught woman enquired.

"Paula, you are more important than you realise. The push to legalise drugs is worrying more people than we can imagine."

Realising he was still naked, Daniel went into the bathroom and returned with a towel wrapped around his waist. Now with him partially covered, Paula realised that this handsome man had been naked all this time in her room and she had been too distraught to notice.

"This will make our case for the legalisation of drugs much stronger," Daniel said. "Now, you get ready, and I'll be back in a few minutes to escort you downstairs."

Paula took a quick look in the dresser mirror and huffed, "I may need a little bit more than a few minutes."

FBI agents and security guards had surrounded the hotel and the neighbouring streets; they were in the foyer and on the roof and even had helicopters circling overhead, lighting up the night sky with their spotlights.

After Paula greeted the American secretary of state and the Australian ambassador in the foyer, Daniel, still dressed in his white suit, escorted her to the waiting limousine. The increase in the security afforded to the Australian prime minister as she headed for the White House was noticeable. Paula felt embarrassed by all the attention.

With outstretched hands, the president and Florence Rose, the first lady, greeted her, and John B. Rose immediately began apologising for the attempt on her life in his country.

"I promise you we will get to the bottom of this; we will find the people responsible for this abominable act," the president assured her. "We are just so relieved that you were not harmed."

"Don't think anything of it, Mr. President; I have a guardian angel looking after me." Paula smiled and took a quick glance at Daniel, who was by her side, acting as her escort. She had to laugh to herself at the way he stood out amongst all the other dignitaries, who were all dressed in black, while he persisted with his ridiculous white suit.

"And talking about guardian angels, please let me introduce you to my adviser, Daniel Leeder."

John B. Rose's grinned and thought, *Well, he is Australian, and they are not known for their dress sense.*

They shook hands, and Daniel, bowing, slightly said, "Mr. President, it is indeed an honour to meet you, sir, and you are dead right on one of two counts, sir."

The president felt a tingle go through his body at the touch of Daniel's hand, and he reacted slowly in replying, "Only right on one of two counts, eh? I can't recall making any counts, but tell me where am I wrong."

"Well, you are wrong about most Aussies; they aren't as bad as me in their dress sense. And you are right about the Colombian drug lords. They were definitely behind the attack on the prime minister. One more thing, sir: you can put your mind at ease; the prime minister will not be killed in your country. I'll make sure of that."

The elderly man with distinguished grey hair glared at Daniel. "Sir, you are a mind reader; that's exactly what I was thinking—darned good guess. I am sure it is the Colombians, but as far as protecting her on your own, well, that's another thing; they are mean sons of bitches, those drug barons."

The invitees mingled, and the president and the first lady introduced them to each other. One introduction stood out for Daniel, when the president's short, large-breasted wife presented him to a dark-skinned man in an obviously expensive navy-blue reefer jacket. It had genuine twenty-four-carat gold buttons on the front as well as the sleeves. His cream-coloured Western trousers and matching shoes made his Turkish black fez, with a shiny gold leaf pinned to the front, seem out of place.

"This is Shahma Habib; he is an adviser to the president on Middle Eastern matters. He was of great help to my husband in the war against the Taliban in Afghanistan. John, of course, was a three-star general over there, you know," she said proudly and with an obvious flirtatious manner towards Habib.

"It is a pleasure to meet you, Mr. Leeder." The barrel-chested man with the goatee beard and the large brown eyes reached out his right hand in greeting. He ignored the tingle he felt. "I am actually not an Afghan; I hail from Iran. My family was forced out of that country with the fall of the shah of Persia—the old name for Iran, as you no doubt know—and we became refugees in Afghanistan."

Daniel had expected him to have a heavy Arab accent, but he definitely hailed from New York. "You certainly seem to have had a very interesting life, Mr. Habib," Daniel commented. "You obviously have lived in this country for most of your life."

"Yes, my heart belongs to the three countries; I was fortunate that my parents had most of their investments in the United States, so they left a sizable fortune for me to be able to afford to live anywhere in the world I choose," Habib bragged. He downed his glass of orange juice before he continued the conversation. "I noticed that you are with the Australian prime minister; where do you fit into this picture, Mr. Leeder?"

"No doubt similar to you, Mr. Habib—an adviser on world issues." Daniel smiled.

Habib nodded in agreement. "Mine is a little bit more concentrated—the forever-warring country of Afghanistan and the troubled country of Iran. Being a descendant of Iranian parents and loving Afghanistan and its people make my job so much more enjoyable. I am able to help all three of these countries, including America, in trying to keep the peace between them."

A bell sounded, and the guests were led into the enormous dining room. All the dignitaries attending had their chairs individually pulled back and pushed forward as they sat at the massive table.

The president sat at the head of the table, with the first lady at his right and Paula at his left. Daniel sat next to her, and directly across from him was his newfound friend, Habib. The president, curious about the controversial views Paula held on many subjects, especially the drug problem, prompted her to explain some of her ideas before they started their dinner.

"Mr. President, if we—and by 'we,' I mean the whole world—do not make a combined effort to eradicate the drug problem, the starvation of millions of people, and the ever-growing AIDS epidemic, not to mention terrorism and so many more equally important problems, we might as well hang up our boots and call it quits."

The president's head lifted higher at the mention of terrorism. "Terrorism—I am one hundred percent behind you there, I can assure you," he interrupted.

"Mr. President, by 'terrorism,' I mean terrorism from all sides," Paula was quick to point out. The president frowned at that remark, not quite sure if sarcasm was the intent; he politically chose to ignore the comment, and Paula, not wanting to offend her host, skipped over the remark and continued.

"And by 'starvation,' I mean an effort by nations such as ours to help the countries less fortunate than us, and—let's face it—their plight emanates from the past deeds of our own ancestors. AIDS has to be stopped from spreading by any means available to us, and drug users must be stopped from addicting others in order to support their own habits. These ideas are not new, but now the time has come when we have no choice in these matters. The time for change is now, and time is one commodity we have little of."

The enthusiasm she emanated was infectious, and the other diners were caught up in her excitement as they listened with interest, waiting for the lectured president's retort.

John B. Rose hadn't asked for a sermon, although he had the feeling that he had just received one. He smiled to reveal a perfectly capped mouthful of teeth. "The urgency in your voice, Mrs. Prime Minister, tells me that these matters are high on your agenda. You sound as if you are predicting the end if we don't solve these problems." He gave out a quiet laugh, but to his embarrassment, no one else laughed with him.

"Mr. President, it seems that it's not only Mr. Leeder who is a mind reader." She grinned.

His smile vanished for a moment, as he sensed there was something grave in the way the Australian prime minister had answered him. John B. Rose felt beaten, and he quickly gave the signal for dinner to begin.

"Paula, if I may call you that, let us enjoy this fine food; we will finish our conversation in my office after dinner." The president ended the serious atmosphere surrounding the table, and only small talk followed as they ate the elaborate offerings.

The president escorted Paula into the renowned Oval Office, followed by Daniel and a few of the White House advisers; they sat and drank port with their coffee as they debated.

Daniel could sense they were not taking Paula seriously, and they only skirted around the edges of the topics she had brought up at the dinner table. After twenty minutes, one of his advisers reminded the president he had another dignitary waiting to see him.

On the way out, the president said farewell to Paula, and as Daniel grasped John's hand tightly, he whispered, "Mr. President, I know you are a busy man, but you will make time to see me before we leave America. We need to talk about an urgent world matter that I need your help with."

"My time is very precious, Mr. Leeder. I doubt if I will have the time before you leave," said the indignant president.

"Mr. President, I predict that by tomorrow, you will change your mind." Daniel turned and left the curious man watching him walk away.

Paula felt humble as she looked down from the platform at the delegates from the many countries that made up the body of the United Nations. She was in wonderment of all around her and had difficulty starting her speech. A subtle feeling of power came over her, and she instantly knew Daniel was with her. With a renewed confidence, she began her talk. "Please, if I may beg of you all, just for today, may we pretend that we are all related to each other? Let's pretend that there are no borders between countries. Let's pretend that the whole world is one country, consisting of one people and one family. If we were one people, would we let our brothers and sisters starve or let them abuse themselves with drugs to which they have become addicted? Would we not try to help them by feeding them or by trying to wean them off these drugs?"

The speech went well over her allocated hour, and she finally finished with a request that they not just forget her talk but start discussions towards solving these massive and urgent problems.

On the conclusion of her talk, silence overtook the assembly until a black man from one of the poorer African countries stood up and started clapping. One by one, the audience members stood and joined the first one, until all the delegates were standing and clapping.

Noticeably, the delegates from the richer countries were the last to stand. The ovation she received on her conclusion lifted her spirits; she knew that her time had not been wasted and that Daniel would be proud as he looked down from the visitors' gallery.

That afternoon, at the hotel, a loud knocking on the door interrupted Daniel's reading of the local news. He donned his jacket and opened the door to reveal the same two American security guards who had guarded Paula the night before. The taller black man gave an abrupt order to Daniel: "Mr. Leeder, the president wants to see you."

"What kept you? I have been expecting you, and I'm ready to go," he told the surprised escorts.

The tall grey-haired president sat leaning forward at his desk, looking at his guest. Daniel, sitting on a comfortable chair on the other side, was fascinated by the ugly bulldog squatting in the middle of the room and eagerly licking his genitals. The president had asked his aides to leave them alone, and he appeared a little flustered over how to broach the subject matter he wanted to discuss.

John B. Rose, obviously perturbed, gave out a loud sigh. "Daniel, that comment you made last night has me intrigued. You were sure I would make the time to see you today."

"Mr. President, you have an autopsy report on your desk about the three dead men and a report from the FBI, and you are perplexed by them both."

"You seem so sure of yourself," the president remarked smugly.

Daniel asked him to turn off the internal tapes recording their conversation. As a hesitant president made a phone call; he noticed Daniel close his eyes, and stillness came over the room. The elderly man hung up the phone, and with a smile, Daniel said, "Thank you, Mr. President; they are all turned off now."

The phone rang, and the president answered. When he hung up, he looked across at Daniel and meekly asked, "You turned off all the tapes in my office?"

"Yes, Mr. President, we need to talk privately—very privately," Daniel sternly replied.

John B. Rose picked up the papers from his desk. "Daniel, these reports are hard to understand; the three dead men were killers—mercenaries who worked for the Colombian drug lords. That we already know, but the way they died is strange; they died of asphyxiation, from lack of oxygen. They were dead before they were shot in the head." He hesitated before continuing. "And your Australian guards were shot up very badly and should be dead, yet they live." He stood up, looked directly into Daniel's eyes, and, in a wavering voice, said, "They spoke to some of our guys and told them they were not wearing vests, and when they took off their clothes, dozens of bullets fell out onto the floor."

The president walked across the room, stepping over the dog, which was still enjoying its genitals, and pulled out some clothing from a plastic shopping bag.

"I have their clothes here, and they are riddled with bullet holes, and another thing that is very puzzling: there is a lot of confusion in regards to the passport you used to enter into this country. The number of that document belongs to a Peter Brand; Daniel Leeder's passport expired many years ago. Can you please shed some light—any light—on what really happened last night and tell me who the hell you are?" The president sounded frustrated.

Deliberating within himself for a while, Daniel tried to pick his words carefully. "John, your country could destroy the world many times over with its nuclear capabilities. Yet I believe that the world is on the verge of destruction by another means—by me. Within me, there will one day be enough power to destroy the world. I have no idea how, but I sense it."

The president smirked and wanted to stop this farce and get back to the subject of the dead men. "Okay! Okay! First things first. Just suppose you tell me what happened to those men last night?"

"I killed the three men with just a thought. I created a vacuum around them, and they suffocated. Then, using the Australian guard's gun, I shot each of them in the head to disguise what had actually happened. I revived the dead Australians, but I couldn't be bothered with those other men; they were scum who killed for money."

There was real authority in Daniel's voice. "John, I need you to listen to me, because I do not have time to waste. Look at your dog—it's dead. And I can kill you just as quick."

Daniel's tone frightened the president; he tripped over his dog as he moved closer to the door. Picking himself up, he realised that the dog was indeed dead. It was slumped down with its tongue sticking out of its head and resting on its genitals.

"Winston, Winston!" he called to the motionless dog as he stood over it. He looked up, cowering, as he saw Daniel slowly walking towards him.

Daniel knelt down next to the dog, touched it, and closed his eyes. In a few seconds, the dog recommenced licking his scrotum and wagging his stubby tail in glee.

The president now sat and listened intently to every word Daniel had to say. After some time, Daniel concluded, "This world has become so fragmented and so unbalanced that I must bring it into some order. We have very little time to unite the world and achieve a balance amongst mankind itself and between mankind and its environment. I believe there is a gauge measuring our progress or lack of progress, and that gauge is the growth or the reduction of the power within me. Our planet and all life on it will end unless my powers stop increasing and actually start to reverse to a state where I have less power. The ultimate would be if I lose all this power and become a normal person again. This would mean that the world is at peace and most of the injustices have been conquered. Unfortunately, this would be next to impossible, so I can't ever see all my power being eliminated. In this unprecedented emergency, the world needs one person leading it, and that is what I have been chosen by the Natural Force to do. I need all the help I can get." Now it was Daniel's turn to show his frustration. "John, the world needs you, and I need you; you are the man who must help me unite the world."

A realisation came to the president, and he quickly looked up at Daniel. "Normally, by now, I would have you in a straitjacket, but recently, an event has been brought to my attention that seems to tie in with what you are saying. Scientists have discovered a comet—Comet Clara—and they predict that there is a possibility it could hit Earth sometime in the next five to six years. If it did, we would not survive. Their calculations were not accurate, due to its inconsistency; its velocity was not constant enough to provide accurate data."

"So that is how the Creator means to destroy us." Daniel was now in shock himself. "It has already instigated the method of our destruction. I am like a magnet or some sort of trigger."

The president, although wary, had no real choice but to temporarily take Daniel seriously. "Scientists are at a loss on where the comet has come from and why it is acting so unpredictably. How do we do the impossible—how do we unite the world? The closest thing to unification is the United

Nations, and that body is next to useless. Do we tell them your story or tell the whole world about it?" The president was now cooperative.

"No, we cannot take any chances of panicking the general public, and the delegates at the United Nations are only puppets to their individual leaders. What we need is to get all their leaders together and start planning for world peace and unification. This needs to occur within the next twelve months or earlier if possible."

The president and Daniel talked for several hours about the major problems that needed resolution and how John would instigate the conference of world leaders. They agreed that the island of Malta, in the Mediterranean, would be the easiest to secure and convenient to the majority of attendees.

The religious group led by Father Andrew had begun to have the desired effect; the group had united as one. Their own personal religions and views didn't come into play; they had one major aim: to spread the unification and respect of all the religions of the world.

Henry had become the publicist for them, and he always managed to have their meetings covered by the news in Australia and abroad. Similar religious groups sprung up in many countries.

Jimmy and his helpers spread the message of hope amongst his people, and they developed a new respect for themselves and for their community.

The People's Party, under Paula, was in the process of writing new legislation to put before the two houses of Parliament—the legalisation of drugs, foreign aid, and Australia's assistance in eradicating AIDS worldwide being on the top of her agenda. Her popularity with the Australian people and worldwide made her one of the most well-known and respected people on the face of the planet.

The world wanted and needed change, and change could only be achieved by implementing radical measures. Making illicit drugs legal was certainly not a new notion; it had been debated worldwide for scores of years, yet governments and law enforcement had persisted with the old way—the illegality of drugs—no matter how much of a failure it proved to be. Paula sought immediate action in implementing these changes.

The wealth of Daniel's group had become enormous. They had a combined wealth of several billion dollars, and their fortune was rapidly increasing. They gave financial aid to many charities that enhanced their cause.

The food supply in the refrigerated warehouses at the Melbourne Port was now at full capacity and ready to be delivered to a country in need. With funds from the group, Peter arranged for a cargo liner to ship this food to Ethiopia. Refrigerated warehouses were being built in that country for such shipments.

Daniel's powers were still growing stronger, and they had not even scratched the surface of the world's problems. The injustices and killings in the world increased at a faster rate than the good that his small group could achieve. He needed to get the world leaders together urgently.

The meeting had already been scheduled, and the majority of acceptances the American president had been able to muster were mainly from the Western world. Daniel arranged for Paula to officially visit Indonesia, where he would travel with her as her adviser.

Daniel instructed Garry Foster to plan a flight to Indonesia in their private jet; with Caris as his passenger, he would rendezvous with them there, and together they would journey on to South Africa and other African nations.

Again using Peter's passport, Daniel entered Jakarta Airport with Paula and her entourage. The Australian ambassador and the Indonesian minister for foreign affairs welcomed them. The president, Mr. Dachamer Islamiyah, was well known for snubbing Western dignitaries, and this visit would be no exception.

The president was in an impossible situation; the Muslims were in the majority, and he needed their support to keep his power. To his people, Australians were Christians, and any show of affiliation with them could be detrimental to his re-election.

They were to be presented to him the next morning, but as soon as they arrived at their hotel, the foreign affairs minister, Mr. Santos, wanted an immediate audience with Paula. As the manager of the hotel personally escorted Daniel and Paula to her presidential suite, Mr. Santos followed them inside. He was a short, stout man with dark hair combed back, a small nose, and a small moustache, but when he talked, the clear tone in his voice somehow made him seem taller.

Mr. Santos informed Paula that the president could not see her tomorrow and that he would endeavour to see her the following day. A rage came over Daniel. He glanced at Mr. Santos, whose legs buckled. He collapsed into Daniel's arms, and Daniel gently lowered him onto a rug in the middle of the lounge room.

Paula watched, horrified, as Daniel slowly rolled him up in the rug and dragged him into the large walk-in robe in the magnificent bedroom.

"Paula, you carry on as if nothing has happened, and whatever you do, don't let anyone into the wardrobe," he told the bewildered woman.

"Don't worry about Mr. Santos in there; he will be all right. You will have your meeting tomorrow with Mr. Islamiyah," Daniel promised as he stormed out of the room.

He walked out of the lift in the foyer, and a lean older man dressed in a white shirt over white trousers immediately confronted him.

"What are your instructions, Mr. Santos?" the man asked as he bowed.

"I need to talk to the president urgently. Please arrange it at once," ordered the new Mr. Santos. In the aide's mind, the order was in perfect Bahasa Indonesia. Out of the hundred languages spoken in Indonesia, this was the official language.

They made their way to the ministerial palace as the assistant made arrangements for an immediate private meeting between the minister of foreign affairs and the busy president.

An hour had passed, and Daniel, now back at the hotel with Mr. Santos's assistant, waited for the lift to take them back up to Paula's room. To some people, the two made a strange couple; they were two different nationals talking in two different languages, yet they were having a congenial conversation. Others saw two Asian men conversing and took little notice of them.

The assistant was confused when the hotel manager walked by; he looked directly at the assistant and greeted him in Indonesian. He then turned to Mr. Santos and, in English, said, "Hope you are enjoying your stay in our country, Mr. Leeder; please let me know if there is anything I can help you with."

The aide glared at the manager as he walked away and, pointing a finger to his head, said to Mr. Santos, "The humidity is bad today; the heat must have affected his brain."

"Yes, it is quite humid today." Mr. Santos grinned.

The Australian guard outside Paula's room knocked on the door as he saw Daniel approaching. The aide waited in the hallway as Daniel closed the door behind him upon entering the suite.

"He is a nice fellow, that Mr. Leeder," the guard said in English to the assistant as a way of starting a conversation.

The older man looked at the guard and muttered, in his own language, "It must be the humidity."

With the worried Paula looking on, Daniel picked up the unconscious Santos from the wardrobe and dragged him into the smaller second bedroom, where he lifted him and laid him on his back on the bed. He put his hand on the sleeping man's head, and in an instant, Mr. Santos opened his eyes and propped himself up on his elbows. He looked around as he focused on the two people looking down on him.

"What happened to me?" he asked.

"You fainted," replied Daniel. "You were having such a nice sleep that we decided not to wake you. I am sure you must be feeling better after such a good rest."

"Yes, I do feel very well—very well indeed." Santos stretched out his arms and yawned.

"My heartiest apologies to you, Mrs. Prime Minister. I hope I haven't inconvenienced you in any way." He turned to Daniel and asked, "How long have I been asleep?"

The door to Paula's room flew open, and an agitated foreign minister berated his waiting aide. "You imbecile! Quickly—I must get back to the palace; the president is not going to be happy with my tardiness. By Allah, I should have seen him half an hour ago; he will have my head for this. You should have made sure I was not late for my appointment with him," he screamed at the confused man.

"But, sir, you rescheduled your appointment; you have already seen him," the concerned assistant pleaded. "Don't worry, sir. It is the humidity; it has affected many people today."

The president told a surprised and agitated Santos that there was nothing to apologise for, and the stout man became more baffled than ever.

"Mr. Santos, please make arrangements for my meeting with the Australian prime minister for tomorrow morning, and while you are at it, I want you to arrange a personal telephone conversation with the Malaysian and Filipino leaders as soon as possible."

"But, Mr. President, I thought you were not seeing the Australian woman," a surprised Mr. Santos said.

"I do not quite understand why, but I must see her, Mr. Santos," a rather vague president tried to explain to the bewildered man. "I had a most unusual but very realistic dream—or at least I think it was a dream. You came to see me before, yet it wasn't you; it was a man in a white suit, and he became my dead father, who instructed me to see the Australian prime minister and to contact our neighbours to ensure they go to that conference in Malta."

With the help of the Indonesian president, the other Asian leaders agreed to attend the world leaders' meeting, and now Daniel's next agenda was to persuade some of the ministers from the poorer African countries to attend.

CHAPTER 4

Garry, with Caris as his only passenger, had arrived in Jakarta to pick up Daniel. They headed west to Sri Lanka as the first refuelling stop towards their African destination. From there, they made their way to Addis Ababa in Ethiopia, where Daniel wanted to get first-hand knowledge of the poverty and the AIDS problem in that country.

Caris's long blonde hair swayed in the gentle eastern breeze that stirred up the dry dust in the main street of the capital. She looked exceptionally beautiful as she walked beside Daniel. They made a striking couple as they strolled amongst the rubble that dotted the sides of the road. The suspicious people of Addis Ababa watched them walking past their hovels, and some, especially the children, followed at a safe distance behind them.

Sticks in clothes walked the streets amongst the dirt and stench of human waste and rubbish. People stretched out their hands, begging for food, and Daniel's heart went out to them—in particular to the children who looked up at him with their oversized eyes and bulging stomachs.

The cargo liner carrying food supplies was due to arrive at the port of Djibouti, a small neighbouring country to the north-east, within two days. Daniel wanted to ensure that the receptacle warehouse in the capital of Ethiopia was ready to accept the first delivery.

Hiring an old blue sedan, which used just as much oil as petrol, they found their way to the modest palace of the Ethiopian chairman of the ruling council. At the gate, Daniel handed one of the many well-armed guards a letter of introduction issued by the Australian prime minister. The guard quickly took the letter into the gatehouse and presented it to his superior, who opened it and laboriously read it. The tall, robust superior rushed out the door of the gatehouse, yelling instructions, and within seconds, the gates opened and the two Australians were ushered into the courtyard.

Phillip Azage welcomed them with open arms; he had been expecting a delegate from Australia ahead of the food delivery, and as the ruler of his country, he wanted to welcome them personally. He felt honoured that such obviously important and busy people would come visit him and his poor country. He was well spoken in English thanks to the missionary school he had attended in his younger years. The aging chairman stood tall and proud; he had a bald-topped head with thick, curly white hair standing high around the sides, and the curly white beard with the absence of a moustache accentuated his thick pink lips.

After a brief conversation over a cup of tea, the smiling chairman, with a contingent of about one hundred well-armed men, escorted his guests to a refrigerated warehouse close to the palace. Workers, guarded by many soldiers, were already there, waiting for the first truckload of food.

A question from Daniel regarding why so many guards were accompanying them and watching over the workers made the chairman's smile turn to a frown. The change in his expression made his weathered face look much older now that his white teeth were hidden. He explained that there had been many attempts by rebel forces to overthrow the council's regime. They took whatever they wanted from the poor villagers, including any food that they had gathered for themselves. The women and young girls were theirs for the taking, and if any of them didn't willingly succumb to the rebels' every request, they were repeatedly raped and then horribly mutilated. Any male villagers who were too old or didn't join their band were hacked to pieces with machetes.

The rebel forces had grown dramatically, and the situation had become critical. It was only a matter of time before the chairman would be killed and whatever law the country presently had would be lost.

"For many years now, my country has had to contend with an ongoing famine, and as the rebels grow stronger, we have let ourselves get weaker. The council has put its efforts in trying to help the hungry, and unfortunately, this will prove our downfall. Maybe we should have simply forgotten the people and concentrated on the army." He paused and then, with a loud sigh, added, "I want to be here to welcome the arrival of the food so that I can see smiles on the faces of my people, especially the children." He concluded with watery eyes.

"Mr. Azage, I will be flying to Djibouti to supervise the unloading of the supplies, but I'll be back to see you again soon. I need to talk to you about other matters that concern not only Ethiopia but many of your neighbouring countries." Daniel and Caris said their goodbyes.

Two days later, the ship arrived, and Daniel watched with pride as three refrigerated trucks, gifts from the Australian people, were slowly lowered down onto the wharf.

Some of the workers loaded the trucks, while others carried the supplies into the refrigerated warehouses. These vehicles would be used in making the many journeys to deliver the cargo to the capital of Ethiopia. Food would be dispersed to villages on the way, and some of the food was gifted to the people of Djibouti, as had been agreed in gratitude for the use of their dock.

The impoverished country of Ethiopia was only one of the many countries being helped in this way, as various richer nations had started to become involved in the scheme Australia had started.

Daniel instructed his pilot to meet them in Addis Ababa, as he and Caris would travel by road ahead of the trucks in a hired four-wheel drive. He wanted to ensure that all the villagers understood the importance of sharing the food parcels they were to receive.

The three large trucks made their way south, following the direction Daniel had taken. One of the drivers would leave a supply of food at the first village in Ethiopia, not far from the Djibouti border, and continue on to the next village until his truck was empty. He would then return to the wharf for more supplies, which he would deliver to the next village in line. The rough, unmade road slowed them down, so it wasn't long before Daniel and Caris were well ahead of them.

In the heat of the midday sun, an elderly headman and the people of his small community stood outside the outer stockade, waiting for a signal from a boy who had climbed a tall tree overlooking the dirt road that passed their village. They knew that they were the first in line for the food they were anxiously waiting for.

A sudden yell from the boy excited the waiting group. Drums started to beat, and the crowd broke into a chant and started dancing to the rhythm, scattering the many goats being looked after by their young herders. They danced and watched as a cloud of dust came over a small hill; disappointment came over their faces as a lone car pulled up instead of the trucks they were anticipating. The beating of the drums and the dancing stopped, and they leered at the strange occupants of the vehicle.

Daniel got out of the car and, knowing how anxious the people must be, called out to them, and they understood his words. "The trucks will be here very soon." Cheers went out from the crowd, and the drums and the dancing started again. The chief ran to the car and welcomed the tall man and the beautiful blonde lady.

Daniel's vivid blue eyes and Caris's blonde tresses fascinated the children as they ran around them. The shy, tall, and bony headman led them into the compound and past many round huts made with earth and straw. He took them to the large ceremonial mud hut in a clearing in the middle of the village, and while the people outside chanted and danced, the women inside served tea. The happy faces of these people pleased Daniel, as he could see that even with the immense poverty they endured every day of their lives, they were still able to manage kind and happy smiles.

A little girl not much more than six years of age, sitting on the floor and clutching the hand of her grandfather, the headman, kept looking at Daniel, almost in fear. She gathered her courage and slowly rose to her feet and walked over and sidled up next to him, encouraging him to lift her up. He hesitated and looked over at Caris, as if asking her if it was all right to do so. He picked up the girl, and with a gratifying smile on his face, he placed her on his lap. Her big brown eyes looked up into Daniel's sky-blue eyes, and the fascination she showed him kindled an affection he had never experienced before with a young child.

A commotion outside the stockade signalled the arrival of the trucks. The headman forgot his guests and, along with the other natives inside the hut, ran to join all the other excited villagers already outside the wall.

Daniel lifted the little girl onto her feet as he casually stood up, and then he helped Caris to rise. Suddenly, a loud rattling noise disturbed his senses. "Stay here," he ordered Caris, and he ran towards the outer fence. Outside the wooden-poled wall were a number of small, open tray utilities as well as a couple of jeeps. Men stood on the backs of the vehicles with automatic rifles in their hands, pointing them at the panicking villagers.

The three truck drivers were on their knees with hands clasped together over their heads and rifles pointing at them. The people, although frightened, moved forward towards the trucks, their hunger overcoming their fear. The thought of losing this food supply to these rebels was more than they could tolerate, and they were willing to risk their lives for the food.

A loud command came from a burly man flanked by a number of other armed men, and immediately, the gunmen on the backs of the vehicles, without the least hesitation, opened fire on the villagers. The machine-gun fire mowed down dozens of them, and blood oozed out of their bodies and soaked into the parched ground.

Something grabbed Daniel's hand, and looking down, he saw the terrified eyes of the headman's granddaughter; her bloodied little body collapsed, and she lay dead at his feet. Daniel's whole body began to tremble, and a fury he had not experienced before encompassed him. A roar emanated from deep inside him; the sound was so intimidating that the petrified villagers moved away from him and back towards their huts. The rebels momentarily froze, and Daniel stood alone amongst the dozens of lifeless bodies, facing the armed men.

"For what you have done this day, you have forfeited your lives." His voice came with a message so loud and clear that it penetrated and petrified all who heard it.

Silence befell the whole area. In the stillness that followed, no one could hear a sound; no one fired a shot. Daniel's whole body became rigid, and the glare that radiated from his eyes was so intense that with one look, some of the rebels clutched their chests, and their excruciating screams of sheer pain broke the silence.

Hand grenades and ammunition stored in the backs of the trucks exploded, and the vehicles burned out of control. Men were blown apart when the ammunition belts they carried across their shoulders and midriffs exploded.

In a matter of seconds, the incident was over; the carcasses of more than fifty rebels were roasting in the debris as smoke rose many metres into the sky, letting off a stench from the burning rubber and bodies.

Daniel's distorted face was locked in the angry trance that had overtaken him, and he appeared oblivious to the carnage that lay around him. His whole body trembled as he fell to his knees in complete exhaustion. Quietly, a soothing voice entered his subconscious, and as he slowly closed his eyes, the concentration on his face dissipated, and he felt a soft hand resting on his shoulder and heard a familiar voice calling out his name.

"Daniel! Daniel! They are dead, Daniel—they are all dead." Caris stood next to him, calming his anger with her gentle, sweet voice. He opened his eyes and saw what lay in front of him; the utter devastation made him feel even weaker. His eyes rolled back into his head, and he fell to the ground.

He opened his eyes and looked down on his naked chest; pushing the blanket back, he found himself to be completely naked. He realised he was back in the ceremonial hut of the village, lying on a mat on the floor, and next to him, on his left, a reclining Caris was watching him.

"About time you woke up," she said.

"How long have I been asleep?" he asked.

"Oh, only about eighteen hours."

"Eighteen hours!" Daniel was surprised; he normally didn't need much sleep, but he recalled the complete exhaustion he had felt after the rebel attack.

"The little girl?" he asked timidly.

The tears that filled Caris's eyes answered his question.

"Daniel, you did your best; God knows how many people you saved by destroying the rebels."

Guilt overtook him. Why couldn't he have done more? He could have saved those innocent villagers. Why had his powers not been stronger? The irony of the situation dawned on him; he wanted more power, knowing all too well that in reality, he wanted to achieve the opposite.

The superstitious villagers were afraid of Daniel; they had surrounded the ceremonial hut but kept a safe distance away from it.

Caris had convinced the black drivers that Daniel was not a devil but a man sent by God to protect the innocent against the evil in the world. With the help of the villagers, they had unloaded some of the supplies from one of the trucks and were ready to head for the next village. Although the drivers were afraid of the white man and his magic powers, they were definitely not going anywhere without him.

Daniel and Caris emerged from the hut; a murmur went through the villagers as the old headman, although frightened, cautiously made his way over to them and looked long and hard at Daniel. He reached out and, holding Daniel's hand, knelt before him and kissed his hand as a sign of great respect.

Daniel felt the old man's grief and his gratitude; he wanted to console him.

"You do not have to be grateful to me for what we bring you, for we have selfish reasons. Please accept our gifts and pass on these words to your people. Tell them to share what they have with those who are in need. Do this for me, old man, and that will be all the thanks we want." Daniel put his hands on the old man's shoulders, and he understood.

"I am sorry for the way my people have reacted towards you, even after saving them. I beg you, do not be offended by them, for they are afraid—not just of you, for they know you are a good spirit. They are terrified of the revenge Amir, the rebel chief, will exact on them when he hears of what happened to his men." The terrified old man trembled as he spoke.

"Do not fear this man, Amir; he and I are destined to meet very soon," Daniel assured the worried man.

"Be careful, my everlasting friend, for he travels with many men, and he will surely kill you." He kissed Daniel's hand again as he bade the pair farewell.

The Range Rover travelled some distance behind the trucks as they continued the journey to the capital. Caris's heart went out to Daniel; his sadness showed on his face.

She looked at his handsome features, and Daniel glanced at her with eyes that showed his love for her. Caris unfastened her seat belt, reached over, and slowly and gently caressed his thighs until she saw a movement in his loose trousers.

The truck driver in front, glancing through his side mirrors, wondered why the white man had suddenly started driving so erratically.

One of the trucks made a few stops and delivered food to villages along the way until it was fully unloaded; it then headed back to the wharf for reloading. A few hours later, the food in the other two trucks was emptied into the warehouse at the capital to be dispersed in an orderly manner.

Mr. Azage arranged a modest dinner for Daniel and Caris.

"I heard some unbelievable things about your journey, Mr. Leeder; they, of course, cannot be true, can they?" a curious Phillip Azage asked.

"Who really knows the truth? As they say, truth is in the belief of each individual. The important thing is that your people have a modest amount of food to help them for a short time." Daniel shrugged off any further questions about an event he would rather forget; he had more-important matters to discuss.

"Mr. Azage, I now need your help; I want you to convince as many of the leaders in your neighbouring countries as possible to attend a meeting that is being convened in Malta. You and the other leaders have already received invitations." Daniel paused, as he anticipated a question from the old man.

"I know the countries in this area are very poor, so all expenses for the leaders and a limited number of their aides will be reimbursed," Daniel assured him.

"I am sure that will please all of us, but I have a much bigger problem." The elderly man was apologetic. "If I leave here, even only for a few days, my country will be overrun by the rebel forces."

Daniel felt his genuineness; he clearly wanted only what was best for his people. Although Azage believed his end was near, he wasn't going to desert his post.

"If I can assure the safety of your office, would you go?" Daniel asked.

"If that was at all possible, I would do whatever bidding you request of me," the puzzled man agreed.

"Grant me power to give amnesty to the rebels if they swear allegiance to the ruling council; I will talk with them and show them the errors of their ways," Daniel told him.

The councillor gave out a loud, nervous laugh he could not suppress. "You will show them the errors of their ways? No, my friend, they will kill you as soon as they see you."

"Let me worry about any killing." Daniel grinned.

Heading south towards Kenya, a lone grey Range Rover sped along, followed by a cloud of dust in its wake. Farther south, a few miles north of the Kenyan border, a convoy of well-armed trucks had surrounded a village of mud and thatched huts. Smoke coming from the village lifted high and darkened the afternoon sky as the huts burned uncontrollably. Mutilated bodies lay in the dust inside the village wall, while hundreds of armed men scrounged for anything of value they could find.

Agonising screams of women and young girls came from all corners of the village as men lined up to take their turn at the limited number of women available to them. Most of the young girls died slowly and horribly as their blood oozed out of their bodies from the haemorrhaged internal wounds caused by the repeated rapes. The invaders hacked unwanted elderly women to death for no other reason than to watch them die.

The male villagers who had opposed them were made to watch the carnage and the rape of their daughters and wives. They accepted their fate and even welcomed the rifle being put to their heads, hoping for quicker and kinder deaths than to be hacked to pieces by the machetes. Their lives were over; they wanted an end to the sights they had witnessed. Their deaths would be merciful compared to what their wives and daughters had to endure before they succumbed and died.

Amir, the rebels' leader, who was massive in stature and had a large head on his broad shoulders, made a point of dressing in the traditional way; only a loincloth covered his lower body. He never interfered or participated in the rape of the women in any of the villages. Amir and his two sons would inspect the females his men paraded in front of them, and they would select the ones they fancied; he gave the rest to his men. The selected females were the lucky ones; they were placed in one of the canvas-covered trucks to be transported back to the rebels' camp up in the hills, where they would join the many other females in Amir and his son's harem.

Amir left the sanctuary of the hills and headed north with a large convoy; his leadership had been threatened, and he had to do all within his power to restore the fear his men and the people of Ethiopia had of him. The white man, with the blonde woman, had killed more than fifty of his men without using a weapon; his own younger brother had been leading the raiding party. He had to revenge his brother's death if he was to have the respect of his men. When they came upon a village, he decided to make camp there for the night and continue his quest for vengeance in the morning.

In the early, bitter cold of dawn, as the sun rose above the ranges to the east, the unruly mob stirred, awakened by the noise of fighting baboons at a nearby waterhole. One of the sentries—a tall, lean youth standing on top of the village well outside the outer wall—yelled a warning and pointed towards a hill overlooking them.

A grey car was meandering its way down towards them. Amir's men raised rifles and aimed at the approaching target. Amir, looking through binoculars, could make out a blonde woman in the passenger seat, and almost in glee, his deep voice boomed out a command to his men not to shoot.

Without the slightest hesitation, the vehicle went past the trucks and came to a halt outside the village perimeter. A white man in an immaculate white suit stepped out and walked around to the passenger-side door to help a beautiful and desirable young woman out of the vehicle.

The rebels made suggestive noises at the sight before them; they had just been handed a worthy prize. The unarmed couple seemed unperturbed as they walked through the gauntlet of men who made way for them as they headed towards the village. The rebels encircling the well and blocking the entrance to the village surrounded them. Some were dressed in khaki shorts, while others only had loincloths covering the fronts of their lower bodies. The men were heavily armed, and they took great delight in waving their weapons in the air as the pair walked past them. Their weapons consisted of rifles, hand grenades, and even a bazooka or two on top of the trucks.

Amir, carrying an automatic rifle, stepped forward and let out a raucous laugh that the rest of the onlookers mimicked.

"Allah is with me today," Amir bellowed. "They have come to me, as I willed," he bragged to his men as he strutted, head held high, around the well; he wanted all to see that his power was great.

"Allah has saved us many days in searching for this man and woman. They have now been delivered to me to do with as I, Amir, please," he yelled as he lifted his right arm, rifle in hand, and fired a shot into the air. He slowly and purposefully walked over to Daniel and looked him in the eye, but his bravado was short lived. A shiver of fear went through his body; he felt the anger searing through the big eyes that glared at him. He quickly turned away from Daniel and placed his gaze on Caris; he felt more relaxed with the man out of his immediate sight.

"What is this fallacy I hear that you killed my men without using a single weapon?" He asked Daniel the question without looking at him, and he spoke in his own tongue, knowing that only a handful of whites would understand, let alone speak, his language.

"That is no fallacy," Daniel answered quietly. A surprised Amir forgot his fear and spun around to face Daniel again.

"You speak my language; that is good," he said with a smirk on his face, trying hard to hide his amazement.

Daniel slowly resumed taking steps towards the village, and the men in front of him stepped aside as he walked past them. The sight of the inhumane carnage before him saddened him. A hand reached out and touched him gently. "Stay calm, Daniel; please stay calm," Caris pleaded.

He nodded, and she could see the sadness in his eyes as he walked back out to face Amir.

The rebel leader still avoided Daniel's staring eyes. "Bring the woman to me," he ordered. "Now you will tell me all I need to know before I kill you. Bring the woman here." He pointed to the well as two men dragged Caris over to him and held on to her. With a motion from Amir's hand, another man stepped forward, grabbed Caris's blouse, and ripped it off her to reveal a pair of perfectly formed breasts. The onlookers screamed encouragement as he tugged at her khaki shorts, and a gasp went through the crowd when they finally gave way. A G-string was all she had left; the excited mob urged the man to pull them off her, but Amir stopped him. "I have never seen a woman with such a thing on her body; it looks very appealing." He leered at her pale skin and blonde hair. "Leave them on her for now."

Amir wanted her for himself, but he could not show any weakness in front of his men. He looked into the mob and called out, "Come, Jinto. Show this white man how your women die—from the sheer pleasure you give them."

A mountain of a man, dressed only in shorts, stepped forward and headed towards Caris. He grunted something to the men holding Caris, and they immediately turned her around and leaned her body forward over the wall of the well. He took off his loosely fitting shorts, and a gasp again filled the air. The man's penis had started to harden; it was abnormally long and as thick as a man's wrist.

Caris was flabbergasted at the sight of the man coming towards her and had no misapprehension about what his intentions were. She feared that Daniel had abandoned her.

"No woman ever survives after Jinto pleases her," Amir said with a laugh. "Now will you answer my question?" Again, Amir would not look into Daniel's eyes; he had walked behind him and preferred to strut around and look at his own men crowding around them. Daniel was silent, and to the onlookers, he appeared to have fallen into a trance, probably from fear.

Amir gestured, and Jinto stepped forward. The massive man had never seen a body so white and so clean. The excitement he felt made his penis grow to its full length, and he took pride in thrusting it up and down to show the onlookers the control he had over it. He rubbed it teasingly on Caris's outer right thigh, and his eyes rolled back in ecstasy as he touched her body. The expression of pleasure that appeared on his face slowly changed from delight to sheer panic as a burning sensation went through his body. Jinto backed away from Caris and looked down in pain and horror; his penis, scrotum, and pubic hairs were alight. He ran around the well, screaming in excruciating pain, before leaping into the well; a splash of water came over the top of the wall, and the crowd heard a loud sigh from within.

"He will never harm another woman by pleasing her." Daniel laughed as Caris came to his side. The muttering from the frightened men made Amir aware that he had to act quickly in some form of reprisal against this enemy. He called out to his sons, who were almost replicas of their father, to come forward and hold the white man.

Daniel did not resist, but as they tried to grab his arms, they found that some unnatural force was keeping them from holding him. They were on either side of Daniel, and as they tried again to grab his arms, Amir stepped back, quickly aimed his rifle at Daniel's chest, and let off two shots in succession. He stood motionless, in a stupor, his mind not accepting what he saw. The white man was still standing, while his only sons were lying on their backs on the ground. His numbed brain finally registered what his eyes were seeing; both of his sons were dead, with bullet holes in their chests.

With great effort, the stunned Amir made his right leg step forward; it was heavy, as if made of lead. He heard a twanging noise, like a twig snapping, and he felt certain someone had hit him on the heel. He turned to see who was behind him and who would dare assault him, and as he did, he took another step with his left leg and heard the same twanging noise again. There was nobody behind him. He stood there for a moment, oblivious to his surroundings, and suddenly, he dropped to the ground and onto his knees. His senses came back, and he tried to stand up. The pain that came from the backs of his legs made him scream out in agony, and he fell back onto the ground. The Achilles tendons on both legs were snapped clean in two, and he realised that this man in front of him—the man he was now looking up at—was no ordinary man.

The mob backed away from Daniel and Caris; only a moaning Amir was in close proximity. Daniel turned slowly and looked at the men around him. "You have seen what I can do, and my first thought is to destroy all of you for what you have done to your own people. You do not deserve to live. Give me one reason why I should let you live," an angry Daniel bellowed at them.

Almost in unison, the entire rebel army dropped to the ground, whimpering and begging for their lives.

"You know your lives are mine to do with as I please." Daniel walked amongst them as they lowered their heads into the dust, cowering before him.

Caris picked up her clothes, put them on, and made her way over to the wailing girls locked in the truck. They had witnessed what had happened through holes they'd found in the canvas that was their prison. They had heard all the screams of terror coming from behind the wall where their families were being butchered, and now they were watching Daniel addressing the hated guerrillas. They had admired the white woman when they had seen her through the peepholes, and now they were seeing her at the open back panel of the truck—an angel beckoning to them.

Daniel's relentless tirade at the rebels sent shivers through their bodies with every word he uttered; finally, his voice calmed, as if coming to a conclusion. "There is only one way I will spare you. Every one of you must swear allegiance to the council that rules your land; but mark you well what I say, because the day that you break your promise is the day you will die."

The terrified men rose to their feet and chanted in unison, "Azage, Azage, Azage."

The sixteen young women prisoners had walked into the village, and after a few minutes, they came back out, and the sombre looks on their faces showed their sorrow. In complete silence, they walked past Daniel and the rebels, and still holding their composure, they walked over and surrounded their quarry. Caris tapped Daniel's shoulder, and as he looked around, he could only see the women's frantic bodies covering that of Amir. The onlookers could hardly hear his muffled screams as the women clawed at him like a flock of vultures. Some held his arms, while others held him by the legs; they had completely overwhelmed him, and Daniel was not going to stop them from exacting their vengeance.

When they were done, they looked down at the bloodied Amir, who was conscious enough to know what had happened to him. The women had blood all over their faces from the many bites they had inflicted on him; two of the girls who stood over him bent down and spat out lumps of flesh at his face. Amir looked down at his body, and his eyes showed his terror. They had spat his own testicles at him; his genitals, scrotum and all, had been bitten off.

They buried only the villagers; they left the dying Amir with his dead sons as fodder for the vultures circling above them. Carrying white flags and a letter written by Daniel and addressed to the chairman, the rebels headed north towards the capital. Daniel and Caris refuelled their car with petrol taken from the rebels' supplies and headed south towards Kenya.

Caris's curiosity got the better of her, and finally, after an hour of travelling, she asked, "Why are we going to Kenya? I thought we would be heading back to Addis Ababa and then flying back home."

"Caris, we have been concentrating on the human animals in need and are forgetting the other just-as-needy animals in this world. Poachers are decimating the rhinos in this part of the country for their horns, which fetch a small fortune in Asian markets. There is only the black rhino left here in the savannah, but like the white rhino, it too is in danger of extinction. I want to do something to stop poaching altogether, and as we are in the area, we might as well see how we can help." Daniel talked like a man who had accepted his lot.

In the early afternoon of the second day, the couple came to a camp where two black rangers had been preparing their lunch over an open campfire. The Kenyans, dressed in their shorts and short-sleeved shirts, had their rifles at the ready when they saw the car approaching. They were surprised to see the two unarmed occupants out there—and more surprised at the perfect dialect of Swahili that Daniel spoke. Over a cup of tea, the rangers explained that they were on the trail of about ten poachers from the Kikuyu tribe but were waiting for more reinforcements before they engaged them.

The rangers sympathised with the poachers; they were only poor villagers who didn't comprehend the reason for protecting animals or the reason why the "slant-eyed people" were willing to pay so much for the horn of a rhino. The payment they received helped their families for many years, and for this, they were willing to risk making the ultimate sacrifice. But the rangers also understood the importance of protecting the endangered animals, even to the extent of killing the poachers.

They said their goodbyes, and against the advice of the rangers, Daniel turned the vehicle west and headed to Lake Turkana. The rangers had warned them that they would be heading in the poachers' direction.

With darkness approaching, they stopped and set up their modest camp on top of a hill looking down into a picturesque valley. After a snack of canned spaghetti, they lay on a blanket, watched the myriad of flickering stars above them, and listened to the various noises of the animals around them. Caris cuddled up to Daniel and whispered in his ear, "I didn't pick you for a liar, but you certainly have proven to me that you are."

"What lie did I tell you?" Daniel wondered.

"You told me that you would never make love to me again, but you certainly didn't mind my playing with you in the car, and I bet it wouldn't take much of an effort from me for you to dirty my insides. Am I right, or am I wrong?"

Daniel couldn't answer, as his lips met hers, and he rolled over on top of her.

Inside their little two-man tent, Caris's light snoring gave the signal for Daniel, completely naked, to slip out of their airbed and quietly leave the campsite.

In the not-too-far distance, a hunting party had set up for the night in a clearing away from the trees; they encircled a large fire, which lit up their modest camp.

No sentries were posted, as none of them had ever encountered any rangers on past hunts, and the roar of a lion in the distance didn't perturb them as they settled for the night. But a slight noise nearby did disturb them; instant silence fell on the camp, and wide eyes looked around, while ears perked up and listened intently. They heard nothing for a while, and then the talking and laughing started again. They now found it hard to resettle.

Occasionally, they could hear the faintest of sounds above the noise they were making, but the sounds were so soft that after a while, they ignored them, and slowly, they fell asleep.

Light broke through the trees onto the clearing, and one of the young poachers stirred and opened his eyes to another cold but beautiful morning. He lifted his blanket to cover his shoulders, and on hearing a snort coming from close by, he casually raised his head and peered around him. His eyes bulged at seeing, only metres away, the rhinos they had been tracking. The big male and the two females were happily eating the tall grass around the camp. The excited young man gently nudged the man next to him, indicating to him to stay quiet and pointing to the other body next to him.

Soon the whole camp had quietly awakened, and they lay there looking at their quarry.

Slowly, each of them reached for his rifle and, with a stunned look, turned to face the others. They were gone; all the rifles were missing. Trying not to scare the rhinos, they carefully looked around the camp for their weapons, to no avail.

A sudden movement in the tall, dry grass to the left of one of the men made him give a subdued scream. He tried to talk, but the words wouldn't come out, and with a shaking finger, he pointed. The others looked in the direction he was indicating. A large lion with a massive black mane had stood up and shown itself. The men were petrified, and their first urge was to run to the trees, but they were men of the jungle and had enough sense to know that to run would be futile and fatal.

Another lion—a female—appeared to the right of the male, and yet another female stood up to the left of him. The men, crouching in the tall grass, slowly turned and started to crawl away from the danger at their rear, but to their utter dismay, there were more lions in the direction they were heading. They lifted their heads as high as they dared, looking all around them for a way of escape, but in every direction, they saw lions. The beasts were only metres away, and they were surrounded.

The three snorting rhinos showed no fear as they browsed amongst the roaring lions that were now closing the circle. The scared men huddled next to each other and prayed to the Christian God to save them. The stench of the lions got stronger as the animals neared, and they were now so close that the poachers could see the yellow colorization of the animals' eyes. The circle of lions stopped their approach and sat calmly down on their haunches, bellowing from deep inside their majestic bodies and yawning as if they were tired of playing a game.

Above their own loud prayers, the doomed men heard an intimidating voice—a voice that spoke clearly and in their tongue.

"Why do you do this to your animal brothers and sisters?"

They looked around and saw nobody except for the animals; they looked up to the sky and again saw nothing. Could the animals be talking to them? They looked at the beasts and were aghast to see a man standing there before them. A white man, completely naked and standing next to the huge male rhino, had his arms stretched out over the beast's massive back. The strange man patted the relaxed animal as he looked at the mystified hunters and spoke to them.

"My golden friends, the lions, are hungry and would like to make you their meal. Is it all right by you if they bite off your noses and leave the rest of your bodies to rot in the sun to be eaten by the scavengers?"

The wide-eyed men shook their heads in unison.

"You have come to hunt my friends here for their horns. You would not hesitate in killing these beautiful creatures just so you can hack off their horns and let their massive bodies rot in the sun. You have made me angry—so angry that I have come down from the heavens to help my friends before their whole species disappears forever. I have made this journey to give you a specific warning, and this warning must be heeded, so listen well, and spread the word to all who would be poachers. If the rhinoceros is wiped out from the face of Africa, then devastation will follow, and all Africans will also perish. The Creator gave you the animals to help feed you and your families. He does not mind you hunting for food to sustain your lives, but now you are hunting for selfish gains, and this has to stop. My instructions come to me from a much higher power, and you must warn all the people who dare hunt for gain. We must have the word of the Kikuyu tribe that you will no longer hunt uselessly and that you will spread this news to all hunters in all of Africa. It is to be your word or your life." The naked man looked at them long and hard, and the cowering men listened to every word he said. "You will be given a mark to show to others so that they will believe your story. Kneel. If you want to live, you will hold still and endure the pain you will feel."

They fearfully knelt and closed their eyes as sweat poured off them. Each lion started to roar and, one by one, came up to a man and instinctively stopped behind him. The men could smell and feel the animals' hot breathe on their backs. With their long claws unsheathed, the majestic beasts' outstretched paws swiped the right shoulder of each man at such speed that initially there was no pain. Within a few seconds, the poachers felt an excruciating ache, but they were too scared not to follow the instructions the man with the sky-coloured eyes had given them. They endured the pain in silence and waited for what other punishment was to follow.

A full five minutes passed before the elder in charge of the poachers had the nerve to open one eye and peek around him. There was nothing there. He stood up and scanned the area before he told his men that they were safe. They were frightened yet so relieved that they were still alive that they temporarily forgot the pain that emanated from their backs until they noticed the marks on each other.

Each man had four perfectly formed parallel lines from the top of the right shoulder down to the middle of his back. Blood seeped out of the gashes, and the depth of the wounds was enough to leave a permanent scar, which they would carry for the rest of their lives as a warning to themselves and to others.

CHAPTER 5

The rotund Archbishop Bradley had listened to Father Andrew's advice and taken it to heart. Over the past several months, he had set an example for the rest of his peers, not just for those in the Catholic following but also for the many clerics from the other religions in Australia. Newspaper stories often showed the big man handing out food parcels to the poor or attending picnics with homeless youths. The Christmas party was a big hit, and the picture of him embracing two old derelicts on the front page of a major tabloid somehow turned up all the way at the Vatican.

Father Andrew was playing his cards right by ensuring that all publicity given to the local church was credited to the ambitious archbishop. The Australian Catholic Church was having a resurgence of active worshippers, and it pleased the pope—so much so that Archbishop Bradley was summoned to the Holy City in Rome for a private audience with the pontiff.

After nearly three years in office, Pope Gregory XVII's popularity with the world remained at a low ebb. The aging pope had little personality, and he held the old church traditions close to his heart. A few days after the archbishop visited the pope—and it came as no surprise to Andrew—Bradley was promoted to the position of cardinal. The promotion of the popular archbishop was a consolidated move by the cardinals in Rome to try to boost the pontiff's image.

Another few days passed, and at the request of the new Australian cardinal, his chauffer picked up Father Andrew and drove him to the airport to meet the cardinal on his arrival back home from Rome.

After a fairly lengthy press conference held at a reception area at the airport, a chauffeur drove the cardinal and Andrew to His Eminence's Melbourne residence. In the back of the stretch limousine, Andrew listened to the man in red as he excitedly talked about his new appointment and how proud Australia should be of his achievement.

"His Holiness expects me to extend the good press we are receiving here in Australia to our overseas churches, and to be truthful to you, my son, I need your help." He pleaded for ideas.

"Anything I can do, Your Eminence, I will do if it will further the good of our beliefs," the young priest assured him.

"Well, do you have any suggestions on what course we should be taking, you understand, to keep things moving?" the big man probed.

Andrew stalled in answering the cardinal too quickly, so he pretended to be deep in thought. He had already surmised the reason he had been asked to meet the cardinal at the airport and wanted him to think that he was coming up with new ideas.

"What we need to do is something that is very radical," Andrew began. "My first thoughts would be for the church to give a reasonable amount of its wealth to the needy of this world."

The cardinal took his cap off, reached into his pocket, pulled out a red handkerchief, and proceeded to wipe the sweat that poured from his face and head. From the top of his glasses, he gave Father Costa a wide-eyed look of bewilderment. "My boy, you can't be serious with such a wild suggestion like that, can you?"

Andrew tried to keep his enthusiasm under check. "Yes, Your Eminence, I am serious. Why not hit the Holy Father with a mind-blowing suggestion like that? Can you imagine the mass publicity he would get with such an announcement? He would go down in history as the holiest of all the popes; he may even be canonised, after his death, of course. Imagine, Saint Gregory XVII—and with the renewed faith in our Church, I envisage a massive growth of the congregations worldwide. The Church's wealth would be replenished in a very short time."

The rampant imagination of the silent, smiling cardinal told Father Andrew that the big buffoon might be contemplating his idea.

Twelve months had passed since Daniel had suggested the world leaders' conference with the American president, and finally, the time had arrived.

Malta, a tiny speck in the middle of the Mediterranean Sea, with its proximity to the African continent and its strategic situation central to the

rest of Europe, made it the ideal place for such a meeting. Over the centuries, the rulers of Malta had made the Valletta Seaport the most fortified port in the world. Valletta, the capital, a World Heritage City, was once a fortress to the Knights of Saint John as they defended Christendom.
The president and the prime minister of Malta were honoured that their country had been chosen for such a historical occasion. The humble Maltese recalled and revered the prominence of their islands in the last world war, after which King George V had presented the whole population with the George Cross Medal for their defiance of the Third Reich. To be in the eyes of the world again made the population of Malta proud, and they made every effort to cater to the needs of the security forces.

The residence of the governor was the principal architectural building of Malta, and it would be used as the meeting place for the summit. Ships from many countries would surround the harbour. America and England would each supply an aircraft carrier, and they would be stationed at the east and west ends of the main island.

Tourism was a main source of income for this country, and to have this avenue of income stop for a few weeks meant a big loss in their revenue. The American president made a commitment to compensate the Maltese for this loss, and he assured the US Congress that many other countries would in turn reimburse them after they realised the importance of this mysterious meeting.

Obviously, the world, by now, knew of this historic meeting, but it appeared that only the US president knew the reason for it. The American people and, more importantly, the people of the world needed to trust him completely on this occasion.

Two weeks prior to the main event, over three thousand security guards from the many nations had invaded Malta. They had scoured the governor's building as well as its grounds and surrounding properties. The guards had evacuated all residences close by, and the citizens had been well compensated for their trouble.

Black Hawk helicopters from the aircraft carriers now in position at either end of the islands hovered above the ancient buildings as they patrolled the skies to accustom themselves to the area.

Over a few days, the delegates trickled into the country; most had to fly to Rome and take a smaller plane for the short flight to Malta. The dignitaries, with a minimum of staff, were set up at the best hotels or the vacated houses close to the meeting place. The security staff managed as best they could by sharing bedrooms in the vicinity.

The Australian prime minister, accompanied by Daniel, Peter, and three security guards, was amongst the first to arrive, in the private jet piloted by Garry Foster. Daniel used Henry's passport to enter the country; he wanted to be there early to check out the security.

Midafternoon, after checking Paula Chan into a comfortable but modest room at the hotel, Daniel and Peter walked the streets of the capital. The two Australians were enthralled by the scenery and its ancient architecture. The fortified harbour made a spectacular sight as one looked over its walls across the clear, deep blue water.

They stopped for coffee at one of the many al fresco cafes on the foreshore of Valletta, watching the passing parade, and in turn, the passing parade watched them. A broad-shouldered, well-tanned, and unshaven young man sat at a table near them. His espresso coffee was served, and as he stirred in the one and a half sugars, he smiled at Peter, who was facing him. When he received a smile back, the man stood up with cup in hand and walked over to their table.

"Welcome to this beautiful country; I hope you are enjoying the view," he said in well-spoken English. "And which country would you be from? I assume you are with the delegates, as there are no tourists here."

Slowly sipping his coffee, Daniel let Peter do the talking. Peter slyly peeked at Daniel, who gave him a slight nod, indicating approval to answer the man's questions.

"Australia, mate." Peter's Aussie accent came to the fore.

"You must be pretty close to the Australian prime minister to be here—maybe assistants, eh?" His enquiring dark eyes matched the colour of his wavy hair.

"Yes, advisers, actually," Peter said.

"Myself, I am a security guard." He pulled his wallet out of his back pocket and flashed a small laminated card with his photo on it. "I am with the Egyptian president, who arrived this morning. With all the secrecy that surrounds this conference, it makes my job, and my men's, very difficult. Can you gentlemen enlighten me with any information you have from your minister?"

"What did you say your name was?" Daniel joined in the conversation.

"I am so sorry to be so rude. It is Adnan Basha, and yours?"

Daniel reached his right hand out and firmly shook hands with the inquisitive man, and as he introduced Peter and himself, the man felt a tingle go through his body.

"So you are Egyptian and are in the security service for your president, and it seems that you too know as little as we do about this." Daniel took a final sip from his cup and asked, "What is your opinion of what is happening here?"

"Most likely it would be about the world's growing terrorism; I can't think of anything else, can you?" Adnan replied.

"Could be the unification of the world—maybe world peace."

Daniel was being honest, but Adnan just laughed at such a suggestion and said in a cutting voice, "That will never happen, my friend—never happen."

Daniel changed the subject and asked Adnan if he had found suitable accommodations.

"Yes, I found a little place that is very convenient for my needs, and talking of my place, I just remembered I have someone to meet; I am sure we will see each other again."

Daniel, deep in thought, watched him walk away, and by just the look on his face, Peter knew something was amiss. "Have we got a problem with that guy?"

"Yeah, we have a problem; it's amazing how, by asking a few appropriate questions, the mind always flashes the truth—and the only truth that came out of his mouth is that he is Egyptian. Firstly, his name is not Adnan Basha but Hussain Bassumai, and he is not with the security forces for the Egyptian president. He belongs to a group known as the Liberation Army of the World, also known as LAW. Have you ever heard of that group?" Daniel asked Peter.

"No. You're saying this is a terrorist group?" Peter had learned not to question any summation Daniel came up with.

"I am afraid so. There are four members here, and they are a sleeper cell for this LAW group. They consist of many different nationalities trying to overthrow Western governments, which they believe are the cause of the world's problems. Their instructions are to disrupt the conference and kill as many of the Western leaders as possible. Their headquarters are on Maria Street, not far from here; I saw their house in his mind, so we should have no trouble finding it." Daniel appeared worried. "I would rather have the local authorities involved instead of handling this matter ourselves; we may need their help at some stage. First thing, let's find a police station and see if we can convince anyone about this."

The waiter gave them directions to the police headquarters, which were in the city centre, not far from the cafe.

The young constable at the desk led them to his superior, who greeted them with a beaming smile and sat them down in his office. The middle-aged, balding, and stocky Reno Cassar looked uncomfortable in his striped dark blue suit; the trouser legs were too long, and the jacket sleeves were too short. He had dressed to impress the many dignitaries visiting his island. After the introductions, Daniel proceeded to tell the short man the reason for their visit.

The inspector was astounded by the Australian's perfect Maltese, even down to the dialect he personally spoke.

Cassar's dark eyes grew larger as Daniel, lying, explained that in his professional opinion, two men he'd overheard talking were undoubtedly terrorists.

"The men spoke freely in Arabic, not realising that I speak many languages, and I understood every word they said," Daniel assured the inspector, who had no doubt about his ability to speak many languages. "You must get the necessary warrants, and then you and your men are to accompany us to their house. You are to let me enter the house on my own; this is vital, and you must agree to this demand if I am to involve you in the arrest of these men. If you do not agree, I will not divulge their whereabouts, and I will have my men handle it."

Before the inspector could object to his terms, Daniel held up his hand to silence him. "I must insist; I will hand these men to you, and you and your men can claim the credit for their arrests as long as you promise me that once you have them in custody, I am to be the first person to interrogate them." Daniel paused, and Peter made a comment.

"Inspector, if you do this, you will become famous as the man who stopped a terrorist attack on the world leaders." Peter spoke in English, and the inspector had no problem understanding him, as most Maltese spoke the English language. Cassar liked the idea of worldly fame.

"You speak Maltese too?" The sweating man assumed Peter must have spoken Maltese as well, seeing that he had kept up with the conversation between himself and Daniel. Peter's answer—"Not a word"—puzzled him even more.

Speaking in English, the inspector reluctantly agreed. "I cannot take a chance with the safety of the delegates, so I must assume that you are telling the truth. If I must, I will abide by your instructions, but if this is a joke, your minister will hear about it, and I will ensure that you are both sent home."

By the time the warrants and the men were organised and instructed in their mission, darkness had overtaken the day. In the moonlit night, Daniel had no difficulty finding the house, and along with a contingent of police officers, they crept up to the high front limestone wall. A padlocked steel gate as high as the fence blocked their progress; Daniel spoke to the inspector, asking him to wait while he took a closer look at it. The inspector nodded at Daniel in consent, and looking over at his men, he indicating to them to stay where they were.

A few minutes passed as they watched Daniel, seemingly in a transfixed position, at the gate. The inspector looked over at his men and Peter, and they shrugged at each other; when they looked back at the gate, Daniel was gone. An eerie, light mist had suddenly swallowed up the footpath where he had stood.

The bewildered and concerned inspector whispered to his men to stay put while he crouched his way over to look for Daniel. The haze engulfed them all and, eventually, the house as well; a strange sensation went through their bodies as heaviness overtook them. Their every sense, even their heartbeats, seemed to almost stop. They could not talk or even turn their heads to look at each other; it was as if time had almost come to a standstill, and even a single breath seemed to take forever to complete.

Frozen in front of the gate, the inspector could see a figure—more like a ghost forming out of the mist—on the other side of the wall. The sprite became a solid mass, and although the inspector couldn't be certain through the haze, he thought he saw Daniel at the front door of the house. The man reached for the handle; the door opened, and he disappeared inside. The men outside saw a flash of light that seemed to increase ever so slowly in its brightness, and they heard a slow, soft murmuring sound that hovered around them as it too intensified gradually in its loudness.

Daniel stepped around the suspended stream of pellets that discharged from the shotgun rigged to fire when the door opened and made his way over to the lounge room. There stood four men in different stances that gave the impression they had just heard something and had been quickly reacting to the situation when they had been caught up in the stillness of time.

Fifteen minutes passed before Daniel emerged from the house, walked over to the gate, and touched the padlock, which opened and fell onto the footpath. The inspector, still unmoving, saw the events unfolding in front of his own apprehensive eyes and could not believe how realistic this dream seemed. Daniel came out of the gate, picked the inspector up, and moved him next to his men by the front wall.

Daniel closed his eyes, and the mist lifted away from the house. In an instant, the night became clear again. They now heard the noise from the shotgun, and a blast of pellets pinged its way through the steel gate and smashed into a car parked across the road.

The rapid heartbeats of the police officers were the first indication that they were now back to normal, and several men made the sign of the cross several times as they looked disbelievingly at each other and at Daniel.

A flurry of commotion began as the people in the neighbourhood came out from the surrounding houses, and on seeing the police, they gathered together to watch.

Daniel led the inspector and his men into the house, and the astounded officers, who were completely bewildered by what already had happened outside, now were even more baffled. Inside, they found four men handcuffed together. The inspector, seeing the handcuffs on the men, reached for his and was not the least surprised that they were gone, as were some of his men's.

A search of the house revealed a variety of weapons. Daniel showed Peter and the inspector a number of briefcases hidden in a cupboard. "They are bombs that could be detonated by a mobile phone; you can see how easy it would have been for them to walk into restaurants, cafes, or anyplace the delegates were, put the case under a chair or table, leave, and then ring a certain number—and *kaboom*."

Daniel instructed the inspector to take the prisoners to the station and put them in separate cells. "I will interrogate them first thing in the morning. You and your men will keep all this to yourselves, won't you, Inspector Cassar?" Daniel winked.

"Who is going to believe us anyway?" The wide-eyed man shrugged, and while muttering under his breath, he motioned to his men to bring the prisoners.

The next morning, Daniel had a cup of coffee ready for Hussain when, with two officers on either side, Hussain was brought into the interrogation room. He momentarily hesitated at the door when he saw Daniel sitting at the table. The constables slammed the door behind them as they left the room, and being alone with Daniel made Hussain's heart skip a beat.

"Ah, Adnan Basha—or should I say Hussain Bassumai. Join me in a cup of coffee, won't you? Black with one and a half sugars—that's how you have it, isn't it?" Daniel wanted him to feel uneasy and to have the upper hand when he questioned the person he believed to be the leader of this band of terrorists. The surprised man had to quickly sit, as he felt a weakness at the knees. Maybe one of his own men knew his real name, he figured. That had to be it. He now felt angry.

"If any of the weak bastards cooperate with you, their lives will be very short ones." Hussain arrogantly started to talk in his Egyptian native tongue, trying to show contempt for the man in front of him, but when the next question came back to his mind in his language, perfectly spoken, he leaned back in his chair and nearly rolled off it.

"Who do you answer to, and why are you doing this?" Daniel asked.

"We do it for the love of Allah and Muhammad's teachings in the Koran," the uneasy man replied.

"Hussain, you are full of shit; you do it because you like the excitement and because it makes you feel important to dictate who lives or who dies. It makes you feel as important as Allah himself," Daniel corrected him angrily.

Daniel softly muttered, "So Bruno Cardi is the man you answer to?"

Hussain stood up and backed up to one of the walls as quickly as his shackled legs would allow him. His knees buckled, and he fell to the floor. "How could you possibly know about him? It is impossible—you can't know." A quivering voice came out of a man who knew that he had suddenly become a condemned man. Daniel wanted to take full advantage of this now-vulnerable man whose mind was racing with fear.

"You obviously think that the LAW organisation will believe that you are the one who betrayed them, and no doubt they will kill you for this." Daniel showed little emotion as he snarled at him. "Well, think of how many people you have killed over the years; what goes around comes around, my friend."

Daniel glared at the prisoner. "Very clever, Hussain; yes, I must admit the way this organisation works is very clever. There are many cells worldwide, like a chain with many links, and each of these cells consists of four members, including one leader. Here in Malta, you are in charge and are the one who recruited the other three. Your men here only know each other and follow your orders, and in turn, you only know the leader of the next cell in line and the man you answer to, and that's Bruno Cardi."

Daniel stood up and thumped the table so hard that the coffee cups toppled over, and their contents spilled onto the floor.

"Where can we find Bruno Cardi?" he yelled at the top of his voice at the cowering man.

"Okay, so the next cell is situated in Messina, Sicily, and you and Bruno converse often to keep up with news he has received from his contact and to give you instructions."

Hussain, now completely flabbergasted, remembered what had happened to him and his men the night before. There was no doubt this man had the capability to read his thoughts. Every question the man asked immediately brought an answer to his mind, and the more Hussain tried to shield his thoughts, the more information came to his mind.

Daniel brushed past a perplexed Reno Cassar; he dialled a secret number that only a handful of people knew.

"John, I need your help in a matter that concerns your safety, as well as the safety of many of the other delegates on their way to the conference."

Daniel and Peter boarded the USA Marine helicopter waiting for them at the small Maltese airport. In less than twenty minutes, the chief of police of Sicily met them in another small airport at Messina, on his much larger island.

A contingent of police vehicles escorted them to an address Daniel had supplied, and with the police cars waiting around a corner from the suspects' house, Daniel walked up to it alone and stopped in front. He quickly gestured for the others to come forward. "They are not here; the house is empty," Daniel told them

A complete search revealed nothing, and after the police talked to nearby residents, it seemed that the suspects had vacated the house only that morning.

The presidential plane, *Air Force One*, would be landing in Rome in less than an hour; from there, the president and his team would board a smaller plane. Within minutes, the plane would be flying over the Tyrrhenian Sea, then across the north coast of Sicily, over the township of

Palermo, and towards Malta. Daniel knew that the terrorists had surface-to-air missiles and that their prime target would be the president's plane. Such was his confidence in Daniel that John B. Rose insisted on adhering to his schedule.

Daniel was certain that the information he had gleaned from Hussain was accurate; the terrorist group would attempt to shoot down the president's plane in Sicily. Now they had to cover over a hundred kilometres of coast, and they had less than an hour.

The pilots, although confused with their mission, had strict instructions to abide by Mr. Leeder's orders. They struck a straight line on their map, indicating the route of the presidential plane, and flew west from Messina to where their line on the map intersected the flight path.

"Follow the coast to the west, and hug the ground; get down as far as you can," Daniel yelled, and the pilots sensed the worry and agitation in his voice.

They approached the township of Palermo and still found no suspicious signs to indicate the presence of any terrorist activities. They passed Palermo and travelled many miles west until a dejected Daniel gave another command: "They are not here, or we missed them. Double back quickly; time is running out."

They travelled back a few miles, still west of Palermo, and as they approached the intersecting line of the flight path of the president's plane, Daniel yelled out an order. There was a sense of urgency in the tone of his voice: "Put this thing down!"

The pilot swooped down low and picked out an appropriate spot, and the helicopter slowly touched down in a small area clear of stones and debris close to the coast.

"When I get off, take her up again, and don't land until I signal you to do so," Daniel told them firmly.

"Yes, sir." The loud and simultaneous reply came from both crewmembers. "We are not to land until we receive your signal, sir." There was a tone of sarcasm in their confirmation.

The pilots along with Peter and the Sicilian police chief watched from above as the man below hastily made his way to the cliffs on the foreshore. Daniel stood looking out to sea. A few minutes passed, and they started to notice the wind getting stronger and making the whitecaps on the waves gradually grow larger and larger. The grass and shrubs on the foreshore swayed from side to side in unison as the waves swirled and hit the coastline with an ever-increasing force. Dust from the rain-starved earth formed unusual yet almost pretty patterns as it blew in all directions. The tempest was not affecting the chopper hovering above, and all on board were dumbfounded and in awe of the man below. Surely he was not causing what they saw happening.

They saw the ground vibrating; rock fences that had been erected hundreds of years ago began to fall, and the trembling earth developed deep splits in all directions. Massive chunks of rock cracked from the cliff's edge and fell into the raging sea, making large splashes before disappearing from sight into the angry water.

The Sicilian crossed himself and asked God to forgive him for thinking that a madman was leading them.

"There! Over there!" Peter pointed to a small clearing surrounded by dry yellow grass and green weeds. They could see a head suddenly appear out of the ground, and they watched as a man laboriously crawled out from a hole. His hat blew off his head as he scampered like a rabbit out of his barrow. The man struggled against the wind as he turned and helped three others out of the same hole he had emerged from.

The four figures fought to stay erect, but the wind was too strong; it blew them down onto their backs, and they managed to turn their bodies over onto their stomachs and cover their faces with their hands.

The people in the hovering craft could see Daniel making his way over to the four bodies on the ground, and they noticed that the strong gale was not having the slightest effect on him. For miles, they could see the grass blowing in all directions, but the grass in Daniel's path was completely still. He stood over the four figures as if talking to them, and after a while, he raised his hands to the heavens, and the wind died instantly.

A plane passing overhead sent a vibration through the body of the helicopter, and Peter let out a sigh of relief, as he had no doubt the American president was on board. A wave of Daniel's hand indicated that he wanted them to land, and again the pilots looked for a safe spot.

The terrorists had set up the surface-to-air missile in a crevice below the ground, and they had been only minutes away from firing it at the passing plane. There was more than enough evidence to convict these men of terrorism; besides the rocket launcher, there were a number of guns and explosives as well as charts of the likely route the presidential plane would take. With the aid of local police officers from the nearby town of Licata, the men were taken away in a police van for transportation to Messina.

Frederico Gullone, the tall, smartly dressed chief of the Sicilian police, sat at his desk in deep contemplation; he was on the verge of becoming a national hero. Not only was he to take credit for capturing the Sicilian terrorists, but also, Daniel had supplied the name and address of the leader of one of the cells in Rome. The Rome police might accept the information and might even act on it, but the only way he was to give this information was if they let the strange Australian interrogate the terrorists once they were captured.

The chief liked the idea of being a hero, but how would he convince the Rome police that a lowly Sicilian police officer such as he was able to capture and interrogate these terrorists and get so much information out of them? He threw his arms into the air, knowing that based on what he had seen that day, anything was possible.

The next morning, as much-needed rain drizzled down, the congregation of world leaders filed into the governor's palace. Each drew a numbered ticket from a container at the door; the number indicated the seat he or she would sit in during this important meeting. This ticketing system had been Daniel's idea, and he hoped it would stop any bickering about favouritism in the seating arrangements. Only the leaders were allowed into the meeting; their aides had to wait in a reception room adjoining the main conference hall.

In silence, they found their seats, and one by one, they sat down and looked indignantly towards the front and waited. The American president made his way to the front of the stage and looked down onto the curious crowd.

A light mist formed adjacent to him, and the form of a man slowly took shape. The delegates' silence was now a roaring murmur as Daniel, in his gleaming white suit, raised his arms, gesturing for silence. When everyone finally settled, Daniel, who was officially known by only three of the delegates, started to speak.

"I apologise to you all for my grand entrance and that I am opening this meeting and not President Rose. My way of entering was to get your attention, and as John B. Rose only speaks in English, many of you would not understand him. I speak all languages, and I speak them all simultaneously."

As Daniel spoke, each attendee understood his words in his or her own language, and it took some time before it slowly dawned on them that he had spoken in their own individual tongue without using an interpretation device or an interpreter to translate his words. It took even longer for the English-speaking delegates to comprehend exactly what was happening.

The president of Indonesia was dumbfounded as he realised that the speaker was the man who had appeared in his dream and convinced him to come to Malta.

Daniel had the full attention of all present; they were intrigued by what had already happened, and they realised that this meeting was going to be far more interesting than they had imagined.

"The world's fate is in the hands of us all here today. All our differences, political or religious, must not be brought to the fore this day, for if ever this world needed to be unified, it is now. We must be as one, for only as one will we be able to have a chance of saving our planet from utter destruction. This day, the future of mankind and the final decision on whether we survive or not may be in the palms of our hands."

A murmur from the large contingent of puzzled men and women slowly gathered volume in the large room. Daniel put his hand out in front of him, asking for quiet, before he was able to continue. "Who I am is not really important, but the reason I am here is of paramount importance."

Daniel could see the intrigue on all their faces, and he knew that he had their interest, but he needed more—he needed their full commitment.

"I have been chosen to be a messenger—a messenger from the Creator of all you can see, all you can touch, and all you can imagine. I know that the reason I was chosen for the task at hand had nothing to do with colour, creed, or wealth. My belief is that I was picked for no particular reason, only that the Supreme Intelligence needed somebody to be its messenger." Daniel hesitated briefly and, almost talking to himself, muttered, "I believe I was at the right stage of my life and at the right place; I should be dead, but the Creator chose for me to live." He again paused. "The right place might be because I came from Australia, which has one of the greatest multicultural societies anywhere in the world and a smaller population, making it a good starting point in my quest to save our planet. I am confident that Australia was picked to set an example for the rest of the world, as I will explain later." Daniel paused and took a sip of water from the glass on the small table to his right.

"We in this room have many individual beliefs as far as religion or as far as politics are concerned. Firstly, let me talk about religion; most of us believe and worship a higher being. Many of us pray to the same God or Allah, who seems to be the same Supreme Being. Others idolise the sun, the earth itself, or even idols that came from their imagination. The point that I am trying to make is that the people of this planet imagine that there is someone or something that makes the world go round—someone or something that has much greater powers than we, as mere mortals, have. We have been right all along; that I can confirm to you. There is a higher and all-powerful something out there. It is a force so strong that our own earth's natural power that already controls us is part of its totality. There are many forces, yet these energies are one. The sun, the sea, the rain, the wind, and the very air we breathe are all part of our world's energy, and we know that without them, we could not exist. Each of the millions of planets in this never-ending universe has its own natural energy, and every object out there has a magnetic force that keeps it in its own place. These many forces are really only one, and that force or energy is our God and our Creator."

For forty minutes, Daniel explained every detail of his mission, and he wound down the first part of his speech by making a quick final statement.

"Please understand that I have been building myself up to you, and there is a specific reason for this; all of you must have a one-hundred-percent belief in me. Before I finish and we have a break, please understand that although the conference itself is definitely no secret, for now, you must be secretive about its content."

After a twenty-minute break, a bell sounded, and the attendees quickly made their way to their seats and waited anxiously for the next instalment. The prime minister of Australia came up to the vacated dais and introduced herself to the crowd; most already knew her. Although not all the delegates understood, she explained her experiences with Daniel and her first trip to America, including the drug baron's assassination attempt on her life. The explanation of her son David's eyesight brought a tear to her eye.

As soon as Paula finished her short speech, Phillip Azage, the chairman of the council of Ethiopia, shyly stood up from his seat and also told of his experience with Daniel.

The American president took over the dais. "This man—Daniel—has no passport and no proof of who he is, and we have no proof that he ever existed here on Earth. I only met him for a brief time, and in this time, I can confirm what these ministers had to say about his powers. Yes, I believe every word he has told us; if we do not listen to him, then we are doomed."

The president motioned for Daniel to come forward, and as he did, he shook his hand and patted him on the shoulder. Looking over the crowd before him, Daniel made a brief statement. "Before we go any further, all who did not understand what the speakers said, please stand up, and I will enlighten you."

Nearly half the people in the room stood up; many of them understood English but needed to reconfirm what they had heard in their own language. They watched Daniel as he closed his eyes and appeared to be meditating. The people were compelled to also shut their eyes, and as if television screens had opened up in their minds, they watched a replay of the latest speakers. Within what seemed only a minute, the people standing sat down in awe, and Daniel, opening his eyes, smiled at the crowd before him. "Now, would anyone who is not totally convinced of what has transpired so far please stand up?"

Nobody moved for a full minute until, suddenly, one man stood up with such force that he knocked over the man sitting next to him.

"I am Boris Zabloski, and you all should know that I am the Russian president." A booming voice came from the moon-faced man who stood at six foot six.

"I have listened, and I have gone along with this charade for too long—much too long. This is nothing but an American trick to gain more world power, and I have had enough of all this, as the American president would say, bullshit." He headed for the exit, not caring what or whom he bumped into as he went.

Daniel was disappointed and angry that this one man, whom he needed by his side, was ruining all the good work that had preceded this incident.

"No! Mr. President, you cannot leave; I have not given you permission to do so, sir." An even louder and stronger voice stopped the big man in his tracks, and he slowly turned around and looked up at Daniel standing on the stage, which was more than twenty metres away. Even from there, the Russian could see the anger emanating from the man he considered a charlatan.

Daniel stretched out his right arm with a clinched fist facing upward, and then he quickly bent his elbow towards his own head as he looked leeringly at the big man. The onlookers heard a hissing noise, like that of rushing air, and a hazy funnel formed between the Russian president and the irate man on the stage. Immediately, the big-framed Russian became airborne and was sucked through a vacuum with such speed that in a split second, his chest was on top of Daniel's clinched fist and his head was only a few centimetres away from Daniel's own head.

To the frightened onlookers, it appeared as if Daniel's hand had reached out, grabbed the big Russian by the shirt, and pulled him across the room towards him. With his arms protruding downward as if trying to break his fall, the Russian's body was still horizontal to the floor, and his eyes were bulging as he tried to inhale from his airless surroundings. With his petrified eyes looking directly at Daniel, a gentle voice said, "What bullshit do you not believe, Boris?"

The anger from Daniel's eyes subsided, and the big Russian body slowly straightened. As Boris stood on his feet, he gasped for the precious air that quickly filled his lungs. The mystified Russian looked down in awe on a face that now looked gentle and calm.

"Boris, everything I am saying is the truth, and I need you to stand by me if we are to win this battle. Please sit down, and let us continue with the meeting, for you are to be a key member of my team."

Daniel spoke forcefully. "The time is running out; we have a short and unknown time frame to reduce the deaths of all living things and the wanton destruction of this planet. I am the one who has been chosen to save Earth. I will not accept any more delays in my quest to save you all. You will do as I bid, and you will do so without question when it concerns this mission."

Daniel waited for a few seconds and then called out in a roaring voice, "I will be your leader, and you will answer to me." The intensity in his voice scared the delegates so much that one fell off his seat.

Daniel's tone was now relaxed yet serious. "I will destroy any one of you or any other person who defies my efforts." Daniel meant what he had said, and the delegates understood that clearly and were confident that he could carry out his threat.

"We first need to consider the major problems that face us and that would reduce the death and destruction of living things on our planet. The major problems are not death and destruction through wars or terrorism, but problems that the ordinary person in the street causes and can solve. The number-one problem is starvation of the people of the third-world countries. The second problem is AIDS. There are over forty million people infected with this disease. Thirdly, the world's forests and the environment are being wantonly destroyed, and this is endangering much of our fauna and flora. Fourthly, the world drug problem is out of control and must be stopped. Together we have to solve these four major problems, and once these are solved, we will concentrate on the many other dilemmas of this world, such as wars, terrorism, and pollution. And talking about wars and terrorism, I realise that the Palestinian people are not represented at this meeting; they did not want to be in the same room with the Israeli prime minister. I will make arrangements to visit them and the others who are not here. The stupidity of the starvation situation is that the people of the Western world are dieting because of overeating, while the people of the third world go hungry. The starvation question will need to be addressed by the more affluent countries. Some of these countries destroy surplus food in order to keep prices up and for the rich to get richer. From now on, this food must be collected and shipped to starving people no matter the distance or the costs. There is more than enough food in this world to go around, and you, in this room, are going to ensure that it does.

"The AIDS crisis is one that will require cooperation from all nations, in particular the sub-Saharan African countries. AIDS continues to spread at an alarming rate. Just in the sub-Saharan group of countries, there are over thirty million people infected and living with the HIV virus. That is more than thirty percent of their adult population. Five million people worldwide are infected each year, of which over three and a half million are in those countries; these numbers will increase each year unless some drastic action is taken. This will be the most difficult and heart-wrenching quandary that will face us, but no matter how hard the solution is, we must take it, and we must make it work. If we can stop or at least reduce the spread of this disease, we will save millions of lives. This alone should please the Creator, as it will be able to sense a reduction of the death rate amongst humans."

One of the leaders in the crowd found the courage to stand up and face the enthusiastic speaker. "Sorry, Mr. Leeder, but you keep mentioning AIDS as a major killer of humans—what about cancer or heart disease? Wouldn't they cause more deaths worldwide?" There was no mistaking the Irish accent in that question.

"Of course, you are right," Daniel replied. "The Creator accepts that we must eventually die from something to make room for the new, just like our cells being constantly replaced. Cancer and heart disease have always been a natural way of dying, mainly by the elderly, but the AIDS virus is wantonly spread by infected sexually active younger humans. The Creator does not accept this as a natural way of dying."

The Irish prime minister wasn't all that happy with the answer, but he accepted it anyway as Daniel went on with his talk.

"The third urgent problem is the world's forests and our environment. We humans are destroying the forests, the fundamental source of the very air we breathe. The many living creatures of this world that depend on this habitat are being threatened by its mass destruction, and they have as much right as we humans to have a home. We have to sustain the living areas of all wildlife. We must conserve the forests of the world and give them time to recover from the many years of abuse by the hands of humans. The continuation of the ecosystems of these forests is imperative; therefore, we must reduce the use of timber, especially by the Western world. We must reduce the emission of oil-based fuel, which runs our industries and our transport systems.

"The last but by no means the least is illicit drugs. Illegal drugs must be made legal; the money factor must be taken out of this epidemic that affects so many people in so many ways. This problem could be solved and reduced and, hopefully, eventually eradicated altogether, if illicit drugs were legalised. Nicotine and alcohol addicts can walk down to their local shop and buy their fixes over the counter, yet the ones who are addicted to other forms of drugs must go underground to get theirs. I say to you that a young person is more likely to take up smoking and drinking alcohol than to take a needle and stick it in his or her arm if he or she is not pushed to do so. Australia has trailed it for some time now, and the results have been very encouraging. We have less overdosing, and burglaries and petty crime have reduced dramatically. Many young people are in therapy to wean them off this terrible habit, and more importantly, the drug centres are reporting a massive reduction in new addicts attending these clinics. The funds saved by the reduction of the police force and the ambulance services and the lower insurance costs to the community and the more productive young people can go to more worthy causes. I want all countries to agree to legalise drugs—after all, haven't we already legalised one of the worst drugs ever known to men: tobacco? The authorities have tolerated the tobacco companies and turned a blind eye as they developed a plant that is more addictive than heroin. They target the youth in their sales advertisements, so once these unsuspecting kids are hooked, they will pay a small fortune over their lifetime to these legalised drug barons. Let's make all drugs legal, but let's ensure that the authorities, not private enterprises, have full control of the distribution and the quality of these drugs. I say ban the lot or legalise the lot."

Daniel looked at the faces before him and spoke his final words in a calm and meaningful tone. "Ladies and gentlemen, this is the greatest race that has ever been run on this planet; it's a race against time."

He looked down on the silent group, turned, and slowly walked to the back of the stage, where he again fell into a deep trance.

John B. Rose made his way to the platform. "Ladies and gentlemen, there is one more thing I need to relate to you, and this one thing is another reason why I know that what Daniel is telling us is the truth. Australian astronomers have discovered a new comet in our solar system, and it is on a collision course with our planet. Scientists are having difficulty in estimating the time of impact or when it will be close enough to affect Earth. Comet Clara, as it has been named, has entered our solar system and is one of the largest ever discovered. Because of its size, it doesn't have to collide with our planet to destroy it; it only needs to come within a few million miles to cause havoc with our weather and effect massive tidal waves that could wipe out all living things. My scientists have taken control of monitoring this comet and have concluded that for some unknown reason, it has slowed down, so this gives us more time. Comets normally have a predictable speed, but this one seems to be driven by some unseen force. We will keep an eye on the situation and monitor it constantly."

The president could tell from the intense faces looking up at him that through Daniel, they understood his words. "My friends, we have no choice in this matter. We must believe that there is this higher natural energy and that if we do as it bids, then it might show us mercy and spare us." John B. Rose looked down at the astonished people before him, and he had to wipe tears out of his eyes before he continued. "Daniel tells us that he has been sent by our Creator to show us the way to save ourselves, and, my friends, there is no alternative here; the only way we can be saved is if there is some heavenly intervention by a very powerful force." The president again wiped his eyes and inhaled deeply.

"Ladies and gentlemen, we have had a ponderous problem lumped onto us." John hesitated, as if he could say no more; he had had enough for one day.

"I propose that we call it a day and consider our options and hopefully come up with some solutions tomorrow when we reconvene the meeting." A few minutes passed before anybody left his or her seat, and then slowly, in deep contemplation, they all made their way out of the conference room.

Peter, who was waiting outside the room, quickly rushed over to Daniel as soon as he emerged.

"We need to get to Rome urgently," Peter told Daniel. "The police there have captured four members of the LAW group, and they are keeping their word to the Sicilian police chief to let you interrogate the prisoners, but only if you get there today. Our pilot has made the necessary flight arrangements; the jet is fuelled and ready to go."

Much to the annoyance of the law enforcement authorities in Rome, Daniel interrogated the four captives. A sullen, attractive young woman turned out to be the leader of this cell; she was an Italian national and was a follower of the world's most-wanted terrorist network, Al Qaeda, and for the first time, the two terrorist groups were interlinked.

Her contact was the leader of another cell located in Lyon, France, and Daniel again obtained names and addresses for the authorities. He stipulated that the Lyon police had to comply with the same conditions the Roman police had agreed to.

Daniel realised that this domino effect would not last and that it was only a matter of time before the whole organisation went deeper underground to lie low, only to re-emerge sometime in the future to wreak havoc on the world once more.

The delegates were seated earlier than the scheduled time, and they waited anxiously for Daniel's arrival; they stood and applauded loudly when he walked onto the speakers' platform.

"It does my heart good to see and hear you greet me in this manner. Your kind reception proves to me that you are behind this mission. Now, has anyone any suggestions on our first priority—feeding the world's hungry?" Daniel asked.

The wealthier countries agreed to help the less-fortunate ones in their own regions first and said they would cooperate with each other to ensure all the needy of all the nations were fed. Engineers would be sent to supervise the building of wells and bores for water and to generally improve the water supply of some of those countries. All acknowledged and appreciated the works of existing charities. Their programmes were for the long-term good of the people they helped. Unfortunately, the world needed immediate solutions to the troubles at hand, so more-dramatic answers and actions were needed.

The leaders would ignore their political popularity and execute whatever legislation was necessary to implement their aid plans.

After a short afternoon break, Daniel again was up on the platform, ready to continue. "Looking at you all during the break warmed my heart; people from so many different doctrines and backgrounds, smiling and cooperating together, tells me that there is hope for us after all. It is a pity that this has only occurred when we face such a dilemma as we do now."

Daniel was pleased with what he had witnessed, and he wanted to encourage these world leaders, but more-important matters were on the agenda.

"AIDS," he called out loudly to get everyone's attention. "This is the one problem that concerns me most of all, as there is no simple solution without being harsh on the very people who need our help the most. A committee will be formed to deliberate this problem further, and there will be a summit in the near future dedicated to this subject."

The meeting ended for the second day, and a saddened Daniel watched the dispirited men and women quietly make their way out the exit.

The third day of the conference started to take its toll. The delegates seemed disheartened with the enormity of the tasks of the first two problems they faced, and there would be even more problems to contemplate that day.

"My friends, I can feel your despair and your resignation at what is ahead of us," Daniel said, trying to assure them. "But we must not give up without a fight. The next problem we have is the environment, and this could be a simple problem if we all agreed—and let's face it, we must agree—to stop clearing the rainforests for timber and agriculture. We must stop this exploitation of the home of most of the world's species of animals, plants, and insects. They need this complex ecosystem to survive. At the rate we are going, they will be destroyed in less than twenty-five years, and this will mean that in the time we have, if we just concentrated on saving only human lives, we will have defeated the whole purpose of why I am here. Saving mankind on its own is not an option as far as the Creator is concerned. The floor is now open to suggestions." Daniel again looked at the despondent audience and waited.

The president of Brazil stood up and shakily spoke in fluent English. "Mr. Leeder, I agree with everything you have told us; I know that this is a great problem for the world and for my country. Sir, can you tell me how I can convince my parliament to pass a bill that would be so unpopular with my people that there would be a revolution if it were enacted? Many investors, mainly from the USA, would bankrupt an already-fragile economy."

Daniel had anticipated such a problem and had only one solution. "Mr. President, I appreciate that just because you are in charge of your country, it does not give you, or any leader of the other countries, the power to enact or even enforce any solutions to our problems, especially in the short time we have. My next step is to visit each country individually, and I will address some of the politicians in your parliaments and the commanders of the armed forces. The armies of the world will not be needed to protect their own shores. I propose that these forces be used ostensibly to enforce any new laws enacted in any country in order to achieve our targets. This has to be done; there is no choice." Daniel was resolute.

The Western nations' leaders reached an agreement to limit the importation of timber from countries that logged rain forests, and all leaders from all countries agreed with the legalisation of illegal, habit-forming drugs. Public opinion of their respective countries was of no consequence for most of the delegates. What was at stake had further-reaching implications than their political popularity.

The major obstacles facing the delegates were the question of passing the legislation through their parliaments and the retaliation of the drug barons on the loss of their markets. The drug lords would stop at nothing to ensure that legislation was not passed, especially in countries such as the USA, which was their biggest market. The American president could face many assassination attempts by these forces.

Daniel spoke quietly and decisively. "The Colombian president is another person I plan to visit, seeing as he did not take up our invitation to attend this conference. Either he is controlled by the drug cartel, is a part of it, or is justifiably afraid of them. I intend to find out which it is. Ladies and gentlemen, this concludes my involvement in our first meeting, which will by no means be our last. As time permits, I will personally be visiting many of you individually to see how your efforts are proceeding. Now the agenda for the rest of the meeting is for you all to discuss amongst yourselves—plans for the implementation of the remedies we have discussed. The urgency of getting things moving to solve our problems cannot be stressed enough. Stay in contact with each other, and assist one another whenever possible."

Daniel concluded his talk and backed away from the dais to allow John B. Rose to have the final word.

"Ladies and gentlemen, I have nothing further to say that has not already been said except for us all to stand and thank Daniel."

Daniel blushed with the ovation that followed.

"Ah! There you are; I have been looking for you for over an hour," Peter called out to Daniel, who was oblivious to his surroundings. He was in the palace garden, which overlooked the harbour, staring out at the clear blue Mediterranean Sea.

"Daniel, my God! You've got that worried look again—have we a problem?"

"Yeah, I am concerned; I would have expected more assassination attempts with all the ministers here. Then again, I guess we did capture a few of the terrorists who were in a position to be a worry." His own reasoning didn't change the concerned expression on his face. "We should have heard from the French police in Lyon; many of the delegates will be travelling across France, including the French president and the English prime minister, and on top of that, John B. Rose has a stopover in England." Peter had been happy, but now he too was frowning along with his friend.

"Peter, please contact the Rome police and get them to follow up on the Lyon police."

Thirty-five minutes later, Peter received an urgent phone call on his mobile from the Rome police, and after hanging up, he ran to Daniel's room. "The bloody arrogant French police didn't take our advice; the bastards raided the house at the address you gave them," he said angrily, panting out his words. "They didn't do their homework; one of their officers was killed, and another two were injured with a shotgun blast as they smashed the door in. And worse still, there was nobody there. I hate to say this, but this smells like the Sicilian cell all over again," Peter blurted out.

A phone call from the French president to the minister of police in Paris had the Lyon police chief inspector and his assistant on full alert and awaiting the arrival of an American helicopter at the local airport.

The immaculately uniformed, tall, and lean chief inspector from the Lyon police station twitched his pencil moustache as he made an attempt at an apology for not following the instructions from Paris in ensuring that the group were all in the house before raiding it. His hooked, thin nose, sticking out of a rather small head, looked down in contempt at these English-speaking intruders. He certainly resented being reprimanded by his superiors in Paris because of them.

Daniel assumed that by now, the terrorist group was probably aware that the authorities were on to them, and he felt that they would more than likely have warned the next link in the chain of terrorists. More importantly, Daniel needed to know where the members of the Lyon cell group were right now. He sensed they were lying in ambush somewhere over the flight paths that some of the delegates would use on their way home.

One consolation was that at least on this occasion, they had some time up their sleeves; if they did not find these terrorists in the next few hours, they would simply divert the planes to different routes.

Daniel wanted to capture this group, as there was always a chance of tracing the next cell in line from any information he could glean from them. He asked the reluctant chief inspector to take them to the terrorist house.

On their arrival, the inspector, with an assistant in tow, talked to his men who were guarding the house, and Daniel immediately walked towards the front entry. Hearing footsteps behind him, he stopped and turned around.

"I will go in the house alone, if you don't mind, Inspector." Daniel was curt in this demand, and the tall Frenchman didn't hide his indignation at this request. He angrily turned to walk away, muttering obscenities to himself. He huffed and spluttered, raised his arms up in the air, and then brought them down, slapping his sides and turning quickly to face Daniel.

"How long will you be?" he asked sternly.

Daniel gave him a stare that sent a shiver up his spine and left no doubt that his question wasn't going to be answered. The smashed door and the blood on the front step told the story of the police officer who had been blasted to death the day before. This angered Daniel, as he knew that if the inspector had followed his instructions, that person would have still been alive.

He looked around the dwelling and walked about, inhaling the air around him in deep gasps and with such intensity that he almost lost consciousness with every breath he took. He inched his way to the dining room abutting the small kitchen and took in the smells that came from the unwashed cooker and the dirty dishes still lying in the sink. He pulled out a chair from the old table and flopped into it as if he had no energy left in him to stand. His eyes rolled back into his head as he slowly reached out and put his hands on the table, digging his nails into its surface.

Daniel's sheer concentration cleared his mind of all thoughts, and his deliberation was so intense that he fell into a stupor so deep that his mind reeled backwards as if going back in time.

"Mr. Brand, it has been over an hour, and we haven't seen or heard anything from the house." The impatient inspector, speaking in an authoritative voice, turned his head from the passenger side of the front seat to leer at Peter, who was sitting in the back of the unmarked police car. "Should we not check up to see if he is all right?"

"No! He will be out when he is ready," retorted an annoyed Peter, who clearly didn't like the man.

"Chief Inspector." The much smaller, rotund assistant, who was sitting in the driver's seat, spoke for the first time since they had met, and he proved to be a considerate Frenchman, as he spoke English for Peter's benefit. "Look at the house—it has trees overhanging it, and today is very windy, but not a leaf is moving. Everything is perfectly still and so quiet."

"The house must be sheltered somehow." The explanation from the chief was simple, and he gave it with an air of confidence.

Another hour passed before Daniel emerged from the house and unsteadily made his way to sit next to Peter in the back seat of the sedan. Peter could see his friend must have utilised a massive amount of energy to make him look this tired.

"Inspector, have you heard of a winery called Pethris—north of here, near a place called Dijon?" a weary man asked.

"Why do you want to know that?" the impatient inspector asked in a tone that Daniel hated nearly as much as the man himself.

"Inspector, whatever your name is—what is your name?" Daniel had just realised that the Frenchman hadn't introduced himself.

"Chief Inspector Maurice Perri, at your service," he replied proudly.

"Look let's get something straight right here and now," Daniel impatiently snapped at him. "You are not the most popular person in my life at this moment, so I don't want you questioning me. You are to follow my instructions to the letter—is that understood?"

"Yes, sir!" the now wide-eyed, sweaty man replied as he fumbled with the GPS in the console of the car.

The assistant drove them north on the main road for thirty minutes, passing many farms and wineries, and then they turned left onto a narrow dirt road. On seeing a small Pethris Wines sign on the rusty gate of a run-down vineyard, the driver slowed down, but Daniel hastily told him not to stop and indicated to a large bush just past the property. The driver slowed the car down, drove off the road, and parked behind the bush. The sound of a 747 Boeing jet overhead suggested to Daniel that this was the right place.

"You are to leave me; go to town and get some food or coffee, and don't come back for at least two hours." Daniel put his finger to his lips to silence the inspector, who was about to speak.

From the road, a long, winding driveway made its way to several buildings, and Daniel headed towards them as he watched the sedan disappear in a cloud of dust. The condition of the old winery indicated that it had not been used in making wine or anything else for many years. In the front yard of a disused, well-weathered old timber house stood a six-tonne open tray truck; a new blue tarpaulin hid the cargo on the back of it. Daniel untied the rope and lifted up the cover and was not the least surprised when it revealed a rocket launcher, armed and ready to fire.

A sudden nudge in the back made Daniel straighten up as a voice whispered in French in his ear, "Do not move one muscle, my friend, if you want to live." From the shadow cast to the right of him, Daniel could see that a man had a gun up against his back. "Now move slowly towards the old shack over to your right," the gunman instructed.

He called out to the house, and a man and two young women with automatic rifles in their hands came running out from inside. One look at the captured stranger put them into combat mode, and without saying a word, the three went in different directions and began to search the buildings and the grounds surrounding the property.

Not finding anyone, the two women jumped into a small red hatchback and drove along the driveway to the dirt road. They searched the road on either side of the property and returned shrugging and shaking their heads. Having come up empty handed, the three came up to the man holding Daniel, as if waiting for further instructions. He motioned with his head for them to go inside, and he pushed the prisoner along behind them.

"Well, my friend, we have a problem." The man with the pistol grabbed Daniel's shoulder and turned him around to face him as he spoke. "If you are here from a neighbouring property just going for a stroll, then I can understand why you do not have a car, but unfortunately, you will have to die. On the other hand, if you know anything about what is happening here, then you might be able to buy yourself some more breathing time." He sat Daniel down on a chair and arranged another seat for himself, facing him.

They were surprised how calm their prisoner was under the threat of death. Daniel needed to get the mind of the man in front of him thinking about what he needed to know, and the only way to do that was to ask questions. "Before I tell you anything, suppose you tell me who you are and why you are doing this?"

Daniel looked at the flat-chinned man with the dark, wavy hair and smiled, as in a split second, his questions had been answered. The man lifted his gun and pointed it at Daniel's head. "My friend, I ask the questions. Do not make it hard on yourself; you tell me what you are doing here, and I will make sure you die quickly."

Daniel was still calm and smiling, even after such a threat; he spoke as if making casual conversation.

"You four are cell members from the LAW terrorist organisation, and you are waiting for tomorrow to shoot down one of the planes carrying delegates from the meeting in Malta.

"You don't even really care which one it is. Chances are that it will be the French president or maybe the British prime minister, but you are really hoping it will be the American president."

Daniel had already known this, and he could see that he definitely had the man's attention. The next piece of information was what he needed in order to decide which way to handle the situation.

"You, Jamas, are trying to make a statement on behalf of the Palestinian movement, and the other three have no affiliation with anything. They just follow you like sheep." Daniel made such an impression with what he had just said that the two who were watching the outside of the building through the dirty windows came closer, and the four looked in amazement at each other, unable to find the appropriate words to utter back to this stranger.

"Oh! Cat got your tongue, eh? Well, let me continue; Jamas Galli was and probably is an honourable man who strongly believes in his cause for a free Palestine. I feel for you and your people, who are fighting a hopeless war that you cannot win—not through violence anyway." Daniel stopped talking and listened to Jamas's thoughts as he reflected on the words that his captive had spoken. Daniel felt a sense of good in this man—good that was hidden deep inside of him and that no one else would think possible from a man who had killed so many. He was genuine in his efforts towards the freedom of his homeland and was saddened for all the killings that he had been involved in while trying to achieve this end.

Jamas finally composed himself and, in complete bewilderment, uttered, "Who are you? How can you know so much about this organisation and about me? You know my name—how?" He didn't wait for an answer from his prisoner, as now his emotions took control and he kept talking. "But you are right about our hopeless fight. I have no country, so I might as well die fighting the ones that caused my people's plight in the first place."

Daniel had empathy for him, and he could see the surprise on his face when he told him in a matter-of-fact voice, "I came here to either kill you all or take you prisoner, but I have changed my mind." Daniel looked at the other man and the two women, who were nervously pointing their rifles at him, unable to think clearly regarding what their next step should be. They saw a pair of large blue eyes peer at them, and the intensity of the glare mesmerised them; their minds seemed no longer theirs. Their thoughts became vague, and the only clear feelings they received internally were sounds of instructions that echoed throughout their body. Although their minds were blurred, they knew that the thought inside them was that of the man looking at them: *You will sleep and only wake up when I tell you to do so.* In an instant, the three dropped where they stood and slumped to the floor.

Jamas jumped up from his chair and put his gun to Daniel's head. "Who are you?" A quivering voice emanated from the frightened man. Daniel stared at him with such intensity that the hand around the handle of the pistol loosened, and the gun dropped to the floor. The trembling man could not stand, and he fell to his knees.

"Jamas, I need your help to bring peace to your homeland. Your people need help to reclaim some of their country, and I want to achieve this in a peaceful way. You are going to help me end the terrorism in this world; it must end, or our world is doomed. I understand why you hate the Israelis, the Americans, and most of the Western world, but we have to accept the situation and change it just enough to stop all this fighting. Both the Palestinians and the Israelis must make concessions, and I am going to make it happen." On hearing the sound of vehicles approaching, Daniel concluded, "Jamas, you are going to be arrested, but I will come for you tomorrow."

The French inspector had radioed for reinforcements, and four cars screeched to a halt in front of the derelict house of the winery. Daniel walked out the front door and onto the decking, followed by Jamas, who had his hands clasped together on top of his head.

With guns drawn, a dozen uniformed police stormed out of the vehicles and, led by the inspector, cautiously made their way towards the house. Chief Inspector Perri, with excitement showing in his eyes and quivering hands, quickly pointed his gun at Jamas and commenced taking control.

"Put that thing away, Inspector," Daniel instructed him as other officers ran past the three on the decking. On entering the house, they found three people fast asleep on the floor.

Peter drove one of the police cars, and as he followed the other vehicles back to the station, Daniel sat in the back seat next to the unrestrained terrorist. He told him his story, and as he did, he scanned Jamas's mind for any information he could learn about the LAW group. He discovered the location and the names of the next cell that Jamas, who was the leader of this group, had contact with.

Daniel stressed to the terrorist that his fight for the return of his country to his people was fruitless unless the world survived. To satisfy his own curiosity and to reinforce what Daniel had been telling Jamas, Peter asked his mentor how he had known this cell was located at the winery.

Daniel's answer astonished Peter but completely confused an already-puzzled Jamas. "Unfortunately, my powers are still growing, and it takes some time for me to grasp what my capabilities have grown to. To cut a long story short, my mind went back in time, and I was able to listen in on the conversations that the occupants had while they were having their last meal."

As they were pulling up at the Lyon police station, Daniel turned to Jamas and, in a serene tone, said, "Jamas, here in France—and no doubt many other places—you are considered a terrorist and a cop killer, yet I want you to work for me. If you agree to help me either capture or convert some of your fellow terrorists into trying a peaceful solution to the Palestine situation, I will arrange to have you set free. Think about it overnight, and I will see you tomorrow for your answer."

The following day, at the Lyon police station, Daniel gave the information he had obtained from Jamas's thoughts about the next cell, which was in Paris, to Chief Inspector Maurice Perri.

Daniel, accompanied by an officer, went down below the station at Lyon to Jamas's dark prison cell, where he sat alone on his concrete bunk. Daniel looked at him and smiled, and nodding in a pleased manner, he signalled to the officer to open the door. Jamas slowly and almost shyly stepped out of his cell and grasped Daniel's outstretched right hand. "Welcome on board," Daniel said with a smile. Jamas was not the slightest bit surprised that this man knew that he had agreed to help.

With the Australian prime minister and her aides on board after having left the conference in Malta, the Learjet, piloted by Garry Foster, was given immediate clearance to land at Lyon. Much to the disappointment of Garry, they were only to stay a short three hours at this south-eastern part of France. That afternoon, Jamas was introduced to Paula, and with Peter and Daniel on board, they took off on their long journey back to Australia. Peter had arranged for Paula's assistants to return to Australia on a conventional flight to give Daniel a chance to talk freely with her and Jamas.

CHAPTER 6

The headlines in the Roman newspapers said it all: "Vatican Garage Sale." To the surprise of all around him, the pope had taken Cardinal Bradley's advice, and the Vatican's publicists, starved for some good news, wasted no time in arranging a conference with the world's press. The pope had agreed to auction many of the Vatican's priceless treasures to the general public. "The billions raised will be spent on the poor from all countries, no matter what their religious denomination," the pope had declared.

The Vatican would work hand in hand with many charities and would endeavour to help ease the suffering of the needy. The first programme would be the alleviation of the problem of contaminated water; unsafe water was killing more than five million people each year.

The pope called for all world religious leaders to join the Catholic Church in this venture and for all religions that believed in a Higher Being, which included the Muslim faith, to have a closer alliance and learn from each other. The world needed unity, and a good start would be for the religious leaders to set an example.

Father Andrew updated Daniel on the good news of Cardinal Bradley and the Catholic Church's gesture. Daniel's only comment on the subject was the following: "Another small step in the right direction. I only hope it's not too little too late."

Daniel arranged a meeting with Tomas Adofo and Henry Cohen at the warehouse. Although unusual for a Jew and a Muslim to become close friends, these two had done so, and now Daniel wanted them to meet Jamas.

The introduction went well at first, until Daniel explained how he had met Jamas. The agitation on Henry's face showed how uneasy he was with having anything to do with this terrorist who no doubt would have killed many Jews.

"Henry, I can understand your uneasiness with Jamas, but you must also comprehend why he is a so-called terrorist and why he was fighting for the return of the Palestinian state to his people. Your people are fighting to retain a country they believe is theirs by supposedly a decree from God himself. There is no disputing that the Israelites lived and ruled that part of the Middle East thousands of years ago, but the Palestinians were the last inhabitants. I am certainly not an expert in their history, so all I am trying to do is simplify a very complex situation. The Palestinians—who, at the time, were ruled by the Ottoman Turks—allowed a great number of Jewish emigrants who considered this their Promised Land to enter their country. Slowly, the Jews purchased much of the land and businesses, and their wealth grew, as did their power. With a promise of independence from the Turks, the Palestinians aided the British in the First World War. The British ousted the Ottoman Turks, and the Palestinians obtained their independence.

"At the same time, the British had promised the Jews settlement in Palestine. Who can blame the Palestinians for rejecting the right of the British to promise their country to another race? As the Jewish presence grew, so did attacks against them by the Arabs. The Zionists wanted to claim all of Palestine, but the British, because of the Arab defiance to their plan, did not allow it to happen. As the Nazis took over in Germany, many Jews from there entered Palestine. The volume of emigrants arriving led to a fear by the Arabs of Jewish domination, so the Palestinians revolted. The Jews were well prepared and, with a well-trained army and world sympathy on their side, won the day. The Israelis endured and took control of the country, exiling all the Palestinian leaders, and with the help of the United Nations, the State of Israel was established. The other Arab countries took up arms to reclaim the lost land of Palestine, and of course, this only gave the Jews more land when they beat the Arabs in the Six-Day War. Now the Palestinians are refugees in surrounding Arab countries or in the new lands that the Jews took from Jordan and from Egypt after the war. Terrorism all over the world has broken out, and I believe that until the Palestinian problem is solved, it will only get worse." Daniel paused as he put his arms on both Henry's and Jamas's shoulders.

"What I want to happen is for the West Bank, which was taken from Jordan, and the north of Israel, including Haifa, to be returned to the

Palestinians. Syria could also relinquish some of its south-eastern land that borders Israel to the Palestinians. The Gaza Strip in the south-west, which was captured from the Egyptians, can go to the Israelites. Jerusalem is the Holy City for the major religions—that is, Judaism, Islam, and Christianity. I propose that the city be made into a neutral zone and that an independent body, such as the United Nations, control it. It should belong to all the people of the world, not to just a few. The fact remains that Israel was taken from Jamas's people, and we have to find enough land that will suit the refugee Palestinian people and that the Israelis would be willing to give up. That's the small problem we have here, my friends; please find an answer." Daniel grinned sarcastically.

Henry, Tomas, and Jamas flew to Israel under a letter of protection from the prime minister of that country. Along with this trio, Henry convinced Rabbi Goldstein to accompany them to the Holy Land.

They were to arrange meetings with some members of the Israeli parliament to consider a possible peace plan without the interference of the Americans. The Israeli prime minister understood the importance of such a meeting to the welfare of the planet, but he also understood the enormity of his personal problem: trying to get any of his ministers to agree to any solution involving giving up land.

After their talk with the Israelis, Tomas would accompany Jamas to visit his people in the surrounding Arab countries and in the captured territory of the West Bank. Their project was to try to stop the suicide bombings that were occurring almost on a daily basis against the Jews. They carried a letter from Sheikh Farho, the head and holy man of the Muslim community in Australia, stressing the importance of heeding any suggestions made by these men, who were on a mission of peace.

A gathering of eight senior members of Parliament was arranged, and Henry Cohen introduced himself and Rabbi Goldstein to them before he proceeded to introduce their other two companions.

It took an imploring Willis Swartz—the small, balding, bespectacled Israeli prime minister—to stop them from leaving the room. "Please listen to these men; they are not just here for their cause. They are here to assist us so that in our small way, we might help save the entire world."

The prime minister's grave words were too serious for the others not to stay. The president went on to give details on the conference held in Malta.

A few minutes into the explanation, one of the Jewish ministers pushed his chair back and, shaking his head, said in a loud voice, "Well, it's obvious that you, with all due respect for your office, Mr. Swartz, were either hypnotised or drugged to believe such a ridiculous load of utter rubbish."

"No, no, that is one thing I can assure you of." The prime minister was beginning to get agitated. "You must listen to me; I am begging you all."

Rabbi Goldstein was just as confused as the rest; he had not heard of the powers of Daniel before, and he watched in amazement as Tomas reinforced Mr. Swartz's words with his own experience with Daniel.

Again, the ministers were not too impressed by the story told by an Arab. An angry Jamas spoke. "I have killed many of your people." The ministers, who were talking amongst themselves, stopped and listened when they heard those words. "And yet I am here before you, risking my life, at the request of this man—Daniel. He is but one man, and on his own, he will not achieve the task before him in time to save us all. Daniel is trying to gather as much help as possible, and from the powers that I have witnessed of this man, he has won me as an aide. In the past, I have fought to have my country returned to my people, but now there is a much bigger cause to follow, so I will postpone my fight with the Israelis and will concentrate on the fight to save our planet. To save this world, it will take many changes from many different parts of it, and we are part of that problem. In the scheme of things, we are not as huge a problem as we may all think, but our area is in crisis, and it's all these small crises that are making up one huge problem that has to be resolved.

"Unfortunately for me, I must do my part to help, even if it means cooperating with the invaders of my homeland, and I am asking you to help us to help each other. To help save the world will mean that we must all cooperate; if we do not work together and do not resolve some of our differences, then you are not giving Daniel any alternative but for him to take direct action." Here Jamas stopped and peered at each of the Israelis present. "What that action will be is not known, but I would not want to be in your shoes if you do not give him any choice. You people believe in God, and you believe that your God could destroy you and the whole world if he chooses to. What if, for just a moment, you believe us that this man—Daniel—is a messenger from God and has been given the power of the Almighty to do with us as he sees fit? I truly believe that Daniel is a human first, but if the world does not get back on God's—or, as Daniel prefers, the Creator's—track, then he will not have the ability to stop the power within himself from destroying Earth."

Jamas stood up and pointed to Prime Minister Swartz. "Your prime minister is not a stupid man; he knows what he has seen and what he has heard, and he now stands before you asking—no, begging—for your help. If your ridicule is the only reaction he is to get for his request for help, then you truly have never respected your leader."

The now-baffled ministers looked at each other for reassurance, and this time, they showed concern.

Tomas and Henry told the group about Daniel's plan for the subdivision of Israel and explained how he expected them to make concessions to make the plan workable. Without further conversation, the two Australian Jews, the Australian Egyptian, and the Palestinian terrorist slowly made their way out of the meeting and left the ministers to debate the issue.

With the letter from the Israeli prime minister, they were able to freely travel from one sector of the country to the next.

The four ambassadors of peace saw first-hand the enormity of the problem. The upheaval of the Jews from the north to the south, if Daniel's plan were implemented, would be a mammoth task. On a visit to the Holy City, they concurred that this place was going to be the stumbling block of the whole peace plan. The Jews would never agree to give up Jerusalem, as they considered this the capital of the Jewish world.

Tomas and Jamas said goodbye to Henry and the rabbi as they headed off to the West Bank, and from there, they would visit Jordan.

The West Bank, with its grazing sheep and goats, was a complete contrast to the rest of Israel. Although controlled by Israel, some of the area was under a limited Palestinian autonomous government. The population density was high, and more than 50 percent of it was under fifteen years of age. More than 30 percent of the people were unemployed, and the ones who were lucky enough to work for their small wages had to find employment in neighbouring countries, including their own homeland, now called Israel. Many of these people lived in absolute poverty.

The luckiest of the people there idled in front of their small stone houses or huts, while others lived in makeshift shacks or tents. They had nothing to do and nowhere to go, and their lives were in the hands of the Jews. Resentment in watching their old country develop in front of their eyes for the benefit of the invaders grew stronger by the day. The irony was that most of the buildings being developed in Israel were being built by the labour of their people.

The elderly and the very young were the only ones to be seen there. The rest of the people, mainly the youths, lived and planned revenge from nearby countries, and their lives revolved around the hatred they felt for the Israelis.

The comparison between the youth of Israel and the youth of the Palestinians was vast. On the one hand, the Jewish youth had the best of education, a wide variety of food, and a social life that they enjoyed to the fullest. On the other hand, the Palestinian outcast youths had no real home and no country they could call their own. Their only social life was to sneak back, dodging the watchful eyes of the Israeli soldiers, into the West Bank to visit their relatives. Their education had one theme: to give up their own lives for the freedom of their land.

With heavy hearts, the two Palestinians, with the help of one of the settlers of the West Bank, who owned an old, well-dented vehicle, headed to Amman, the capital of Jordan, to make contact with the refugees there. The driver took them straight to a relative of his, Adami Shari, who would be able to introduce them around the Palestinian community there. The young man, draped in his Arab garb, hailed a taxi and took them to a hotel of his choosing, and Jamas impressed him considerably with the names of contacts he wanted to see while in Jordan.

Adami left them at the cheap hotel and told them that he would make contact the following morning. Jamas knew the city well, and after he showed Tomas some of the many historic sites, they went to a restaurant and had meal of lamb. They had a little laugh when they were told it was imported from Australia.

Back at the hotel, they entered the dingy room they were sharing, and even though it was still only late afternoon and quite light outside, the room was as dark as night. Tomas flicked the lights on, and before their eyes could focus, powerful arms grabbed them and threw them roughly to the floor.

Their hands were vigorously pushed behind their backs and forcefully handcuffed. Two men looked down on them while two others went through their pockets and searched them thoroughly. Strong hands lifted them up and made them sit down next to each other on the only couch in the room, facing their captors.

"So which one of you is Jamas Galli?" A tall, unshaven man wearing a turban and a soiled white suit looked down at Jamas and pointed at him. "I think that would be you—yes, for sure. I have a description of you at my headquarters. Now, the last I heard about you is that you were arrested in France, and now you are here. I don't understand this; maybe you can teach me how you are here and not in a French jail."

"You must be Hazzan Camilli, and of course I am Jamas; you will find my explanation hard to believe, and I am not sure we can convince you of why we are here. We are trying to bring peace to our country, and we need help from the chiefs of our people to do so."

One of the other men searching through their luggage found the letter from the Israeli prime minister and quickly called Hazzan over to see it. With a glance at the letter, he swiftly pulled out his gun and put it to Jamas's head.

"Traitor—this answers my question, doesn't it?" he yelled in a screechy voice at Jamas.

Tomas saw him squeezing the trigger and called out in a wavering, desperate tone, "Stop, before you make a terrible mistake. I beg you—look at all the letters we have. There are other letters there; look and you will also find one from the Jordanians and one from the Egyptian president."

Hazzan's men brought more letters to him, and this confused him. He sat on the closest single bed to think. "This has me baffled," said Hazzan as he scratched the back of his head. "I will let you live for now, but you will need a better explanation than the one you are giving me about peace."

"Well, I am sorry, but that is the only reason we are here. I was freed from jail even though my group was caught red-handed in the act of trying to shoot down a plane and even after the murder of a French policeman. I joined a man who is a prophet no less than Muhammad himself. He is based in Australia, and he took me there in order for me to help him with his mission. This man next to me is Doctor Tomas Adofo; he migrated with his family to Australia many years ago. We have come all the way from there to seek help from such men as you."

Hazzan cut Jamas's explanation short. "I have had enough of this stupid talk of a prophet. This is not for me to comprehend; you will come with us to our people's camp, and our holy men can decide what they want to do with you. We will leave now so that we will get there before darkness sets in."

A short trip in an old black Mercedes brought them to a large camp in the desert not far from the West Bank. Hundreds of people milled around the many fires that dotted the scores of tents. Women were cooking their evening meals, and some of the men played cards in the twilight, while others cleaned their rifles.

The clear sky was darkening quickly as the sun descended. When the Mercedes entered the camp, some of the people came to welcome the occupants, but when the onlookers noticed the prisoners, whispers went through the crowd, and many more curiously gathered around.

Hazzan motioned to his captives to sit on the sand near one of the fires and left his men to guard them as he made his way to a larger tent that stood out amongst the much smaller ones. They sat huddling by the fire to keep warm as they watched the sun disappear over the sandy horizon. The moon and the stars appeared one by one until they took over the sky. In the bright moonlight and the light from the fires, they saw a group of men come out of the bigger tent and make their way towards them.

The mullah, the man who called this unruly group to prayer each day, stopped in front of Tomas and Jamas and beckoned for them to stand before him. He was a short, fat man with an unkempt grey beard under a dusty black turban. He arrogantly strutted, with a copy of the Koran in his right hand, before the prisoners.

"Hazzan has been pleading your case. He tells us that you are Muslims but you have found a prophet who is as great as the man who founded our faith. Is this true?"

Jamas knew that whatever they now said in their defence would be fruitless, so he thought if he were going to die, he might as well go out telling the truth. "Yes, there is such a man, but that is not to say that Muhammad was not a great prophet also. It is only that this man is here now, and Muhammad was from a time that has passed. I am stressing to you, by all that is holy, that if we do not listen to this man of today, there will be no tomorrow."

The holy man took this answer as an affront to his belief. "That is enough! By your own words, you have blasphemed against our faith, and for that, there is only one punishment: death. You have one minute to prepare yourselves by asking Allah for his forgiveness, and maybe if you are genuine enough, he may accept you into his fold."

The crowd was so intent on what was happening that nobody noticed that the moon and the stars were no longer visible; instead, a massive black cloud covered the sky like a blanket. Some heard a distant rumble and briefly looked in the direction they thought the sound had come from; however, the execution of the two men was more interesting, and they paid little heed to the noise.

The prisoners were given copies of the Koran and made to stand next to each other beside a large campfire that gave off a bright glow that lit up the area around them. From where they stood, they could barely make out the shapes of a number of men standing in front of them. They knew that their time had come; they were facing a firing squad with rifles at the ready.

The holy man, standing on a knoll of sand to the side of the condemned men, raised his right hand, holding the holy book towards the sky, and called out at the top of his voice, "May Allah forgive these blasphemers and bless the executioners for keeping the faith true. Allah is great."

The onlookers were all shouting, "Allah is great," when instantly, the sky lit up as bright as the day itself, and a lightning bolt, in a blaze of light accompanied by a deafening clap of thunder, struck the raised Koran. The body of the holy man vibrated uncontrollably and was illuminated so brightly that the people watching were temporarily blinded, and most fell, cowering, to the ground.

A few moments passed before they regained their senses. The sight of the smouldering remains of their holy man in a heap on the sand and the stench of burning flesh terrified them even more. The six men from the firing squad still held their positions. Their rifles were no longer in their burned and badly blistered hands but were on the ground before them, bent and on fire. Mouths were moving, and terrified people were speaking and screaming, but it took several minutes before their hearing returned to them.

At dawn, Hazzan entered the big tent and awakened the two men from an exhausted sleep. "Well, my friends, I hope you had a good night's sleep in the mullah's tent. You should have made use of the fat bastard's wives last night, although I don't blame you for kicking them out."

Hazzan had brought them breakfast and proceeded to make Tomas and Jamas coffee. "My people believe you to be messengers from Allah."

A hesitant Hazzan then coyly said, "I just want to ask one question: Did you have anything to do with the lightning last night? I mean, did you make it happen?" He lifted his arms in front of him and gave a sheepish smile.

"Let's leave it to every individual's imagination. What happened last night happened for the right reason," Tomas replied as he lifted his eyes to the heavens.

When the two men stepped outside, they were agog to see the hundreds of people who had propped themselves quietly in the sand, waiting for them. The crowd consisted mainly of young men and women who were nursing old and badly kept rifles, and their silence made the two men nervous.

Jamas looked over at his companion and stepped forward; he bowed his head slightly as a gesture to the crowd and said in a loud yet humble voice, "I am Jamas Galli, and I am considered a terrorist by the enemies of my people. My friend over here is a Muslim doctor, and we both have come here from far away. We were sent here on a mission by a new prophet who has set up his headquarters in the country of Australia. He has sent us here to prepare a path towards peace for the Palestinian people with their archenemies, the Israelis."

A murmur came from the crowd, and Tomas started to sweat; he envisaged being torn to pieces by a rampant mob. Jamas waited until the noise died down before he continued. "The past is gone. No matter how hard we try to bring it back, it will not happen. I am here to pass on a message to you from this new prophet. This message is simple: forget the past, and concentrate on the future. Wrapping yourselves with explosives and blowing your bodies into a thousand pieces to kill a few Jews will not change our lot. All the goat shit that is being fed to the youth of our people, especially the young men, that they will go to paradise and have many wives and live a life of luxury is just that—shit—and I am sure that down deep in your hearts, you know that what I say is true. We must go forward with a plan of reconciliation with our enemy if we are to have any future as Palestinians. We need you to cooperate with us and give peace a chance to work. I say this to you: if some resolution is not reached in the near future, I too will go back to my old way and fight our enemy to the death. This I promise you." Jamas raised his right hand in the air, and a roar came out of the crowd. He calmed them down and added, "We have tried our way, and this has not worked. Can we now try the way of Daniel from Australia—a peaceful way? Can we lay down our arms and give peace a go?" Jamas stopped talking and looked at his people.

There was silence for a minute, and then a young woman stood up and looked deeply at an apprehensive Jamas. She spun around and faced her people and yelled to them, "I would like nothing better than to settle down in my own home in my own country so that I can marry and raise my children in peace. I, for one, will try anything to resolve this never-ending killing; although our battle is righteous, I know in my heart that all our fighting will not achieve an end to it."

A young man sitting next to the young woman looked up at her as she looked down at him. Their loving eyes met, and he jumped up, hurled his rifle out in front of him, and called out, "Give peace a try! Give peace a try!"

Another stood up, and slowly, more and more of the youths followed suit until a mountain of rifles was stacked up in front of the man preaching peace.

Jamas, with misty eyes, looked at Tomas and said quietly, "These people deserve much more than they have been dealt. They have lost their will to fight and have now put their trust completely in us; please help me not to let them down."

Phillip Azage from Ethiopia was elected spokesperson for the African countries, and a meeting amongst them was to be held urgently in South Africa to implement the AIDS plan the committee had agreed to set up to tackle this enormous crisis.

Caris, Peter, and Daniel were to attend, and from there, they would go on to the Middle East to meet up with Tomas and Jamas.

To Daniel, the difference with this conference was the few white faces amongst the many black ones. Phillip welcomed all, especially Daniel, who opened the meeting.

"The starvation issue is being addressed by many nations, and already, results are being noticed," Daniel began. "Now we start the next leg of our programme: AIDS. This will be the most contentious of all our issues, but we must be strong and persistent with what will appear inhumane to your own people and most of the population of the world. Already we have over three thousand doctors, including pathologists, and ten times that number of nurses committed to us by many countries. The use of your own armies and the many thousands of extra personnel from other countries will help ensure that this massive undertaking is successful. To help start our task, here in my hand is a bank draft for one billion US dollars, which my associates and I are donating towards this important cause. Now it is up to you to figure out how to solve this dilemma we face." Daniel ended with the enthusiastic cheers of the delegates.

The slim Ethiopian thanked Daniel and took over the meeting. "We want to take quick and decisive action. Each country on the African continent will issue a decree that every citizen is to be tested. Individual countries will take turns establishing clinics all over their land for the use of the medical staff being supplied to us. The clinics will be fitted with the latest state-of-the-art computers and technology to allow us to keep records and to print out photo identification cards. All, except for infants, must be tested. Millions of people already know that they carry the AIDS virus, and we have records of many of these infected ones, so they will not have to be tested, which will save us much time. All infected persons will be isolated into camps, which will be partitioned cities and towns. They will be medically treated and educated about their disease. The uninfected will be given photo identification cards that they must carry with them at all times; these will be their proof that they have been tested. Anyone who refuses to be tested will be isolated and kept under guard until he or she agrees. We envisage problems getting our new laws through to some of the bush people, but they are in the minority as far as population and infection; just the same, they will eventually be tested as we come across them. This project will take many months to complete—maybe even years—and each country will vary in time needed for the task, depending on its size, its population, and even its terrain." He gazed across the room at the quiet listeners.

"Libya and Egypt are to conduct their own testing, as they don't have a massive AIDS problem. When they have completed their testing, they will send their teams over to Algeria and Morocco to help the authorities there. We will start this operation from the south coast of this continent and work our way up north. The thousands of soldiers we have under our control will form a human chain and slowly work their way north in conjunction with the medical staff tending the clinics. In this way, nobody from the north who has not been tested can escape to the south to an already-tested area. The individual can only escape farther north, where we, hopefully, will catch up with that person sooner or later. The few arriving south by air or by sea who have no proof of testing will have to do so before they leave the ports. This plan is, unfortunately, not one hundred percent foolproof, but hopefully it will ensure that the bulk of the people will be tested. The soldiers will have to be careful to allow the wild animals to have their freedom in wandering back and forth past their lines."

The Ethiopian chairman looked over at the other leaders to ensure that they were in tune with him before he carried on with his speech. "Obviously, South Africa will be the starting point, and it is already prepared and has commenced informing their citizens. Many helpers are calling on villages all over that country to advise them of this new law. As the lines of soldiers move farther north, we might have clinics manned in three or four different countries at the one time." Mr. Azage took a breather and looked down at the audience.

"Does that cover all or most of what we agree on?" he asked.

"Our soldiers are bound to come across rebels, and I am sure they will be shot at. What will our boys do—do they retaliate?" a concerned delegate asked.

"We thought of that, and I thank you for reminding me; we will offer amnesty to all rebels as long as they agree to disarm and to be tested. If they want to fight, we will have many armed helicopters standing by to help our soldiers. I am sure that most of these rebels will agree that giving a little blood is better than giving up their lives. This exercise might achieve more than just help us wipe out AIDS; we might get rid of many of the rebels as well as poachers. We will look at each option as we come across it. One major situation is the question of the dictatorship of Zimbabwe. They have not attended this meeting, and as yet, we cannot get a response to our communications with them. Nevertheless, we are starting the testing programme, and I will personally keep trying to contact the dictator in an effort to get a commitment from him. If they do not cooperate, we will surround that country to ensure that nobody leaves that land—by foot anyway. If there are no more questions, we will adjourn and get behind South Africa. Let's get this whole project started for the benefit of the whole of our continent," the jubilant chief councillor of Ethiopia said, concluding his talk.

Daniel was pleased with the way Phillip had taken control of his assignment and had every confidence in him in completing this massive undertaking.

While Daniel attended the meeting, Peter was hard at work; he had organised the next point of call for them. He contacted Henry to find out what stage he was at with organising the Israeli prime minister and selected members of their parliament for the joint meeting involving themselves, the Palestinians, and the three other surrounding Arab nations. The Israelis had agreed to the meeting, provided it was held in the Holy City, Jerusalem.

Henry contacted Tomas and Jamas; their task was to convince the leaders of the Palestinian Liberation Army to attend a meeting with the Israelis on peace talks.

Peter, as Daniel's representative, had no difficulty in making contact with the Jordanian prime minister with a request that he speak to his king about attending this special meeting in Jerusalem. The Egyptian president and the Syrian president were pleased to be included.

A week later, the Israeli prime minister, flanked by four members of his cabinet, sat uncomfortably on high-backed solid-oak chairs around a long, old oak table; they deliberately ignored the other people in the large, ancient room.

The Egyptian president, along with his deputy, sat down to their left, joined by the Syrian president and vice president to their right.

Peter, Tomas, Jamas, Henry, Rabbi Goldstein, and three members of the Palestinian Liberation Army, including Al Bahda, the leader of the PLO, and Hazzan Camilli sat directly in front of the Israelis.

The elderly Israeli defence minister didn't hesitate in showing his contempt for the people sitting across from him.

"Al Bahda," he taunted the PLO chief, "you are no Yassar Arafat. Who is pulling your strings—maybe his ghost, eh?" He had despised the long-deceased former PLO leader Arafat, but he at least had respected him as a soldier. Al Bahda had no charisma and came across as a weak man. "Who is really leading your people? Which terrorist group is giving you orders?"

The PLO chief, to his credit, kept his composure, and with a slight snarl in his voice, he retorted, "May the ghosts of Arafat and Osama Bin Laden descend on you and all your people for the misery you have bestowed on my people. My strings can be pulled by anyone who will help us rid our land of our persecutors."

Jamas came into the conversation before the Jewish defence minister had a chance to retaliate, and to the surprise of all, he admonished his own colleague. "Do not speak of Yassar Arafat in the same breath with the terrorist Bin Laden, for there is no comparison between the two. Arafat fought for the freedom of his people, whilst the other fought for his religion. Any man who leads freedom fighters, who fights for the right of deposed people, is not a criminal in the eyes of the people he protects; he is only a criminal in the eyes of the invaders. Anyone who kills in the name of religion is a hypocrite and an enemy to his own faith."

After a few uncomfortable minutes, Peter was glad for any interruption and was pleased to see the king of Jordan entering the room, followed by his meek prime minister. They sat at the head of the table, to the right of Peter.

Again, the gathered waited in silence, and Peter, feeling the tension growing, hesitantly started the meeting.

"While we wait for the main speaker, may I introduce myself? My name is Peter Brand, and I hail from Australia."

The indignation showed on the king of Jordan's face as he stood up. "I am not accustomed to waiting for any man." He beckoned to his hesitant minister to follow him out through the thick wooden doors. "Come, we leave," he abruptly uttered.

Halfway across the room, the king stopped as he watched the massive, solid doors move on their own accord and suddenly slam shut. The loud crash sent a shudder throughout the room, and it startled the king so much that he fell backwards, losing his silk turban as he landed on the floor.

A hazy mist appeared in front of the closed doors, and slowly, it became denser and denser until it began to form a shape, and within a few seconds, the amazed onlookers were staring at a new person in the room.

The terrified king sitting on the floor used his legs to push himself backwards, almost knocking over his prime minister, until his back collided with the wall on the other side of the room.

The others, except for Peter and Henry, were now standing at the other side of the table and cowering behind the chairs. A blue-eyed man walked over to the petrified king, stretched out his arm, and grabbed the king's right hand. He helped him to his feet and, at the same time, spoke to him. "Please be a good man and sit down so we can get the meeting started." A soft-spoken Daniel led the king and his prime minister back to their seats, and the other attendees cautiously followed suit and made their way back to their chairs and sat down. Tomas and Jamas gave sighs of relief on seeing Daniel, and if they'd had any doubts whatsoever about him, those doubts were now completely gone.

The leaders from Israel, Syria, and Egypt and the Jordanian prime minister hastened to Daniel's side, and they took turns embracing him and welcoming him.

"Sorry for the theatrical way of entering, but I wanted to make sure I got everybody's undivided attention—and now I believe I have."

"This man is the prophet—Daniel," the Egyptian president said with pride. The other three men confirmed this to the other wide-eyed men in the room.

They all had questions, but they abstained from asking any, as they suspected that their queries would be answered soon enough. It took Peter quite some time to explain their mission.

Daniel was assertive in what he wanted. "The Israeli problem is one that will never go away unless a decisive plan of action is undertaken. The hate of the Palestinians for the Jews is a hate that can be justified and understood. The Israelis and their allies call the PLO terrorists, and they in turn call the Israelis and their allies terrorists. Who is right here? The Jews have taken over this land, claiming it is theirs as decreed by their God, Yahweh, thousands of years ago. The Palestinians want what they consider their country back. The Jews had no country to call their own, and now they have, but now the Palestinians have no country to call their own. There is a lot of irony here; I am sure you will all agree. One irony is that once, the Jewish race was persecuted, and millions of them were killed. The world was in sympathy with them for all the atrocities committed against them, and they deserved a homeland. But now the Jews have become the aggressors and have persecuted the Palestinians to the extent that they have been deposed out of their own homes. The Palestinians are the ones who have paid for the atrocities that were committed against the Jews under the Nazis. What did they have to do with the Holocaust? Nothing! How ironic is that? The other irony is that both sides have used terror, currently and in the past; this must stop, and you Israelis surely must have noticed that there have been no suicide bombings for the last three weeks, which I am sure is a record for the last few months. The Palestinians have agreed to give peace talks a chance, and I am here to help resolve this crisis once and for all." Daniel slammed his open hand onto the table to emphasise this point.

"Gentlemen, today we will come to a solution one way or another. Today you people are here to agree to a plan I have in finding an answer to this ongoing problem." Daniel took a long, hard look at the Israelis sitting at the table, and except for the prime minister, he gathered that the others were not in agreement with any reconciliation with the Palestinians if it involved giving up land.

He ignored them and continued. "Jordan has already conceded the West Bank, and Egypt conceded the Gaza Strip. This area is already occupied by Palestinians. Syria is to sell some of its south-eastern land to the Israelis, who will no doubt be able to afford to pay for it through future savings on defence. I want Israel to be split in two."

The Israeli ministers were flabbergasted with this suggestion, and even Swartz was surprised, but their wariness of Daniel stopped them from objecting. "The north, including the West Bank, is to become the new Palestine, and the south, including the Gaza Strip, is to remain as Israel.

"Jerusalem is a holy city for the world's main three religions—Islam, Christianity, and Judaism; therefore, I want it to become an independent city. It is to be a free city for the world's people who want to worship or visit there. A separate ruling body made up of all religions will run this city and will do so in a congenial way. It is to be administered by the United Nations."

The Israeli prime minister slowly made his way to his feet and reluctantly spoke. "Daniel, I appreciate that we must do everything in our power to restore peace in this region and that, in turn, in our own way, we are helping save our planet, but you are asking too much from my people. They will not agree to any of this, especially giving up Jerusalem."

"I also appreciate your concerns, Mr. Swartz"—Daniel was still being assertive—"but you, the Israelis, have been trying to find a solution for over eighty years. I will consider any plan that will solve this problem, so if you can come up with anything better, let me know."

The Syrian president understood the gravity of this matter, but the vice president didn't and wanted Daniel to know of his feelings. "Why should we contemplate selling any of our land? It is our land, so why should we inconvenience our people to help out the Jews?"

An angry reply from Daniel was enough to send a shiver through the bodies of all present. "Mr. Vice President, the inconvenience to a few thousand Syrians means nothing when you compare it to the possibility of no planet. Sir, land will not mean much if there is no world. The inconvenienced people will be well compensated by the State of Israel, and they may well be better off than they are now. We must pull together to solve a problem that will not go away."

The Syrian president confirmed that he was behind this plan and would do everything in his power to ensure it was implemented. The Israelis were still concerned. "To convince the people to give up nearly a third of their country is going to be a mammoth task," the prime minister pointed out. "Firstly, we would have to convince the rest of Parliament and then the generals of the armed forces; even if we convinced them, the people would revolt, and there would be anarchy. It is going to take a miracle to implement this plan."

Daniel said, "There is no need to panic your people. We do not have the time to try to convince the masses of what our mission is. So I agree with you, Mr. Prime Minister; we need a miracle, and the good Rabbi Goldstein is going to provide it for us." He didn't expand any further with his plan; Daniel winked at the stunned rabbi, and with everyone's agreement to keep communications open, the meeting was adjourned.

The next day, the Israeli parliament gathered for an extraordinary meeting. The main executive body consisted of a cabinet of twenty-five members, and the Israeli legislative body was made up of 120 members. All 145 parliamentarians were present and eagerly waited for Willis Swartz to begin his oration on the latest peace plan. Surely, every conceivable notion had already been explored.

He told the audience about the meeting he had attended the previous day with the neighbouring Arab countries and the Palestinians. Swartz wasn't far into his speech, when, at the mention of the division of Israel, the whole of Parliament erupted into a roar of hostility. The people's representatives, who were now all standing, let out gasps and shouts of dismay.

Prime Minister Swartz found it difficult to maintain order, and he could not continue with his talk. He looked at the irate faces and knew that they would not listen to him any further. In despair, he turned and looked at the man waiting to be introduced to Parliament.

A tall man dressed in black, with a hat to match, approached the president, and they swapped places. He raised his hands, giving a sign for silence. The curious assembly slowly quieted down, and they sat down to listen to this stranger with the scruffy white beard.

"I am Rabbi Goldstein, and I came here only a few days ago from Australia. In the old days, we rabbis were legal authorities, but these days, we are just plain old preachers. You will more than likely not believe what I am about to preach to you, but I must say what I have to say, for all our sakes. We are of the faith of Judaism, and therefore, we are believers in a higher God. Our history began with God speaking to our ancestors and guiding us through the ages. Now our belief in God is to be tested again. This test will show whether we still are believers or whether we are just pretenders. I am here to warn you that if this special assembly does not vote for the plan your prime minister has just tried to unfold to you, there will be a sign from God—a sign of great significance—within two days of the rejection of this plan." He halted to ensure the audience digested what he had told them.

"I ask you to calmly listen to your head of state and then vote with your head and not with your heart. We must attain everlasting peace for the good of the Middle East and for the good of our people and for the good of the Palestinian people. Please listen to the plan that will achieve this goal, and after the vote is taken, please do not leave this assembly, as I will have more to say on this matter."

The members cast their votes by a secret ballet within minutes of the conclusion of the prime minister's speech. After collecting and counting the votes, the clerks handed the results to the prime minister, who looked at the note and slowly stood up. With unsteady hands, he read them out.

"These numbers were expected—only twenty-three of you voted for the plan, and obviously, the rest of you have overwhelmingly rejected it. I ask you to again listen to Rabbi Goldstein and listen well, for if his warning is not accepted, then many of our people will die." The red-eyed prime minister looked at the assembly and, in dismay, sat down.

The rabbi stood up and pointed a finger at all before him. "You have made your decision, and now you must face the wrath of God, the Creator, for the destruction of Israel is at hand."

He was silent for a full minute, letting the minds of the listeners absorb whatever fear he had conjured up. "You will respect one last order from your prime minister: have the armed forces clear every person from within three hundred metres of the Western Wall of Jerusalem. This most holy of places for the Jewish people, the Wailing Wall, will be utterly destroyed within two days hence."

A murmur rumbled through the assembly hall, and abusive shouts taunted the rabbi, but he kept his composure and uttered a final order: "We will reassemble in two days' time."

The rabbi looked down at the gathering, turned, and, with head held high, walked towards the exit, through the gauntlet of abusive parliamentarians.

Two days later, under a clear blue sky, the soldiers formed a perimeter around the Wailing Wall. This wall, built in the first century BC, was the remains of the great temple erected by Herod, king of Judea. The huge, eroded limestone blocks at the bottom and the smaller ones at the top were evidence of its age and its strength. Jews from all over the world made pilgrimages there to pray and pay their respects to their ancestors.

Most of the people who were evacuated assumed that there must have been a bomb threat and didn't question the authorities; they stood facing the wall, waiting until the area was declared safe again.

Rabbi Goldstein and the entire Israeli parliament, led by Willis Swartz, stood in silence on a hill overlooking Jerusalem, where they could clearly see the threatened area. The frustrated prime minister finally broke the silence. "Have you heard from Daniel at all?" he asked the rabbi.

"No, I haven't. It's eerie, though—I think my thoughts are not entirely mine. I seem to know what to say about this whole matter. At the assembly, I stood there in front of everybody, frightened to death because I had no idea what I was going to say. My whole body and my mind were no longer mine; they appeared to be controlled by someone or something else. Words came out of my mouth, but they weren't my words. I had imagined everybody walking out of that meeting as soon as I started to rant and rave, but no—they all kept their seats and listened to me, even if they did jeer me in the end."

In the middle of the afternoon on this beautiful day, an eerie shadow began to creep over the land. Looking up, the rabbi mused, "Isn't that odd? That large cloud has come out of nowhere. And how quickly it is growing in size, and how black it is."

Darkness covered the Holy City as a continuous rumble, more like cannon fire, emanated from the sky, and lightning lit up the land spasmodically. An illuminating flash came from the cloud, a lightning bolt reached down, and in the blink of an eye, the top corner of the Western Wall turned to dust and disappeared. The enormous roar of thunder that followed instantly was so loud that it scattered the screaming crowd and the soldiers on guard duty in all directions.

Members of the ruling assembly watched in awe. Was this the sign the rabbi had warned them about? As if in answer to their thoughts, a second bolt hit the top of the wall, and another section was turned to white powder. More strikes followed, and more of the wall vanished.

Up on the hill, the rabbi had a compulsion to count the number of lightning strikes out loud, ensuring that the prime minister could hear him. An hour had passed since the first strike, and half the wall had become rubble. "That's seventy-eight bolts of lightning, and I believe there will be another forty-four to go," the tall rabbi muttered to the amazed prime minister.

"How would you know that there would be another forty-four?" he asked.

"Remember what I said before about receiving thoughts? Well, I think that was one of those. At the assembly, one hundred twenty-two members voted against the peace plan, and that is how many lightning strikes we are going to get."

The two men looked at each other, and together they instantly came to the same conclusion. Mr. Swartz called his cabinet to gather around him, and with the rabbi standing next to him, Willis Swartz silenced the whispering and frightened people before him. "The cloud is still there, but the lightning strikes have stopped, and the entire Western Wall has been turned to powder; the rabbi wants to talk to you again, as he requested two days ago."

Goldstein sneered at them as he raised his arms and spoke in a clear, booming voice. "One hundred twenty-two of you voted against the peace plan, and it took one hundred twenty-two lightning strikes to destroy our Wailing Wall. That black cloud you see above us will not go away until each and every one of you agrees to the plan that was put before you two days ago. Another vote is to take place immediately. Be warned: the lightning will keep destroying parts of Jerusalem until the Creator is satisfied that you all have accepted the plan unconditionally." The rabbi instructed the ministers to vote by a show of hands, and this time, the result gave the peace plan an overwhelming majority.

The prime minister, although happy, was still concerned. "But I do not know if this is good enough to please the one above. There are still five of you who have voted to reject the plan. Could those people please tell us why in heaven's name they have not understood the message or ultimatum we were all given and have witnessed?"

Four men and one woman who were milling together came forward, and the woman spoke first. "We are sorry, but we do not believe that what we saw was a message from God. We believe it was just a coincidence, and we are not in agreement in giving away any of our country to those terrorists."

A massive brilliance of light streaked across the sky, followed by a deafening, echoing boom that made the delegates dive to the ground. They sat up and watched helplessly as the lightning strikes started again, but after the fifth, all was quiet.

The woman jumped to her feet and screamed, "I vote for the plan! I vote for it. I believe in God, and I ask for his forgiveness for doubting him."

The other four followed suit and gave their consent.

The day slowly turned from a completely bleak one to a bright, sunny one, and the clear blue sky appeared again. The dark cloud was dissipating in a northerly direction, and it soon vanished over the horizon.

No one heard from Daniel for the next few days, but news came from the West Bank that a strange man dressed all in white had appeared in the midst of a battle between Israeli armed forces and a hundred stone-wielding Palestinians. Word was that the stones thrown were suspended in midair like stars in the midday sun, and some unknown power wrenched the weapons out of the Israeli soldiers' hands and piled them on top of each other in the middle of the battleground. The two Israeli tanks at the scene went out of control, crushing all the weapons before careening off on their own towards a ravine. The crew abandoned the tanks before they plunged over the edge.

The Israeli newspapers had an exceptional day for news with the lightning strikes, the total destruction of the Wailing Wall, and the dark, menacing cloud that had slowly headed north. They called the first event a phenomenon of nature, but now, with more miracles happening, they were reporting that these occurrences must surely be the work of God and his dissatisfaction with the Middle East debacle. One paper's main feature ran a story that the Messiah had come to bring peace to the area.

An interview with Willis Swartz explaining what had occurred at the Parliamentary Assembly, including the correlation between the number of lightning strikes and the negative votes on the proposed peace plan, had much of the population congregating at their synagogues.

Other politicians from both sides of the House confirmed what their prime minister had explained, and they expanded the story.

Henry, Jamas, and the rabbi stayed behind in Israel to assist with the implementation of the peace plan, while Tomas headed back to Australia and his family. The other three—Daniel, Caris, and Peter—headed for America. John B. Rose was having difficulties in convincing Congress to accept the idea of legalising illicit drugs.

On their way, they would be stopping in Paris so that Daniel could interrogate terrorist members that the French police had captured a few days ago. Daniel's prediction that the terrorists would scatter had been right; at this juncture, the French constabulary had been able to apprehend only two members of the Paris terrorist cell. They were hoping that with Daniel's special abilities at interrogation, they might be able to locate the other two as well as discover the whereabouts of the next cell.

Daniel was pleased with Jamas when he gave him the name of an arms supplier in Paris whom he had often utilised.

The commissioner of police and the tall, skinny chief inspector, Maurice Perri, from Lyon met them at the airport. They took Caris to the hotel and then headed off to the prisoners' holding centre.

The terrorists were of no help; they were only followers and could not assist in tracing the next cell, bringing an end to capturing any more terrorists by this method. Daniel requested that the commissioner put the inspector from Lyon and a couple of his men at his disposal; he had another lead to follow.

Jamas's lead was an industrial area close to Paris, and two unmarked police vehicles headed for it. They drove through the potted road they were seeking and parked three hundred metres away from their destination. After Daniel instructed Maurice and his men to wait until he called them, he and Peter drove one of the cars to the address.

The outside revealed nothing more than an innocent cabinet-making factory and two vacant buildings on either side. The pair boldly walked through the open roller door into the workshop; the machinery looked as if it hadn't been used in a long while, and the floor was covered in sawdust that had hardened into clumps. There was no activity, and the place seemed empty, but Daniel sensed danger and quickly instructed Peter to stay close behind. A large, shabby man appeared from behind a pile of pallets and approached them.

"Good afternoon, gentlemen," he called out to them in bad French. "Are you lost, or do you want some work done for you?"

The unshaven man was close to seven foot tall, and he looked down on them through squinting eyes. Although it was a cool spring day, the huge, unkempt man, who had a round, shaven head, wore dirty green shorts and a matching short-sleeved shirt that was too tight for him and stretched over his large stomach. He appeared confused; he could have sworn that the man at the rear had been fair-haired, but now that the two intruders were closer, he could see that they were of Arab appearance. Daniel suspected that the manner of the man's greeting was a code. He scanned the big man's mind as he mulled over the reply he was waiting to hear.

The man perceived Daniel speaking to him in French with an Arabic accent. "No, we are not lost; we want a special writing desk made for us. It is to be in mahogany and have no drawers."

"Ah, gentlemen, we have just the thing for you, if you will follow me." The big man's attitude changed, and he turned and walked towards the back of the workshop. They entered a small office, and he motioned for them to sit at his desk, while he stood and leaned his massive frame against a corner of the back wall. The open door was at their back, which made Daniel restless.

"Before we sit, I would appreciate it if you would get your two men out there to lower their guns. We will not sit here with rifles pointed at us," Daniel politely but firmly said. The surprised fellow slowly raised his right hand, and two men clutching rifles climbed down from a storage loft on top of a scaffold structure overlooking the office. They entered and took the place of the man in the corner while he moved to sit at the other side of the desk.

"Now, what is it that I can do for you?"

"We need equipment for a very big project we have. Some you may have on hand, and some you may have to get for us from your suppliers." Daniel looked intently at the man and bore into his thoughts. A picture of a cellar beneath them appeared in Daniel's mind; it was full of arms and explosives. The supplier and the town came to him: Kladno, twenty-five kilometres east of Prague, the capital of the Czech Republic. The street name and the warehouse became clearly visible to Daniel.

The badly spoken Frenchman took offense at the Arab's assumption that he did not have all the supplies on hand, and he abruptly let Daniel know so.

"You goat fucker, what makes you believe that I have not got all the supplies you need?"

"Well, do you have six command-guided missiles with radar tracking beams as well as a control station with computer processors on hand?" Daniel indignantly asked.

With his mouth gaping wide, the big man stroked his unshaven chin with his right hand as his mind wandered to the industrial city of Kazan in central European Russia, a port city on the Volga and Kazanka rivers, where aircrafts were included in their manufacturing industry.

Russia was the only place possible to find these items, especially the control station. Since the break-up of the Soviet Union more than four decades ago, almost anything could be bought on the black market there.

"My friends, I offer you my humblest apologies." The mountainous man found it hard to utter those words, but he now realised he was not dealing with amateurs. "You are right; I would have to order these and have them delivered."

"Now, if you could show me your wares, we will pick what we need from your current stock." Daniel wanted to see the cellar below them.

A fourth man ran into the office, shouting with excitement, "Police, police—there are police out there! Three of them, and they are coming this way."

The big man and his two henchmen glanced at the now unlikely customers and reached for their weapons in unison. Daniel waved his hand, and the room hissed with a torrent of rushing air, making it impossible for the men to move or even breathe. The walls, the roof, and the floor expanded under the immense air pressure, and Daniel instantly lifted his right fist and smashed it onto the desk. The office shattered in all directions, making the timber floor collapse from under their feet. With swishing air currents around them, the arms dealers landed heavily twenty feet down on a hard concrete floor. They groggily looked up to see two men clutching each other, slowly descending on them, floating through the thick air.

Gritting his teeth, the large man fought to clear his mind as he struggled to his feet; he rushed at Peter, who was the closest to him. Peter stepped aside, and the big man crashed head first into the shelving. Heavy boxes of ammunition fell off the shelves, crushing him into unconsciousness. The other three men had had the wind knocked out of them from the fall, and they were in no shape to fight.

"Are you all right down there, Mr. Daniel?" the inspector called out.

An angered Daniel looked up, and the inspector fell, somersaulting through the air and landing heavily on his buttocks. He held his bottom as he stood up and tried to walk as his two assistants found a ladder and climbed down to help.

"You were taking so long that I got worried you were in trouble," the frightened inspector said apologetically.

To Daniel, this little excursion had proven fruitful; three sources of arms suppliers and dealers had been eliminated. Stopping the supply of arms was more important than actually apprehending the terrorists themselves. There was always someone to replace the human element of terrorism, but weapons were a much more important commodity, and if they were harder to find, then terrorism might slow down at a faster rate.

CHAPTER 7

John B. Rose welcomed the three Australians as guests at the White House and personally escorted them to the third floor, where three separate rooms were ready for them. An obviously embarrassed president whispered into Daniel's ear and received a smirk in reply. The president shyly turned to the maids, and smiling sheepishly, he raised two fingers.

They sat in Daniel and Caris's room, and after the maids served coffee and left, the president brought Daniel up to date on the progress of legalising illicit drugs. "There is no way we can get the two-thirds majority we need from Congress to pass this bill. We have a strong lobby group amongst the Senate and the House of Representatives against this legalisation, and they are fanatical about it. It's as if their lives depend on this bill being defeated."

Daniel thought for a moment before asking, "Can you arrange for a meeting here in the White House with this group, especially the ones who are the most outspoken? Invite the directors of the FBI and the CIA and a couple of their assistants, and please arrange to have a few armed guards assembled at the library doors after we close them."

Two days later, the president led Daniel and Peter into the library while Caris went shopping. Assembled inside were a number of men and a few women; some sat alone, while others congregated in groups. A hush came over them as they watched the three men enter.

The president addressed the attendees. "Ladies and gentlemen, would you please be seated, and we will get started? Firstly, let me welcome you all, including the directors of the FBI and the CIA and their aides. I would like to introduce and welcome our special guests all the way from Australia, Daniel Leeder and Peter Brand. Mr. Leeder here, along with the prime minister of Australia, is a man who has been leading the world in an effort to legalise illicit drugs. You people, on the other hand, are against it for one reason or another. Daniel wants to get an insight into your reasoning as to why you feel so strongly against this proposal."

An elderly gentleman dressed in a cream-coloured suit, sitting comfortably in a lounge chair, made no effort to stand as he demanded to be heard. "With all due respect, sir, do we really need to have a foreigner tell us our business? I, for one, will not change my mind on this issue."

Daniel walked over to the arrogant man and looked deeply into his eyes. "Senator William Barrett, why are you so against this legislation going through?"

The senator was pleasantly surprised that this stranger knew his name. "Obviously, you have done your homework; good for you, sir."

Daniel needed to make an impact on the rest of the group. "Tell me, Senator, have you ever been paid any monies by the drug barons?"

"I don't have to take this from you or anybody else." The outraged Senator tried to rise but seemed to be glued to his seat.

Daniel berated him. "There are few words that describe a man such as you, sir. You have betrayed the youth of your country, and that makes you nothing short of a traitor—a traitor who is in the pay of the drug barons of Colombia."

Daniel had astounded not only the man sitting before him but also everyone in the room, including the president.

The senator's face showed fear as he stared up at his accuser.

"Why not tell us all about the Swiss bank accounts you hold and the millions of dollars paid into them by the drug cartels, Mr. Barrett?"

Leaning over the senator's wriggling body, Daniel reached over and grabbed a pen and a writing pad from the desk behind him. He concentrated on the senator's thoughts and wrote down the information he obtained.

Ripping the page from the pad, he walked over to the tall, lean man with the bad comb-over. "Director Bob Wilson"—Daniel extended his right hand, and the man quickly accepted it—"you will follow this up, won't you?" Daniel handed him the piece of paper. The CIA director just nodded and, after a quick glance at the note, turned and handed it to a serious-looking aide who stood at his side. The middle-aged, unsmiling assistant nodded and left the room quietly. Daniel indicated to Peter to follow the aide.

The silence was deafening in the library, and although the room was relatively cool, sweat poured from the faces of some of the fidgeting people present. Daniel sensed the fear, but the fear of one person was paramount.

He walked amongst the people and asked the same simple question to each. He entered a note in his writing pad before seeing the next person in line. At times, he would detect genuine concerns, and he would ask them to expand on their thoughts. "Congressman Walker, sir, why are you against the legalisation of illicit drugs?"

"I worry that we will have a problem similar to cigarette smoking, and by making drugs legal, we may actually encourage the youth of America to take up drug use rather than not."

Daniel needed to answer these concerns. "With cigarettes, the youth only have to worry about peer pressure and the saturation of advertising by the large cigarette companies. These companies concentrate their advertisements towards the youths of the world and hook new generations on an ongoing basis. Unfortunately, they have taken full advantage of their drugs being legal and being privatised rather than being government controlled. This has been a massive mistake, which now is very difficult to rescind. Current drug addicts rely on addicting others so they can sell them drugs to maintain the cost of their own habit, or they steal or prostitute themselves to raise funds. This same scenario does not occur with cigarette smoking; because it is legal, the price is relatively low."

He gave another example. "The United States tried abolishing alcohol in the 1920s, and that didn't work. They made the problem worse rather than better when a whole new industry started with bootlegging. Money came into play, and the new illegal-alcohol game ended up with so much corruption and killing that alcohol had to be legalised in order to control it."

He progressed through the room, surprising them all when he called them by their full names. He asked the same question to each of the politicians, and most of the answers were in the same vein, with little or no variation. When Daniel came face-to-face with the first congresswoman, he looked at her for some time, and without saying a word, he passed her by.

When he finished interrogating the people in the library, he gave his handwritten notes to the president, who immediately asked eleven men to move to the left of the library and forty-one men and women to the right. One lonely woman sat in the middle, along with the first senator Daniel had talked to, who was still squirming, trying to get up from his seat.

"Some of you people disgust me for many reasons. The ones who are ruled by the mighty dollar, especially the drug dollar, are nothing but scum, and you are going to be treated as such." Daniel's fury was frightening, and unrest started to build amongst them. "We have armed guards outside in the hallway, so nobody is leaving this room until I say," Daniel commanded.

"Most of you are honest people who genuinely believe in your cause, and I salute you for standing by your beliefs. Some of you have gone along with the lobbyists because they have helped you financially with your election campaigns, or they have simply influenced you. Others have been physically threatened, and worse still, there is one amongst you who has a son being held prisoner in Colombia by the drug lords. Such is the power of these monsters; they have enough clout through their tainted dollars to influence the so-called democracy of this powerful nation."

Daniel looked at Senator Barrett. "You—wriggling worm—over there. Get up and join your mates on the left."

The disheartened looks of the group on the left told their own story; with Barrett joining them, they knew that their days were numbered in more ways than one.

The CIA aide, followed by Peter, came back into the room, and Daniel was able to tell that they had been successful in the task he had set for them. He handed another eleven account numbers to the unsmiling assistant, who again nodded and rushed out of the room.

Daniel stood in the middle of the decorative room, behind the congresswoman, who now sobbed uncontrollably; he looked into the eyes of the others present.

"The life of this woman's son, Michael Bryant, is at stake; he is being held by one of the barons, who has been forcing her to vote against the bill we want you all to support. The power of these people must be broken, and the legalisation of illicit drugs is the only way it can be done once and for all. I again ask you to reconsider and also help us to convince other congressmen and senators who are against this bill to also try a new approach to this ongoing problem."

The group of forty-one were allowed to leave after Daniel made one more comment to them: "Remember what you have seen here today; sometime in the future, you will be called upon to help your president and me in a very important mission." He smiled at the forty-one politicians for the first time since he had walked into the library. The ones remaining shamefacedly looked down as they wondered what had happened.

The homely Congresswoman Bryant turned and looked at Daniel, tears flowing freely, as she cried, "Mr. Leeder, you have just killed my only child."

"Sarah, if I may call you that, your son will be found—and found alive. I promise you this." Daniel was convincing in his assurance to her.

"I received a DVD of my son. He was tied to a chair; he told me that he was being held somewhere in Colombia and that if the bill for the legalisation of drugs went through, they would mail me his head. I have it here in my bag. I carry it with me because it makes me feel like he is close to me. He is only nineteen years old, Mr. Leeder—only nineteen. He's just a baby really, just a baby." She sobbed as she brought her handkerchief to her face.

Daniel made the corrupt politicians sit in front of the wide-screen television and view the footage with him.

The DVD didn't give any clues as to where in Colombia Michael was being held. The footage showed a scared, skinny young man in front of a white wall, reading from a prepared statement.

Daniel turned to the corrupt men before him. "Gentlemen, you are all in deep shit, and you all know it. Your bosses, the Colombian cartel will want your blood and that of your families as soon as they discover that you have been detected and are of no use to them any longer. They will want a refund of the hundreds of millions of dollars they have credited to your Swiss accounts, and you know what? They are not going to get it back. They won't get it back, because the money will not be there; even as we speak, these funds are being transferred out of your accounts and into one of my friend's accounts. This money will help fund the establishment of clinics for the drug addicts you scum helped to put into that position."

A sweaty, trembling man stood up to speak, and the others followed suit. "You can't do this to us; you can't let us, our wives, and our children be slaughtered by those butchers. You don't know these men; they will stop at nothing to get to us, especially if we can't return their money."

Daniel appeared to snigger as he told them to keep quiet and sit. "This dilemma is your doing and, therefore, your problem; but I will suggest a few things that might help. Firstly—and this goes without saying—you will all resign your positions, and you will sell all your assets and give two-thirds of the proceeds to the drug rehabilitation programme. After helping the FBI and the CIA with their inquiries about the Colombians, they might help you and your families establish new identities."

He felt a new power within himself, as nobody appeared surprised or even bothered to ask questions as to how he had obtained the information from these people. They simply accepted what occurred without question.

Daniel paraded in front of the twelve, and they felt the contempt he had for them with every word he uttered. "You are all getting lodgings in the White House for a few days, and any attempt to leave or communicate with the outside world will get you shot. You will be escorted to your rooms now." Daniel pointed to the door, indicating that he meant right away. "That is, all except for my friend over here, Senator—correction, *Mr.*—Barrett. I need your help with an important matter."

Sitting the petrified man in front of Congresswoman Bryant, Daniel leered at him. "You, sir, are one person who is not getting off as lightly as the others, you son of a bitch. You look at this mother, and you tell her that you are the bastard who arranged for the kidnapping of her boy—tell her!" Daniel shouted at him, and Barrett cowered in his seat.

"I'm sorry! I'm sorry. I didn't have much choice; we had to ensure that this bill didn't go through, and your son was conveniently in Brazil, so it was easy to get him to Colombia. You are a much-respected member of Congress, and with your influence, many would vote your way."

Daniel already had most of the information he needed, except one unclear point: the exact whereabouts of the boy.

"You are not sure where Michael is being held, but you think he is in a plantation near Pasto, in the south of Colombia, close to the Ecuador border. The drug lord responsible is Alvaro Vargas, the most powerful man in that country, and he is the one who controls the drug cartels in Colombia."

The hapless man looked up at Daniel and simply nodded in agreement; he had no idea where this blue-eyed man was getting his information from, but he had gotten everything right, as if he were reading his mind. The frightened elderly man again looked up at Daniel, and his eyes narrowed as suddenly it dawned on him that that was exactly what he had done; this man had read his mind.

The library was now empty except for the Australians, the president, and the CIA director. Daniel told them that he and Peter intended to fly out the next morning for Ecuador's capital, Quito, and from there travel the 150 kilometres to Pasto by helicopter. They would attempt to rescue Michael Bryant before any of the White House prisoners were taken to another facility for questioning.

The CIA director, Bob Wilson, running his right hand over his comb-over to ensure it was still in place, had an astonished look on his face as he drew closer to Daniel. He shook his hands vigorously in the air, trying to get his point across to him. "You have to be joking! Do you have any idea what you will be up against? Man, besides the drug gangs, there are the rebels." He stopped to gasp for breath, and the undeniable smell of a heavy smoker made Daniel draw his head back. "There is a lot of guerrilla activity in that area, and they love kidnapping Westerners. You will be right on the equator, so if the rebels or the drug cartels don't get you, then the heat will." He stopped again and gasped for more air. "You will never make it; there is not a chance in hell of you making it out of there alive."

Peter made the final comment: "Mr. Director, never underestimate what this man can achieve."

On the outskirts of the town of Pasto, at the villa of Alvaro Vargas, a well-dressed and well-groomed man sat in a comfortable settee, reading one of the many newspapers and magazines he had especially flown in from America. He loved dressing in black, as this was the colour he considered best suited his film-star looks.

His wealth afforded him any luxury he craved, including a bevy of young women who saw to his every need and desire. His wife and three children lived in Bogota, the capital of Colombia, while he spent most of his time with his harem in this magnificent mansion.

Guards patrolled the fortified walls, which were over six metres high and covered the perimeter of the house and gardens. The balconies that encircled the top floor of the two-story hacienda had bulletproof glass around them.

Vargas spent much of his time sitting out on his deck, looking down on the large plantation he had built up over the last fifteen years. The fifty-plus well-armed security guards ensured his safety and the smooth running of his cocaine operation.

German shepherd dogs roamed freely in the enclosed grounds; they were well trained, and only Vargas and some of his trusted personal guards were allowed through the area they protected. They would attack and savage anything to death on the command from any of the three trainers.

Vargas considered himself to be handsome with his dark beard trimmed to perfection and long, thick black hair slickly combed back and tied at the nape of his neck. He sat and read one of his newspapers as two of the girls sat half naked next to him, rubbing their hands on his legs. Vargas was still tired from the romp he'd had with two of the other girls earlier, but now his blood was stirred up, and he wanted to be pleasured again. The wink he gave them made the girls scamper to their feet and run upstairs, but before Vargas had time to put his paper down, another well-dressed man walked hurriedly but quietly into the room.

He had a bead of sweat on his brow, for he knew the temper of his patron, especially when he was interrupted during his reading time. The house servant tried hard not to look directly at his master, so he looked down to the floor as he stuttered out his words.

"Patron, Patron, I am sorry to disturb you, but I thought that you should know that there is a man at your front door."

An angry Vargas stood up and shouted sarcastically at the cowering man, "What do you mean there is man at my door? Is he selling encyclopaedias? I suppose he knocked first?"

"Yes, yes, Patron, he knocked first, and when I opened it, he said that he wants to see you about—"

An agitated Vargas interrupted the servant by slapping him across the face and making him reel a couple of steps backwards.

"Let me get this straight—there is a man at the gate outside the perimeter of my well-secured, intruder-proof villa. Is that right, or is that not right? It had better be right, or someone's head is going to roll."

The sweat now poured out of the servant profusely, and it took him a few seconds to swallow all the saliva that had built up in his mouth before he could answer.

"Pardon, Patron. I am so sorry, but that is not right; he is at the door to the house. He looks like a gringo, but he doesn't sound like one; he tells me that he wants to talk to you about a Mr. Michael Bryant."

"Mother of all saints, how can anybody get past all my men and all my security?" The disbelieving man stared at the sweaty servant. "What about the dogs—where are the dogs, you stupid fellow? The dogs would have eaten him alive."

"They are with him, Patron."

"With him? What do you mean 'with him'?" Vargas shouted.

The anger that came from Vargas made the servant shake as he tried hard to find his words. "They are licking him as if he is their master, Patron."

"Get some of the men here quickly, and subdue this man."

The cowering servant ran off, and Vargas shouted after him, "Do not kill him—I need to find out much about him." A frowning Vargas was, for the first time in a long while, worried. He went over to a dresser in a corner and opened a draw to pull out a small pistol.

He couldn't resist looking at his own image in the mirror of the dresser, but this time, the reflection looking back at him wasn't only his own. He screamed in fright, dropping the gun to the floor; there, staring back at him in the mirror, was someone else—a stranger with big blue eyes and dressed in a white suit.

Vargas turned slowly and slyly looked at the man while, at the same time, trying to look down for the gun.

"Here, this must be what you are looking for." Daniel bent down, picked up the gun, and passed it over to Vargas, who snatched it out of his hand and quickly pointed it at the intruder's chest.

"Who are you? How did you get inside my house?" The confidence of the powerful man had waned, and a feeling of intimidation overtook him.

"I have come to take Michael Bryant back to his mother, and I was hoping that you would cooperate." Daniel peered into the man's mind.

"What has this Michael, eh, whatever his name was, to do with me?" Vargas said nervously.

"He is the man you have hidden in the cellar of that large work shed you have on the other side of your property," Daniel retorted. "It would be to everybody's benefit if you freed him; your life and the lives of all in this household are in your hands, Mr. Vargas," Daniel threatened.

Six of his armed men entered the room, and Vargas's confidence returned. "Grab him." He pointed at Daniel with his left hand as he held the raised pistol in the other. The closest man to Daniel moved forward, and immediately, a deafening shot rang out. The big man grasped his chest and fell forward onto the tiled floor, blood oozing out of his limp body. The other henchmen instantly stopped their charge towards the stranger and looked at their boss in astonishment.

Vargas's mouth was gaping in an amazed stupor as he looked down on the smoking gun he held in his hand. With a shaking head and a trembling voice, he gave the order again. "The gun went off accidentally, you fools—get him."

When the two men rushed forward, two shots were fired in rapid succession, and they too fell to the floor with bullets lodged in their hearts. Vargas, looking at his gun, tried to point it in a different direction, but he was frozen in place. He tried to drop the gun, but he could not open his hand. The gun still pointed forward, and no matter how hard he tried to release it from his grasp, he couldn't.

"Get him, get him!" He commanded the three remaining men as he desperately wrestled with his own hand. The baffled men looked at the gun in their patron's hand, panicked, and ran out of the room, falling over each other on the slippery tiles as they made their hasty retreat.

Vargas's anger subsided as exhaustion took over, and with his arms limply at his sides, his right hand still holding the gun, he found that he could not move. With a look of bewilderment, he stared at the man in front of him.

"You keep the gun, Mr. Vargas. I might still need you to protect me from your men; they may return." Daniel showed no remorse for the three bloodied men who lay at his feet.

"Now will you release Michael Bryant?"

"Who are you, and what are you? I shot my own men." Vargas felt defeated by this stranger. "You made me do that, but how? I knew I was doing it, but I could not stop myself," the confused man rambled, mostly to himself, when suddenly, he came to his senses again and realised that he was the powerful one there. This was his world, and he had the manpower to defeat one lone man.

"No! You cannot have him; I will have him shot first!" a defiant Vargas now screamed at Daniel.

"Yes, maybe you could, but at the very moment Michael dies, so will every living thing in this evil house, starting with you." A calm and focused Daniel looked right through the petrified eyes of Vargas.

A commotion came from outside the house as Vargas's men surrounded the place. "Now we are going outside, and if any of your men shoot at us, their bullets will kill you. Be strongly advised that what I am telling you is the truth; if they shoot at me, you will die." Daniel gave his warning, and Vargas unwillingly headed towards the front patio.

He stood outside the door of the villa, still clutching the gun in his right hand, and shouted orders at his men. "Do not shoot! Do you all hear me? There is to be no shooting! Is that understood?"

The barking of restrained dogs deafened the rumbling that came from the many security guards acknowledging their patron's request. Daniel walked boldly up to Vargas, and together they headed for the smaller gate at the rear of the garden.

The dog handlers took it on themselves to release the dogs, and with a command to kill, they charged forward towards the two men near the gate, but instead of savaging the stranger, they walked by his side, looking up at him, almost in admiration.

To the amazement of the drug baron, the large security gate magically opened; the dogs sat down and watched the two men walk through to the field.

In the distance, Daniel could see the massive industrial steel plant about half a kilometre away from the main house. The armed men followed them, but a word from Daniel and Vargas ordered them back to the perimeter of the villa. The huge field they walked through was covered by the coca plant, whose leaves contained the chemical alkaloid cocaine, from which the drug was extracted. There were no machines there; instead, the peasants from the local villages were picking the leaves, which were similar to tea leaves, off the plants and placing them into sacks on their backs. The workers took the full bags to drying bays at the rear of the factory.

The factory ahead of them processed cocaine and crack, and the workers in the facility laboured under atrocious conditions. Their overseers wielded whips as they walked amongst them, and they had no hesitation in using them, especially when they saw their patron walking towards them.

Another group of armed men appeared at the door of the plant, trying to fathom the scene before them; the other men in the villa had alerted them.

"Move away from the door, and do not use your weapons." Vargas gave strict instructions.

With the man in black leading, Daniel followed, seemingly unperturbed, through the line of thugs. A muscular man wearing a tight singlet that showed off his pumped-up body took it on himself to impress his boss; he lunged forward at the unarmed intruder, but as soon as his arms touched Daniel's shoulders, he was instantly repelled, as if shot from a cannon. The big man's body flung five metres upward and landed more than fifteen metres away on the hard ground. The sound of breaking bones told the utterly surprised onlookers that he was either dead or badly injured.

Vargas headed towards a better-maintained area on the far side of the facility, where the laboratory was located, and Daniel followed him into the immaculate room in time to see the lab technicians and bookkeepers hastily leaving through a side door. The pair walked over to the far side of the well-equipped lab and into Vargas's personal office. The room was fully furnished and air-conditioned and had plush wall-to-wall carpeting. Video monitors adorned one of the walls and showed every aspect of the factory and laboratory. Daniel looked at the only monitor not working, and it instantly lit up to show a dingy room with a scruffy young man sitting on the floor. The cell consisted of only a bed, a washbasin, and a toilet that badly needed cleaning.

Vargas was resigned to the fact that this unusual man had beaten him and that his empire was finished; his inner sense accepted his situation. The dejected man reached above his head and pulled down a lever; a trapdoor in the floor opened to reveal a ladder leading to the room below, and immediately, a sickening stench flowed up into Vargas's office.

"Michael? Michael Bryant, I am a friend; I have come to take you home," Daniel called out to the prisoner.

Unkempt, tangled black hair was the first sight Daniel had of the young man as he struggled up the ladder. With his head above floor level, Michael looked up through his dirty glasses to see who his rescuers were, but the brightness of the day, which he had not seen for a number of months, blinded him.

The frightened boy saw Daniel, and a sigh of relief changed his anguished face from one of despair to one of hope. "Who are you? How did you find me?" he asked in a feeble voice.

"There is no time to explain everything to you right now, Michael; I am a friend of your mother's." Daniel felt a kindness in this boy. "You will have to trust me; I still have to get you out of this place safely, and there are dozens of armed men outside."

"You are saying that you are on your own? Oh my God! We'll both be killed." The scared youth turned when he heard a noise behind him, and for the first time, he noticed that another man was in the room—an armed man he instantly recognised.

"Vargas," he screamed, and he quickly turned back to Daniel. "What sort of trick is this?"

"Michael, this is no trick; you are going home, but I need you to trust me."

The look in Daniel's eyes reassured him and put him at ease, but his wandering mind was still puzzled. "But Vargas has a gun in his hand, and you look like you are completely unarmed."

Daniel again tried to reassure the bewildered youth. "Michael, believe it or not, he is helping me. I need you to keep your wits about you, okay?"

"Yes, yes, I understand." The desperate youth nodded wildly.

"Come; it's time to start for home." Daniel looked at the distraught drug lord still sitting in his plush director's chair, looking down and unaware of what Daniel had uttered.

Michael watched as Daniel made an upward hand movement, and some unseen force lifted Vargas onto his feet. Daniel walked out onto the factory floor, followed by Michael, with Vargas at the rear. The dozen or so armed men were still waiting, confused by the fact that their patron was walking behind the other two with a gun in his hand. Did he want them to take some action, or did he have everything under control?

The oppressed workers were milling around behind their guards; they were seething with hatred for Vargas and his men. The aura that the man in the white suit gave off inspired them, and the overseers were apprehensive by what they saw around them. The workers somehow looked different. The supervisors could see their faces; instead of walking around with lowered heads, they were holding them high in defiance, with pride and hope.

A tense look came over Daniel, and he made a sudden hand movement that frightened all who saw it. The guards' weapons were instantaneously wrenched from their hands and flung into a large vat of water. One by one, the workers and the now-vulnerable overseers fell to their knees and crossed themselves several times.

With Vargas in the lead, the three made their way towards the villa under the scrutiny of the drug baron's men perched on the outer wall and on the roof. There were dozens of high-powered rifles pointing at Daniel, but not one of Vargas's men had the confidence to take a shot.

In the simmering heat of the perfectly still day, the approaching men stopped, and the people in the villa watched as the man at the rear raised his arms and looked across the field of coca plants. They were only four hundred metres away from the big house, and with eyes only on the three, nobody noticed the stirring of the trees in the far corner of the field.

A small gust of wind blew some dead leaves off the ground and swirled them upward amongst the trees, making the foliage sway to and fro. More leaves and dust funnelled up off the ground, and the density of the debris grew rapidly. Trees swayed back and forth, and leaves and smaller branches plucked from them joined the ever-darkening mass surrounding them.

A steely faced man with a large cigar protruding from a corner of his mouth had positioned himself on the roof of the villa—a spot he considered the best vantage point for a clear shot. The man had a powerful long-range rifle, and he was by far the best shot of all the guards in the villa. Vargas had specifically employed him because of his sharpshooting skills and his prowess as a sniper. Although the target was at the rear of the three approaching men, his position gave him a clear shot at any of the group; he adjusted and readjusted the telescopic sights until he had the perfect shot at the intruder.

With the sights directed at the chest of the approaching man in the white suit, he caressed the trigger, when a breeze blew some dust into his face and blinded him for a few seconds.

"What are you waiting for, you motherfucker?" A shout came from one of the men on the wall. "Just make sure you shoot the one in white."

The shooter looked through his telescope again and was surprised to see that the man in white had changed position from the back to the front of the group. He rubbed his eyes and looked again.

The sound of the rifle shot echoed through the valley, and the sniper watched with glee as the man in the front dropped onto the track. He saw the second man dive to the ground and lie there with his hands protecting his head, and he saw that now only one man was still standing out there in the field—the man in black.

"You stupid fool! You idiot, you shot the patron! You shot Vargas!" one of the men cried.

"What are you saying, you blind father of a sheep? I shot the man in white." He took another look at the man standing next to the two bodies on the ground. "The man in black is still standing there." He pointed wildly for them to see. "Are you blind?" the shooter shouted angrily. "The patron is standing there."

"No, it is the man in white that is still standing; you killed Vargas, and he was the one in black." Another shout from a different direction confirmed the first man's call.

Their bickering and confusion was of no consequence, as a sudden darkness came over the villa, and a deafening, roaring noise of shattering glass overtook the men's baffled faculties. They looked up to the terrifying sight of a dusty, swirling sea of rushing black air, and they suddenly felt the enormous power a tornado could unleash as it set upon them from behind. It had approached the villa without the slightest warning. In a flash, the funnel sucked up the front outer wall and gates of the villa, followed by the sides of the fortress.

The dogs, still being restrained by their trainers, had been barking, aware of the pending danger that neared, but their masters had ignored them, and they now suffered the consequences as they vanished into the darkness. The main house was swallowed up piece by piece, and it disappeared into the mire, followed by the men standing on the roof and the back wall. Everything vanished into the blackness of dust and debris that was the tornado.

Michael, with eyes shut tightly and covering his head as he lay on the ground, had heard the enormous noise that had followed the blast from the rifle, but he was too frightened to look up to see what had happened. Within what seemed only moments, the noise stopped, and quietness came again.

The young man rose to his knees and looked around him. There next to him lay Vargas, on his back, covered in blood, and with some of his black shirt imbedded into a gaping hole in his chest. His rescuer stood behind him in deep concentration, staring towards the villa. Michael looked in the same direction and was completely flabbergasted; the villa was gone. What had been there only moments ago had vanished, and only parts of the outer wall remained.

Michael stood up, wanting to ask so many questions, but the sight of Daniel, seemingly so distant, made him refrain from asking any. He heard screaming and shouting coming from the plant where he had been held prisoner for the last few months, and he saw the oppressed workers hacking into their overseers; they had taken control of their workplace, and now they were exacting their revenge.

From the far side of the plantation, where the tornado had originated, hundreds of armed men appeared from between the defoliated trees and headed towards them. One of the many rebel groups that plagued Colombia approached and formed a long line ten deep in front of Daniel and the petrified youth. Two opposition forces were formed; on one side six hundred soldiers stood and on the other side, two lonely men faced them.

A horn tooted from the rear of the rebels' line, and the men moved aside to let an army jeep through. There were two other men besides the driver in the old green vehicle; one stood at the rear, holding the latest British Bren light machine gun with one hand and hanging on to the roll bar with the other. The jeep came to a screeching halt, and the broad-shouldered passenger, wearing an American Marine cap and green fatigues, alighted and walked out between the rebels and the two men.

He was taller than all the men around him, and he walked with the assured stride of a man who was full of self-confidence and obviously in command. Looking around him and seeing the long line of his men on one side and the two foreigners on the other made him give out a loud belly laugh. His men understood the cause of his merriment, and they too burst into laughter.

"What an interesting day this has turned out to be." He spoke loudly in his educated Spanish language, ensuring everybody could hear him. "Here, on the one hand, we have a friend and a benefactor holding a gun in his hand, and he is as dead as a squashed ant, and I am positive his own men—why, I do not know—shot him. These other two, on the other hand, have no weapons, and they have taken on all of the patron's men, and they appear to have beaten them with the help of nature—not just beaten them but killed every one of them. Now these two are facing an army of more than six hundred men, and I am not sure what I should do."

Daniel understood that the head of the rebels was in a quandary as he turned to face him. The tall man had a reserved fear; he sensed that what he had witnessed was beyond explanation. He could see in the clear blue eyes of the man in the white suit that he showed no fear at the odds that were facing him.

"Who are you? You are not one of our people, so where are you from, and why are you here?" the curious man asked.

"You may call me Daniel, and this is Michael." The mind of the questioner received Daniel's quietly spoken English answer in perfect Spanish. "Where I come from is an interesting question, and as to why I am here, that is quite simple: I am here to take this boy back to his mother, and I will do so at all costs, including the lives of your men as well as yours."

The tall man wanted to laugh at the thought that this one unarmed man could destroy his entire army, but he didn't laugh. He and his men had taken position on the outskirts of Vargas's property as soon as they had heard the first shots coming from the villa. They had seen the tornado forming, and they had seen Vargas being shot by one of his own men. They had watched the way the tornado had torn the big house to pieces and taken it—and all within it—to who knows where. No, even to this educated man, what had happened that day certainly was not a natural occurrence.

"You are trying to tell me that you caused that tornado?" The tall man tried hard to sound sarcastic, but his eyes showed that he had an open mind about what he had witnessed.

"I do not have to tell you anything, but if you care to look back to the trees you were hiding in, you may have your answer." Daniel turned and faced the distant trees at the rear of the rebels facing him. The trees were swaying from side to side, and the few leaves that remained on them, and the debris from around them, again swirled in a menacing action. Blackness formed over the trees as the distant wind grew stronger and louder.

The assembled rebels saw the menace that had destroyed the villa being reborn, and they became restless and began to huddle together in an ever-tightening group.

"You are sending a very strong message. Are you doing that?" the unsure man asked. "How can that be possible? How can you have so much power over nature?" The rebel leader had already accepted that a single man against a force of well over six hundred had beaten him.

"What do you want from us?"

Daniel pointed to the trees, and the tall man looked over to see everything was calm once more. The wind had stopped, and the darkness around the trees had changed back to the clearness of the day.

"I am sorry about the death of your brother, Colonel Antonio Vargas, but I do not think there was much love lost between you two. You hated what he had become, although you accepted his dirty money to aid your cause, and in turn, you were obligated to protect his drug empire. Now you have lost a powerful ally, and that is concerning you much more than the loss of his life."

"Who are you?" the flabbergasted man queried. "You are a stranger here, and yet you seem to know much too much about me."

"Colonel, there is not one thought that goes through your mind that I do not know about. So at this stage, I will just continue with what I was about to say," Daniel said, confusing the colonel even more. "You were going to lose his support anyway, Colonel, as soon as illicit drugs were legalised all over the world. Your brother and many like him have spent a fortune trying to stop this from happening, but it will happen just as sure as he is dead. Within a few weeks, the drug trade and the drug barons will be no more."

Daniel appreciated that the colonel believed in his revolution against the corrupt politicians who were controlled by the drug barons, but in order to achieve his aim, he had no choice but to protect the very men he hated.

"Colonel, your country needs men like you with strong convictions and a strong will to back those beliefs. A man such as you would ensure that you achieve your goals for a just and law-abiding Colombia; many of your politicians are honest, but they need the help of strong people such as you to clear out the corruption. Many of the needy of your country work in the cultivation of the coca plant, and unless immediate action is taken, this industry will be lost to them. The world will still need the drugs from this plant for many decades to come. They will be administered legally to the addicted people all over the world. Men like you must take control of plantations such as this one and others that will be abandoned when the money dries out of the illicit drug industry. The peasants can go on working them for a fair wage and in much better conditions. You can amass enough manpower to rid your country of much of its wrongs, and if you could get the cooperation of your government, who no doubt will be willing to try to stop any revolutionary group in a peaceful way, your task would be made much easier." Daniel foresaw that this could work well for Colombia and its people for quite some time in the future.

Colonel Vargas had known about the efforts of many countries in legalising drugs, and he knew of the great concern this policy had brought to the industry in his country. He also realised that this impressive man might have given him a direction not available to him in the past.

At the local airport in Pasto, Peter's curiosity rose at seeing Daniel in the passenger seat of a jeep driven by a big man in a Marine cap, with a haggard-looking young man in the back seat. After a brief introduction, Michael was taken to an office in the small terminal, where he contacted his mother. Later, he enjoyed a well-needed shower in a small private restroom reserved for the manager of the terminal.

Peter, with Michael in tow, took the colonel's car into town to purchase food and clothing for the young man, while Daniel and the colonel sat at a small table in the reception area and continued their previous conversation, which now had the big man excited at the prospect of a more respected Colombia.

"I do not know who you are, my friend, but you are an extraordinary man." The colonel marvelled at Daniel and wanted to know more about him.

"Antonio, we have some time before my companions and I leave you, so I am going to tell you who I am; I need your help."

In less than an hour, Antonio became convinced of Daniel's tale and of his quest to save the world. One thing intrigued Colonel Vargas more than anything else he had just heard, and it also surprised Daniel that no one else had asked the question.

"You are telling me that there is no devil, so I won't be spending eternity down in a fiery inferno?"

"No! There is no such thing as a hell—or a heaven, for that matter. We make our own heaven and hell throughout our living years on Earth. When we are happy and have a clear conscience, we are in heaven, and when we are sad and have an unclear conscience, we are in hell. Thieves, murderers, and anyone who goes against their own feeling of what is right and decent have a very disturbed inner sense, and they are the people who are always restless and unsatisfied with life; they are already in hell. Their consciences play havoc with them, and they suffer within themselves until they can right the wrongs they committed. The people who live full lives helping the community they live in, seeing happiness in their children's eyes, and enjoying the love they share with their spouses, offspring, family, and friends are already in heaven."

Colonel Vargas could have listened to Daniel talking for many hours, but the sight of a clean-shaven and well-dressed Michael following Peter out of the colonel's jeep halted the conversation.

As the pair approached, Daniel had one more item to divulge to the colonel.

"Antonio, in your brother's office at the laboratory, there is a false wall on the right as you enter the door. Behind this wall, there is a secret room that has millions of US dollars and gold stashed inside it. I now know that you are a man to be trusted, so use these funds to purchase the plantations we talked about before. Colonel, in the next few days, I want you to contact your president, Garcia, and arrange a meeting with him for conciliation talks."

"Conciliation talks? He will have me shot," the astonished colonel stammered.

"I will talk to him, and he will be waiting for your call," Daniel assured him. "I will say goodbye for now, but I will be in contact with you in the near future. Tell your men of most of what I have relayed to you so they can spread the word of what is needed from the people of Colombia and the neighbouring countries."

The colonel waved to Peter and Michael as he drove past them and headed back to his men.

"As you suggested, while you were on your adventure, I did some homework," Peter told Daniel. "I made contact with most of the leaders of the south and central American countries.

"The Brazilian president has a few problems he is finding difficult to overcome. Illegal timber cutters and the thriving illegal fauna trade are two of his concerns; apparently, millions of birds and reptiles are taken each year from along the Amazon River and are smuggled out of the country. More than half of them die in transportation. The area is so large and so dense with vegetation that it is next to impossible to police. We are talking about a river that carries a greater volume of water than any other river system in the world; the total forest area along it is over five and a half million square kilometres."

"What about deforestation—are they implementing any further plans to combat that?" Daniel enquired.

"Well, there has been an environmental bill in force for many years, making deforestation and pollution illegal, and offenders can face hefty fines and even jail. They have extended this bill and have also made the penalties much harsher, so they are hoping this will stem the growth of any new illegal wood-chopping activity. One problem here is that much of this rainforest land is privately owned, so again, it is hard for the authorities to police.

Anyway, the president's other concern is about the homeless youth. There are groups of traders called death squads hunting down these kids and culling them to try to reduce the crime rate, which affects the tourist trade and, therefore, their bottom line. They are being hunted like animals, mostly at night, and shot as they sleep." A saddened Peter had a sip of his soft drink; he sighed at the thought of how helpless the whole situation seemed.

While in this country, Daniel needed to have a meeting with the president of Colombia, and through the neighbouring Brazilian leader, Daniel arranged an urgent conference in Bogota with him.

Two days later, Daniel was pleased with the cooperation President Garcia afforded him and his agreement to having conciliation talks with the rebels and pardoning their past indiscretions. Colonel Vargas had always been considered an honourable man and was well respected by his people and by the president himself; the president felt that to have Vargas at his side to help run the country would be a privilege. He had heard many marvellous things about this man, Daniel, from the many meetings he'd had with his friend the president of Brazil.

Daniel understood and accepted the Colombian president's apology for not attending the meeting in Malta. He stressed how he would have forfeited his life and the lives of his family to the drug barons, had he gone. President Garcia understood that the days of the easy money and power of the drug cartels were numbered, and Daniel could see the president's sincerity in the belief that for once in his term in office, he might at last be free from the fear of the men who really ran his country.

With Michael enjoying his newfound freedom, they boarded the helicopter and flew back to Quito in Ecuador, where their jet awaited them.

Garry Foster was instructed to first take Daniel and Peter to the city of Iquitos in north-eastern Peru, and from there, he was to take Michael back to Washington to his anxious mother.

Garry was to return to South America with Caris and rendezvous with the pair in two weeks' time at Macapa, near where the Amazon River exited into the southern Atlantic Ocean on the northern coast of Brazil.

Daniel explained to a puzzled Peter, "As you may know, Iquitos is a port on the west bank of the Amazon—the start of this mighty river—and from there, you and I will commence our journey down the Amazon to its end."

CHAPTER 8

Daniel and Peter made their way out of the Iquitos airport and took a run-down taxi to an old hotel near the water port on the west bank of the Amazon. The locals looked inquisitively at the strange duo walking along their narrow, steep dirt road on this beautiful and sunny morning.

They stopped at an unsanitary-looking cafe for coffee, and the unkempt proprietor took extra care to ensure the mugs were clean.

"This is our best blend, and it is much better than that Brazilian shit they call coffee," the fat, balding man said in poor Spanish as he placed the mugs on the table. "What would two great gentlemen like yourselves be doing in this out-of-the-way place?" he enquired as he pulled up a cane chair and sat next to them.

"We have come to see your town and also to see the place where the mighty Amazon River is born." Daniel's voice came through to the surprised man in a dialect of Spanish he understood—one spoken amongst the people of that area.

"Do you know where we might be able to hire a boat and crew that could take us to the very end of the river?"

"Gentlemen, the end lies many weeks from here, and it is a very dangerous trip. I myself have lived here all my life, and I would never undertake such a journey," the proprietor replied.

"We are willing to take the risk; we want to reach Macapa in two weeks' time, so we do not have much time to waste," Daniel persisted.

The man slammed his hand on the table in glee and laughed out loud as he shook his head in a condescending way. He noticed two men on the other side of the road, and still laughing, he stood up from the table and called out to them. "Francesco, Francesco, come over here if you want a good laugh!"

The two men walked over and stood next to the proprietor. One, a small, unshaven man sporting a pencil moustache, had a majestic blue-and-yellow macaw perched on his right shoulder; the head of the bird reached well above the thick, wiry silver hair of his master, and its tail went all the way down to the man's buttocks.

The other, a straight-faced, barefoot man, was undoubtedly of Peruvian Indian descent; his long black hair reached past his shoulders, and he exuded pride in the way he stood—tall and straight. His sleeveless shirt revealed his huge biceps, and his tight-fitting trousers, much too short for him, bulged with his muscled, trunk-like legs.

"Ah, Carlos, my friend, what is so funny that you invite us to your cafe for coffee and maybe a cigar or two?" The small-featured Francesco spoke in a fast, shrill voice. "For me, black with two sugars and with a little spirit, and just black for my friend Mucho, thanking you."

"No, no, you don't, you thieving bastard—no coffee for you. I thought, seeing that you have made the trip to the Atlantic before, you might want to talk to these naive men. They think they can make the trip to Macapa by boat in just two weeks."

Daniel motioned for the two men to sit at their table. "Get them coffee, please, Proprietor."

Francesco sat across from Daniel, while the broad-shouldered Inca stood with his huge arms folded, behind his small friend, looking down on the group.

"Don't be offended by my big Indian friend, but he rarely sits, especially at a table. This is my other friend, Long John." Francesco pointed to his right shoulder. Peter gave a chuckle as he noticed that the bird had a peg leg.

"Now, what is this foolishness fat Carlos is talking about?"

"We want to hire a boat and crew to take us to Macapa, and we would like to make it there in as close to two weeks as possible, so we need someone who has no commitments and can start on the journey straight away," Daniel explained. "I gather you have a boat, and you have made the trip before, so is there any reason why we can't hire you?"

"Ah, my friend, there are many reasons: one, we cannot do it in two weeks unless we have a speedboat, and two, it would cost you a lot of money. Of course, you would need to find the stupid men who would want to take such a dangerous journey and own a good boat." Words came out of this small man at machine-gun pace.

Daniel jumped in while Francesco drew breath. "The two weeks is not set in stone, money is no object, and we will take care of any danger."

The proprietor came back to the table with the coffees; he stood there for a moment, trying to understand the situation. The man in the white suit was speaking in what seemed to be English, and the scallywag Francesco was comprehending every word and answering in Spanish. Why was this man who had spoken to him in local Spanish a few minutes ago now speaking in a foreign language, and how could this uneducated peasant understand him?

He put the coffee down on the table and sat close enough to listen.

"Eh! Carlos," called out the little man, "where is the cigar?"

The proprietor looked at Daniel, but he didn't get any reaction from him.

"Okay, no cigar for the captain." Francesco gestured with his hand at the proprietor and turned back to Daniel. "So the only thing that is stopping us from attempting this adventure with you is that our boat is out of commission. Unfortunately, the motor of our old but very sturdy boat suddenly decided to stop a few months ago, and we cannot get it started again." A dejected yet somewhat relieved Francesco shrugged and gave a wily smile.

"Ah, my friend," Daniel said, sarcastically using the little man's own words, "so what you are saying is that you would go if your boat was not out of commission?"

The little man looked up over his shoulder and winked at the Inca behind him, who seemed oblivious to what they were talking about. "Yes, that is what we are saying."

"Okay, let's go get the supplies we need, and if I get your boat going, we will leave this afternoon. Is that agreeable?" Daniel asked.

"And do we get to keep all the supplies if you can't get the motor running?" He followed this question with another wink over his shoulder at the unsmiling Inca, who definitely had no idea what was happening. Peter, on the other hand, was only half confused, as he at least understood Daniel.

"That's a deal," Daniel agreed. "I gather you do not have to say goodbye to anyone before we leave."

"Is it that obvious?" a dejected Francesco said. "Maybe I have a wife and a dozen children or maybe many girlfriends I will need to say goodbye to." With the small man still rambling, they left the cafe, leaving a puzzled proprietor scratching his head and watching them walk towards the strangers' hotel.

Two hours later, in a small truck borrowed from the supply store, Mucho, Long John, who was sitting on his lap, and a young man from the store who held on tightly in the back with the supplies made their way to the boat mooring. Daniel and Peter sat in the cabin while Francesco drove erratically, swaying from one side of the potholed road to the other. They soon turned onto a bush track and pulled up adjacent to a narrow walkway that meandered its way down to the river.

With arms full of supplies, they came to a wreck that resembled a boat, which was firmly secured to trees on the bank of the Amazon. Peter took one look and abruptly turned to Francesco, who had quickly walked up the plank and boarded the wreck. "You lying little bastard, this boat has been out of action for a lot more than just a few months—more like a few years. There can't be one thing working on it."

Francesco didn't have to understand what Peter was saying; seeing the anger in his face and hearing the tone of his voice were enough to make him stretch his arms from the deck into the cabin and reach above the door. He produced a pistol, which he placed in his belt, and a serious look replaced the smile they had become accustomed to.

"A deal is a deal, my friends; you did not seem too worried about the condition of the motor or if the boat was even sea worthy when you bragged about fixing it for me." He put his hand on the handle of the pistol as he talked.

"My Inca friend and I could not afford to keep her shipshape once the motor ceased, so we have just been living in it, waiting for a miracle to happen."

Francesco's cheeky smile overtook his face again as he pointed at his benefactors. "You, my friends, are our small miracle; at least now we will have enough to eat for a while. The fuel is a bit of a waste, but I am sure we will be able to sell it." He stopped smiling, looked at Daniel, and shamefacedly said, "I am very sorry, my friend, but a deal is a deal; you said we could keep all the supplies if you could not fix her, and as you can see, it is no good even trying. You better get a lift back to town with the boy—after we get the rest of the supplies, of course."

"What's the little bastard rambling about?" Peter asked Daniel.

"Don't concern yourself, Peter; leave this to me," Daniel replied.

As an indignant Daniel started to make his way on board, Francesco backed away and reached for the gun. Inexplicably, the gun flew out of his hand and disappeared in the river. Francesco looked down at his empty hand, still expecting to see it clutching the gun; he looked up at Daniel and then over at Mucho, trying to get confirmation of what had happened, and for the first time in a long while, he noticed a puckered brow on the Inca's face.

"Now you"—Daniel pointed at the Inca—"Mucho, take the boy with you and bring the rest of the supplies on board; you, Francesco, start getting this boat ready to sail while I see to the engine and the electrics." Daniel gave his instructions, and Francesco, mumbling under his breath, obeyed without the slightest hesitation.

A bewildered Mucho, for the first time in years, understood what was being said, and in the excitement of the moment, he accepted the situation and hurried to follow his orders.

After the young man from the store drove away, Peter ensured that the reluctant Francesco, with help from the Peruvian Indian, buried all the rubbish that had accumulated on and around the boat. They scrubbed the deck and removed as much of the built-up grime as possible while Daniel, still in his immaculate white suit, meditated over the engine.

By midafternoon, Francesco, although exhausted and sweating profusely, admired the boat he had inherited many years ago. He had saved the old owner from pirates who used to cruise the Amazon, and Francesco had nursed the man back to health after his ordeal. They had travelled the river together for many years, and on the old man's death, as the man had promised, Francesco inherited the derelict thirty-footer.

Well, he thought, *at least it looks good, even though it is not going anywhere.*

Daniel interrupted his daydream. "We are ready to sail," he said as he reached for the ignition keys hanging from the wall.

"No, Mr. Daniel." An apologetic Francesco shrugged and stretched out his arms in front of him. "What about the motor? The batteries are no good; they cannot be charged up. We could buy new ones and even a new motor, but they will take some time to have delivered and installed. And the wooden hull—I am not too confident that it will be in good condition to withstand the strong currents; she will leak and sink. Maybe we could fix everything first and then start the trip in a few weeks' time."

The noise of the motor kicking over drowned out Francesco's voice, and instantly, choking smoke covered the whole boat, making the crew cough profusely. They waved their hands wildly, trying to clear the air around them; Daniel lifted his arms, and immediately, a strong wind swept over them, taking the smoke away.

Francesco guided his boat downstream to the middle of the water and listened in disbelief at the smoothly running inboard motor. He checked the boat for leaks, and astonished that there were none, he took control of the wheel as the captain of a riverboat once again.

He looked out from behind the wheel and over at Daniel, who was holding a conversation with the Inca. The little man turned to Peter, who was standing by the cabin. "He cannot be talking to Mucho; he only speaks Loreto-Ucayali Spanish, which is jungle Spanish, and it is a Native American language that not many people speak. I have never heard my friend speak to anyone else before, not even to me. How can they be speaking together like that? Your friend is speaking English, is he not? And my friend is answering him back in jungle Spanish. Who is that man, that Mr. Daniel? I just cannot understand what is happening here."

"Accept it, Francesco; I have seen many such miracles since I first met Daniel, and I guarantee we will see many more before our journey is ended," Peter said, consoling the puzzled captain.

Long John leaped onto Peter's shoulder and turned to face his master inside the cabin. "The name you have given your parrot is certainly appropriate for a one-legged bird," Peter told the little man.

"I don't understand what you mean."

"You know, Long John Silver—the pirate from *Treasure Island*."

"An educated friend of mine suggested Long John, and I liked the name. Who is this Silver person anyway?"

They had been holding a conversation for some time before Francesco turned to Peter and said, "You speak very good Spanish, Mr. Peter."

"Me? Speak Spanish? No, you speak good English, Francesco."

They both looked at each other and then turned to look at Daniel.

The old boat had found a new lease on life, and once more, it churned up the water of the Amazon. Her acceleration increased, with the V8 motor seemingly improving the longer it ran. They went at least 150 kilometres in the first three hours, and the small captain suggested they should stop before sunset.

They moored the boat in a little alcove close to the bank and secured it to overhanging branches; Francesco didn't trust the anchor alone in the rushing water.

The Inca and the captain shyly glanced at each other; they had been together for many years and had never held a conversation. Their communication had always consisted of hand signals or sheer instinct of the knowledge they had of each other. Now they were faced with the dilemma of the possibility of being able to converse together. Peter understood their dilemma and tried to help ease the situation. "Well, Francesco, what do you think of your boat now?"

"Magnificent. It is unbelievable that this is the same boat that Mucho and I have lived on for so many years. My big friend here"—Francesco touched Mucho's arm—"is going to love travelling up and down this mighty river."

A large smile broke out on the Inca's face. "Yes, my friend." He put his hand on Francesco's shoulder. "We will have great adventures together."

Their conversation started from that moment and carried on, mainly by Francesco, as they prepared the evening meal.

The four sat on the splintering old deck, under the stars, and ate the fish Mucho had expertly caught on his first throw of the net. Francesco, as expected, did most of the talking. "I still cannot understand anything that has happened and is happening to us this day, but I don't care. You know, Mucho has been with me for nearly eight years, and we have never talked. I found him on the riverbank not too far from here, more dead than alive, with two bullet holes in his body. I couldn't lift him to put him in my boat, so I built a shelter over the spot where he lay. I am small, but I am strong—but not strong enough to lift such a big man, no sir. Now that we can talk to each other, he told me what happened to him. It seems that he broke a law that is very sacred to his people. He fell in love with the youngest wife of his uncle, the village chief, and he was going to be put to death. I think he more than just fell in love with her; I think he got caught with her, doing something they shouldn't have been doing. Anyway, he ran away, and they chased him for days and took many shots at him, hitting him twice. He recalls coming to the riverbank but cannot remember what happened after that until he woke up to find me tending his wounds. I now even know his real name—Iguino—but he told me he doesn't mind the name I gave him." The little man shed a tear of relief at having finally solved the mystery of Mucho.

"Now I understand more of why he stays here with me; he can never return to his own people, so I am his people. I can say I have two very good friends, even though one is a bird." Francesco reached out and grasped the big Inca's hand.

"Francesco, you realise that Long John is not really your friend; you have clipped his wings, so he is your prisoner," Daniel admonished him.

The little captain felt pain at this suggestion. "I found him hurt and with only one leg, thanks to one of the traps that the poachers had set. How long do you think he would last out there in the wild with only one leg?" Francesco shook his head almost violently as he looked at his accuser. "No! No! Mr. Daniel, he is my friend, and I will look after him."

"If he grew his flight feathers back and could fly wherever he wanted to but decided to stay, then you could say he is truly your friend," Daniel persisted.

"Well, that is not going to happen, so we will never find out, will we?" Francesco concluded, and he, mumbling to himself, walked into the cabin and sat on one of the six berths.

In the blackness of night, they could see a glow above the forest canopy.

"Mucho, where do you think that light is coming from?" Peter asked.

"That would be from the campfires of timber cutters; they would have many barges anchored in the smaller rivers that come to meet their mother, the Amazon. These bad people are slowly destroying all the jungle tribes' hunting land. The law does not allow this, but money makes the authorities turn a blind eye to the whole thing. If I had the power within me, I would destroy all the men who desecrate the forest." The agitated Indian, with his mighty chest expanded, looked angrily at the bright glow above the trees.

"Daniel, do you see the light above the tree line over there?" Peter pointed. Daniel was sitting in the dark, close to the pair, and on not hearing a reply from his friend, Peter turned and called his name again.

Daniel had been there only moments before; now he was gone. A worried Mucho looked around the deck, while Peter went down to check below. The sleeping Francesco snored so loudly that the noise made Peter's ears vibrate. Daniel wasn't on the riverboat.

"He must have fallen overboard and maybe hit his head or something. The water is not too deep here; get a torch quickly," the distraught native called out

Peter calmed him down, saying, "Do not worry, my big friend. Daniel is safe, and I think I know where he has gone. He will be back when he is done."

Half an hour passed, and then a sudden burst of light made the sky above the forest canopy even brighter. The men heard several explosions. Soon the brightness above the treetops returned to its previous glow, and an eerie, ghostly sound echoed through the forest. The sound became a distinctive voice in a language that could be understood by all who heard. "Why do you do this to me? Am I not the one who provides protection for the many plants and animals that live within me? Am I not the one who supplies the water that flows throughout the land and the one who cleans the air that you breathe? The one who stops the erosion of the earth that gives you the food that you eat? Leave my domain, and do not return, for if you do, you will surely die—that is my warning to you all." The voice stopped only to come back louder and more forceful than before. "Be gone before the sun rises." The ground throughout the forest vibrated as the loud, booming voice echoed throughout the area. The message was direct and to the point; it had lasted only a few seconds. The eerie silence that followed for the rest of the night hours was more frightening than the voice itself. For the jungle night to be devoid of insect and animal sounds was a haunting experience.

Francesco, wrapped in a blanket, crossed himself as he stood with a kerosene lantern stretched out in front of him. He stood close to the Inca as he looked out into the darkness, wondering what had caused those explosions and that frightening, booming voice—a voice that had awakened him from his deep slumber. A rustling from the back of the boat made him gasp and turn his light towards the noise. He held the lantern out as far as his small arms could reach and, on recognising Daniel, gave a sigh of relief.

"Did you hear that strange voice? I think it was the spirit of the forest warning the woodcutters; I did not believe such things existed. The natives have always talked about such things, but I never believed it." Francesco looked up at a subdued Mucho, waiting for confirmation about the forest spirits, but his friend wasn't paying attention to him; instead, he was staring at Daniel as if seeing a ghost.

At the break of dawn, the crew were all awake and ready for another day on this majestic river and for unknown adventure. Mucho looked at Daniel, who mystified his senses. The man's white suit and polished shoes had not a mark on them. He understood that Daniel was no ordinary man but someone or something much more—more like the air itself. He was simply a natural part of his surroundings.

They had only been on their way for a few minutes, when they came across three empty barges following each other. The men on board were frantically urging the pilot to go faster as they looked at the forest around them in anticipation.

The small boat made good time; by early morning, they had crossed the Peruvian border and had been in Brazilian territory for some two hours. Francesco could not believe how good it felt to be piloting such a powerful boat. He glanced over his left shoulder and saw Daniel running his hand over Long John's clipped wings. The bird was perched on his left arm, when suddenly, it let out a screeching squawk as it excitedly stretched out its beautiful blue plumage. The little captain looked around just in time to see Daniel fling his arm. The bird flapped its mighty wings, lifted its body into the air, and ascended up into the clear sky, circling eagerly above the boat in a teasing manner.

Francesco smashed his head on the glass panel in front of him as he tried to look out the window to follow his parrot's flight. "What is happening here? He cannot fly; he has no wings to fly with."

Long John flew higher and higher and headed away from the river, soaring over the forest like an eagle.

Daniel saw Iguino looking at the distant hills, which they could see across a rare clearing for the first time since they had started their journey. He felt the sadness within the big Indian, knowing that his people and the woman he loved were up there.

With the sun on their faces, the gallery of trees on the banks of the river whizzed past them for another three hours. Francesco could still see his beloved parrot as a dot against the clear sky; it stopped its forward flight and started to circle persistently in one area. Daniel asked the captain to find a spot as close as possible to where the parrot was circling and to moor the boat there.

"I have been thinking that it is possible to make it to Macapa on schedule, but if we keep stopping, we will definitely not be able to, Mr. Daniel." Not receiving a reply, Francesco grudgingly headed downstream and slowly edged in towards the left side of the river to try to find an alcove in the bank.

As the boat slowed, still fifteen metres from shore, a sudden splashing from the starboard distracted all on board. Two large male alligators were fighting over territory and the servicing rights of the females that went with it. Francesco returned to his task of mooring the boat and instructed

Mucho to throw out the anchor, as the water was getting too shallow to get any closer to land.

"There, Mr. Daniel—now what do you want to do here?" asked the small captain, curious as to why they had stopped. No answer came back to him; he turned his head to repeat his question, but he could not see Daniel anywhere on board.

Mucho looked for him again, as he had the night before, and not being able to find him, he gave out a mighty laugh. "This man is a spirit; he comes and goes as he pleases, just like the wind."

Not more than a kilometre away from where they were moored, a big blue-and-yellow macaw looked down from the tree branch it had perched on. Down below were many men sitting around a campfire, sipping coffee and eating fruit that they had picked from the forest. Over a hundred cages of different sizes were at the campsite, and many species of birds were imprisoned in them. The creatures ranged from exotic, smaller birds to larger parrots, mostly macaws and a few toucans, frantically trying to escape from their poky enclosures.

More men were coming in from the dense forest, carrying squawking birds they had caught earlier in the day. The larger parrots had bags over their heads, which the men removed as they shoved them into the few remaining empty cages. Another four men were feeding the birds with fruit and seeds, while one man threw beetles, worms, and even dead lizards into the cages of the non–seed eaters.

The private zoos of the world would pay a high price for the birds, and these men stood to make a small fortune, by their standards, which would make them and their families financially comfortable for many years.

"Our boat will be here tonight just before sunset; we start loading our cargo as soon as it arrives." A man wearing a pistol in his belt rolled a cigarette while standing and leaning on a tree as he talked loudly for his men to hear. "We will leave at first light tomorrow morning, so let's make sure we fill the remaining cages."

Hearing a loud squawk from above, the men looked up to see a majestic macaw watching them.

"He is beautiful—we could get a small fortune for him if we could catch him!" an excited young lad no more than fourteen years of age exclaimed.

"Raphael, you get the sunflower seeds and spread them under the tree." The man put the rolled-up cigarette in his mouth as he instructed the boy. "With some luck, he may be hungry and fly down." He tried lighting his smoke, but for some reason, he could not get his lighter to work.

As the youth spread the seeds, which were laced with a native potion that would have put a grown man to sleep within minutes, an unusual groan came from the large branch the macaw was perched on. Another even louder groan made Raphael look up just in time to see the large branch snap, and as if in slow motion, it started to fall. He dove for cover as it crashed to the ground, showering the men below with wooden splinters that shot at them like spears.

The macaw flew to the next tree that encircled the clearing, and as soon as it landed on another large overhanging branch, that branch also creaked several times and came toppling down towards the men below. The parrot appeared to have a pattern behind its every movement, as each time it landed on a branch, the branch would snap and splinter into many pieces, and like arrows shot from a bow, the fragments of timber would fly downward at the petrified men. They ran to the other side of the clearing, in the only direction the falling branches allowed them to run.

The terrified men at the front halted so quickly that the ones at the back crashed into them, sending the whole group rolling onto the ground. They looked up, and there, in their way on the forest path, stood a majestic Incan warrior. The exotic feathers on the band on his head enhanced his proud, stern face, and the long spear he held in his right hand demanded respect.

The men huddled together, unable to move at the sight of the giant Indian standing amongst the trees; his well-defined body, almost naked except for a lap-lap that covered his loins, gave him the appearance of a mighty god. Sunlight beamed down from the canopy of the forest and shone on him like a spotlight, which pronounced his muscular body and exaggerated his stature even more. To the frightened men looking up from the forest floor, the man in front of them appeared as an apparition of days gone by.

The chief of the bird smugglers, although frightened, drew the pistol from his belt and aimed it at the figure in front of him. A golden spear flew through the air and impaled him to the ground, killing him instantly.

Horrified, the other men watched as the warrior raised his hands, stretching them over his head as far as he could reach, and, in an eerie voice, called out to the men in front of him.

"I am Iguino, the protector of the forest, and men like you have been depleting my land of the creatures I am destined to protect. The god of the sun has resurrected me to destroy all who dare enter my forest with wrongful intent, and each of you is now condemned."

Some of the men leapt to their feet and ran back to the cages; they started frantically freeing their captives, which quickly flew into the surrounding trees.

"Please forgive us! We will release them all and never come back again; please forgive us." Men, down on their knees, sobbed out loud and begged the warrior for their lives.

Still with his arms stretched to the heavens, Iguino spoke again. "There is only one reason I would spare you for your misdeeds; you are to go back to your homes, and you are to warn others that if they dare ever enter any part of the forest to harm any living creature or tree for financial gain, they will surely die. Go quickly before I change my mind. Leave now while you can and wait for your transport, and as you wait, pray hard that my master, the sun god, does not instruct me otherwise."

They lifted themselves off their knees and ran towards the riverbank, leaving all their supplies and empty cages behind them.

Two men walked through the forest; one, a native Indian, had a large blue-and-yellow macaw on his shoulder. The almost fully dressed Inca with bare feet had many questions he wanted to ask his companion as he trod along beside him.

"Daniel, your message came to me in my thoughts, and I came to you, as you instructed me. I knew exactly what you wanted of me without you saying one word to me—how can this be?"

"I thank you for your help, Iguino, but there are too many things to explain to you. All I ask of you is to believe in me and understand that what I do is for the benefit of all," Daniel assured him.

"My people have a legend that tells a story of a man who comes from the sun god to save our world. Are you that man, Daniel?"

"Yes, Iguino, you could say I am that man." Daniel had no hesitation in reinforcing the belief of this man and his people.

"Iguino, you have been away from your people for many years, and now your uncle, the chief of your village, is in very bad health and has not long to live. Ilina, the young woman you love, believes that you are dead and has been mourning your passing for many years."

Iguino stopped walking and looked at his companion in complete awe. "How do you know all this? I have never mentioned Ilina's name to anyone, for the sound of her name hurts my heart, and I want to die every time I think of her and that I cannot be with her."

Daniel reached out both his hands, grasped Iguino's arms, and looked up at him compassionately. "I have been to your village, and I have seen your people. I have listened to their thoughts, and they still remember the tall, strong youth and his love for Ilina. They regret that he is not with them to lead them and wish for his return."

The usually stern face of the Indian mellowed, and tears fell down his face as he listened to Daniel's words.

"My friend, when this journey to the end of the river is over, I want you to return to your home in the high hills. Your village will be looking for a new leader, and you will be welcomed back by your people to lead them. Your uncle only had daughters, so you are the one in line to be their chief, and therefore, you will inherit all that he had, including his wives. When you become the leader of your people, I want you to spread the news of my coming and what you have seen. Tell your people to protect the forest the way you did, and always, whenever they face evil men like the ones we met before, a light from the sun god will shine on them and shield them."

"What about my friend Francesco? How can I leave him, when I owe him so much?" the big man, with his head hanging low, asked.

"Your village is not too far from the river, and Francesco will have one of the best boats on the Amazon. You take him to your people, and he will live a life between you and the river. He will find a woman in your village, and she will make him a better man. His life will have much more meaning than it has at present; this I promise you."

"There you are, you stupid pair of idiots," shouted a relieved Francesco at the sight of the two men standing on the bank. "I have aged ten years worrying about you both. First, one disappears, and then the other jumps overboard and runs into the forest. If it weren't for Mr. Peter, I would have left you both to be eaten by the alligators. Don't ask for my help; you can make your own way on board, and I hope the alligators get you." The macaw left its perch on Mucho's shoulder and flew to his master; Francesco offered his arm to Long John, and the bird screeched loudly as it grasped his arm with its feet.

The amazed man turned back to the men on the shore, but they were no longer there; they were on board. A flustered Francesco didn't know which question to ask first. His bird had acquired a new leg and new wings. The men had gotten back on board, and there were wet footprints on the deck, but they were not the slightest bit wet.

This proved too much for the little man; he reached into the cabin and brought out a half-full bottle of whisky and started guzzling it down. Peter laughed his heart out at the spectacle of their confused captain.

Mucho took the parrot and sat in the cabin, out of sight, as their boat passed many men on the bank of the river. The stranded men waved and begged frantically, trying to entice the boat to come to their aid; they had several hours of waiting in sheer apprehension before their rescue boat arrived. A large branch nearby creaked and fell behind them with such force that most of the men jumped into the water. Daniel was pleased; they were more scared of what lay behind them in the forest than whatever might have been lurking in the dark water.

After travelling many miles, they moored the boat for afternoon tea. While they sat, Francesco noticed something odd about his old boat. "I must be going crazy, but I am sure that this decking looks in much better condition than a few hours ago."

He leaned over the railings and peered over the side. With widened dark brown eyes, he looked across at Daniel. "The paintwork—I can see the colours blue and yellow on her hull, just like Long John, and there is some writing on her side, but I can't make out what it says. Even when I saw her for the first time, she had no paintwork." The confused man finished his coffee in silence and in deep contemplation.

With the sun setting behind them, they started looking for a place to stop for the night. Ahead of them, moored on the left bank, were three large barges heavily laden with timber. Approaching the rear barge, they could see that the vessel had been designed to carry more than just timber. The front of the barge had been built for comfort, with luxurious living quarters, while the aft, as was the case with most of these ships, held the illegal cargo.

A police launch, with a sign on top of the canopy advertising the River and Forest Patrol, was tied to the side, and four uniformed rangers were sitting with two other well-dressed men at a table on the deck while a crewmember served them drinks. Alligators abounded, waiting for scraps of food that the men constantly threw overboard.

On noticing the approaching boat, the rangers, who were obviously drunk, clumsily hastened to hide their drinks and quickly stood at the rails to give half-hearted salutes as it sailed by. They had not noticed the vessel until it was almost alongside them, and they were surprised by its quietness and speed.

"Those bastards—they are there for the night, and they will leave in the morning with money in their pockets," Francesco said angrily. "Their job is to stop the illegal woodcutting, but the hypocrites actually help run it and will let anyone cut the wood as long as they pay enough."

"What about their superiors—wouldn't they be suspicious if they didn't prosecute some of these people?" Peter asked.

"Their superiors—those bastards—supervise the whole operation from the river town of Manaus. Who do you think sends these dogs of men out here to fetch the bribes? They make sure they arrest anyone who doesn't pay their dues or any new cutters who dare enter their well-controlled areas. The rangers have such a business going here that they earn more than the wood thieves themselves." The little man shook his head and spat overboard through the open window in disgust. "They have permanent machinery set up in the forest—mostly generators and front-end loaders, always on the ready to cut down the young native pines. These trees are not big in diameter and are cut to lengths that their men can carry down to the barges. Tomorrow empty ones will come to be laden and will replace the loaded ones we just passed; they will probably leave here in the morning."

Daniel came up to the despondent Francesco and asked him to find a spot for the night, close by but out of sight of the barges. A little smile came across the small man's face.

A curious Peter sidled up to Daniel as the boat made its way to the bank. "You seem to be doing things the hard way. Can't you just simply will these guys to leave and not come back instead of scaring the shit out of them?"

"Yes, Peter, I could do that, but that will only take care of these men. What I want to do is, as you said, scare the shit out of them—not only so they don't come back, but also, more importantly, so they spread the word to others who will hear that the forest is protecting itself and its inhabitants. Now there are also other protectors of the forest; every time an Indian or a blue-and-yellow macaw is spotted in the woods, it will send a shiver through any intruder who has heard the story of the warrior sent by the sun god. Peter, I can't be in every corner of the world, so I am recruiting anybody, whether a wilful volunteer or an unwilling one, to help us."

The full moon cast mysterious shadows across the slow-moving water, and the haunting noises from the woods made the atmosphere eerier. Two of the rangers on the rear vessel were with two native girls down below in one of the large cabins.

The bigger man of the two lay naked on top of the bunk, trying to catch his breath as he leered at the frightened girl lying next to him. She moaned from sheer exhaustion and the pain she had endured over the last few days. A scream from the next bunk made her look over at the other girl; the younger and slimmer man, who was lying naked on top of her, had slapped her across the face. The first girl tried to reach her, but she too felt the backhand of the man abusing her. They were drained of strength and in total despair; the many men who had used them showed no pity to their crying and pleading. They only spoke in their own native tongue and could not understand the Portuguese language of their tormentors. At a complete loss, they prayed to their God to show mercy and take their lives.

A loud, dull sound right above them on the deck made the men and the girls stop and listen. "Must have been a branch falling onto the deck," murmured the skinny ranger.

"That was no branch," the older man gasped as he slipped into his shorts and motioned to his younger companion to do the same.

With the fat ranger in front, they grasped their pistols and slowly headed up the stairs leading to the deck. Cautiously, the man in the lead, standing on the third step with the other ranger pressed hard against him, peered onto the deck. It took a few seconds for him to register the scene before him.

On the moonlit deck stood the two well-dressed men, three members of the crew, and the other two rangers, who had their guns pointing at what seemed an apparition. The majestic demeanour of an Incan warrior god stood tall with muscles glistening in the moonlight that highlighted him. Seven puzzled armed men faced the Indian, who held a golden spear in his hand and appeared unperturbed by the odds against him.

The fat ranger, with his shorts under a protruding stomach, pushed his way to the top of the stairs and, waving his pistol in the air, made his way to the front of the group. He screamed at the others, "What in the name of Jesus is going on here? How did this Indian get on board?"

"He just landed there, Sergeant," said one of the crew in a timid voice. "He didn't come up the plank; I was sitting on it. Maybe he jumped down from the tree, but that is so high. I heard a loud noise, and he was standing there." He pointed.

A shadow skimmed over the water, and the distinct cry of a macaw shrilled through the night air as the bird dove across the barge between the Inca and the onlookers. The surprised men ducked as the massive bird passed them, swung upward, and landed on a jutting branch high above the barge.

The big Inca raised his arms, and a voice emitted from deep within him, shaking the people facing him. "I am Iguino. You have violated the forest and angered the sun god; all will be destroyed."

The sergeant raised his gun, aimed it at the Indian, and shouted at him as he squeezed the trigger, "Nobody is going to destroy me!"

The Inca looked at him, and the sergeant's right hand twisted out of shape and snapped loudly, and the pistol fell onto the deck.

The fat man dropped to his knees and grasped his right wrist, screaming in pain. "My wrist, my wrist! It is broken."

The Indian pointed to the other armed men, and the menacing look on his face was enough to make them throw their weapons overboard.

"Mendoza, you and your men have been commissioned by your president to protect the Amazon and all its beauty, but instead, you help to defile it." The Inca looked down on the man, whose left leg jerked out from under him, followed by an even louder snap. The man cried out in agony as he fell face first onto the deck.

"What reason could there be for not killing you? You have forfeited your life for betraying the position of trust that was bestowed on you; you do not deserve to live." The angry Inca raised his arms.

The petrified man, anticipating more pain, screamed, begging for mercy.

"Please—I beg you. Please don't hurt me anymore."

The Indian called to the macaw above, "Destroy these boats," and with that, the massive branch the bird was perched on broke and plunged down towards the barge and the men on board. It came down like a giant spear and hit the deck between where the Inca and the other men stood.

The sheer size and weight of the branch forced it through the hull, and it disappeared into the mire below.

The macaw flew to the tree closest to the next barge and landed on another huge branch, which was not directly above the craft. The Inca again raised his arms, and a gale blew through the treetops—a wind so strong that it bent the tree until it was over the deck of the barge. There was another loud creak, and the branch tumbled down and fell through the barge, leaving a gaping hole in the deck.

The commotion awakened the men on the middle barge, and they jumped off their bunks into the water that had risen inside their boat. Yelling loudly, they ran across the gangplank and scampered off the barge and into the jungle, quickly followed by the crewmembers of the first barge, which had experienced the same dilemma as the others.

Two frightened and naked girls came running and screaming up the steps of the rear barge. They stopped at the top of the stairs and stood gazing at the glistening, handsome warrior holding their tormentors at bay.

Slowly, the three fully laden workboats sank and settled to the bottom of the two-metre-deep water. The girl at the rear of the two felt the water lap at her feet and pushed the first girl onto the deck. The Inca looked at them, and disgust filled his senses at what he saw. They were young women—maybe seventeen to nineteen—and he could see that they had been badly abused. The Indian's face distorted with anger, and instantly, the men in front of him doubled over in agony, holding their groins. The Indian again looked up and called out, "My feathered friend, go—search out their machinery, and destroy it all."

The macaw flew through the night sky as the Indian turned his attention to the cowering sergeant. "You have begged me for your life, and I hope you were also begging for the lives of all on board, as there is only one way I would spare you all. You and your so-called rangers must honour your employment. You must arrest the timber pirates you have dealt with in the past, and you will use the proceeds that they and you have made from your illegal dealings to feed the poor of your towns." The Indian walked amongst the men, who were crouching and holding their testicles. "Your duty of protecting this forest must be diligent and without question. You do this, and I will spare you."

"Yes, yes, my men and I will do whatever you ask of us." The sergeant agonisingly looked at the faces of his petrified men.

"Yes, we will do anything you want—anything." A unified and pitiful reply came back rapidly.

The older of the two well-dressed men painfully stood up, still holding his crotch. "Arrest me and my son, Sergeant. I will promise to abide by the Inca's instructions."

The Inca plunged his spear into the chest of the man, lifted him above his head, and threw him into the murky water. The man screamed as the waiting alligators tore their meal to pieces.

"I listened to his mind, and the mind does not lie; I heard his voice, and it lied."

The silence that had befallen the immediate area was suddenly broken again that night as another loud shriek from the macaw sent chills through the horrified men awaiting their fate at the hands of the messenger of the sun god.

The giant Inca's face transformed into a deep trance, and he raised his arms to the night sky and called out, "Father, give me the strength to forgive these men; keep an eye on them, and if they do not do my bidding, destroy them and all that is holy to them. This I ask of you, my father, the mighty sun god who is one and the same Creator of the universe." He stopped talking, but his arms remained stretched upward; a number of enormous explosions rocked the night air, followed by flashes of light.

"There will be no more woodcutting with those machines, and you people take heed that it is that easy for me to reach you wherever you are; you cannot hide from the sun god."

The Indian let out a chilling laugh. "It is always good when justice is done, and today it will be done. All you men who have forced yourselves on these young girls, be warned; one of you is very concerned that the rest of you might find out that he has syphilis. So that person has undoubtedly passed it on to the girls, and they in turn will have passed it on to the rest of you. Now you can go home and explain to your wives or lovers why you won't be sleeping with them for a while."

He glanced at the rangers' boat tied to the side, and immediately, the mooring ropes snapped and its motor roared to life; it began moving, making a complete circle until it was adjacent to the sunken barge. The girls understood every word the warrior had spoken and followed his instructions to board the boat.

The Inca leapt into the speedboat, and as his feet touched the deck, the boat sped away with the three on board and with nobody at the wheel. The terrified rangers watched their boat disappearing into the night, followed by a large macaw.

The naked Indian girls had never been on a boat that went so fast, and they cowered in the back, huddling together. In the bright moonlight, they had been watching the warrior manoeuvring the boat around the bend, and as it started to slow down, to the girls' bewilderment, he was no longer there. Instead of the massive frame of the Inca, they could see a pale man in white clothing holding the steering wheel. He turned to them and spoke softly in their own language, assuring them that they were in safe hands and that they would be looked after. In the last few days, the girls had gone through so much terror that they welcomed any changes to their situation. What had happened and was still happening that night was beyond their comprehension, and they just accepted the magic around them and the feeling of being safe again.

Daniel manoeuvred the boat closer to the bigger craft and pulled up alongside it. The girls' eyes widened in surprise, and they muttered to each other in excitement as the Inca warrior who had rescued them reached out from the bigger boat and helped them on board. The circling macaw squawked and landed on the cabin roof to be welcomed by a scruffy, small man who proceeded to feed him sunflower seeds.

The girls turned to Mucho and knelt before him, kissing his feet and shouting their gratitude to such a brave man and a man of magic, the messenger of the sun god. He turned to Daniel with an enquiring look on his face, but he only got a smile back from him. The Inca was even more confused when, embarrassingly, the girls asked his permission to bathe in the river, for they needed to get all the evil out of their bodies and try to cleanse themselves of the many men who had disgraced them over so many days.

Mucho didn't trust the river, especially at night, so he opened a hatch and brought out a bucket, which he dunked into the river and filled with water. He gave the girls sponges and soap, and they immediately squatted down and started rubbing the soapy water between their legs as hard as they could. Their pain intensified when the cold water made contact with their open wounds, and they could only stand the aching from the rubbing for a few minutes before they reached out for the big Indian to help them back to their feet. They were in agony with every step they took as Mucho led them below to the sleeping quarters while Daniel explained to the others the events that had occurred on the barge and how he had ended up with the two Indian girls.

Mucho emerged from below, and to everyone's surprise, he joined in on the conversation. "I have seen the markings on their faces; I know the girls' people. They will kill them now that they have been defiled. We must not take them back to their family; when this journey is over, I will take them back to my people in the hills."

With a heavy heart, Francesco, the man with a lot of words, looked up at his big mate and said nothing. A rare smile came from Mucho as he put his arms across the saddened man's shoulders. "You will always be by my side, my little friend."

The night was a restless one for the men on board, especially Daniel. The cries of pain from the cabin below were more than he could stand. He rose, looked at the other men, who were awake, and entered the cabin. When he switched on the lights, the girls sat up in fright, and when the nervous man explained that he wanted to examine them, they whimpered loudly. He tried to explain that they had a bad sickness inside them and that he wanted to heal them. The girls shook their heads in despair. They imagined that they were back in the same situation as before; they were helpless and had no choice but to accept their fate.

Daniel had to take control and end their misery and apprehension as quickly as possible. "Imaka, you are the older sister, and I want you and Iluma to be brave and trust me.

"You know our names. We have not told you what they are, and you, a white man, can speak our tongue as if you were from our tribe." Imaka, although scared, was intrigued. *There certainly has been magic this night, so maybe he is telling the truth,* she thought. Maybe he wanted to help them.

Daniel carefully and gently lifted the blanket that Imaka held so tightly over her body. He laid her down on the bed as her frightened sister looked on, and he slowly parted her legs. Daniel saw the painful open cuts she'd had to endure for the last few days. He remembered what he'd had to do to cure Caris, and he feared that he might have to do the same with these girls.

He ran his finger across the old wooden floor until it snagged on a splinter and started bleeding. Daniel inserted his bloodied finger into the frightened girl's vagina, and within a few seconds, he could see a look of relief come over her face.

A disillusioned Mucho had kept to himself and watched the sun break over the trees; the sound of someone coming up the steps made him turn to see two smiling girls wrapped in blankets come and stand next to him. Mucho's sad and disappointed look changed to a smile as he looked at the girls' beautiful faces. He bent down to get a closer look at Imaka, and he put his hand out and ran his fingers up and down her cheeks. He wanted to make sure that his eyes were not deceiving him; the swelling and bruises and even the cuts that she'd had all over her face were gone. Not only had the injuries disappeared, but also, the two tribal scars that he had seen the night before were no longer there; they had vanished, and her skin had become immaculate. He saw in her face that she was no longer in pain and that she felt good about herself. He pulled away the front of the blanket and looked over her naked body; there too all the cuts and bruises had healed.

The doubt that had built up inside him about the man he revered came rushing back, and he was compelled to rise to his feet. With outstretched arms, he faced the sun, and in a booming voice, he welcomed the new day and the messenger of the sun god.

The boat, now with six on board, made good time, and on days when Daniel didn't insist on them stopping for him to venture off into the forest for one of his adventures, they could easily travel five hundred kilometres.

Francesco had made long journeys down the river on several occasions, but never had he seen so many men on the banks of the Amazon, trying to escape the forest. He had no way of understanding the events that had taken place before his eyes or the man Daniel. This person appeared human, and he appeared to have a kind heart; however, Francesco suspected that this kind heart could quickly turn into a cruel one if provoked. To the small man, there was something that made Daniel more than merely human—something pushed him towards a goal, and nothing was going to stop him from achieving it. Whether human or a god, one thing was for certain: Daniel had changed his life forever, and he was grateful for it. For once, his life seemed to have some meaning—what exactly, he didn't know, but his attitude had changed for the positive towards the future.

The name Mucho slowly lost its meaning, and the men used it less; Iguino emerged as the rightful name for the big, proud Inca. The two Indian girls doted on him and were by his side at all times; he unwittingly became their master, and they belonged to him, whether he liked it or not. Iguino now felt that he once again belonged with his people and that he would make a good and just chief for his tribe, and with his wives, he would have many children to be proud of. Under his rule, his people would obey the bidding of the messenger of the sun god, and they would protect the forest and its inhabitants.

On the fifteenth day of the travellers' journey, the many people who stood on the pier at the port of Macapa had the opportunity to watch a sparkling blue-and-yellow boat with a macaw circling around it proudly approaching. The rotting and weathered timber of the old boat had been regenerated to nearly new, and the spotless paintwork shone in the bright midday sun.

The clean-shaven captain took pride in manoeuvring his boat into the small harbour and blew the now-working horn with gusto to ensure that all noticed her. Amongst the onlookers stood an attractive blonde woman; Caris had had a strong urge to be at the pier.

Once on the pier, the six crewmembers looked back at Francesco's pride and joy; the name *Sun God* stood out in yellow against the blue colouring of the hull.

That night, the whole group, including Caris, ate their last meal together on the *Sun God.* Caris had taken the girls shopping, and they looked presentable in their bright new clothes. Francesco loved the cold beer and the wine, and it didn't take long before he was merry and reminiscing about the last two weeks' adventures he'd had with his two new friends. The little man laughed as he filled his glass with red wine and clicked the bottle of pineapple juice in Iguino's hand; he put his arms around the big man and toasted, "To friendship."

Daniel explained that from that night onwards, they would no longer be able to openly talk to each other and would have to revert back to their sign language. The little man again raised his glass and said, "Don't worry, Mr. Daniel. Iguino and I already figured out that might happen. In the last two weeks, we have done a lot of talking, and we understood each other verbally for a short time; we have learned much about one another, but that really doesn't change anything about how we felt before. Our eyes and our actions always told us a story of respect and friendship for each other, and that will last until we die. So let me thank you from my heart, Mr. Daniel and Mr. Peter, for your friendship and for the faith you have given us for the future. And I must say one more thing: thank you for our new boat; she will last for at least my lifetime."

The next morning, after refilling the empty fuel tanks and containers of fuel and food, the four in the boat waved goodbye to the three on the pier. With Long John circling overhead, Iguino stood tall on the cabin roof; his outstretched arms reached for the sky, and facing the rising sun, he again welcomed the arrival of the messenger of the sun god.

Daniel and Peter, along with Caris, headed for the airport to fly to the capital, Brasilia, for a visit with the president of Brazil. He personally met them at the airport and insisted they stay at the presidential palace, where they would be able to converse openly and privately.

At the palace, Daniel explained the reason for his journey down the Amazon. He requested that the president follow up on the four rangers led by Sergeant Mendoza; they would be willing witnesses against their superiors, and with their help, the president could wipe out most of the illegal timber trade in that area.

The next subject of conversation was the death squads, mainly centred in Rio de Janeiro. This tourist attraction—the most popular in Brazil—had children constantly arriving from the poorer rural areas. The traders' concerns about a decline in tourism and the many thefts from their stores had given rise to the death squads.

"These young people can be found wandering all over the city," the gentle elderly president explained. "At night, you will find them sleeping under trees in the parks, under bridges, in drain pipes, at the beach, and in the doorways of shops. The traders compare them to locusts; to them, they are nothing but pests to be rid of, and they shoot them down as if they were culling feral game. Obviously, most of these kids are from families that cannot feed them, so they are sent out to fend for themselves. Most are of Negro descent, and it saddens me to see this; the whites all over the world, even though they are a minority, hold most of the riches of this planet and have wrecked many lives in order to achieve this wealth. The ancestors of these children were slaves, and even though they are supposedly free, they are really not so; they are prisoners of our society, which will not give them a chance to achieve what the whites have achieved. They need help, but my country does not have the resources to eliminate this problem."

Late afternoon the following day, on the sparkling beaches of Rio de Janeiro, Daniel, Peter, and Caris played the role of tourists. They were able to see first-hand not only the problems with the youth of the country but also the alcohol and drug abuse amongst the adults, mainly the blacks. Prostitution was rampant all over the city, and many young girls and boys offered their services to the tourists who walked by.

They were touched by the poverty and the sense of complete hopelessness amongst so many of the people. While the three were walking along a beach road, they noticed a number of young children loitering around the area. Some of them had shoeboxes and long, springy wooden twigs in their hands. Daniel chuckled to himself at the ingenuity of these kids in their fight for survival. He asked Peter to walk ahead on his own; it didn't take long before a young black girl approached Peter and proposition him.

A barefoot black youth standing close behind her reached into the shoebox he held and brought out a clump of a sticky mixture of mud and clay and put it on the tip of the rod he carried. The youth walked past the girl, and in an instant, he expertly flicked the concoction onto the top of the unsuspecting Peter's left shoe.

The girl, having done her part by distracting the tourist, left Peter, and he walked on, unaware of what had occurred. Another black youth walked up and, facing him, produced a rag, which he tried to hand to him. "Mister, mister," he called out. "You have dog shit on your shoes." He pointed down to Peter's left foot.

Peter looked down and was astonished at the mess on his new runners. The boy again offered the rag. "Here, mister. You clean off—no charge."

Peter took the rag, got down on his right knee, and started getting the stubborn mess off his shoes. Another youth, who had been inconspicuously close by, suddenly made his move; he quickly walked up behind Peter, and reaching down, he grabbed the exposed wallet in Peter's shorts' back pocket.

Before Peter realised what had happened, the youths bolted in the direction of Daniel and Caris, who were watching the charade. The thieves' legs suddenly stiffened, their run became a walk, and by the time they were adjacent to Daniel, they could not move at all and came to a complete stop.

"Here is your wallet, my friend," said Daniel with a grin on his face as he took it from one of the boys and handed it back to Peter. "If these boys had the opportunity to use their cunning to make an honest living, God knows how far they would go."

The boys kept trying to run away, but their bare feet would not move from under them. They grabbed their legs in an effort to lift them off the ground, but to no avail. Frustration overtook them, and when the youngest one started crying, the other one joined in, hoping for some sympathy.

The trio stepped back and watched their futile efforts, but once the children started to show real fear and the crying became genuine, they moved forward to comfort the distraught youths.

"What should we do with you boys?" Daniel asked. "Should we take you to the police, or should we just leave you here to rot?" Daniel's words came through their minds in Portuguese, and the boys were surprised at how calming his voice sounded.

"Boys, we want to talk to you, so if you promise me not to run away, I will release you. Do you agree not to run away?" asked Daniel

"Yes, mister; please let us go and we talk with you," the taller and obviously older of the two agreed.

"Okay, you are free," Daniel told them, but as soon as the boys realised they could once again use their feet, they were off. However, they only managed a few steps before they were incapacitated again.

Daniel freed them once more, and they were now too frightened not to be obedient; besides, they felt strangely comfortable with these tourists, and cooperating fully, they happily answered all their questions.

These particular boys and their gang of well over one hundred had claimed the local rubbish tip as their home, and there they spent the nights. Peter looked at Daniel and twitched his nose, indicating that now he knew why they smelled so badly. The youths apparently took turns guarding their territory against other gangs and, mainly, the death squads that often raided their home and killed any of the kids who were too slow in making their getaway.

The only way they could feed themselves was to live by their wits, and they'd had no choice but to become thieves. The gangs consisted mainly of boys, and the majority were of Negro descent. Parents of girls made good money by selling them as sex slaves, and the family would then have money to feed themselves as well as their younger children. At least, they reasoned, the girls were usually well looked after by their masters for as long as they cooperated and stayed pretty.

The few girls who were members of the gangs were ones who had run away from their parents before being sold or had escaped from their purchasers. After taking Caris to their hotel, Daniel and Peter walked the boys to their home at the dump.

Sunset approached, and the day began to darken; the two men and the two boys waited amid the rancid smell of the decomposing offal, and as night fell, many more of the young inhabitants made their way back home for the night. At first, they were suspicious of the two white strangers who were being protected by two of their own. They were wary but felt comfortable enough to accept them without question as they milled around them. Intermingled in the crowd of mostly black lads were some white boys and a handful of black girls, and as they gathered closely, Daniel explained that he wanted to protect them and help them make a future for themselves.

In the pitch darkness of the night, the encouraging words of the stranger stimulated the children, and they chattered excitedly amongst each other. Some of them turned to face the distant lit-up statue of Christ the Redeemer looking down on the city from Corcovado Mountain. Most of them knelt down, making the sign of the cross, and offered prayers that echoed through the rubbish tip.

A sudden flash of light burst out in the blackness, and a shot rang out; a shrill scream from one of the boys suddenly turned their joyful excitement into the excitement of terror. They had been so absorbed by Daniel and their prayers that they had neglected to put guards up for the night; now it was too late.

Several vehicles had entered quietly into the tip area, and the occupants suddenly turned on spotlights. In the confusion, the vehicles quickly surrounded the group of youths. The men in the vehicles were armed, but they held their fire for fear of hitting their own comrades in crossfire. They had the gang of street kids completely encircled, and they would have started their executions if not for the two well-dressed men with the boys.

Daniel was kneeling over a wounded, bleeding boy, and when the executioners saw the blood oozing out of the youth, they congratulated the man who had fired his rifle in the pitch-blackness with such accuracy.

The man over the boy stood up, and to the surprise of the onlookers, he helped the wounded boy to his feet; he had blood all over him, but he didn't appear any worse for the ordeal he had suffered.

The men disembarked from their cars, and with rifles aimed at their targets, they waited for instructions from their leader. A loud voice called out of the darkness, "Wait!" A big man stepped forward and walked towards Daniel and Peter. "Before we shoot you two along with this filthy scum, I would like to know who you are and what you are doing here. You are obviously not a Brazilian." He pointed at the fair-haired Peter, and turning to Daniel, he shouted, "And who the hell are you, all dressed up like a gentleman just to visit the local rubbish dump?" He talked loudly, ensuring his men could hear him above the noise of the running car engines. "I think what we have here are a couple of paedophiles; I think we shoot them along with the boys and do the world a favour. Some of you men get the girls; we might as well get some money for them—maybe enough to cover the cost of the bullets."

The big man looked down at the boy next to Daniel and bent down for a closer view of the wound; he shone a torch on the boy and saw a hole in the chest area of his small shirt. He poked the hole with his finger and squeezed where the bullet should have entered the small body, but the boy felt no pain.

"That's weird," he murmured to himself. "This little bastard should be dead."

The older boy of the two pickpockets was still crouching next to Daniel, and he looked up at Daniel and with tears in his eyes sobbed out a few words of accusation. "Why? Why you trap us with your promises?" His head drooped down onto his knees as he sat in the dirt, awaiting his fate.

Daniel was so livid that his whole body stiffened up and started shaking violently. The onlookers felt a slight vibration of the earth. Suddenly, the slight vibration turned into a tremor, and the ground around them shook so violently that it knocked all who were standing off their feet.

A fissure a metre wide and ten metres long opened up in the hardened track next to Daniel, and with one sweeping motion, he reached out and grabbed the man in front of him. With a powerful force, he picked the man up, turned him upside down, and jammed him head first into the hole. Then Daniel turned towards the other stunned men, and with just a thought, their weapons were wrenched out of their hands. The rifles and handguns flew through the air and landed one by one in the grave of their leader, and in another instant, the fissure closed up, burying everything within it, leaving no evidence that there once had been an opening in the hard ground.

Nobody moved; the men and the youths were too dumbfounded to comprehend what had happened in that brief moment of time. The angry man in the immaculate white suit now spoke in a quiet and deliberate tone. "Most of you men are traders, and some of you are loyal employees of these traders of this city. You spend a lot of time and money hunting down these youths so that you can shoot them down like rabid dogs." The voice was now loud and angry. "I am here to tell you that this will stop, and you are to help the homeless youths of your city. You and all the other traders are personally—and gladly—going to donate money to start up shelters for them. You will employ them, pay them, and ensure they are clothed and fed. Help them become useful citizens. Your businesses will grow, and this growth in your profits will be achieved with the need for less security in your businesses and with the increase in tourism as the city becomes safer. You will assist me without question, for if you don't, I swear by Christ the Redeemer looking down at us from that hill that what you have seen here will be nothing compared to what I will do to each and every one of you." Daniel hesitated in order to enable them to take in the fear that he felt in the air all around him.

"As for all of you young people, you too are to ensure that my words are heard by you and all your friends, and you too will play your part in making the city tourist friendly. Do this, and you will all benefit; defy me, and you will all feel the wrath of Daniel, for I am the messenger of the Creator."

These last words echoed loudly and clearly throughout the rubbish dump, vibrating deeply in the minds of all present; they covered their ears for fear of their eardrums bursting. The headlights of the vehicles and the globes from the spotlights exploded in one loud bang, and instantly, there was complete darkness. The man in the white suit said no more; the traders and the children stayed in the same position, too frightened to move, until the break of dawn brought light back to the land.

CHAPTER 9

The Palestinians overwhelmingly accepted the plan to divide Israel, but the Israelis' evacuation of the north was proving to be more difficult—not only in the acceptance of the situation but also in its implementation. The mammoth undertaking of transferring the administration and the infrastructure of Haifa to the south was complex enough, but convincing and moving three hundred thousand people from their homes proved even worse. Haifa was also the chief seaport and Israel's main industrial city.

The population of Israel was aware of the destruction of the Wailing Wall and the destruction of the tanks by the man in white. Most of the people strongly believed that this sign came from God to end the deadlock in the peace talks. The people wanted to accept that God had sent them a message and a confirmation of their faith.

But the belief in a message from God for the majority of the people who were directly affected by the division of Israel was not as strong. For the last few days, a black cloud had approached from the south, and now it had positioned itself over the slopes of Mount Carmel. Scientists confirmed that they had been following the course of this cloud and that it was the same one that had destroyed the Wailing Wall. Now it intimidated the people of the whole city, which was built on or around the slopes of this mountain. Every night, the flashing of silent lightning lit up the sky, and the low murmur that followed sent an ominous fear throughout the city.

Industry was moving to the south, encouraged by favourable taxation treatment and the reimbursement of all costs. The majority of employees had no real alternative but to accept the move and follow their work to new premises in the south.

Africa and the fight against AIDS had come to a standstill at the Zimbabwe border. The line of soldiers sweeping the country and protecting the medical staff had started from the southernmost tip of South Africa, and they had now reached the southern border of Zimbabwe. The combined multinational forces had been moving north in a straight line from the west to the east coast of the continent. They had completely swept the country of South Africa and had finished the southern halves of Namibia to the west and Botswana in the middle. The people of the small country of Swaziland were tested, but only a small part of south-eastern Mozambique was completed before the line of soldiers was halted at the rebel country of Zimbabwe.

Zimbabwe, a landlocked country with a population of approximately twelve million people, was controlled by a tyrannical dictatorship. A feared despot, Dadi Malawa, and his rebel force had taken control of the country over a decade before.

On a mild afternoon in Harare, a tall, well-groomed black man casually walked amongst the shops on the main street of the capital. People admired his immaculate white suit and wondered how it was possible for this stranger to keep his clothes so clean on such a dusty day. He stopped across the street from an old, run-down pink shop that was badly in need of painting. The signage on the awning had faded, but the word *Chemist* was discernible.

He watched a smaller black man with a grey goatee, dressed in a dusty white caftan, walk nervously in front of three well-armed soldiers. The more he looked over his shoulder at the big men following him, the more unsteady his stride became.

They stopped at the chemist's shop, and the little man, carrying an attaché case, entered, followed by one of the soldiers, while the other two stood guard on either side of the door. Five minutes later, the soldiers, one carrying a cardboard box, were again following the little man into a side road and towards a residential area.

Stopping at a house that was better kept and somewhat larger than the others in the surrounding area, the small man looked up at the soldiers as he reached into his pocket and handed a number of Zimbabwean dollars to one of them, who, after accepting the money, pointed towards the house. This motion appeared to be an order to the other two soldiers, who quickly ran to the back of the house. The man with the black case entered the residence, and the remaining soldier took up position at the front door.

"Clissa! Clissa!" the little man called out frantically in English as he ran towards the kitchen. "Clissa, where are you?" he called even louder.

"Emmy, I am here in the lounge room," came the reply. "Come in here; I have a surprise for you."

He hurried into the room just as middle-aged woman emerged to meet him. She was slim, tall, and attractive and looked much younger than her years.

"What you all flustered for, Emmy Banda? You look like you are ready to have a heart attack; maybe you should follow some of your own advice and relax." She berated him with a large smile that showed her perfectly formed white teeth.

"Clissa, listen very carefully; I am in big trouble—big trouble," he muttered as he hugged her.

"What do you mean trouble? What sort of trouble could a doctor like you get himself into?" she said, trying to comfort and reassure him.

"I don't have much time, Clissa; there are soldiers at the back and the front of the house. They have come to take me to see President Malawa at his country palace. They came to my clinic and made me go to the chemist to get drugs, and they want me to help the sick at the palace." The little man sweated as he rambled on. "I had to bribe them"—he pointed to the front of the house—"just to let me come and see you to tell you this."

The woman's smile turned into a frown. "Oh Emmy, no, you must get away from them. Oh my goodness! Please, Emmy—you must hide," she said, panicked.

A cough from inside the lounge room made them both turn, and Doctor Banda saw a man sitting on one of the seats.

"Oh, I am so sorry," Clissa apologised. "I forgot all about you—please forgive me, Mr. Leeder." The woman turned to her wide-eyed husband and said, "Emmy, this man said he is your friend and said you will be happy to see him; I am so sorry, Mr. Leeder, but this is a bad time."

"Who are you?" The doctor stepped forward to have a closer look. "I don't recall ever meeting you before. Do you work for the president?"

"Doctor, you don't know me, but I am going to prove to you that I am your friend," the black man in the white suit told him.

The small doctor raised his hands in front of him and waved them about as he yelled at the stranger. "Go! Please go. I do not have time for this." He quickly calmed down as he realised there wasn't much time. "You had better leave now, please; I want to say goodbye to my wife alone. You can wait outside with your friends," the doctor demanded quietly.

"Doctor, you are not going anywhere; I will take your place and go see this tyrannical president of yours," the stranger asserted.

"This is no time for stupidity!" the flustered doctor yelled at the stranger. "And even if you could, why would you do it? It would mean that you would never be seen again." He ran out of words for a few seconds, and a despondent look came over his face as he took a long look at the man in front of him.

"Don't you realise that more than ten doctors have disappeared over the last two years alone? So I guess they have killed the last one they took to the palace, and I am the replacement." A knock on the front door interrupted the doctor; his time had run out.

"I want you out of here right now before I leave," he called out to the stranger. The downhearted man looked up at his wife, and with a tear in his eye, he reached up and kissed her goodbye. He picked up his bag that he had placed on the floor and turned to walk towards the door, but the sight in front of him made him stop: a white man stood where the tall black man had been. The man reached out and took the bag from the stupefied doctor and, with a hand motion indicating that the doctor should stay where he was, walked to the door.

He grabbed the door handle, hesitated for a moment, and gazed at the utterly puzzled couple; he smiled, and his image changed into the doctor himself. The wife looked at her husband at the door and at her husband at her side and fainted. Doctor Banda tended to his wife as he watched his replica open the door and close it quickly behind him.

During the half-hour drive from the capital to the palace, Daniel could see the devastation that this once-rich country had been reduced to. The starving people walked along the side of the road, looking for any rubbish thrown out of cars that might have been edible. This saddened Daniel and reminded him of the people of Ethiopia. The difference here was that Zimbabwe didn't have the same excuse as the much poorer country of Ethiopia, with its never-ending famine and the constant upheaval with the rebels. Zimbabwe's own rebels had overrun this country, and they had been in power for over ten years—surely that should have been ample time to get the country running in some sort of order, especially in feeding the population.

They slowed down, and the army jeep turned onto an immaculately brick-paved road with a star pattern through the middle of it. Millions of pavers were used, and it must have taken thousands of workers to complete the mammoth task and to maintain it. After travelling for another ten minutes on this magnificent road, a surprised Daniel found it hard to believe the ugliness of the huge structure before him.

The army jeep stopped at a checkpoint at the white brick perimeter wall of the palace, which looked more like a medieval castle. Armed soldiers were marching up and down a pathway along the outside of the long wall surrounding the estate, and there were more soldiers marching along the wall on the inside of the perimeter, also guarding the well-fortified palace.

The structure they entered did not suit the character of the surrounding area. Water was a major problem for Zimbabwe, but not there; an Olympic-size swimming pool adorned the front courtyard, which contained manicured lawns and spotless gardens.

The three escorts marched Dr. Banda up a long passageway that seemed never ending. The interior of the palace was not in keeping with the medieval appearance of the front; pure opulence and modernity marked the inside. No amount of money had been spared in the palace's construction. They passed many doorways along the way until the inquisitive little man stopped at one of them and reached out to open it. One of the soldiers tried to stop him by grabbing his arm, but instantly, an unseen force slammed the guard heavily against the wall, rendering him unconscious as he fell to the floor. The other two looked in trepidation at the doctor; they stood back and let him enter.

The massive room was being used as a hospital, and many patients were lying or sitting up in the beds. Children of all ages, white and black and of both sexes, made up the majority of the patients, and many nurses comforted the ailing little ones. The thoughts from the people in the room filtered into Daniel's mind, and the stories he received from them horrified him. He slammed the door behind him and hurried down the corridor with the two remaining armed guards trying to keep up. He manoeuvred around the palace as if he knew exactly where to go, and when he came to a large reception area with two armed guards posted at either side of huge double doors, he hastily turned towards them.

The guards stood before him with their rifles pointing at his chest. He lifted his arms up, and the two guards were simultaneously flung through the air. They hit the ceiling with such force that their bodies fell back to the floor lifeless.

Before his two armed escorts could recover from the shock, the doctor stood before the large wooden doors, which automatically opened, and the little man boldly entered the room.

The lights of the enormous room were dimmed, but he could make out the room's details. He stood at the bottom of a raised platform that covered the whole width of the room. The structure was a fortress with only one large entry at the front side, where Daniel had entered, and a smaller exit at the rear. In one of the corners, a massive spa bath bubbled away with nobody in it. But the main function of the building was that of a cinema.

There were over a hundred men sitting in large, comfortable chairs with their backs to the amazed intruder. They were all facing the rear wall, laughing and snickering at what they were watching.

The massive room was elaborately furnished; it included a throne made from gold, which sat in a dominant position on the platform. The elegant chair faced the back wall, which consisted of a huge movie screen and slightly smaller plasma TV sets on either side of it. The side walls were also covered with many more of these entertainment monitors, and each screen was showing explicit pornography, mostly involving children.

The scene on the bigger monitor showed a sickly looking man with young boys and girls who were not much more than seven or eight years of age. Daniel abhorred the sight before him; he closed his eyes and turned away, but anger quickly overtook him as he turned back to reinforce the obscenities he had witnessed. "You despicable excuses for human beings!" Daniel shouted, and silence befell the room.

A hissing noise came from the gold throne, close to where he stood, and the chair slowly spun around to reveal a fat, grotesque man whom Daniel perceived to be the president; the man peered down at him in quiet indignation.

The dimmed lights of the many chandeliers were turned on fully, and the diamond-encrusted golden caftan that adorned the president glistened blindingly. One from the group, watching the little man's reaction to the sights coming from the screens, laughed at him. Taunting him, he called out, "Keep looking—the show only gets better from here on." He laughed even louder as he grabbed the remote control and increased the volume, which made the painful screams of the children echo throughout the room.

Daniel leered at him, and not surprisingly, the man turned out to be the paedophile shown on the screen.

By now, the whole group had turned to face the intruder, and to Daniel's surprise, they consisted of many races—Negro, Caucasian, and Asian. The group stared at the little black man in their midst as the man on the throne pointed a fat finger at Daniel. "You have just killed yourself, little man; no uninvited person may enter here and live." He looked across to the entrance to see two scared soldiers peering in, too bewildered to know what to do. "Now, how did you get past my guards without them shooting you down like a mangy dog?" He motioned to the guards to come into the chamber, and they hesitantly followed each other and headed towards the president.

The petrified guards stood at Daniel's side and bowed in front of the president, who, without any hesitation, produced a gold-coloured pistol and shot the closest man in the head.

"Now, you get some more guards and clean this rubbish; I will take care of you later," he instructed the remaining guard, and unperturbed, he turned back to Daniel.

"Before I have you killed, you insolent little peasant, tell me who you are."

"At the moment, I am Dr. Banda, the one you sent your men to fetch, and I am your final nightmare."

"Well." He turned his face sideways to look at the other men in the room. "What we have here is a very confident man, and I am finding him amusing." He turned back to the doctor, and looking down at him, he sneered, "I think I will let you live—for a short while anyway—just to break the monotony of our boring lives. Come up here and watch the rest of our show. I want your opinion on how we might be able to improve our entertainment; we need some new ideas."

Daniel stood on the platform at the side of the throne as it spun back to its viewing position. The man who had taunted him previously was the centre of attention as he proudly walked up to Daniel and laughingly said, "Watch and learn, little man; I will show you how I get those little brats to do everything and anything I want them to do." He laughed in harmony with the rest of the perverts as he walked out through the small door at the rear.

After a few seconds, the large screen changed scenes, and the laughing man appeared on it, waving as he walked down a flight of stairs. At the bottom, he entered what appeared to be another large entertainment area directly beneath where they stood. He went over to a large steel cage, and what Daniel saw made him cringe in horror. The cage was a prison, and it held a group of young children who were huddling together, terrified at some event about to befall them.

"Cousin Edi is a very clever man," the president assured the new onlooker. "He loves the young ones, and he looks after them very well—as long as they do as they are told, of course." A bellow of laughter came out of the big man, and the others in the room echoed his glee.

"After the brats see the show he has for them, they are going to give Edi and the rest of us a very good time today—and for a long time to come." He laughed again.

The surround sound of the amphitheatre echoed the screaming and the sobbing of the children, but soon an even louder noise arose. Daniel could make out the new sound, and his fears were confirmed when the scene on the wide screen changed from the children to five roaring lions. The condition of the beasts, with their ribs protruding from their sides, showed that they had been starved for a number of days. The view on the large monitor zoomed out to show the entire scene; the lions' cage adjoined the one the children were in, and the frenzied, starved lions were jumping up against the iron bars of their cage, trying to reach the terrified young ones huddled together against the far wall of their enclosure.

Daniel found it hard to fathom what he saw next; in a corner of the children's prison, another smaller cage butted up to the lions' pen, and squatting inside, a lonely black boy squeezed his small body up against the far wall of his small cage. One of the lions desperately stretched his paws through the bars of his enclosure and only missed the boy by a few centimetres. The petrified child shook so violently that he gasped for each breath he took.

The small pen holding the boy had an opening adjacent to a steel-barred door on the lions' cage, and two of the many guards were at the sides of the enclosures. They were pulling on ropes attached to pulleys and slowly raising the lions' den's door. Cousin Edi took great delight in prodding the child with a spear. The sharp point made the boy bleed, and the smell of the blood made the starved lions go into a wild frenzy. They started to leap against the wall of the cage and fight one another in anticipation of the coming meal. The door kept slowly and teasingly rising, and as the gap became bigger, Cousin Edi, still prodding with his spear, forced the boy forward.

The intense group upstairs watched the gory show, too busy to notice a sudden mist appear in the room next to the president. The haze vanished just as quickly as it had appeared, and the small doctor no longer stood amongst them.

The group upstairs thought something was wrong with the screen they were watching when it suddenly went hazy; a mist had formed and was blocking their view. They started to worry at the thought of missing their show, but they gave out sighs of relief when the mist instantly cleared. Their relief turned to astonishment, and they yelled and shouted over each other as they pointed to the screen, which now showed a white man in a white suit in the middle of the lions' cage.

They watched in amazement as the lions bellowed and slowly backed away from him and sat quietly on their haunches in a corner of their cage. The man walked towards the two petrified guards who had been pulling open the lions' door attached to the boy's enclosure. They dropped the ropes, and instantly, the door slammed shut again.

Daniel made an upward motion with his right hand, and the door flew up into the air with such force that the top of it lodged in the concrete ceiling above and became suspended there.

The paedophiles upstairs watched the intruder reach over to the trembling boy, take his hand, and calmly pull him through the door into the lions' den. All the guards around the enclosures were standing motionless, too frightened to move—but not Cousin Edi. He started prodding the lions from outside the cage with his spear, trying to get them to attack the stranger. He screamed at the beasts to do their duty, and tears flowed freely down his face as he tried to make the lions understand that they were ruining his show, but no matter how hard he tried, the lions would not budge.

The stranger looked at the pitiful man and shook his head in disbelief and anger; he made another gesture with his hand, and the steel bars next to where the hysterical Cousin Edi stood strained and, as if in the grip of two powerful arms, magically opened wide. With another gesture from the man, Edi was pulled inside the cage, and he stood next to Daniel. He looked back over his shoulders to where he had entered the cage, and wide eyed in horror, he watched the gaping bars close again.

Magically, the little cage the boy had been in slowly moved backwards away from its position to enable Daniel, with the little boy in tow, to walk out of the lions' enclosure and join the other children.

Cousin Edi made a futile attempt to follow. He took a hurried step forward, when suddenly, the steel door jammed up in the ceiling came back down into its original position, severing half of Edi's extended right foot as it did. With horrified eyes, he looked down to see the perfectly clean cut that had left his toes and part of his foot on the other side of the door, which now closed off his exit from the lions' cage.

The terrified man heard the roars coming from behind, and turning slowly, he fell down; there was no foot to support him. He grasped the bars of the cage and pulled himself up to face the beasts that were again in a feeding frenzy. They cautiously crept towards their meal as it cowered in the corner; the lead lion clawed at Cousin Edi, ripping the caftan off his body, while another started to lick the blood seeping from his foot. Slowly and playfully, the five lions began to enjoy chewing on the limbs of the screaming man.

The soldiers guarding the children's cage seemed completely unaware of what was happening around them; they stood like statues, with their weapons lying on the ground near them.

Upstairs, the group watched with glee as one of their own screamed in agony while being slowly torn to pieces. They were so engrossed with the show that they didn't notice the misty cloud and the reappearance of the little doctor, who again stood next to the president's throne.

The entertainment was over in a matter of minutes as the still-hungry lions gorged on the last remains of Cousin Edi's body.

"Well, that was certainly a show with a twist at the end," the bemused president said, almost to himself, as he turned towards the entry. "Guards," he called out, and immediately, two came running up to him. "Go downstairs, and tell the soldiers to find the white man and bring him to me." A big grin came over the ugly man's face, and he excitedly yelled at them, "You must find him; he was magnificent."

He turned to the small man next to him. "Well, what did you think of our show? I had hoped to let you join that boy as a worthy meal for the lions, but as Cousin Edi has taken your place, I'll have to reconsider how you are to die." The president laughed.

"If you will indulge me, Mr. President, before we begin on my demise, I want to clarify a few things by listening to your mind. You keep kidnapping doctors from the towns to attend first to you and your cohorts and then to the children. I imagine you probably killed the doctors, who undoubtedly objected to what is happening here. This place you have built is a safe haven for paedophiles from all over the world. You buy children from anywhere you can, and if they get too sick and can't be healed, you dispose of them just as you would a commodity. You all, without the shadow of a doubt, are the most despicable group of men I have ever come across."

This honest assessment of the men in the room captivated them, and they gathered closer to the throne. A lapse in Daniel's concentration made everyone in the room gasp loudly, and the closest ones took a few steps backwards. Daniel came back to his senses and immediately realised that they now were viewing him as himself. The well-groomed white man in the immaculate white suit who had mysteriously appeared in the lions' den was suddenly in their midst.

"None of you deserve to live, and you certainly don't deserve to have a quick death. Your time for hell is close, and your death should take many weeks to give you plenty of time to reflect on all your misdeeds." Daniel raised his arms above his head, and the features on his face changed; he had a look of sheer anger as he faced the huge main entry doors. The doors slammed shut and welded together in the middle, becoming one.

He looked at the bewildered onlookers. "Those doors are now sealed shut, and nobody will be able to open them. You, Mr. President, I am going to spare for now; you are to come with me while the others remain here." Daniel's angry voice warned the listeners that he had a much more sinister plan for them.

"Now, Mr. President, make your way to that door." He pointed to the same exit that Cousin Edi had taken previously. "We are going downstairs."

The fat, ugly man found he had no choice; his tall, grotesque body shook with the massive blubber that covered it as he moved to follow Daniel. The thick wooden side door automatically opened as they approached, and once they were through, Daniel took the large key from the inside keyhole and shut the door from outside.

The lions were still eagerly licking and crunching the remaining bones of Cousin Edi, and they growled and intimidated each other in their hunger. He went over to the cage and touched the steel-barred door, it slowly opened; the lions looked up, and with a roar from the lead lion, they cautiously followed him out of the cage and up the stairs.

He unlocked the door to the entertainment room and stepped inside to face the curious paedophiles. He shook his head at the worthless occupants. There was no pity in his heart for them; today he was judge, jury, and executioner. His sadness was more for the lions, for they too had to die; they were man-eaters, and they could never be released back to the wild. Daniel stepped away from the door, and the first lion timidly entered the room, quickly followed by the other four. The men's screams of sheer terror pierced Daniel's mind as he locked the door behind him.

The young boys were still in their cage, wondering about their fate and, at the same time, preoccupied by the events taking place around them. Daniel looked at the door to the boys' enclosure, and it instantly opened to let them out.

He turned to the defiant President Dadi with a stern warning; if he didn't cooperate fully, he would be joining the others in the entertainment centre. Daniel looked at the guards, and they were instantly awake. The startled gazes on their faces turned to immediate fear when they saw their president in front of them, and they immediately jumped to attention.

"Tell me, President Dadi—out of all the people in some form of authority in your country, who do you fear the most?" Daniel queried.

"I don't fear anyone in my country; they fear me," he angrily replied, but a name he did not want to divulge came to his mind.

"What about General Zarin? Why do you fear him so much?" Daniel hesitated to allow the time to get an answer from the surprised man. "Is it because he despises you and because he has the respect of his men? You are very lucky that he respects the office of the president, and he is the one man who is really holding the country together. He makes your life easier, and that is the only reason why you have let him live."

Daniel motioned to the captain from the line of stunned soldiers, who quickly came up to him and saluted. "Get a message to General Zarin. Tell him that his president wants an immediate audience with him, and ask him to bring a Dr. Banda from Harare with him."

The captain looked across to Dadi, who nodded confirmation of the orders.

"Come on, Mr. President; let's go prepare for the general. Take me to your office; there is a letter I want you write. Of course, you must have many experienced cameramen filming your entertainment; we'll need one of them too."

Only an hour had elapsed before the general was announced to the president. A tall, stocky man with a shaven head, dressed in a freshly ironed green uniform covered with medals, entered the office of the president and saluted.

"Come in, General, and please bring in Doctor Banda with you," Daniel said, welcoming him.

The general looked with intrigue and suspicion at the white man sitting across from his hated fat president, and he unenthusiastically stuck his head out the door and motioned for the little doctor to come in.

The president's mouth opened wide when he recognised the little doctor who had changed into the man who now held him prisoner. In turn, the little man was agog to see Daniel sitting in the same room with the most hated men in Zimbabwe, and what surprised him most of all was that Daniel was alive.

"Sit down, the two of you." Daniel, now standing, sounded as if he were giving a command, and the resentment showed on the general's face. "General, you may change your attitude after you see what I have to show you and hear my explanation of why I am here."

The general was intrigued by the whole situation; a white man who spoke their language fluently was dictating to the president, and what had the doctor to do with all this? He sat down anxiously, awaiting the explanation.

Daniel looked at the DVD, and it automatically started to play a speech to the nation by the president. In a brief statement, he told his people that due to a major illness, he would be resigning as president and that General Zarin would take command of all the armed forces and, therefore, the country. The general would eventually conduct elections to appoint another worthy president, he said.

Daniel gestured to the surprised general to refrain from saying anything at this stage. He replaced the disc with another and flicked through it, stopping at different intervals to reveal the vile acts that the president had been involved in.

After watching the horror for only a few minutes, the general ran out of the office, and they could hear him dry retching. He walked back into the room and told Daniel he had seen enough. The man, visibly shaken, had tears of grief for the children he had seen being abused in such a horrible way.

"I had heard rumours that such things were going on." He wiped his eyes with a clean white handkerchief and sniffed out more words. "But I never imagined it to be true, and certainly not to this extent. This man I have had to call my president is a beast."

Dr. Banda had his head in his hands; he was too ashamed to look up at the others, as he wondered how the people of this land had allowed his country to come to such a despicable state.

"General, I wanted you to bring the doctor for two reasons."

Daniel started to explain, but the general jumped to his feet and stopped him. "Who the hell are you, and how did you get to be in control here?"

"Dr. Banda is here to vouch for me." Daniel turned to the bewildered doctor, who had been sitting quietly, trying to understand the situation.

"I know that you don't know me, Doctor, but I think that you appreciate what I did for you today."

The little man turned to the general, and with hands outstretched and pursed lips, he tried to explain how he had met this man.

"He took my identity and came here in my place."

The big general laughed. "I knew that Dadi is a madman, but I didn't know he was also blind. Doctor, I am sure he would have noticed the difference between the two of you."

The flustered little man waved his hands in front of him. "No, you really don't understand. He was I—he became me."

Turning to Daniel, the general shook his head and said, "Look, I have no idea what he is talking about, but I have no choice but to listen to you so that I can try to make some sense of all this." The frustration showed on his big face, and he intentionally stopped talking to allow himself to take several deep breaths to get his composure back. "Before, you said that you had another reason you wanted the doctor here," the general uttered.

"Good, let's keep going with this." Daniel was getting impatient, but at the same time, he was happy that the general wanted to listen. "I want the doctor to treat the children who have suffered so much under this monster and turn the whole place into a properly run hospital. And you, General, as the president stated in his resignation speech, are to take control of your country immediately."

The frustration returned to the big man. "You want me to take control of Zimbabwe? You—a white man who has nothing to do with this country—are ordering me to take over my own country?"

"Come with me, and I will show you what has been happening here; bring that poor excuse for a man with you." He pointed to the still-defiant president. Daniel turned to Doctor Banda. "You may want to acquaint yourself with your nurses and patients."

Daniel walked ahead of the two with the general at the rear, pushing the president before him; any soldiers they came across saluted the man in uniform, and they took little notice of the others.

They came across a couple animal enclosures; one held big wild dogs, and another had a large silverback gorilla. Movie cameras had been strategically placed around the cages to entertain Dadi and his friends.

"General, if you keep watching those DVDs, you will see how this madman disposed of some of those children. The dead ones were fed to either the lions or these wild dogs, while some of the healthier kids were put with the silverback just for the simple fun of watching them being killed by it."

The general looked at Dadi and reached for his holster, but Daniel intervened. "Killing him that way would be too simple," Daniel snapped at the general. "I want him to live in hell and suffer the way the children did. I think the ape needs some company."

Dadi collapsed to his knees at what he'd heard, and he started to grovel and beg for his life.

Daniel felt no pity, only annoyance at seeing this defiant man finally show his true colours; he wanted him to cower in the dirt and show the same fear he had put so many people through. He imagined how much pain and suffering the disgraced president had bestowed on his countrymen and others, especially the young boys and girls.

Dadi Malawa was an ugly man in appearance and uglier still in his demeanour. With one look from Daniel, Dadi was plucked from the ground and propelled through the air and over the electrified fence of the enclosure housing the silverback. He plummeted to the ground, panicking the big gorilla into running around its cage, beating its chest, and throwing debris into the air.

A wide-eyed and terrified Dadi, now on all fours, with his lower lip dangling down his chin, turned and looked towards Daniel. "How can you be this cruel?"

"This is your time to be in hell, and you need to be there for as long as possible."

Daniel's cruel justice came to the fore when he instructed the mystified general that Dadi was not to be rescued. He was to spend whatever life he had left with the gorilla. The rest of his cohorts were enclosed in the entertainment centre, and they would die the slow death they deserved, waiting their turn to be devoured when the lions got hungry.

The general assembled the soldiers at the palace and ordered them to return to their normal duties at the Harare army barracks. The palace would now be under the control of Doctor Banda as chief medical officer. The resignation letter and the recording of Dadi Malawa stepping down from his post were shown to the people of Zimbabwe, and as expected, they gladly received the good news. The people rejoiced, but in reality, they didn't care who had the power as long as they were left alone.

The first directive the general gave was the permission for the AIDS test clinics to enter Zimbabwean territory, and he decreed that all his soldiers and all public servants were to be tested first. The soldiers with negative results were to join the team of the allied armed forces already involved in this important venture.

Both the general and the doctor were intrigued by Daniel's last words to them: "I will contact you soon, and when I do, you will understand more of who and what I am, and you will assist me in a very important mission."

In the early hours of the next day, the sun crept into the bedroom through the partially open curtains. Caris stirred, and a satisfied smile broke across her face. She raised her head, and the smile vanished and turned into a frown when she realised that he was gone, but the sound of a shower made her grin. She quickly leapt out of bed, and letting her negligee fall to the floor, she hurried into the bathroom.

Peter joined them for breakfast in their modest Harare hotel room, and as he ate his bacon and eggs on toast in silence, he wondered if Daniel would enlighten him on yesterday's events. As usual, Peter had been keeping track of world affairs affecting Daniel's programmes, and another problem had surfaced regarding the AIDS venture.

"You know, Daniel, sometimes I feel like maybe we should let Mother Nature destroy the bloody lot of us; God knows we deserve to be."

Daniel reached out, put his hand over Peter's arm, and gave him a condescending smile. "We seem to be getting on top of things; we have many projects in progress that will ensure a good chance of success. Now, tell me what's troubling you."

"Sometimes it is so hard to fathom the mentality of humans." Peter sounded depressed. "Do you realise that there are over one hundred million unexploded landmines buried all over this world? The next African country to the east of Zimbabwe is, as you would know, Mozambique; well, about fifty-five years ago, the government of that country approved of, and probably helped the resistance of, the blacks in Rhodesia—now Zimbabwe—against the ruling minority whites. The white Rhodesians, in turn, backed the rebel forces of the Mozambican National Resistance in a civil war against the Mozambique government of the day. In the 1980s, this war became very brutal, and millions of mines were laid all over the countryside. By the time a peace treaty was signed in 1992, they estimated that over three million landmines still remained buried all over the rural areas of Mozambique. About fifteen people a week are killed and hundreds are injured because of these mines, not to mention the many animals that are killed or maimed each day." Peter shook his head; he was obviously finding it hard to comprehend the enormity of this new challenge facing them.

"There are over forty threatened species inhabiting that country, including rhinos, lions, and elephants. This country is one of the poorest in the world, and its people had to endure that long civil war, and to this day, they still face the threat of the mines." Peter walked over to the window and looked out onto the crowded street below. He walked back and faced an impatient Daniel, who was waiting for Peter to impart the rest of the information he had for him.

"Now our soldiers and the AIDS clinics have reached the capital of Mozambique, Maputo, which is at the southern tip of the country. Two of our soldiers have already been killed by landmines, and the rest are not willing to move any farther north into that country until the bombs are cleared." With a shake of the head, Peter concluded, "To sweep the whole country will take years, and we don't have years to spare."

"No, we don't," Daniel agreed. "At least we won't have to travel far to get to Mozambique."

The president of Mozambique was puzzled by Daniel's request to pass on certain instructions to his people that they were to follow to the letter and implement within the next three days.

The following afternoon, the short flight in their jet from Harare was two hours behind schedule by the time it landed at the Maputo airport. Daniel wanted to inspect the landscape of the country.

The limousine had been waiting for them for several hours with instructions to bring the president's guests to his residence, and as usual, Garry stayed behind to ensure the safety and the servicing of their plane.

A banquet held for the three proved entertaining, as the fair-skinned, blue-eyed Caris infatuated the president to the extent that he offered to buy her from Daniel.

The president had sent out the small fleet of army helicopters and others he had commandeered from civilians to pass on Daniel's message to the people in rural areas. The crew of each aircraft was allocated certain villages, starting from the capital and heading northward. The president assured Daniel that they should complete this task by the following day.

The president asked no questions, and having attended the leaders' conference in Malta, he was well aware of the enormity of the task that faced Daniel, not only in his country but also worldwide.

The sun made its way down westward towards the hills that separated South Africa, with Mozambique silhouetting the large animals that were feeding in the cooler evening air. A lone figure of a man dressed in a Western suit moved deliberately to the centre of a series of low, rocky hills. He stopped and looked around as if taking in the beauty of the sunset; he stepped forward a few more paces and again stopped. Appearing to have found the right location, he faced the darkening sky, stretched out his arms over his head, and pointed his fingers upward towards the sky, simulating a conductor about to summon his musicians. He solidified that position and appeared to become one with the rocks he stood on.

Many miles to the north, a heavy mist was lifting over the surface of the Limpopo River. The vapour became dense, like some gigantic grey blanket lying over the water. The low-hanging cloud began to change shape as a strong wind blew under it and started to lift it upward away from the surface. The mist kept rising until dark grey clouds started to form, and the wind grew stronger and circled the enormous mass until it became so dense and black that it became one with the darkness of the night and was not visible anymore. The wind mustered the gathered clouds and herded them south.

The black mass moved over the land, unseen by the creatures it blanketed, but all the inhabitants of the land could hear the murmuring it was emitting. The cloud slowly reached its destination and amassed over the hills where the man was patiently waiting, and with his whole body stretched, his arms wavered. As if on cue, the murmur from above became a deafening roar.

His arms, which deliberately and for a long time had been pointing towards the heavens, instantly pointed to the ground. Lightning flashed all around him, silhouetting his taut frame, and the rain commenced pounding the hills with such constancy that the brightness created by the lightning reflected off it as if it were a mirror, making the darkened sky sporadically daylight again.

The ground beneath the low-lying hills shook in a violent rage that scattered all the animals, big and small, away from the area, and they could be seen running in the distance with every lightning strike.

The hills crunched and contracted as if in a vice-like grip, and the grass holding the soil peeled away as the rocky outcrop from underneath slowly lifted higher above the ground. The concentrated rain teemed down so heavily that it washed the surface soil, grass, and debris away from the black metallic rock still slowly rising and protruding from the surface of the earth.

People could see and hear the intermittent lightning and the ear-splitting crash of the thunder many miles away. The wild animals' instincts took control, and they began to migrate out of the area and head in all directions, except for north.

Most of the humans from the villages huddled in the many surrounding rocky caves in the hills, and the ones who had ignored the instructions from their president soon joined them. They stacked all metallic objects in clearings away from the huts. They had thought that their leader had gone insane, but now they could see that he must have had a vision of this lightning storm; he was indeed a wise man and one to be listened to.

The man remained standing on top of the highest outcrop as it inched its way out of the ground. Lightning bolts crashed to the ground all around him, reflecting a bright glow up from the dark, wet magnetite lodestone, while the torrential rain teemed down, cleaning all before it. In the blink of an eye, the rain and the lightning stopped simultaneously, and an eerie darkness fell over the land. The roaring thunder from the clouds above grumbled louder with each passing second until it too fell silent.

An unexpected small bolt of lightning lit up the sky, silhouetting the lone man standing to the side of the newly formed magnetic outcrop. Pitch-blackness again fell on the land, but this darkness only lasted for a few seconds; suddenly and abruptly, in one mighty swoop of light, the area around these few acres of rock lit up in a blaze of glory. All the electrical energy that had built up inside the massive cloud erupted in one powerful blast of lightning. It came to earth in an almighty sheet of light, and when it hit the rocky outcrop, the whole mass of earth exploded like a volcano into the clear light of the night sky.

The outcrop broke off into millions of small rocks as it was hurtled upward and outwards into the surrounding countryside; some of the rocks landed close by, while others were hurled hundreds of kilometres away.

The night took back its domain as the rocks that had been hurled so high and far started to fall back down to the earth. As the millions of small rocks plummeted downward, the ultra magnetised stones meandered towards any metallic objects they were attracted to. Some clung to metal that was on the ground and came to rest there, while others hit landmines, which exploded on impact, flinging the rocks up through the air again to seek another metallic target.

The terrified villagers heard many strange noises that night, including swishing sounds that passed high in the sky above their shelter and many loud explosions; some were far away, while others sounded close. There was little sleep that night for man or beast, but slowly, the night passed, and when daylight came, all became quiet again. The people timidly made their way out into the open. They noticed many small black rocks scattered all over the land. Back at their villages, they were even more amazed; their iron treasures they had put in a heap the day before were completely covered with the strange dark rocks that glistened with a metallic lustre.

Yes, their president was indeed a wise and mighty man.

Caris awoke to the ruckus coming from outside the hotel; she looked across at Daniel, who was fast asleep, and felt bad at the thought of waking him up, but her curiosity got the better of her, so she shook him a couple times. When he opened his eyes, she quickly blurted out, "There is an awful racket coming from outside. I think we may have a riot on our hands; you'd better get up."

"No, no, don't worry," he assured her. "They're just still excited over last night's fireworks."

"What fireworks? Shit, I slept like a baby and missed them all together?" She gave him an angry look as she said, "You're telling me there were fireworks, and you went without me?" She picked up her pillow and hit him on the head with it as she jumped on top of him. "So that's where you disappeared to yesterday afternoon, you bastard."

"Sorry." He laughed as he grabbed her, drawing her closer and rolling over on top of her.

CHAPTER 10

The major worry for Daniel was the unknown time factor; year three had passed, and the new year had begun. Many worldwide projects were in progress, but something more decisive to unite the peoples had to be done. The tension between Muslims and non-Muslims had worsened, and the world was on the brink of war.

Most of the Christians in the Muslim-dominated countries had left and were now refugees elsewhere, and the ones who remained changed their beliefs and became followers of Islam. Muslims in Christian-dominated nations were in turn persecuted by the Bible-carrying zealots, who stopped short of murder not because of their beliefs but because of the law. That was the only consolation the Muslims in Christian nations had over their Christian counterparts in Muslim countries—at least they had some protection from the law of the land.

Newspaper articles flourished worldwide, and the themes of the stories were in the same vein: the return of the Saviour.

The Israeli papers were the most prolific on the return of the Messiah—so much so that an exodus had started out of Haifa, and the people headed southwards to resettle there. The destruction of the Wailing Wall and the ominous black cloud that hung over the city of Haifa had convinced most of the population that they had to obey this directive from God.

Rumours in Peru and Brazil of a messenger from the sun god also made the news in the South American countries, more as a satirical taunt at the ancient ways of the native population. Tales of strange events enabling the Italian and French police to capture many terrorists appeared as small articles in many of the syndicated papers worldwide.

The *New York Times* ran a story about a man who was in the entourage travelling to the United States with the Australian prime minister; this man, witnesses alleged, possessed special powers. The story told about how he had brought two men who had been shot several times back from the dead.

These articles from the newspapers ran through Daniel's mind many times before he decided his next move. He needed to bring the people of the world together and to have them be in harmony with nature. Daniel didn't want to follow in the footsteps of his predecessors; he wanted to be different, but now he began to understand why they had no choice but to preach to the people and try to convert them to their understanding of what the Creator wanted from them.

Unfortunately, their intention, no matter how good, failed because all they achieved was to start another following that rivalled the other beliefs of the day. To start another religion would be counterproductive; therefore, if he had to follow that line of thinking, he would need to do something drastically different.

Early in this new year, through Father Andrew Costa, Daniel organised a meeting with the religious group that was still having their weekly gatherings. They were firm believers in the good they were achieving and had formed a strong bond among them.

On a beautiful February morning, they gathered in the large and well-fitted boardroom at the warehouse. As usual, they looked forward to their meeting, but they were a little concerned at the new venue Andrew had picked. They preferred their usual restaurant, but they reluctantly gathered there out of respect for the Catholic priest.

They sat looking up at Andrew, who was standing at the head of the oval table. Some of the clergy wore street clothes, including Andrew, while others were never seen out of their own religious garb, especially the Buddhist monk in his bright orange attire. The tall, slim Muslim mufti, Sheikh Abdul Farho, in his white robe and matching fez, always seemed uncomfortable amongst the infidels, but to his credit, he had persisted with the group and had never missed one of the meetings.

As always, the short, round Indian holy man was late; he apologised to the group and made straight for the seat facing Andrew at the other end of the long table. The Hindu tried pulling the chair back, but to no avail; it would not move. The two clerics closest to him stood up to help him, but they too were mystified by the chair not budging. They inspected it closely and could not see any reason why it should be stuck; they gave up, and the dark-skinned man took another seat.

The door opened again, and one of the warehouse security guards pushed in a wheelchair. The silver-haired man in the chair, dressed in a blue-striped suit, held his head high as he was pushed towards the table. As usual, the unsmiling, stern look on his scarred face made him appear much older than his age, and as he approached, the others moved to allow the wheelchair to be pushed up against the table. Andrew welcomed him and immediately started the meeting.

"My dear friends, I welcome you all, and I will start by making a statement. Today your life will change forever; from today, you will be questioning your innermost faith and your values about your life and your life's teachings."

"Andrew, if I may interrupt you." The apologetic but curt chair-ridden man, representing the Lutheran Church, raised his hand in a half-hearted way. "Not meaning any disrespect, but you appear to be starting to preach your Catholic creed to the rest of us; now correct me if I am wrong, but my understanding is that we do not talk about our individual faiths at these meetings."

The cleric from the Greek Orthodox Church and the casually dressed Baptist nodded in agreement with the Lutheran pastor.

"Pastor Nicholas, I appreciate that I may be coming across as if I am about to start preaching to my congregation, but please believe me—that is the furthest thing from my mind," Andrew said, quelling the group. "I am not the only one to be talking to you today; someone else will explain why we are here, and he will explain in a much better way than I am able. Please bear with me while I ask this one question of you all." He paused and looked at each man at the table before restarting. "I need you to put aside all that you have been taught in regards to your individual religions. Put aside all the teachings that have been passed down from your ancestors over the centuries, just for one hour. Do this, and we will all be in the foreground of the biggest challenge ever faced by our planet."

A question from the rabbi broke the tension that followed his dire statement. "Andrew, is the person coming to talk to us a Daniel?"

"Yes, Rabbi Goldstein, it is," Andrew replied.

"Then yes, I am willing to put aside my beliefs for him." The others were surprised by the statement from the Jewish rabbi, who well remembered Daniel in Israel.

Andrew shocked them further. "I thank you, Rabbi, and I will confirm to you that my religious teachings are no longer my faith. I am a follower of

Daniel, for he is the only way we can save our world. I have seen first-hand what he can do, and already the world has started to change for the better."

The group sat in silence, their curiosity aroused.

"Jesus is my Saviour," the man in the wheelchair called out. "The Bible is my way, and all that I need to know is written inside the Holy Book. God and Jesus have inspired the words of the Bible. Get your security guard to wheel—"

Before the Lutheran could finish his sentence, the door opened, and Daniel walked into the room.

Sheikh Farho let out a gasp as he recognised the man Tomas had introduced to him two years ago at the mosque. Daniel's blue eyes looked over at the apprehensive man and gave him a smile that immediately relaxed him. He walked over to the only seat left at the table, and to everyone's amazement, Daniel only had to touch the fastened seat for it to slide back to allow him to sit.

"Sorry for my interruption, Nicholas. I believe you wanted to leave, but I would ask your indulgence on a matter so important that it goes far beyond any of our religious beliefs. Please give me a few minutes, as this is a long-overdue introduction as to the reason why you have all been groomed for an extremely important mission."

The words "groomed for an extremely important mission" intrigued even the staunch Lutheran.

"I am Daniel Leeder, and I am here to ask your assistance in saving our world." He came right to the point, but he quickly detoured from this alarming statement and turned his attention to the rabbi. "Rabbi Goldstein, welcome back from Israel, and I thank you profusely for the important part you played in bringing peace to that region. Henry has advised me of all the good work you did there."

The group members around the table were astounded. Rabbi Goldstein had helped to bring peace in the Middle East? This meeting was certainly getting interesting. Daniel then turned to the Muslim cleric.

"Sheikh Abdul Farho, how is Tomas's elderly mother? Is she still going strong and looking after her grandchildren?"

"Yes, Mr. Leeder, she is still running around chasing the two little brats." Daniel was pleased in the change in this man's attitude, which was much different from the first time the two had met.

"Mr. Leeder, since the day our paths crossed, I have had many questions to ask you, and no matter how hard I tried to get information from Tomas, he would not tell me anything regarding you. Will you please answer one question?" he pleaded with Daniel. "How did a very old woman who only had hours to live suddenly become revitalised to such a degree that she not only lived but also got up and made you a meal? This she told me herself." Farho talked excitedly as he stood and waved his arms around to stress every word he said. "Did you save her from death to help her widower son raise his children?" He stopped talking when he realised that he was the centre of attention and shyly sat down.

Daniel looked at him and gladly answered his query. "I needed Tomas Adofo, so I did what was necessary; I saved this woman's life in order to give Tomas more freedom to help me."

The rest of the men around the table were astounded but sceptical. Daniel went on to tell his tale of the natural Creator, and so engrossed were the ones present that not a murmur could be heard from them. No one in the room interrupted his tale, and he was able to relay his information in a short time.

He concluded with some more thoughts for them to mull over before they undoubtedly would throw a myriad of questions at him.

"What is more wondrous or more powerful than nature itself? Alive or dead, we belong to nature, for it controls every moment that goes by. The greatest question that I can think of that would baffle clerics such as yourselves is probably the simplest one to ask and yet the hardest one to answer. This question would be 'What is God?'" Daniel looked at the faces before him, and he could hear their thoughts—thoughts of surprise. They were individually having trouble answering this question even to themselves.

"God is my Saviour!" called out the indignant Lutheran.

"I thought Jesus was," Daniel answered.

"Well, yes, they are one and the same."

"Okay, then we are on the same wavelength; I am talking about the Creator, God is the Creator, and obviously, according to your teaching, Jesus is also God and, therefore, the Creator himself, so let's not split hairs. Let's talk some more." Daniel continued with the subject at hand. "God is everything we see and everything we touch. Each time you look into a mirror, at another person, at an animal, or at a bee taking nectar from a flower, you are looking at a part of God. Yes, he—or it—is everything and is everywhere. It has no shape and yet has many shapes that we can see before us; the Creator is all the creations of the entire endless universe, and

I am telling you that the Creator is the universe itself—and that includes Earth."

"Your story is indeed an incredible one, and you are obviously asking us to believe all that you have told us, but what proof is there that all you say is the truth? You may have convinced our Catholic friend here, but I need more conviction than words." The abrupt Lutheran fidgeted restlessly in his chair as he spoke. Daniel could see that he was a proud man who would have once stood tall—a man with an intimidating attitude and a voice to match.

"Nicholas, you have complete faith in your beliefs, do you not?" Daniel asked.

"Of course I do. I have given my life to follow Jesus, because Jesus is the way to everlasting life, and that is why he died on the cross for us." An angry tirade came from the pastor.

"Well, I will ask you the same question: What conclusive proof have you that your teachings are the truth?" Daniel retorted.

Nicholas leaned back on his seat, reached into a side pocket of his wheelchair, and produced a small Bible, which he raised above his head. "This is what tells me that my teaching is the way. All I need to know is in this holy book; in here, all that God did for us has been recorded, and everyone can read it. My faith lies in the Bible, while yours lies in clever words," the angry man concluded.

"You are right, Nicholas—clever words are not enough, and I do not expect you to simply have faith in what I say. We could argue all day long about the Bible being only words too, written and translated many times over the centuries by many different people from many different countries. What has been lost in all these translations by the different interpretations of each individual understanding and belief is something that we can only speculate. I do not have the inclination or the time to debate all these aspects with any of you, for time is our enemy, and we cannot afford to waste it. My intention all along has been to demonstrate who I am, not for you to have faith in what I say." Daniel looked at the Lutheran, and the wheelchair rolled back away from the table.

"Nicholas, you were involved in a terrible car accident that left you a paraplegic, and you have been confined to that cursed wheelchair for the past fifteen years. Your bark is a lot worse than your bite, and I know that you are a good man. I need you and everyone else here to help me. But I need a man who is whole." Daniel sounded cruel. He walked past the glaring gazes and stood in front of the wheelchair of the disheartened man. Daniel raised his hands out in front of him, and the Lutheran, construing this as a gesture for his forgiveness, shook his head in defiance. Ignoring Nicholas's effort to push him away, Daniel placed his hands on the big man's shoulders, and Daniel's large eyes looked down into the apprehensive bloodshot eyes of the invalid.

Daniel then walked behind the wheelchair, and to gasps of horror, he lifted it and tipped Nicholas out—but instead of falling, Nicholas found himself leaning forward and bent at the knees but standing on his feet unassisted. He automatically straightened up and stood to his full height, and as he did, Daniel ordered him to walk, which he did with ease.

Nicholas was confused and bewildered, and then a feeling of awe came over him as he turned to stare at the man behind him. With a smile that made him look much younger, Nicholas spun around to face his stunned comrades. Daniel sat and indicated to Nicholas to also sit down.

"Sorry for the dramatics, but like I said, I do not have time to waste. The preceding messengers, like Jesus or Muhammad, had much more time than I, so there is a need to be more direct with getting the required message across to the world."

"Am I healed?" the happy yet apprehensive Lutheran asked. He was too preoccupied to even realise that Daniel was talking.

"Yes, you are; like I said before, I need a whole man to help me," Daniel replied.

The eager group began asking questions that they previously had not dared to ask of their own faiths for fear of showing any doubt about their teachings. The United Church layman had the first query. "One thing that has always puzzled me is why God lets so many babies be born with defects, such as Down's syndrome and cerebral palsy. Is this natural Creator any different from the God we believe in?"

"Well, why do you think your God allows this to happen?" Daniel asked the same question back to the ginger-haired man.

"It is his will," he answered ignorantly.

"There is no such thing as 'it's just his will'; there is always a reason for why anything happens in this world. Nature made all its creatures on this planet to a definite plan or DNA with the intention that time would improve the genes with every new generation born. There was and still is a natural selection that is practised by animals; males fight each other for favour of the females, and the strongest and fittest will always win.

This means that the strongest and the healthiest of the male species will be the ones who spread their seeds through the many females whom they control. This natural selection doesn't stop there. Those minute living seeds that are ejected into the female race to be first to fertilise the eggs within her, so even at this point, we have the strongest seeds carrying on the best bloodline of the best donor available. The females accept this, and their offspring are normally strong and healthy, carrying their sire's genes.

"We humans are no different from the other animals in the jungle, but we gradually followed a path different from nature's way. Slowly, our societies became more sophisticated and changed our way of thinking. Instead of human females being only interested in the strongest and healthiest males, they became very materialistic, and suddenly, wealth was what measured men's standing in society. The greatest hunter of the tribe has now been replaced with the greatest thinker, so we now have a society that has grown mentally but is lacking physically and in its general health. The way it is now with the majority of humans, only the seeds from a particular male still follow the natural selection process." Daniel saw, as usually happened with most of his explanations, that this answer was intriguing and, at the same time, confusing his listeners. "Look, I am not saying that humans were wrong in changing this natural process. What I am saying is that we can't blame Mother Nature, our Creator, for us going against its intentions, and therefore, we—our society—has to accept responsibility for the many defects in our general health."

"Why does it allow so many people to be killed by wars?" Another question came from the table.

Daniel pondered this query for a few seconds before answering. "War is not caused by nature; it is caused by greed or trying to protect the material possessions that men have. Greed could mean material gain, such as more land, or maybe it's just simply trying to prove one's power or to save face. Throughout history, the greatest cause of wars has been religion. To be a Christian or a Muslim or to have any other divine belief is a good thing, and those people following these beliefs are good people. The problem comes from fanatics—ones who believe that theirs is the only religion and who will not tolerate any other, even if it means killing the nonbelievers of their faith. To be a Christian or a Muslim means that you follow the teachings of Jesus or of Muhammad, and they certainly didn't want us to go around killing our fellow men in their name.

"Currently—and the reason for our meeting—there is the threat of a religious war between the followers of Islam and the non-Muslims, although the Muslims and the Christians are the main instigators. Can you imagine a war between these two religions? One third of the world's population is Christian, and one fifth is Muslim; it would be a complete disaster—much worse than the last two world wars combined. If this occurred, it would mean the certain end to all life on this planet."

Daniel ignored the raised hands of his listeners; he hoped that they would find most of the answers to their questions during his explanation. "The ten of you here are representative of the majority of the religions of our planet. There are literally hundreds of different creeds all over the world—Christianity, Islam, Hinduism, Judaism, Buddhism, Shinto, Confucianism, and many, many more, including some very primitive religions practiced by African tribes, Pacific Islanders, and the Australian Aborigines. At least these primitive people were worshipping the sun, the moon, oceans, or even mountains, and some, like our Aboriginals, worshipped Earth itself. They at least were worshipping their natural environment or the natural universal objects they could see. Most current creeds being practiced have merit, and each encompasses some of the same beliefs; for example, we can learn a lot from Hinduism, as its ideals are of peace and respect for all living things.

"If we took the best from each and combined this with another religion practiced by very few—pantheism—then we could have an ideal doctrine. This group follows the theory that God is all things in the universe, as opposed to, say, Christians, who claim that God is everywhere. This religion is the closest to the one we need to follow. We don't have to be going to church every Sunday or facing the east and praying every day. There is only a need to respect everything and everyone, and there should be no divisions, such as countries, making up our globe; we should only be concentrating on the total well-being of the whole planet."

"Daniel, are you asking us to start a new religion?" the Orthodox minister asked as he scratched his head.

"Well, Constantine, in a way, but not so much a religion—more of a following or a belief that nurtures the notion that our Creator is the universal natural force, which includes our own Mother Nature. But to simplify this whole matter and to answer your question, the answer would be yes. That is exactly what I—or should I say *we*—need to do; we must combine all religions into one. If people work together for the benefit of all, we will have a chance of saving ourselves. You people here need to convert all your own parishioners to this new way of thinking. Australia is the best country to initiate this new doctrine. You in this room are the ones who must get it off the ground. Gradually, we will recruit the many helpers from overseas who are aware of my existence."

The astounded faces before him worried Daniel; they lacked the confidence of their convictions. "Your thoughts tell me you believe in what I have told you, but you are wondering why I can't will this new teaching onto everyone on Earth. I can't will my beliefs onto others; I could achieve some conversions by creating miracles here and there, but I will never be able to face all the challenges before me. Because of the unknown, limited time frame we have, I need to instigate as many programmes as possible, working towards the common goal. Your goal—changing the world to one religion—is only one of the many projects required to give us some hope."

The Muslim, Farho, stood up, and his face was ashen. "Daniel, I believe in what you are telling us, but can you imagine how my people will react if I start to preach against the Koran? My life will be over within a minute of opening my mouth."

"I agree with you, Sheikh Farho. We will have to tread carefully in your case; I expect to meet with you and Tomas soon to discuss the matter," Daniel said, calming the worried man.

"The rest of you are to start in a small way, with people from your congregations who trust you and would be willing to at least debate the issues. I will be there with you, even if only in spirit." Daniel handed the meeting over to Andrew and quietly left the room.

Over the next week, the ten clerics were busy. They had agreed that each of them would recruit ten new prospects and convene for a joint gathering. For obvious reasons, the warehouse had to be kept secret, so they rented a small hall for Friday night.

The one hundred or so intrigued and puzzled people met at the designated hall. They had some inkling of what the meeting was about, and most had read articles or seen current-affairs programmes mentioning a prophet. Of course, to most, this was a far-fetched story, but if these reports had the slightest chance of being factual, then they wanted to see for themselves. Sheikh Farho was able to persuade some of his own reluctant family members to attend.

The peculiar thing about devoutly religious people, especially Christians, was that they believed that prophets had come to Earth in the past and that Jesus would return, but when someone dared to mention that this had taken place, they were the first to disbelieve such a thing could have possibly happened.

Daniel appeared before them in a misty cloud, and he explained his mission from the Creator. He asked the people who wore glasses to come to him; thirty-one of them were able to attest to a miracle. With a touch of Daniel's hand, their vision became normal, and they did not need their glasses anymore.

It took only a few minutes with him to convince them of his mission, and he left them in the hands of his apostles, who would answer questions and help plan for the next stage.

Each attendee agreed to bring at least ten members of his or her family and friends to the next meeting, which Andrew would hold at his own parish. They estimated at least one thousand people would be in attendance the following week, and St. Bernadette's could cater to that many.

The following dark and overcast Friday night, the clerics were pleasantly surprised to see people already entering the church two hours earlier than scheduled. The crowd inside slowly grew until all the pews were taken and the standing room at the sides and the rear was filled. The outside entry was overflowing, and unruly queues of people spewed out onto the main street and started to block the traffic heading to and from the city. The grounds surrounding St. Bernadette's were full, and people climbed the trees in the garden for a better vantage point.

Police arrived to redirect the traffic away from the church and to find the cause of the commotion, but their efforts to enter the cathedral through the crowd were in vain. Newspaper reporters and television news crews arrived at the scene. They had received a tip—something about the return of the Saviour.

The Baptist minister ran over to Andrew, who was standing near the altar with the others, to inform him that bedlam was occurring outside his cathedral.

Father Andrew was panic-stricken, and his fear worsened when instantly, all the lights went out, and darkness befell the surrounding area. The meagre light given by the few candles adorning the altar only dimly lit the immediate area and made little difference to the overall darkness. The screams from the people brought Andrew to his senses, and remembering the public speaker system, he hurried over and turned it on. He then realised that it needed power to work, but an inner sense told him to try it, and he was not surprised that the speakers were still operating. He calmed the crowd as best he could and told them that he would distribute as many candles to them as he could.

Andrew, with a candle from the altar in his hand, made his way to a storeroom close by and came back with four small boxes and a torch.

"This is all we have," he told the others. "Two hundred in total." He gave one box each to four of the clerics and instructed them to hand them out to the people. "Two of you start at the front rows at either side of the aisle, and the other two take this torch and start as far back as you can and work your way through the crowd."

"We'll run out after about five rows—and what about matches?" the gruff-voiced Lutheran asked.

"Don't worry about matches; I am sure some of the smokers will have lighters. Just hand them out—quickly now," Andrew retorted.

The Lutheran and the Baptist handed their boxes to the front row and asked the people to take one candle and then hand the box to the next person in line. The rabbi and the Anglican chaplain worked their way into the dense crowd; they gave up the struggle and reluctantly gave their boxes to the nearest people to pass on to the rear of the cathedral. Every time a person took a candle and handed the box to the person next to him or her, a surprising thing happened: the candle gave a little flicker, and a glowing, small flame appeared. Each time a wick lit up, it made the place of worship a bit brighter.

Slowly, every candle held by the people lit up, giving the impression of a line of dots appearing out of nowhere and growing longer and longer. Something else now dawned on the astonished clerics at the front: there must have been a lot more than two hundred candles in those boxes. They could see well over a thousand little flames, and more were being lit as they stared down on the congregation.

"Daniel is here," an excited Father Andrew whispered to the others. "Look at all the lights at the back—they go all the way outside. I bet that the people out there are also receiving candles."

One young boy in the crowd tried to blow out his candle, but no matter how hard he tried, he could not do so. His father next to him saw his son's efforts and, thinking this odd, tried to do the same, and he couldn't extinguish the little flame either. Slowly, all the people were trying, until they excitedly realised that this might be a sign.

Andrew again stepped up to the microphone and followed the bidding of his own mind; he asked the people to lift the candles high in the air. A sea of small, flickering flames immediately rose above everybody's head, inside and outside the cathedral, and they eagerly waited for the next sign. The rustling of the leaves on the trees outside made the silence of the night feel eerie. A strong wind blew across the heads of the outer crowd and gently made its way inside the church. The onlookers could hear a swirling noise and the flapping of loose articles coming from above the altar as the hissing of the wind grew louder.

Suddenly, with a mighty whooshing sound, the wind blew through the gasping crowd inside, and in a split second, it was out in the church's gardens again, blowing over the heads of the crowd outside and causing all small, unfastened items to be strewn about in the night sky. The rustling of the leaves in the trees a few seconds ago had heralded the arrival of the wind, and now the stillness of the same trees told the crowd that the wind had now passed.

It took a little while for the people to realise that something strange had taken place in the few seconds the wind had caressed them, and they marvelled at the wonderment of it all. The wicks on the candles no longer had flames on them, but the glistening flames were still there, only now they shone on the head of every person present.

People turned to gaze at each other, and the flames followed their every movement. Some crossed themselves in the true Catholic way; others knelt and prayed, while some raised their arms into the air, praising the Lord God. Outside, forbidden from entering an infidel's house of prayer, a small number of Muslims with the little flames over their heads were on the ground, facing Mecca and calling out, "Allah is almighty." As they bowed and raised their heads, the little flames bobbed up and down, following their every movement.

The sky lit up when lightning streaked across it, and a deafening clap of thunder echoed through the night and vibrated the bodies of the people at St. Bernadette's. They looked up to see the clouds abate, and a stretch of clear, starry sky appeared alongside a full moon. A calming voice echoed out from the brightness above them, and the minds of all present at the church heard the words in their own language. The people inside and outside the cathedral looked up towards the heavens, and their faces showed smiles of gratification. The voice made them all feel at ease, and they were in awe of it, for now they had proof that their faith was real.

"I am a messenger from the universal natural Creator. I have come to bring peace to all the inhabitants of this world. Listen to the words of my followers, for they will show you the way."

The message was brief; all was silent, and the night faded into darkness again. The crowd outside saw the clouds closing the gap that allowed the light from the moon and stars to streak through. Once more, lightning lit the sky, and another enormous crash of thunder shook the earth, followed by pitch-blackness that frightened all outside and inside the church. The thousands of little flames on their heads were extinguished in one swoop. Instantly, the electric power returned, and the blackout was over; all the lights inside the cathedral and the surrounding area were back. The people were restless, trying to fathom the events that had occurred.

The voice of Father Andrew coming over the public speaker eased the built-up tension. He spoke about Daniel, and he reiterated what the prophet expected from them.

The night wore on, and the crowd slowly dispersed as the dawn gave way to the start of a new day—a day that was to be the start of a new movement that would change the concept of what religion was and should be to the whole world.

The headlines in the morning papers splashed the words *prophet* and *messiah*, whilst the text described the events of the previous night at St. Bernadette's Catholic Church. The reporters themselves admitted that at first, they had been dubious about the whole meeting, but before long, they had been left with no doubt that what they had witnessed was genuine.

More profound than the newspapers was the video footage that the television channels were broadcasting. The footage showed the extent of the small miracle of the candles. The commentator fuelled the spectators' minds further as she told them that initially, there had been only two hundred candles dispersed strategically amongst the crowd. Instead, more than six thousand had been handed out. The stations graphically showed the lightning and the claps of thunder, but more intriguing were the various interviews with people citing the same message they had received; the interviewer herself confirmed that she too had received this message.

Father Andrew Costa led the clerics in an interview, giving an account of their experiences with the man sent from the universal natural Creator.

The controversy that followed the broadcast had far-reaching consequences that went all the way to the Vatican. The pontiff and the cardinals were greatly concerned by the upheaval effect that this false prophet could have on the mother church if he were allowed to freely preach this new creed.

To the dismay of Cardinal Bradley, his peers shunned him; one of his own priests had used one of the churches under his control as the platform to launch this so-called prophet. The pope himself demanded that Cardinal Bradley return to Australia and put a stop to all this nonsense before it got out of hand. The pontiff and the cardinals all agreed that had this prophet been genuine, then he would have called on them before he had announced his presence in their world.

After landing in their private jet at Washington airport, Daniel and Caris were ushered to a waiting presidential limousine.

"Good to be back here," Caris confided in Daniel. "I love the shopping in this country, but I'm a bit surprised that we are here at all. I didn't think we would be going anywhere after last week at St. Bernadette's. I would have thought that your anonymity would be over, and I presumed we would be in hiding somewhere."

"Technically, I don't exist; I don't own anything in my name, so I am not that easy to find, but I agree that my life will not be private for too long." Daniel sighed.

The short visit to America was twofold. First, he wanted to meet the incoming president, as John B. Rose had now completed two terms in office and, under the American constitution, could not stand for re-election. The new elected president was a much younger man, a well-known ex–army general. The theme of his whole election campaign had been ridding the world of terrorism even if it meant war against Islam. This premise was a popular one amongst the majority of Americans, and the hate he'd generated for the Muslims had made many of them abandon their homes and leave the USA. The majority of the citizens felt that if a religious war did break out, their country would be in the forefront and the new president was the right man in charge.

The second reason for Daniel's visit was to try to promote the new religious movement and to ensure that the ex-president would be the man to lead the movement.

John B. Rose welcomed them to the White House, and the incoming president agreed to a meeting with the Australian, rather begrudgingly, for the following day.

One of the aides escorted Caris to her room, while the president and Daniel went directly to the library. Daniel had a prearranged meeting with the anti-drug-legalisation lobby group he had met there less than a year ago. The only other invitee outside of this group was the ex-director of the CIA; he sat, trying to straighten his comb-over, at the rear of the group. He looked haggard and pale; Bob Wilson had had to reluctantly take early retirement due to illness. The heavy smoking over most of his life had taken its toll, and he now suffered from emphysema so badly that he carried a nebuliser, which he had placed on the floor beside him; his face was covered with an oxygen mask, and even with this aid, he still struggled to breathe.

"You have all met me before." Daniel got straight to the point. "And no doubt I left you all with a few unanswered questions. I am here to answer some of those queries but, more importantly, to enlist your aid in an immensely important project—a project that if it fails, the world will end."

The forty or so men and women were spellbound at such a statement, and many questions quickly went through their minds. Daniel left them with their thoughts as he walked across to the ex–CIA director and looked down at the pitiful man. Daniel reached over, and whipping the mask off Bob's face, he angrily picked up the nebuliser and heaved it across the room, smashing it into one of the large pillars in the middle of the library. The horrified group in the room gasped at such a callous act, but more horror was to follow. The ailing man had his mouth wide open, gasping for air. Daniel, still standing over him, inhaled deeply, grabbed Bob's head with his two hands, forcibly lifted him off his seat, and placed his mouth on his. The exhalation of air from Daniel into the lungs of the sick man was loud enough for the people in the room to hear.

Daniel stood erect, and the ailing man, with his comb-over flopping on one side of his head, staggered and slumped lifelessly back into his chair. Daniel placed his right hand over the scalp of the seemingly unconscious man and whispered to him, "Sleep well, Bob—sleep well."

Even John felt apprehensive at what had occurred, and the group members were unsure what action they should take; they were mystified by this man and the power he possessed. What had happened was wrong; it was not the American way. Something had to be done about this murder.

"Don't concern yourselves about Bob Wilson," Daniel commanded. "He is not dead; he will join us shortly, so why don't we get on with our meeting?"

For the next half hour, Daniel explained his mission and the threat to Earth without leaving out any details. With these representatives of so many Americans, he strongly stressed the reason they had to join him; time was of the essence. He turned to the incumbent president and, with a smile, said, "John, I know that you are writing your autobiography and that it is nearly complete, and I thank you for your discretion in not mentioning me. But I need you to include our meetings and the details of my mission; however, as usual, use your discretion concerning the consequences in the event of our failure."

Again, John B. Rose was in wonder of Daniel; he had been secretly writing his memoirs from the first day he had entered politics many years ago, and now with the end of his tenure as the president, the manuscript was nearly ready for publication. To have Daniel's permission to include him in the book would be the highlight of all his experiences in his colourful life.

In the excitement, nobody noticed the lean man on the couch stir and open his eyes; he desperately tried straightening out his hair as he slowly regained all his senses.

"When are you going to tell us exactly why you are here?" an alert and sprightly man at the rear of the room asked. The members of the group were elated to see Bob Wilson awake and, more importantly, still alive.

"Welcome back, Bob," Daniel greeted him. "I guess you must have been asleep; John will bring you up to date later." The ex–CIA director stood up and inhaled deeply several times. He found it difficult to understand what had happened to him, but he now could savour every breathe he took. The pleasure of simply feeling the air entering his lungs brought tears to his eyes. He felt invigorated as he walked over to Daniel and, with complete wonderment, looked up at him. With trembling arms, he embraced him and started to cry uncontrollably. Daniel put his arms around him and comforted the highly emotional man. "What I have done for you was a selfish way for me to make all the people in this room believe in me by deed and not by faith alone. Please accept this gift I have given you and help me to help all of us."

The tall, lean, broad-shouldered former general, dressed in his immaculate uniform adorned with his war medals, marched through the hall of the White House, smiling and shaking hands with any of the staff he came across. He was ushered to the Oval Office, and as he entered, he ran his hand through his curly blonde hair, and his smile widened even more to reveal a perfect set of capped teeth.

"Ah, President Elect Chuck Foreman, please come in and meet my special guest, Daniel Leeder," the incumbent president said, welcoming his successor.

The general grasped Daniel's extended right hand. The boyish man squeezed Daniel's hand as hard as he could, and the only reaction the Australian showed was a smile that revealed a perfect set of uncapped teeth. The general turned red in his effort, and he embarrassingly released his grasp and sat in the chair next to Daniel.

John B. Rose started the conversation by reintroducing Daniel. "General, we are in an extraordinary situation, and at this time, Daniel is the most important man in the world."

A roar of laughter came from the uniformed man. "This Aussie—the most powerful man in the world? I would think that at present, it's me."

"Chuck, this is so serious that we are not even following the usual protocol of taping all conversations held here. What is said here stays only with us—is that understood?" The outgoing president was adamant.

"This all sounds very secretive and exciting. What's this all about, John B.?" the general enquired gleefully and sarcastically.

"I have followed your career for a long time, General, and to be quite candid, I am more than a little concerned about you replacing me." The president hated being called John B., and he didn't particularly like this man. "You have a reputation for being a bit of a cowboy, and I know that you are dedicated to the Catholic Church—and please don't misunderstand; there is nothing wrong with you being a zealot for the Catholic faith. I'm concerned that during this unsettling period of world history—and it's mainly religious based—I just don't believe you are the right man to be running this country. Nevertheless, there is nothing I can do about it; the people have spoken, and they have elected you as the president. I honestly do not think that you will accept what we are about to tell you, but we must try."

John began to tell the grinning man about Daniel and his mission, but he was only able to utter a few sentences before the general stood up, called the president a nutcase, and headed for the door. He had only taken three steps before his left foot tangled with the right one, and he fell to the floor. Red faced with embarrassment, he leapt to his feet, and as he did, his trousers fell down around his ankles. He again fell down.

"Now, Chucky," Daniel said disrespectfully, "we can keep doing this all day. Sit down and listen to what John has to say," he ordered.

The frowning general, with his back to the other two, staggered to his feet and pulled his trousers up over his legs. He was confused with what the Aussie had said. Had he indicated that he'd made him trip and drop his trousers? Before he had time to gather his thoughts and turn around, the chair he had been sitting on slammed into the back of his legs with such force that it made the big man fall into it. The chair turned, and with the general hanging on, it slid back into its original position next to Daniel, facing the president.

"Now, General, mind if I continue?" the president asked the disorientated man.

Before the president could say another word, a gasp of pain came from Daniel, who was standing and grasping his chest. He doubled over and slumped onto the presidential desk.

John B. Rose ran to Daniel's side as the general looked at them both indifferently.

"Daniel, are you all right?" John asked.

Daniel stirred and slowly rose to his feet. "John, I have to leave; I must get back to Australia urgently. Please tell Caris to fly back at her leisure, and in the meantime, please do your best to convince this cowboy about our mission."

Daniel fell into a meditative trance, and the two men watched as his body slowly faded into a mist. The vapour dispersed and became part of the air inside the room, and an eerie breeze sprung out of the air vents and into the office. The captive wind gathered speed and blew around the room, tossing the papers on the desk in all directions and causing the flag behind the president to flap uncontrollably.

The two men hung on to the arms of their seats tightly as their hair swayed with the breeze; their ties twirled around their necks, and loose flying objects bombarded them from every angle. The deafening hissing noise concentrated at one part of the room, and it died down completely as it headed out through one of the air vents. The papers now covering the wire mesh over the vent slowly floated to the floor. The wild-eyed general tried to straighten his tangled hair and come to terms with what he had witnessed.

Outside above the White House, the swirling breeze straightened, and the windy noise started again as the wind picked up tremendous speed and headed south-west across the American mainland.

CHAPTER 11

On the other side of the world, Andrew Costa was standing over the workbench in the middle of the modest kitchen at the presbytery, preparing his evening meal. He was cross with himself for not changing out of his black priestly garb, but he was hungry and had had a busy day, so he couldn't be bothered.

The front doorbell ringing disturbed his undivided attention on dicing vegetables for the stir-fry he was looking forward to. Hesitantly putting down the sharp paring knife and hoping this caller was not one of his parishioners seeking help, he went to the door and reluctantly opened it.

"Cardinal Bradley." A surprised Andrew invited him in. "I certainly didn't expect you to be the one ringing my doorbell."

"I need to talk to you, Father Andrew. Do I still call you Father or just Andrew these days?"

A sarcastic opening remark didn't surprise the young priest. "You can call me whatever you like, Cardinal Bradley," Andrew replied. "I have been expecting to be called in to see the bishop or archbishop but certainly not to be visited by the cardinal himself. Last I heard, you were in Rome. When did you get back?"

The huge man seemed redder than ever as he restlessly followed Andrew into the kitchen. "I had my driver bring me straight here from the airport," Bradley answered as he looked around the small kitchen.

"Hope you don't mind if I continue with my cooking; I am rather famished." Andrew grinned and added, "Would you like to stay for dinner?"

"No! No, thank you. I won't be staying long."

"Now, Cardinal Bradley, I am assuming that this is not a social call, so what is so important that you came straight from the airport to see me?"

The cardinal could not hold his agitation any longer; he slammed his open hand down on the kitchen bench. "What is this nonsense that you have been preaching to your parishioners here at St. Bernadette's?"

The big man's anger didn't make Andrew even flinch, and he turned to his once superior and calmly stated, "One thing is for certain: what I am preaching is no nonsense, and I guarantee you will be following this new creed before too long."

"You are ruining my career with all this paganism you are spreading, and you have the audacity to use one of our cathedrals for your sermons!" the cardinal shouted as he started to lose control of his emotions. "I could have been the first Australian pope, but you have made me the laughing stock of the Vatican. The pontiff himself admonished me because of you; you must renounce all the hype you have been preaching, and you must tell the people that what happened at St. Bernadette's was a trick—mass hypnosis or something." He raved and waved his arms around, his face now nearly blood red, and he was gasping for air. The huge man slumped down on a small stool in a corner of the kitchen, and the cheeks of his massive buttocks hung loosely on either side of the seat.

Taking a few deep breaths, he reached inside his large robe pocket and pulled out a handkerchief to wipe down his sweaty face. A look of horror came over him as he looked at his right hand; it was covered in blood. At first, he thought he must have burst a blood vessel, and he started to anxiously run his hands over his head. In his frenzied reaction, he didn't realise that he had dropped his small eyeglasses onto the floor. He remembered where he was, and a great fear came over him; he stared out in front of him, too scared to turn his head in any other direction.

"Andrew, Andrew! Please answer me, Andrew," he called out in a wavering voice. All was quiet. Slowly, he looked towards the bench top where the young priest had been cutting the vegetables, but he wasn't there. With great effort, the cardinal stood and shuffled slowly around the workbench. His feet hit something on the dark slate floor; he looked down and at first didn't notice anything, but with squinted eyes, he could make out the shape of a man lying there. He screamed, and realising his glasses were missing, he dropped onto his hands and knees and frantically searched the floor for them.

Finding them, he nervously put them on and crawled back to the man on the floor. Andrew was face down on the kitchen floor, with dark blood oozing out from under his clothes; he had the small paring knife protruding out of his back. The cardinal's second scream was much louder, and it sent a chill through the body of his awaiting driver. The frightened man gathered his courage and slowly made his way into the small dwelling. Hearing someone whimpering, he cautiously headed towards the sound; he stopped at the kitchen door and gave out a womanish scream when he saw the big man kneeling over the lifeless body of the young priest.

Peter Brand thought he might have an early night after enjoying a magnificent grilled snapper specially cooked for him by Ang, the chef at the warehouse. He had a shower and prepared for bed but now felt refreshed; he turned on the television and lay in bed to watch.

With Daniel away, things around the warehouse were a little dull, and he looked forward to Daniel's return. He was starting to doze off and only half listening to the television, when a newsflash interrupted the normal programme. He opened his eyes on hearing the mention of a priest.

"The priest, from an inner suburban church, was well known in the community, and the police are baffled for the reason of his murder. They have detained a male suspect who is helping them with their enquiries," the newsreader announced. "No further details are available at this stage; we will keep you informed as more news comes to hand."

Peter sat up, and a sickening feeling came over him; he picked up the phone, and using the quick dial, he pressed Andrew's number. It rang for a while before someone answered, and not recognising the voice, he asked briskly, "Who's this?"

The other person's reply was also curt and just as brief: "Who are you after?"

"Have I got the right number for St. Bernadette's Presbytery?" Peter retorted.

"Yes," the person answered.

"Father Andrew—is he all right?" Peter asked.

"What are you to Father Andrew, sir?" the stranger said, answering Peter's question with a query of his own. Peter didn't bother answering; he jumped out of bed, donned his clothes, and, within seconds, was in his car and heading for St. Bernadette's.

The short trip only took minutes, and Peter arrived in time to see a stretcher being wheeled out of the presbytery and into a waiting coroner's wagon. He ran towards the two men with the stretcher and straight into the arms of an intercepting police officer who had seen him approaching.

"Is that Father Andrew?" he asked the solemn-looking young man who held him by the shoulders.

"And who are you?" the policeman asked.

"I am a very good friend of his. What happened here?" Peter was getting distraught. The uniformed police officer nodded to a plain-clothes man who quickly came over and introduced himself to Peter. He wanted him to accompany them to the Melbourne Central Police Station to help them with their investigations.

The time dragged for Peter as it approached midnight; he was alone in the computer room back at the warehouse. He missed David, who had gone on one of his many visits with his mother to the capital. A couple security guards were at their stations at the other end of the building. He had never felt as alone as he did at this moment, and he urgently needed Daniel. He had contacted Caris on her mobile, and she'd told him that Daniel had vanished, saying that he was going back to Australia. "He left me here on my own, except for Garry, so he didn't take the jet back, and nobody knows if he did get out of America or how he got out of the country, if he did. He must be coming back there by airmail." She laughed.

Peter couldn't see the sense in worrying Caris, so he omitted telling her about Andrew. Sometime before dawn, a sudden noise woke him from the restless sleep he was having on the couch he had been sitting on. He was startled to see loose items flying through the room all around him. His hair swayed from side to side as the breeze got stronger, but suddenly, the wind subsided, and as it did, all the debris that had been flying around in disarray settled down to the floor.

A hazy mist formed, and as it thickened, it slowly took the shape of a man. Peter's initial fear turned to excited joy as he realised that Daniel had arrived. A thought came to him, and he gave out a half-hearted laugh. He looked at Daniel, and for the first time, he put his arms around him and hugged him.

"What's so funny?" Daniel asked.

"Oh, just something Caris said about you coming home by airmail," a smiling Peter answered.

"I am so glad to see you, my friend." Daniel was relieved to see Peter, and he timidly patted him on the shoulder. "I had feared the worst. I had a premonition that someone close to me had been badly hurt."

Peter's smiling face turned into a grievous look as he came back to reality and remembered his dead friend. "It's Andrew, Daniel—Andrew is dead," Peter told him.

"Dead—how?" a distressed Daniel asked.

"Of all things, he was murdered by that fat Cardinal Bradley," Peter explained. "He says he can't remember doing it, but the police say there is no doubt whatsoever that he is the murderer."

"Where is Andrew's body being kept?" Daniel demanded.

"His body is currently at the morgue down in the cellars of the Central Police Station in the city." Peter had already been to the station to assist the police. "A forensic pathologist determines the cause of death after conducting a post-mortem examination, so apparently they have to do an autopsy on his body tomorrow morning."

"How long has Andrew been dead?" Daniel asked in a matter-of-fact way.

Surprised at the attitude Daniel was taking, Peter answered coldly, "About six to seven hours."

"Take me there," Daniel insisted.

The five-minute trip saw them outside the station, and at that time of the morning, they had no trouble parking right outside the main entry. Daniel got out of the four-wheel drive and, as he did, turned to Peter and asked him to wait for him, no matter how long it took. Peter watched Daniel walk up the wide, curved steps of the old building and saw him slowly disappearing in a mist that formed around him; the doors to the police station opened and closed again.

The night had been reasonably quiet, and the trainee constable at the reception counter read a novel, while another two police officers were sitting at their desks and doing paperwork. The pages of the book that the young red-headed boy had open on the counter flickered, and he felt a breeze. Looking up, he noticed a haze before him, and he watched it as it headed down the passageway.

He noticed the papers pinned to the notice board halfway along the aisle flicker, and one piece of paper dislodged from the board and fluttered along the hall and down the stairs heading to the morgue. The lad reassured himself that the other officers were still behind him, and as he started to say something, the other two raised their heads and looked at him. He timidly said, "Nothing, nothing," and gritting his teeth, he looked down the hallway again.

The thick steel door of the morgue opened silently and then automatically shut tightly again in one slow movement. The mist that had entered the room had dispersed, and a man stood in its place.

An hour had passed, and Peter had laid the car seat back and had fallen asleep; he was completely oblivious to what was transpiring in the morgue below the building his car was parked adjacent to.

The red-haired officer at the front desk was once more engrossed in his book, while the other two were deep in conversation and sipping on cups of coffee. He lifted his head and listened; he turned to his fellow officers and asked, "Did you fellows hear someone knocking?"

"No," they swiftly replied.

"There it is again; it seems to be coming from down below." He grimaced and again looked at his workmates, who now were more attentive, as they too had heard something.

"One of those guys in the morgue must have woken up." The bigger one of the two older men laughed nervously.

This time, they heard the distinct knocking, but more than that, the knocking was followed by someone calling out.

"It is coming from the morgue," the third apprehensive officer remarked. "You don't suppose one of those pathologist nerds locked themselves in there, do you?"

"Come on, Smithy; we'd better check it out." The bigger man led the way out the side door of their office and walked around to the front counter. He smiled at the uneasy young man who was leaning over the counter, looking down the passageway, and said, "Give us the keys, will you, mate? And one more thing, Blue: you'd better stay here and hold the fort. And whatever you do, if it's a ghost, don't shoot it—it's already dead." He laughed as the two officers made their way down to the morgue.

They hesitated at the door and jumped back when they heard a knock, followed by a desperate voice.

"Who the hell are you?" the larger apprehensive man called out nervously.

"I've been locked in here," an anxious voice replied.

The big man indicated for his mate to open the door, and as Smithy carefully did so, the other officer stood back in anticipation.

Smithy pushed the steel door ajar, and in fright, he jumped back, elbowing the bigger man in the stomach; a pale hand had reached out from inside the morgue and opened the door the rest of the way to reveal a man wrapped up in a white sheet standing on the other side. The two police officers gave out loud screams and ran up the stairs and headed for the front counter, where they stopped to recover their breath. They looked wide eyed at each other, drew their guns, and waited to see if the corpse would follow them up the stairs.

Young Blue stared at the senior constables, puzzled by their apparent frightening experience, and he too now felt wary, but before he could ask any questions, he heard a voice coming from the staircase: "Hey, guys, don't panic; I'm Father Andrew Costa. Where in heaven am I? Looks like the morgue to me. God, they must have thought I was dead or something, but as you can see, I am still alive. I am coming up, so don't go and bloody well shoot me, will you?"

The man covered in the sheet walked up the stairs and headed towards the petrified officers. Blue saw the pale and sickly looking man with the darkened eye sockets and collapsed in a heap right where he stood. Smithy cleared the counter in one massive leap, while the bigger constable staggered up onto it stomach first and rolled over to land on the other two already on the floor.

The older policemen were on their hands and knees, hiding behind the front counter. They timidly checked on Blue, and gathering some courage, they forced themselves up high enough to see over the counter just in time to see the front door close and the man in the sheet, thankfully, leave.

Peter was in a deep slumber, and he didn't hear the car door open and slam shut again; he woke abruptly with someone shaking him by his left shoulder and shouting at him. "Peter! Peter, wake up. Wake up, man. Come on—I am so tired and thirsty. Let's get going."

Peter, in the early morning darkness, could not see who had woken him, but he assumed it to be Daniel trying to make a quick getaway from something that had occurred inside the police station. Without hesitation, he righted his seat, started the car, and accelerated away, going straight through a red traffic light as he made a right-hand turn and headed for home. "What the fuck is happening? Daniel, what did you do?" Peter queried as he hunched up against the steering wheel.

"Peter, it's me—it's Andrew, not Daniel." A confused reply came from the passenger. With smoking tyres, the car came to a screeching halt, almost hitting the kerb, and hesitantly, Peter reached for the interior light and switched it on. He let out a loud shriek and felt the hair at the back of his head stand on end. He frantically tried to open the car door, but a familiar voice soothed him enough to prevent him from following his instinct to run away.

"Peter! Peter, it's me—it's Andrew. What the hell is wrong with everybody? I'm not a ghost; bugger it, what the fuck is going on here?" That was the first time Peter had ever heard Andrew swear, but it was what he needed to relax him; he turned and had another look at a friend who, only a short time ago, had been dead.

"Andrew, you're alive," Peter sobbed as tears flowed down his face.

"Of course I am alive; Peter, please tell me what is happening. My God, man, the last thing I remember, I was at the presbytery, preparing my dinner and talking to that hypocritical, fat bastard Bradley." He hesitated for a moment, and squinting, he recalled something else. "I felt an excruciating pain in my back and chest, and the next thing, I wake up completely naked at the morgue. I was so cold I wrapped myself up in this sheet I found under me, and Daniel was talking to me, but he wasn't there; I couldn't see him, but he was there talking to me. He told me that you were outside waiting for me." The confused man had never felt so weary, and he started to wheeze with each breath he took.

"Where is Daniel? Andrew, do you know where he is?" a distressed Peter asked.

"I have no idea; please take me home before I collapse. I need to rest really badly, Peter—really badly." The last few words were only a mumble, and Andrew slumped back into the car seat and rolled over onto Peter's lap.

In the New South Wales town of Parkes, Clara had urgently called her mentor, Professor Morey, back to work. She had disturbed the romantic candlelit dinner he was having with his wife as they celebrated their thirtieth wedding anniversary, and he let her know in no uncertain terms how he felt about this interruption.

Ten minutes later at the conservatory, his annoyance subsided, and the anniversary dinner was the last thing on his mind. After looking through the telescope into the night sky at Comet Clara and doing some quick calculations, he reached the same conclusion as his young assistant. He immediately rang his colleagues in America. They asked him to stay on the line whilst they checked out the figures he had given them.

Panic mode came over the Americans as they confirmed Professor Morey's calculations; the comet had again set a course directly for Earth, and at the present accelerated velocity, the anticipated collision was going to happen well within twelve months. Unfortunately, this comet's rate of acceleration was unpredictable. If it continued to pick up speed at the same constant rate, then it was feasible that it would reach Earth much sooner than that.

They had a dilemma on their hands; there was no scientific explanation for why the comet had changed course again and, more importantly, how it could pick up so much acceleration. To the scientists, Comet Clara defied all logic, and past theories put forward by astronomers did not apply to this comet. The only conclusion they could come to was that an unnatural force was guiding this mass of destruction towards Earth.

Nine o'clock the next morning, a chirpy middle-aged man walked into the city's central police station and rapped his knuckles on the front counter to attract the attention of the police constables who were usually busy working at their desks. On this fine morning, there was nobody behind the front counter. He could see several of them through the glass partition at the rear of the reception area; they were all in a deep and animated discussion in the office of the station's chief sergeant.

He went down the passageway and headed down the stairs into the morgue.

Ten minutes later, the head pathologist, now in his white coat and with his younger assistant beside him, was knocking at the front counter upstairs.

"What is going on here?" he demanded. "Where is the cadaver of that priest?" He slammed both hands down onto the counter. "If someone is playing a joke here, it will be at the cost of their job."

The men deep in conversation at the rear all looked up at the ruckus from the front, and the chief sergeant indicated for the doctor to come to his office. The men from the night shift and their day replacements returned to their debate, but they were abruptly interrupted.

"Everybody, shut your gobs," the big-bellied sergeant yelled at his subordinates as the doctor and his assistant entered the room. "Now you three"—he pointed at the men from the night shift—"tell Doctor Bell here the bullshit you've been telling me; I want it exactly the way you told me."

The older and bigger man from the previous night looked at the doctor and swallowed hard before he muttered, "He went home."

"He went home? What do you mean by 'he went home'?" the agitated doctor screamed at him.

"Just that, sir—he went home," the man reiterated. "About five this morning, he knocked on the door of the morgue. We opened it, and he walked out of here and left."

The doctor took a deep breath and shook his head as he looked at the three men in front of him. "Just let me explain this to you; firstly, the coroner pronounced him dead, and secondly, he would have been in that fridge for around seven hours. Now, even if there were the slightest chance that the coroner made a mistake, the cold would have finished him off. Oh! And one more thing: you can't open those drawers from the inside, so he would have had to have help." He stopped and slowly looked at each man individually. "Now, do you men want to tell me what really happened here?" he screamed in complete frustration.

The sergeant concluded that they were not getting anywhere, so he suggested they go down into the morgue and look again.

The sergeant and the officers from the night shift followed the medical staff into the morgue; the room wasn't large, and it had been searched from top to bottom several times. The dumbfounded group stared credulously at the floor in front of them; there, lying on his back and completely motionless, was a man neatly dressed in an immaculate white suit. The six, cautiously following each other, approached the body and peered down at it. No, this was not the missing cadaver. They were mesmerised by the mysterious man, and as they peered at him, two startled eyes opened wide and stared up at the men looking down. The surprised men jumped back in fright; the sergeant fell over a chair and landed heavily on the concrete floor, and one of his subordinates had to help him up.

The men hesitantly made their way back to the man on the floor and were relieved that his eyes were shut; the mysterious stranger was unconscious. The doctor opened a drawer in his desk, found a stethoscope, and started examining Daniel.

"Well, one thing is for sure: he is definitely not dead; as a matter of fact, he has the strongest heartbeat I have ever heard," the doctor pronounced.

"Do you reckon he is going to be out of it for a while?" the sergeant asked.

"Your guess is as good as mine," replied the doctor, "but I certainly don't think he is going to die any day soon."

"There's one fucking thing I plan to do, and that's get to the fucking bottom of what the fuck is going on here." The sergeant yelled at the top of his voice and felt embarrassed when he realised how loud he was shouting; he calmed down and, red faced, continued. "Now, we don't want the papers to get hold of any of this; my God, they would have a field day with all the kerfuffle that's been happening here. Imagine it all; they are aware that a priest has been murdered, but they don't know we are holding a cardinal as the suspect. Now the priest's body has disappeared, and in his place, we have someone else." He thought for a while and gave a command. "You two"—he pointed at Smithy and young Blue—"carry this man upstairs, and put him in one of the cells for now; I'll interrogate him when he comes out of whatever is wrong with him."

Daniel stirred and opened his eyes; he had been coherent enough to understand what had been happening around him. Reviving Andrew had been entirely against nature, and he'd had to fight for his friend with every ounce of his will and strength. The weary Daniel had come to the realisation that he had taken a stupid chance; not only could the Creator have stopped him from reviving Andrew, but also, he could have forfeited his own life and, worse still, the lives of the entire world. His bodily strength and his will to survive had all but gone, and at one stage, he had dematerialised into thin air with little chance of reconstituting himself back into reality. But his will had returned to him, and it had grown strong enough to fight against nature itself—and somehow he had survived. He sat up on the bunk of the small cell, and although he felt his power returning, he had some reservation about this energy within him. He now had the knowledge that there was a limit to how far he dared use these powers.

Daniel became aware of someone else in his vicinity, and he turned and looked at the cell to his left. There sat one of the fattest men he had ever seen, and he immediately recognised Cardinal Bradley. The big man, full of remorse, sat on his bunk, looking down and contemplating his uncertain future.

Daniel almost felt sorry for the big man. "Cardinal Bradley, fancy meeting you here. I have been meaning to call you for quite some time."

The cardinal unenthusiastically lifted his head and looked across to the adjoining cell. He gave a couple small nods in answer.

"Do you mind if I come visit with you for a while? There is a lot I want to talk to you about, Cardinal," Daniel said, playing with the despondent man. The big man wasn't interested in small talk and returned to looking down at his shoes and feeling sorry for himself.

From the corners of his eyes, the cardinal noticed a haze. He took his glasses off and rubbed his eyes vigorously. Taking his hands away from his eyes, he could distinguish that a pair of white trouser legs and two white shoes were at his side. He donned his glasses and looked up to see a handsome man standing next to him in his cell. The cardinal, although naturally slow, leapt to his feet, and with disbelieving eyes, he looked at the man and then at the cell next door. It was empty, and the cardinal could only think that his imagination was playing tricks on him. He quickly turned to face Daniel, thinking the man wouldn't be there, but the stranger now sat on the bunk where he had been a second ago.

"There is no need to ask any questions, Cardinal Bradley, because I am going to give you most of the answers you will be seeking," Daniel told him. "You know, people talk about luck, but there really isn't any such thing. It's all coincidence; that's all luck is. Being in the right place at the right time is considered good luck, and being in the wrong place at the wrong time is considered bad luck." Daniel stood and pointed at the big man. "But in your case, I have to say that if there was such a thing as luck, you have it." He walked over to the bars and leaned his back on them as he turned to face the dumbfounded man. "You know all the things that Father Andrew Costa has been preaching about? The prophet sent here by the Creator? Well, guess what? Here he is." Daniel pointed his open hands towards his own body.

Cardinal Bradley's eyes grew, and he looked flabbergasted; Daniel ignored the state of the big man's bewilderment and casually told him his story and his plight with saving the world.

When he had finished, he sat on the bunk next to the cardinal and stressed another point to him. "The reason I am telling you all this is that you are going back to your boss, and you are going to convince him that I do exist."

The cardinal didn't really care for the nattering coming from this madman; he already had enough problems of his own to cope with. But to his dismay, the man continued talking.

"My plan is not to be worshipped like all the other prophets before me, but to ensure that people realise that it's the natural energy within us all and the entire universe that must be adored and respected. Tell the pope that the natural force can be called whatever people want to call it; it doesn't comprehend names, so call it God, Allah, the Creator, or whatever you want. All I am trying to achieve is to have one teaching within all religions so that the Catholic Church and all other religions, including Islam, will still be able to exist and worship in their own manner, with only minor changes to their creeds."

The obese man's stomach began to roll as he broke out in uncontrollable laughter.

He had tears flowing down his huge face as he looked up at Daniel and tried to talk, but his hysterical laughter prevented him from being coherent.

"You think that I have forgotten about the murder charge you are facing?" Daniel asked the cardinal. "Well, that's something I will let the authorities handle." He put his hands on the cardinal's shoulders and tried to soothe the inner pain and guilt the big man felt.

"Although you are an ambitious, overbearing glutton of a man, down deep, you are not a bad individual, and that is one of the reasons why I will help you. I will make use of you.

"I know you didn't intend to harm Andrew; it was a spontaneous reaction from you. I would have known if you had intended to harm him, and I would have stopped you. I will be leaving now, but very soon I will be sending you a visitor who will enlighten you further and who will undoubtedly help to convince you of my mission."

Cardinal Bradley had to use his handkerchief to blow his nose and wipe the tears from his eyes, and as he put the wet cloth back into his pocket, he realised that the man was no longer in the cell with him. He struggled to his feet and looked across into the adjoining cell; he wasn't in there either. The man had mysteriously disappeared in the same manner he had appeared in his cell. The cardinal convinced himself he had gone mad with the guilt he had inside him.

With a throbbing headache, the massive man crossed himself, dropped to his knees, and started to pray.

The results of the calculations being discussed across the globe through the computer link-up between the Australian Parkes Observatory and the American scientists were completely astonishing. Comet Clara had slowed her acceleration and was back to her original velocity. The new calculations proved the comet was back on the original time frame for the possible collision with Earth.

One of the American scientists made a statement that the people involved found unscientific, but they could not argue against it: "This comet seems to have an agenda to rendezvous with our planet at a specific time, and it is doing all it can to keep to that time. There is something impelling it to pick up its pace, as if time has been cut short for our planet, and then, all at once, this something puts it back to the original targeted time frame. We must try to discover what this something is."

Silence followed for a few moments before Dr. Morey spoke of something else that puzzled him. "Have you guys heard anything about our weather? I have a friend at the weather bureau, and this morning, he told me that yesterday, as far as he knows, is the only day on record when there was not one single drop of rain recorded anywhere on Earth. Just thought I'd share that with you so that you can mull over that phenomenon too."

A familiar voice made Peter stir as he lay on the couch in the computer room. "Hey, sleepyhead, feel like a cup of tea?" He opened his eyes, and a broad smile appeared on his face as he rose to a sitting position.

"Where have you been? God, you're stressing me out; Daniel, you have to stop doing this to me. I don't know how much more I can take."

Drawing a chair close to the couch, Daniel spoke seriously. "I am glad you brought Andrew back here instead of taking him to the presbytery," he commended Peter. "His body needed to recover from the ordeal he has been through, and when he wakes up, he is going to be facing a more perplexing situation."

"What perplexing situation?" Peter asked.

Daniel seemed concerned. "His body will no doubt fully recover and probably be better than ever, but his mind is another matter; he might find it difficult to accept that he actually died."

Daniel ignored a sigh coming from behind him, and with a wink, he continued talking to Peter. "We must convince him that he is still the same man he was before and that he will be the focus of the world news when his resurrection comes to light. They will call it a miracle, and all the news media in the world will want to hear his story. It's as if nature itself realised the implication of Andrew's death and the enormity of allowing me to bring him back against its own natural intentions. You know, Peter, at one stage, I too faced death, and I was willing to take the chance of daring the Creator to either let me bring my friend back or take me and the rest of the world into oblivion. In this way, by Andrew being revived, nature admitted that his death was a mistake and that he was needed amongst the living." Daniel stopped talking and leaned back in his chair.

A throat clearing put a smile on Daniel's face; he stood up and turned to see Andrew timidly standing behind him. They faced each other, not knowing how to start an awkward conversation. Daniel was well aware that Andrew had overheard the conversation, and in truth, Andrew probably realised that Daniel knew he had been listening.

The thickset priest had enough faith in Daniel to accept what he had heard, and he understood that to let the world know about his revivification would create nearly as much publicity as the knowledge of a new prophet. He would now be able to help Daniel with his mission at a much higher level. The tag in Andrew's hand fell to the floor, and with misty eyes and a small grin on his face, he said, "I found it tied to my big toe."

With no further words and with tears running down his face, he stretched out his arms, and the two friends embraced each other devotedly and respectfully.

A few seconds later, the three friends were laughing uncontrollably. "Found it tied to my big toe!" Peter spluttered out between the laughter.

The Melbourne Central Police Station was a hive of activity. They set up a temporary reception area in a different section of the station to cater to the public, as they had closed the permanent reception counter while two plain-clothes CIB detectives were interviewing the night watch officers for about the tenth time.

The detectives were convinced that these men had played a practical joke that had backfired. In another room, two more detectives were talking to Cardinal Bradley about the missing body and the missing man from the cell next to his.

"Excuse me, Senior Detective Sergeant." The dark-haired young woman from the front counter tried in vain to interrupt the interrogation of the three men from the night shift. "Excuse me, sir." This time, she was loud enough to make all the men in the room turn towards the door.

"What?" the man in charge curtly yelled. The young woman, although intimidated by him, appreciated the frustration that showed in his face. "Well, what is it?" he demanded.

"Senior Stokes, there is someone here who said he is the man you are looking for," she blurted out.

The detectives nearly knocked the young woman over in their haste to get to the front counter.

"Who are you?" the senior detective demanded. He had expected to see the man who had vanished from the upstairs cell, and from the description he had been given, this was not him.

"Father Andrew Costa. I believe you are looking for me?" replied the stout priest dressed in his black attire.

"No, we're not looking for you—just your body," the senior detective, who figured he had a nutcase in front of him, retorted sarcastically.

"I am Father Andrew Costa," the man reiterated.

"Of course you are Father Costa, and I am the Hunchback of Notre Dame." Senior Detective Stokes shook his head and turned to leave, followed by his man. He stopped abruptly upon seeing two terrified and ashen-faced men from the night shift gaping at the priest. The red-headed junior constable had again collapsed onto the floor.

"That's … that's him," Smithy managed to stutter out as he pointed at the smiling priest. "That's the man from the morgue."

The detectives turned to face Andrew, and the senior detective quickly gave out an order.

"Get that fat bastard out of the interrogation room, and bring him here. If he tells me that this is the man he murdered, I'm taking early retirement."

The detectives and the police officers had to move aside to let the big man through to the front counter. They were anxious to see his reaction at the first sight of the priest. The cardinal looked at the man on the other side of the counter, squinted, and looked again; he took his glasses case out of his pocket, opened it, and removed the cleaning cloth, and to the frustration of the senior constable, he commenced to casually clean the glasses. Then, as he moved closer, he put them on and gazed at Andrew, and without saying anything, he stumbled backwards until his buttocks came to rest on one of the desks.

After a few moments of complete silence, he raised his arms to the heavens and called out, "Daniel, Daniel! I believe in you, Daniel. Thank you, thank you."

"For God's sake, man! Don't bring anyone else into this. Do you know this guy?" the man in charge called out.

The obese man sobbed openly as his trembling lips blurted out, "That's Father Andrew Costa. Andrew, Andrew, please, please forgive me. I didn't mean to do it; I can't even remember doing it. Please forgive me."

The senior detective had worked on many murders over the course of his long career, and many remained unresolved, but there had always been some logic to every crime. For the first time, he was completely baffled by the illogical nature of this case.

His frustration showed when he yelled at his subordinates, "Okay, I want you two"—he pointed at the priest and the cardinal—"in my office, and you"—he pointed at the young woman—"get the doc here. I want him to take a blood sample from the priest, and he can compare it to the blood samples the coroner obtained at the scene of the murder. Nobody is leaving here—nobody—until we get a result of the DNA test. Is that understood?"

Every person in the room, including the cardinal and Andrew, nodded consent.

"And who the fuck is Daniel?" the senior detective screamed as he followed the others into his office.

Two hours passed, and the night shift officers were fast asleep on the various couches in the surrounding rooms, while the pathologist, his assistant, and the plain-clothes men waited impatiently in their senior's office as he read through some papers that had been handed to him. The results of the tests were in the senior's hands, and he read and reread them several times before he handed them to his subordinates. He gazed at Andrew and was in complete awe of the whole situation.

Throughout the confusion, Andrew had kept quiet, but now, for the first time, he decided to try to alleviate their concerns. "Look, obviously you must all realise that there is something odd or divine happening here. Detective Stokes, please trust me, and soon you will understand how important your contribution will be towards this world's survival," Andrew pleaded. "Tell the press exactly what has happened here—no more and no less, just the truth. Please ensure you mention Daniel when you talk to the press."

"Daniel, mention Daniel. For the last time, who is Daniel?" The senior detective was almost screaming.

"The man who disappeared from your cell is the prophet, Daniel, and he is the one who resurrected me," Andrew replied. The senior detective looked at Andrew and was at a loss for words.

"Obviously, I am not going to lay any charges against the cardinal, so you will have to let him go, but you are to implicate him as my murderer," Andrew concluded with a smile.

The presses were running hot. The stories about the prophet had been front-page news for some time, and now they had more fuel for their articles. A new miracle to compare with the revival of Lazarus had occurred, and photos of Father Andrew Costa forgivingly shaking the hands of his murderer, Cardinal Bradley, were shown all over the world.

The Vatican was now even less impressed with the cardinal who had been sent back to Australia to quell the rising fame of the young priest and the prophet; in fact, the opposite had happened—they were now much more renowned. Cardinal Bradley was not in the least surprised by his urgent recall to Rome for a briefing on the situation.

CHAPTER 12

Late on Friday, prayers were held at the mosque close to the city, and word spread amongst the worshippers that Sheikh Farho, their well-respected holy man, had a special sermon after the evening prayers.

A nervous mufti walked up to the pulpit and looked down at the expectant crowd; he cleared his throat several times before he gained the confidence to speak. "My people, I have been calling you to prayer for many years, but what I have to say to you tonight will question your beliefs, and undoubtedly, this will not be pleasing to your ears. I ask for your understanding and for your tolerance to enable me to have the courage to divulge a new religious movement that has started right here in our adopted country. Some of you may have already read about or seen television reports on a new prophet who has been sent to us by what he claims is the natural Creator of the universe." Farho felt great discomfort at the murmuring that came from the people facing him. "Allah gave us our great Muhammad to be his messenger to show us the way, so why is it now so difficult for us to believe that our beloved Allah, or our Creator, has in its wisdom decided to send us another messenger? I have had contact with this prophet personally, and I have seen his power and have heard his logic. He has come to guide everyone, no matter what belief they follow, be it Islam, Christianity, or even Judaism. Daniel, this new prophet, wants us all to change our attitude towards each other and to form one universal religion." Farho knew that that would be the last word of his sermon, as the noise from the crowd grew to a roar, and he could no longer be heard.

The more fanatical worshippers started to stir the crowd by citing passages from the Koran and calling for the stoning of the blasphemer who had been known to fraternise with the Christian infidels. The crowd pushed forward towards the pulpit, and the hatred they suddenly engendered for their holy man showed in their wild eyes. Sheikh Farho watched his congregation and found it difficult to understand how easily and quickly hearts could be turned from love and respect to hate; worse still, this hate was instigated by only a handful of the more militant in his flock, who now urged the crowd on. It had taken some years for his people to learn to respect him, but in a moment, that respect had vanished.

The first line of the rioters reached the steps of the pulpit and were about to grab Farho, when suddenly, a tremendous roar sent an earth-shattering rumble across the iron roof of the mosque and the terror of Allah through the mob. Silence fell amongst the agitated crowd, and looks of uncertainty came over them. Farho looked up to the heavens and whispered, "Daniel," and then he took advantage of the sudden quiet.

"My people, I ask you not to blemish the very place where we worship Allah; make room for me, stand aside, and let me go out into the courtyard." Farho walked down the few steps of the pulpit and headed out towards the large courtyard as the apprehensive mob stepped aside to let him through.

With subsiding fear of the loud thunder they'd heard only moments ago, the fanatics amongst them in the courtyard called out, "He comes! Get stones ready for the blasphemer."

The holy man again saw the hatred being regenerated by a mere handful. How easily the many good could be swayed by the bad few.

Sheikh Farho walked backwards away from the pushing crowd and found himself against a brick wall; he tried to hide his fear and face his accusers. A big man came forward out of the rowdy crowd, and Farho, on recognising him, regained some of his courage. The man reached out his arms, grabbed Farho's shoulders, and pulled him towards him. He kissed the holy man on both cheeks and slowly turned to the crowd. Tomas Adofo raised his hands, and they, recognising their doctor, quieted down to listen.

"Today I am ashamed to be one of you—ashamed to be a Muslim, a member of a people with minds that are shut like steel traps. Can you not concede that it is possible for Allah to send us another messenger? I know that Sheikh Farho speaks the truth, for I too have seen this prophet; I will stand by Farho's side, and if you still have it in you to shed blood on this day, then shed mine too."

The crowd was confused. Their anger started to subside, but one of the fanatics picked up a dish-shaped river stone from the garden and, holding it firmly in his large right hand, stepped out in front and screamed, "By your words, you are ashamed to be a Muslim, and by your words, you have blasphemed, and by our law, you have condemned yourselves to death.

Today you die, and tomorrow we will line up to piss on your graves." He laughed loudly, drew his arm back, and threw the stone with all his might at the men in front of him; the stone missed Farho's head, striking the wall with such force that sparks flew in all directions. The stone ricocheted back faster than a bullet and hit the instigator on the forehead, splitting his head almost in two.

The man stood in the throwing position for some moments before his body, by some unseen force, turned slowly, faced the crowd, and collapsed onto the ground. The people closest to him yelled in terror at the gruesome sight in front of them.

A shocked Doctor Adofo apprehensively made his way to the man on the ground and was amazed at the damage he had sustained. The top of his skull looked as if it had been sliced open by a machete. Tomas stood up and, with his head hanging low, pronounced him dead.

The many who had seen what had occurred spread the news throughout the frenzied flock, and in a short time, the murmur coming from them subsided from one of anger to one of fear. Their uneasiness grew to terror when an eerie fog formed around them, and they were engulfed so tightly that they felt as if they had been wrapped in a blanket. A voice came from within the fog: "Why do you want to kill the two men I have instructed to teach you the amendments that must be made to your Koran if the human race is to survive? Listen to my holy men, and follow their instructions to spread the new way to your brethren all over this world."

The voice died down to a distant whisper as it faded along with the mist.

The hush of the crowd felt more intimidating to the two men facing them than when the people had been screaming. The doctor and the mufti stood frozen with fear at the sight of the many eyes that looked piercingly at them; a gentle wisp of air whispered in Tomas's ear, and a smile came to his face as his confidence returned to him. He knew that they were not alone.

"My people, you have just witnessed first-hand the power of Daniel. He has come to us not to denigrate our mighty Muhammad but to enhance—to continue on—his training and to correct the human mistakes that have been made in our interpretation of his teachings." The doctor's words flowed freely; the voice was his, but the words were not.

"Muhammad was a prophet sent to us by our Creator hundreds of years ago, and now we only have the Koran to remember his words. Those words were spoken many hundreds of years ago, and the world that

Muhammad existed in has changed much. Are we so naive that we cannot accept that if Allah sent us Muhammad, perhaps he would send us another prophet to change our way to a more modern path that we must take? All religions have some merit and, in most cases, have some common aspects of our teachings and beliefs. The Christian Bible and our own Koran have many similarities, and our two beliefs are the main religions in this world, yet we have a hate for each other that should not be part of our teaching. This hate must end. The prophet, Daniel, is here to guide all religions towards a path that will unite them into one so that all mankind will know and adore the same Creator of all the heavens."

The people were too engrossed in the events taking place to notice that darkness had overtaken them. "Let us venture inside, and let us all rejoice at being alive at a time when a new messenger has come to us right here in our new country," Tomas shouted with confidence.

Sheikh Farho switched on the lights to enable the people to silently enter their holy place of worship. The members of the congregation were mesmerised by the holy man and the doctor as they told them of Daniel. Their interest and curiosity grew, and they began asking many questions. Sometimes they found the answers hard to understand, too far removed from their old teachings. They debated for many hours, and by the end of the night, they were in agreement to spread the words of that day not only to all their family and friends in Australia but also to all their relatives in the many respective countries of their origin.

The people of the nation flocked to hear the clerics from the different denominations. People now perceived these elite few as blessed men who had been selected to preach the word of Daniel. The churches, mosques, or temples—wherever these men conducted meetings—were always overflowing. In the few weeks that followed Daniel's first conference with the clerics, hundreds of thousands of people heard of Daniel, his teachings, and the miracles he had performed.

Witnesses to these miracles, whether live or on television, did not have to rely on faith; this messenger was there in their time of history, sent to them by the natural Creator of the universe. Daniel gave them proof that a great energy existed that was everywhere and in everything, including their own bodies and senses. The idea of the planet they lived on being their everlasting abode and of the regeneration of their decaying bodies into cells of other living things that were forever bound to be part of Earth made more sense to the disbelievers of the old religions. This new concept of divine belief started to spread worldwide, and most media in the Western world wrote and talked about or televised little else.

Cardinal Bradley was now back in the Holy City, holding court with the pope and the other cardinals. He tried to convince them that if they were to get the upper hand for the benefit of the Catholic Church, they would have to act quickly. They would need to hop on the bandwagon and accept that Jesus had been a prophet sent by the Creator. The Creator had sent him to Earth to change the direction mankind had taken from one of sin to one of loving thy neighbour. The cardinal sarcastically pointed out, "Is this not what Daniel is also teaching? You need to acknowledge that when humans went astray again, the Creator sent other prophets, such as Muhammad, to the world to help direct us in the way we were meant to be heading. After all, isn't Daniel here to follow in the footsteps of all the prophets sent before him to ensure we are put back on track? Are we not all human, subject to making mistakes? Can we not accept or contemplate that it is possible that we made an error in our interpretation or in the translation of our Bible? And likewise, the Islamic religion could have also made mistakes with their Koran."

The Catholic Church had the biggest following of all the Christian religions, and if it wanted to maintain this status, he insisted, it had to be proactive in the amalgamation of the different Christian denominations and the many other creeds.

Most of the cardinals agreed to consider all that Cardinal Bradley had put forward. He had become known as the murderer who had been saved by Prophet Daniel so that he could deliver his message to the leaders of the biggest and richest religion in the world. The pope and some of the older hard-line cardinals had their doubts.

John B. Rose's term of office had now ended, and Chuck Foreman became the American president; Daniel was a little perplexed about the power this man was inheriting. The outgoing president had published his autobiography, which included his meetings with Daniel and Daniel's mission on Earth. The book was by far the best seller ever published in the USA.

Over the next few days, there were many surprises for most of the people who had met Daniel. He made contact with many of them, appearing to some in their dreams or in the shimmering sunrays that shone in the day as a mirage in the Middle East. The many leaders and politicians worldwide who had been involved with him were asked to follow John B. Rose's autobiography and start spreading his teachings amongst their people. Daniel had a large army of disciples at the ready.

At the warehouse, Peter watched his friend sitting on the couch, staring into space, immersed deep in his own thoughts

"Daniel, you seem preoccupied. Is there any problem you may want to run past me?" asked Peter.

Daniel half-heartedly smiled. "I don't think it will be long before our location is found."

"What if this place is discovered? What can happen?" Peter was confused as to the reason a man with the power of Daniel would be so concerned.

"There are a few reasons why I am afraid, Peter. We would never have a moment of peace with the multitude that would descend on us, and there is their safety to consider as well as ours. But of a greater concern is that, whether we like it or not, we undoubtedly have enemies—enemies such as religious fanatics, the drug cartels, and even people we may have considered as friends."

The heavy grey snow cascaded down to make the tough Moscow life even harder for the eight and a half million people living there. Dirty, low-hanging clouds covered the fortified triangular walls of the Kremlin in the centre of the city. A blanket of snow lay over the entire area, and somewhere on the outside of the eastern wall, underneath the white mess, lay the famous Red Square. There the seat of the Russian government was run in the many government buildings within those walls.

These buildings could not compete for beauty against the magnificent multicoloured domes of Saint Basil's Cathedral, which was the centre of the Russian Orthodox Church, or the majesty of the Great Kremlin Palace. Within the walls of the main chamber of the largest government building, the tall, greying, big-framed Russian president stood before the

Federal Assembly, which consisted of two chamber bodies: the state lower chamber, which had 450 members who were elected by popular vote, and the upper chamber, which had 178 seats.

He thanked the head of the Russian Orthodox Church, who was the religious patriarch of Moscow and all of Russia, for opening this important joint meeting of both chambers. Boris Zabloski looked across to the other guests representing the many religions in Russia.

"Thirty-five years ago, we passed a law allowing the freedom of religious beliefs, but for eighty years prior to that, we discouraged religion. Now, as I look down, I am proud to welcome all the leaders of our varied religious groups, from the Russian Orthodox Church and the many other Christian denominations to the followers of Islam, Buddhism, and Judaism, just to name a few. I thank you for coming to a meeting that will change the beliefs of all your teachings as well as the religious attitude of the three hundred–plus people's representatives who could make it here today. Unfortunately, on this miserable morning, our planes are grounded, so there is very good reason why only half of the people's representatives are here." Boris took a sip from his glass, and the clear vodka immediately warmed his body and gave him more confidence to continue.

"No doubt you have all heard about this new prophet who has been the topic of world news recently; this prophet claims that he has been instructed by the Creator of the universe to change the way our world is heading. What is facing us is the most serious matter that has ever come before all mankind."

The whole assembly was engrossed with this statement, and the clerics especially were shocked that the president was not only bringing up this prophet in discussion at this prestigious place but also giving this rumour credence.

"What we are facing is a worse scenario than that which faced us during the two world wars—combined. These wars devastated our land and most of the world, but over time, we got over them and got on with our lives. Let me tell you that what is confronting us now is the utter destruction of the whole planet."

Boris took another sip of his vodka. "What I am about to tell you is easy to say, but convincing you will be another matter." The president had everyone's complete attention. "The rumours about the prophet have led most of you to suspect another plot being hatched by the Western world. Let me tell you, you are completely wrong. The fact of the matter is that

I have met Daniel, this prophet, and this is not a Western ploy; he exists." He looked down on the listeners, and the absolute silence intimidated him.

"Most of the heads of this world have met Daniel and have accepted him to lead us through this crisis; he is on a mission to save us. Accept that there is a messenger from God amongst us." The huge man stressed these words as only he could.

"Let us not react in the same way the ignorant people of the world of Jesus's time did; let us react as people of knowledge and accept that throughout history, most of the people of this world have been expecting some message or messenger from God. Well, my friends, that time is now. He has come, the message has been sent, and we must listen."

A clap of thunder interrupted him, and Boris looked up and smiled broadly. "Go to the windows, and look up into the heavens; you will be given a sign of the power of Daniel, for he wants you to believe your eyes, not just your hearts, that he does indeed exist."

With shaking hands, Boris pointed to the windows as the gathered people's representatives, like little children, eagerly did as they were told. The heavy snow falling made it difficult to see more than a few metres out the windows. Instantly, as if someone had turned off a switch, the snow stopped, and they could see the ugly grey clouds hovering low in the sky.

As they watched, a straight, thin blue line appeared in the dense clouds. The line grew wider until it looked as if a river flowed through the heavens. The clouds had split in two, and they were travelling in two different directions. Half went westward, while the others headed eastward, until both sides vanished out of the sight of the people of Moscow.

Within the next two to three hours, more of the people's representatives were heading for the joint meeting of the two chambers.

The unusually beautiful day had a magical appearance in its composition, and it befit the president's speech. Boris now had almost a full house as he launched into the reason for this meeting: combining all the religions of this once-great nation into one belief.

Colonial Antonio Vargas had been promoted to general, and he was proving a great asset to the Colombian president, Garcia. The president gave the general and his rebel force a special commission to take control of the cocaine industry in Colombia.

The neighbouring countries of Peru and Ecuador, in consultation with President Garcia, had requested that General Vargas be appointed in the unification of the drug industries in their countries with that of Colombia. This would ensure that they reaped the opportunities and benefits of legally supplying the drugs, mainly to the Western world, which had now legalised their use by the addicted under strict government supervision.

Antonio Vargas had also received a message from Daniel for him and his many men to start spreading his teachings throughout Colombia and the adjoining South American countries.

Shopkeepers and their staffs in Rio de Janeiro had premonitions and started confirming their encounters with the prophet.

On the other side of the world, a small black man sipped a cup of tea and ate his lunch as he sat in his office, watching a closed-circuit television monitor. He suddenly heard a knock, and the door opened. The massive frame of a man in a green uniform entered, making him jump to his feet. Bowing humbly, he extended his small right hand, which disappeared in the grasp of a gigantic black hand.

"General Zarin, welcome to our hospital." Dr. Banda looked up at the uniformed man.

General Zarin looked across to the monitor and, with an amazed look on his face, pointed to it as he sat on the vacant chair next to the doctor. "Is that Dadi? He is still alive?"

On the small monitor, they watched a naked man with protruding ribs crawling on all fours in a large enclosure. His large companion, a huge silverback gorilla, was tearing bamboo shoots that lay all around him, and they watched the man sneak up behind the animal and grab a couple of the bamboo sticks. He made a hasty retreat as the ape roared and made a lazy attempt at chasing him away from its food.

The president turned to more-serious matters. "I wonder why our friend Daniel wanted us to meet here."

As if in answer, the small screen on the doctor's desk flickered, and they both looked across to see the images in the gorilla's pen turning fuzzy and being replaced by a man in a white suit.

"Ah, my friends from Zimbabwe, good to see that you are both well, and it is also good to see that Dadi is still in hell." Daniel seemed elated with Dadi's pain. "It has been over eight months since I met you both, and you may recall two things from that meeting: one, many unusual and unexplained events occurred, and two, I said to you that I would contact you sometime in the future for your help."

Dr. Banda rolled his eyes to the ceiling and gasped out loud. "How could we ever forget? My goodness, I think about what happened on that day every second of my life."

Zarin was more direct. "We know what happened, so hopefully you have contacted us to explain how it happened so that I can stop trying to make sense of the whole thing."

The eyes of the two men were fixed on the screen, watching the image of Daniel; it took them a few seconds to realise that the image was now life-size and had started to move around the room. The amazed pair stood up and stepped back, knocking their chairs over. Daniel laughed and quickly assured them that what they were seeing was nothing more than his image and that they could interact just as if he were really there. The confused pair just nodded in agreement and listened intently to what Daniel had to say.

"I have a story to tell you. With what you have already witnessed, I envisage it will not be too hard to convince you of the reality of it all and to make you trust me. Trust is something I need from you both, so please have an open mind. The fate of our entire planet lies in the hands of people such as you."

For the next hour, Daniel reiterated, as he had done many times before, nature's plan for Earth and the reason why he urgently needed all the help he could muster from as many people as possible. Daniel concluded by asking the two Zimbabweans to recruit the soldiers who had witnessed his miracle with the lions to spread the words of the new prophet amongst their people.

The doctor had a question he needed answered before Daniel left them again.

"The big room that you sealed with all Dadi's friends and relatives—can we now open it? We could use some more room for our patients."

Daniel began, "That room is a tomb, and it would take—"

But before he could finish, a loud whirring noise drowned out his voice, and someone frantically screamed out his name. "Daniel, Daniel, Dan—"

The image and the sounds started to fade intermittently and then disappeared.

CHAPTER 13

Peter vigorously shook Daniel, who was sitting on the couch in a deep stupor. "Daniel! Daniel, come out of it. Come on—come back to us," Peter screamed, frantically trying to be heard above the deafening noise coming from above the warehouse. Even through the dense curtains, they could see flashing blue lights in the starless night, intermittently brightening the already-well-lit interior of the warehouse.

"What's happening?" Daniel, confused, called out as his senses came back from a vision to reality.

The sight of Peter and Caris panicking in front of him and the overbearing noise made Daniel jump to his feet.

Peter screamed at him, "Daniel, we are surrounded by dozens of police and military vehicles! I have no idea what is happening."

"What they are after is quite obvious." Daniel sighed. "I guess the fear of the unknown has panicked someone in high places into taking action against me."

Caris grabbed Daniel and hugged him tightly. "Well, can't you just disappear or something? Go—just go."

"No, Caris, I have to find out who is behind all this and, more importantly, why. Clearly even the prime minister herself doesn't know about this operation, or Paula would have warned us." Daniel conversed with Caris philosophically as he made his way to the security room.

David called out, "I can't get hold of Mum! They won't put me through to her; they always put me through to her, but this time, they won't."

"It's okay, David; they probably have taken over our telephone lines or something. Don't worry about it," Daniel consoled him.

They heard the noise from above distancing itself away from the warehouse, and an immense light flooded the area around the warehouse.

The security cameras positioned around the roof revealed the situation: a twin-engine tandem-rotor Chinook helicopter, which was designed to transport cargo and troops during the day or night, had dropped off men, and they had taken positions at various points on the roof. The chopper was now hovering above its quarry, and a search light from beneath it exposed the whole area. Police cars and military vehicles had taken over the entire main road at the front, and the small laneway at the rear had been blocked.

A man dressed in plain clothes with a bullhorn up to his mouth started to call out. "Attention! Attention, occupants of the warehouse! For your own safety, please pay attention to what I have to say." The voice, which had a distinctive American twang, paused slightly before it gave out further demands. "We want everyone in there to come out with their hands clasped together and on top of their heads; start coming out now." The voice hesitated for a moment and then, in an almost pleading tone, restated, "Please start coming out now."

Caris embraced Daniel and whispered, "I have seen you wipe out many men who threatened you. Why can't you do the same with this lot?"

"No, Caris, I can't do that. The people out there are a lot different from the others; these people are doing a job they believe in. They are following orders, which they think is of national importance. You see, Caris, to them, I am the villain in this scenario, and you wouldn't want me to harm somebody following orders that they consciously believe in, would you?"

She looked into his eyes and nodded in dejected agreement.

Peter's voice quivered. "Look, I know your capabilities, but there are an awful lot of well-armed men out there, including what looks like a crack army unit." Peter was getting frantic again. "Why not let me go out there, and I'll talk to them? That would probably be better than you going out there. Let me find out what they want."

"Peter, I appreciate your concern far more than you will ever know, my friend, but I need to find out first-hand what is happening." Daniel was adamant and headed for the door as he indicated to the others to get back. "Peter, I am having trouble fully understanding the reasons for this exaggerated operation of theirs. My mind is gathering that they have been ordered to capture me alive and take me back to base." Daniel was concentrating as he talked. "There are agents out there from the Australian Security and Intelligence Organisation, and they don't have any idea why they have been given the order to arrest me. Weird. They are being led by an American—a CIA agent, to be exact. I have to go along with it until

I get to the bottom—or should I say the top—of the whole thing. Now, please, Peter, get back with the others; I will see you soon."

He opened the door slowly and stepped out into the well-lit street.

"Put your hands on your head; do it now." The gruff instruction came through the bullhorn from the man across the road.

Daniel ignored the order and walked directly towards the man giving the instructions.

Another frantic order came from the bullhorn: "Get him!"

A dozen burly soldiers ran at Daniel, but when they were almost on him, some unseen force repelled them and threw them onto the road. Daniel was now face-to-face with the amazed American holding the bullhorn. The police officers had their guns drawn and were shakily pointing them at Daniel.

"Gerald Waite, how about telling them to put their guns down? Your orders are to take me alive," Daniel calmly suggested.

"Who—or what—the fuck are you?" the American said.

The American pointed to two plain-clothes men standing on the other side of him. "You two ASIO agents," he stuttered, "put cuffs on him."

"I don't recommend that they even try," Daniel threatened.

Gerald remembered what had happened to the soldiers and stood the two men down. He also indicated to the police to lower their guns.

"Look, I don't know who or what you are." The man was clearly intimidated. "All I know is that I have my orders, and I have to take you in."

"And that would be to the army base at Puckapunyal?" Daniel commented.

"Yeah, good guess," the impressed man answered.

"No guess, CIA Agent Waite. Your instructions are to take me there, and you have no idea why or what for." Daniel was connecting with this man. "But I do understand that you must obey orders."

The amazed agent looked at him in wonder. "How do you know all that?"

"Never mind, my American friend. Time is a wasting; let's go meet your superior and find out what is happening here," Daniel said impatiently.

Puckapunyal Army Base was approximately a three-hour drive by road from the warehouse, but in the helicopter, flying directly overland, they were landing within thirty minutes of boarding. Agent Waite and his men led Daniel towards a large building with a contingent of armed personnel outside its doors. They motioned for the group to come forward, and on entering, they were led towards a small steel room in one of the corners. Daniel deduced that all the personnel around him were following orders and had no knowledge of the reasons behind their instructions. Although wary of the solidly constructed container, he followed Waite inside. They looked around at the empty room and at each other, realising they were each as confused as the other.

On the inside, the container was reinforced with steel ribs; it had been built to take massive amounts of pressure. "Definitely wasn't built for comfort," the CIA agent muttered as he waited impatiently for further orders.

A young uniformed private from the Australian regular army came to the door and, standing at attention, yelled out his orders. "Sir, General's orders, sir. The prisoner is to stay here, sir; General Pollard would like to see you, if you could please follow me, sir."

Waite took a step towards the exit; he hesitated and turned to face Daniel again. "I have a feeling that you could leave here anytime you want, but you have chosen to stay. I'll see you soon, Daniel—I hope." The despondent CIA agent gave a half-hearted wave to Daniel, who walked out of the small room and followed the private and the two ASIO agents towards the stairs leading to the offices above. They had only gone a few paces, when the steel door of the small container slammed shut behind them, and they immediately heard the sound of rushing air.

The CIA agent did not like what he saw. Why they would seal off this prison tighter than a sardine can was beyond him. The three men walked up two levels of steel stairs to an area where several soldiers were going about their various duties. A number of Australian army personnel as well as a few Americans, dressed in civilian clothing, were watching closed-circuit television monitors. Seeing Waite approaching, one of the soldiers entered the office of a uniformed man. "General, sir, everything is in working order. CIA Agent Waite is here, sir."

"Just keep monitoring that pump." The general stressed his orders further by pointing his finger and thumb in a cocked-gun position at him.

The craggy-faced General Pollard, in his fatigues and a black beret, saluted and congratulated Waite for a job well done and gestured for the CIA agent to sit in the chair next to him.

On the monitor, Gerald could see Daniel floating off the floor in his prison. He had an oxygen mask, which had obviously fallen from the ceiling, over his face, and Gerald could tell he seemed confused.

"General, what's happening here? That room is a vacuum. Who is this guy?" he asked in a concerned and earnest tone.

"Agent Waite, to be honest, I don't have any idea why we have taken him prisoner; I was hoping you could enlighten me, but it sounds like you are being fed bullshit and kept in the dark too. There is so much secrecy surrounding all this." The general was genuinely baffled as he opened a sealed envelope and pulled out a manila folder, which he opened on the desk in front of him, and he started perusing its contents.

He removed his black beret and ran his left hand over his clean-shaven head as he concentrated. Looking inside the large envelope, he found a key, and then he left the room and went out to the hallway. He found a small steel door on the wall, and using the key, he opened it and immediately pressed a green button and then shut the door again.

General Pollard, back in his office, whispered to Gerald Waite, "Whoever is giving these orders is fucked in the head." He was somewhat surprised that he didn't get any reaction from the man sitting next to him. "Don't you think this is odd?"

"General, whoever is giving the orders isn't fucked in the head—far from it." The CIA agent now seemed to have a better grasp of the events occurring. This guy we are looking at is not normal. I saw a dozen soldiers charge him, and they were dispatched without him raising a finger. And one more thing: he knew my name—my full name. It was as if he was reading our minds."

"Who the fuck is he?" the general stressed.

"I think he is that prophet on the news." Gerald was adamant. "They are doing to him what they did to Jesus."

"Are you really being serious here, or have you gone bananas too?" General Pollard retorted.

"No! For God's sake, General, just think for a moment. Why all this secrecy with the finer details of this mission?" Waite's mind was racing. "They don't want him to read our thoughts to find out who is behind all this. Look at the room he is in—maybe they are worried that he could vanish right before our eyes and walk out of it. He must use the elements around him or something like that—doesn't that make sense to you?"

Agent Waite didn't bother to wait for the general's reply. "Fuck it all. I'm too tired. I'm going to bed—good night."

Midmorning the next day, the irate Australian prime minister sat in her office, talking to her foreign affairs minister. He could only give a limited amount of information on the reason the American CIA—working in conjunction with ASIO, Australian army personnel, and Melbourne police—had captured Daniel Leeder.

"Paula, all I know is that the CIA got in touch with ASIO, who in turn contacted my department about a man they wanted to extradite back to the US for questioning," the minister explained. "We checked this fellow out, and the only thing that came up under the name Daniel Leeder was a death certificate. Daniel Leeder was a wealthy industrialist who died about twenty years ago, so naturally, we assumed this guy was impersonating a dead Australian citizen and had illegally entered our shores to escape the CIA. As far as we were concerned, they were welcome to bad rubbish." He began to show some concern when he noticed a tear trickling down Paula's cheek.

"You know this man?" he cautiously asked.

"That bad rubbish that you are referring to is the greatest person who has ever been put on this earth, and believe me, our world needs him badly."

The Australian prime minister wasn't mincing words. "Find out who has him, where he is being held, and why they took him away in the first place, and arrange his release immediately. I will take full responsibility for him."

By late afternoon of the same day, a nervous General Pollard, with his beret in his hands, sat in Parliament House, waiting outside the prime minister's office. The foreign affairs minister's request that he attend an urgent conference with the leader of the country could only be for one reason: the man in the white suit.

"Sorry to keep you waiting, General, but running a country is not an easy matter." The small woman extended her arms and shook hands with the sweating man in the fatigue uniform. She gestured for him to sit in one of the leather chairs away from her desk; Paula sat across from him and sternly looked him in the eyes. "General Pollard, where is Daniel Leeder?"

"Mrs. Prime Minister, I wish I knew; last night, he was back at my base in a type of cargo container the Americans brought with them. The room was completely sealed, a bit like an astronaut-training module that they use at NASA. They had me personally anaesthetising him every two hours." The general appeared genuinely worried.

"When was the last time you saw him?" Paula asked.

The general leaned forward as far as he could stretch his sitting body. "Midmorning, I went to bed for a nap, and in that time, the CIA agent and the ASIO guys took complete control of the facility. In the short time I was absent, they took him, along with the container he was in; I have no idea where." The man pursed his lips and said, "Madam Prime Minister, you obviously know this man. Would you be able to enlighten me as to what is going on?"

"General Pollard, I do know a lot about Daniel, but that is not what is important right now. We need to find out where he is."

The general looked across at Paula and inhaled loudly before he uttered what he surmised. "My feeling is that he is on his way to the United States."

"Well, if the CIA is involved, the person ultimately responsible would be the president himself," Paula concluded. The general closed the door on his way out, and immediately, Paula picked up the phone and pressed a button.

"Get me John B. Rose on his private line straight away." Paula listened for a moment and then angrily retorted, "I know it's the middle of the night there! Just get him—now!" she screamed as she slammed the phone down.

The door to the steel container opened, and two men wearing gas masks entered; Gerald Waite rushed to the side of the man lying unconscious on the floor and checked his oxygen mask. The other smaller man, who was wearing a white smock, looked down on them. He put his attaché case on the floor next to Daniel and took out a large syringe. "This guy has had enough chloroform to kill ten elephants, and he's still alive." He was surprised at the condition of the clothes the man wore. "There is not one wrinkle or one speck of dirt on this guy's clothes, and you told me that he has been in this cage for over twenty-four hours—all the way from Australia," the observant doctor uttered. He pushed up the right sleeve of Daniel's jacket, found an appropriate vein, and proceeded to insert the syringe into it. To his frustration, the needle would not touch the skin of the unconscious man. He grabbed the syringe in both hands, and using all the strength he could muster, he still could not force the needle into the arm. "What the fuck have we got here?" the astonished doctor exclaimed. "I'm getting out of here, and I advise you to do the same." He made a hasty retreat to the exit and gave an order to the three soldiers outside the door. "Do what you have to do in there, and lock this fucking door behind you—fast."

Agent Waite walked up a short staircase and into a dimmed room, and on seeing the many-manned closed-circuit monitors, he thought, *Here we go again.*

"Over here, Waite." A loud voice came out of the dimness, a voice he recognised immediately. "Come on—take a load off, and tell us what you know about this guy." The loud-voiced man gestured from the door of a small office. Gerald walked over to him, and the man pointed to a screen inside the room, showing the motionless body of Daniel floating in midair. Daniel had an oxygen mask covering his face; a long hose attached to it coiled its way up through the ceiling. The balding man with a grey ponytail down the back of his neck had always looked ridiculous to Gerald Waite. He was close enough to sixty, but even Gerald had to admit that he looked well for his age.

"Come on, Waite—what have you discovered about him?" he reiterated as he closed the door after Gerald entered.

"I think he is human." Gerald mused for a moment and murmured, "Not being able to get a blood sample—now that's what has me intrigued."

"You're not on your own there, I can tell you," the ponytailed man said loudly. "I was watching from up here."

"It's as if there is something protecting him from harm," Gerald said, adding to the intrigue already surrounding the prisoner. "I have a feeling deep inside me that that man"—he pointed to the screen—"is very special." Agent Waite turned to his colleague and commented, "For them to put Chief Agent Howard Green over me makes him special—wouldn't you say, Howie?"

"Well, he can't be too extraordinary; he is still our prisoner." Agent Green reacted with a superior tone in his voice.

Gerald gave him a bewildered look and scoffed at him. "Come on, Howie. For God's sake, man—you know it's totally impossible for anyone or anything to escape from that chamber. Not even air can ooze out of it. The steel barricades on the outside of that steel door are two inches thick. Why this much precaution?"

"Yep, this is a bit beyond me," Howie said almost apologetically. "I don't know what our next move is supposed to be; I'm just gonna do what I was told—wait for my boss to come and take over." Howie gave out a sigh. "I can't get my heart into anything I don't believe in, and I certainly don't believe in ETs, but then again, I've been reading up on this guy—the new messenger who claims to have been sent here by our Creator, whoever or whatever that might be, to accomplish a mission of peace and goodwill to all on Earth."

The two men gasped as the image of the prisoner's face took up the whole screen on the monitor, and the agents heard the image talk. "Howie Green and Agent Waite, talk with me? I don't want you feeling bad over me, Howie. I am doing exactly what you are doing—waiting for your boss."

"How the fuck did he do that? He is comatose! He knows my name, and he knows that the two of us are up here together?" Astonished CIA Agent Green tugged nervously at his ponytail.

Gerald nudged Howie and pointed to the other manned monitors outside his office; they had a different image on their screens. Inside the office, they were seeing the face of Daniel, while the outside monitors were showing a man asleep and floating.

"What do you want to talk about?" a nervous Howie asked.

"I hope you will forgive me for invading your privacy." Daniel smiled.

"How do you mean—invading our privacy?" They both asked the question simultaneously.

"Well, one can't get more invasive than scanning someone's mind—wouldn't you say?" Daniel explained. "Unfortunately, there is not much more that you can help me with. All you know is what they, whoever they are, are willing to let you know, which is not a great deal."

"Sorry, Mr. Leeder," the puzzled Howard Green apologised. "But I have no idea what you are talking about."

"Well, Howie, Gerald here only knew that he had to take me prisoner and bring me here, and he didn't even know that you were in charge of this case. And as for you, Howie, you report directly to the assistant CIA director, whom you are currently waiting for. From there, I would assume that the new CIA director would be overseeing the whole thing."

"You certainly have your facts right," Howie agreed. "Mr. Leeder, what the hell is this all about?"

"While we are all waiting, I am going to tell you two a tale that will astound you."

Daniel felt that these two men were in a position to be able to assist him in many ways. Their knowledge of the security of the world's greatest nation would be a huge asset to his fight against terrorism, so he held nothing back.

The two men stared at the monitor silently with eyes open wide and in sheer contemplation. Assistant Director Terrence William Teasdale interrupted their thoughts. He was tall and lean and not well liked by his subordinates. "How's the prisoner holding out?"

"Look, Mister Assistant Director, why have we taken him prisoner?" Howie started on the wrong foot, but he didn't much care, as he knew that he would no longer be working for the CIA after what he had learned from Daniel. "We need to tell you what we have learned from Daniel. Let me say from the outset, we are making a huge mistake."

The surprised Teasdale quickly sat down next to Gerald and keenly urged the man to continue.

Fifteen minutes later, the baffled assistant director stood up, put his hands on his hips, and walked around the room in a rage. "You are telling me that that man in there reckons he is Jesus Christ, and you both—fully accredited CIA agents with years of experience—believe all the bullshit he told you?" The man was at a loss for words for a few seconds. "You are telling me that I am in charge of a case looking after a madman—is that what you are telling me?"

Howie stood up and looked across at Gerald, who instinctively rose from his seat. "Mr. Teasdale, what we have told you is what we believe is the truth; we are off this case as of right now."

"You can't just walk away, you idiots!" the assistant director called out as the two headed for the door. "You're fired."

"That's okay with us," Howie retorted as they walked out the door.

John B. Rose called an urgent press conference. "Most of you will know that I have written my autobiography, and in this, I mention Prophet Daniel. He is the one who instigated the peace treaty in the Middle East between the Israelis and the Palestinians. It was through him that we were able to legalise illicit drugs, and it was through Daniel that we were able to gather the world together to tackle the AIDS problem. He was largely responsible for the legislation changes encouraging hydrogen cars and the massive reduction in the importation of rain-forest timber. The clearing of the landmines in Mozambique was single-handedly tackled by Daniel to allow the continuation of the AIDS programme. Now this great man has disappeared, and currently, I have only my suspicions as to where he may be. I believe he has been taken prisoner and that he is somewhere here in our country. I have put the question to our CIA director, and he tells me that his department is not involved. Knowing the director personally and trusting him the way I do, I believe that he doesn't know Daniel's whereabouts. But by the same token, we have it on good authority that Daniel was taken prisoner from his home in Australia, and we also understand that the CIA or someone claiming to be from that department was involved. That's why I have good reason to believe that he is somewhere in America." The ex-president started to take questions from the reporters present.

"Why would we do such a thing? Why take him as a prisoner? What law has he broken?"

John was quick to reply. "One bad trait we Americans have is that we are suspicious of anyone or anything that is different. We want to tear it apart to find out why it is different; we just can't accept that this man was sent to us by our Creator."

"Well, it is a bit hard to accept—wouldn't you say, Mr. President?"

"So what you are saying is that we Christians are only pretending to believe in Jesus coming to us from God? It's all show?"

"How long has he been missing?"

"We haven't heard from him for the last four weeks or so."

"I hate to sound morbid, but couldn't he be dead?"

"He's not dead," John replied sharply.

"How can you be so adamant about that question? Isn't it possible?"

"No, it's not possible; believe me, the whole world would know if he was dead."

"Mr. President, you are scaring us; there seems to be more to this Daniel than you are saying."

The president stopped answering questions and took control of the conversation.

"I am here tonight for one reason: I ask whoever has my friend in captivity to listen well to what he is saying to you, and for your sake and the sake of all mankind, set him free."

With that, John B. Rose concluded his press conference.

The following day, a chain reaction began worldwide. World leaders were making State of the Nation announcements. The controversy that followed within each country varied widely.

The cultured Western country officials were outright and told of their meeting with the prophet, Daniel, and how they had no doubt that the universal Creator had sent him. They talked freely about the call to unite all religions, starting with the different Christian denominations and eventually encompassing all the other forms of creeds, including Islam.

The Indonesian president had to be more diplomatic; he announced that he had met Mr. Daniel Leeder and that Daniel had some ideas that warranted looking into.

Most other Islamic countries allowed small articles to appear in their main newspapers, presenting the possibility that Allah had sent a prophet—a brother to Muhammad—to the world. This was a way to create curiosity amongst their people.

Even the American people who were sceptical of their ex-president had to reconsider the possibility of a new prophet when many of their political representatives started to back John B. Rose's story.

The movement to unite the religions had commenced.

John B. Rose roared out his secretary's name from his study at his home, and she came running as quickly as she could. He stood up from behind his clean desk, which had a large, neat pile of letters he had been reading on it.

"This letter—how long has it been here?" he screamed at the distraught woman.

She had never seen this normally gentle man so upset. The middle-aged woman reached out and took the letter from his outstretched hand. She read through it and hesitantly handed it back. "I am so sorry, Mr. President; I assumed it was another of those letters from the many people who have been writing to you about Daniel," she stammered. "That pile of letters has been here maybe a week, sir."

Without further hesitation, John B. Rose picked up the phone and, looking at the letter, started dialling.

Within twenty minutes, a yellow cab pulled up in front of the old, majestic Tudor house, and a huge, well-dressed black man met the two men who emerged from the back. He opened a small steel door to the right side of the larger security gate, which had another two guards manning it. The two visitors were shown to the front door of the mansion, and they stepped inside to a waiting and anxious man. John B. Rose extended his hand and introduced himself to Gerald Waite and Howard Green. He led them into his office and pointed to the chairs in front of his desk. Before they even had a chance to sit down, he blurted out, "Okay, gentlemen, tell me where Daniel is."

"Well, we did know, but the place he was being held in is now empty, so we can't tell you where he is," Gerald answered. "But we do know who has him."

"Who the hell has him?" The anger that came from John's voice frightened the ex-agents.

"Well, Terrence Teasdale, the assistant director of the CIA—he was in charge of Howie here, and that bastard seemed to be in full control of the whole thing."

A worried expression came over the aging face of John B. Rose. "In that case, it would be hard to believe that the director himself would not be involved. I have always trusted that man—just goes to show that you never can tell."

John again picked up the phone and pressed a button on the quick-dial menu. "This is John B. Rose; put me through to the director." He listened for a moment and then said, "Sweetheart, I don't care if he has someone with him. Put me through—now."

He looked at the men in front of him and told them that he was putting the phone on speaker.

"John, what's the urgency?" A slow, drawling voice came from the speaker.

"Bill Baxter, let me start by saying that I have you on speaker and that I have two ex-agents of yours with me."

"Which ex-agents would that be?"

"Gerald Waite and Howard Green."

"Two good men. I didn't know that they had left the agency."

"Bill, I have to say that I am very disappointed; I recommended you to replace Bob Wilson when he retired, because I honestly trusted you and believed you to be the man for the job."

"John, John, what the hell are you talking about?" A distraught voice came over the speaker.

"You were there in the library when right in front of our eyes, he exposed the corrupt representatives and senators, and you were the one who checked out those Swiss bank account numbers, remember? I wanted you as the director because you believed in him, and I have explained the situation we are in to you and about his mission."

"John, of course I believe in Daniel, and yes, I know he is missing."

"Don't play the innocence with me, Bill; these men of yours were partly involved in his kidnapping, and they have implicated Teasdale as being in charge of the operation."

"Oh! My God! Now I am beginning to understand." A voice conveying comprehension of a situation came across the room. "John, I am not saying any more; get here as quick as you can, and bring those men with you." Dial tone sounded as he hung up.

A knock on Bill Baxter's office door brought the CIA director to his feet, and he hurried to open it.

"Come on in, gentlemen." The unsmiling man gestured for them to enter. "I want you to meet someone."

The man sitting on the guest side of the director's desk stood up and looked around. His mouth opened in disbelief as he saw Gerald and Howie with the ex-president.

"What is this?" he demanded of his chief.

"Where is Daniel, and why have you got him?" his superior demanded.

Teasdale realised that it was futile to deny anything; he sat down, and after pondering for a few seconds, he looked up at the director and made one quick comment: "I'm not saying anything."

"You don't have to; I know exactly what is going on here!" the stern director shouted at him. "It's you and the cowboy; the president knew my views on Daniel, so he bypassed me and recruited you to do his bidding. That Christian fanatic is convinced that Daniel is either the devil or an alien, maybe a creature from Mars."

John tried in vain to convey his concerns to Teasdale, who would not have anything to do with the thought that another Jesus had come to Earth. After all, he didn't believe the first Jesus had ever existed. His laughter at the whole situation made them all realise that this man was of no use to their cause.

Although constantly anaesthetised, Daniel's mind was vague, as in a dream, but alert enough to slowly comprehend his situation. He could not feel his body and wondered if he was still contained within it. He had some idea of the location of his new cell from scanning the minds of his overseers; he knew that he was in a warehouse on the outskirts of the capital. Teasdale visited the prison regularly, and from his thoughts, Daniel had deduced that the American president was responsible for the predicament he was in. The chamber was a vacuum, and the limited oxygen being fed to him through the tube coming from the ceiling was barely sufficient to keep him alive—this worried him most of all. What if he died?

Daniel had overestimated his own powers and underestimated his enemies; they knew his weakness and had taken the elements out of his control.

He had been incarcerated for five weeks and had had no news from the outside world; with every hour that passed, he grew more concerned for the programmes he had instigated. Were they still on track, or had everything fallen apart? Did his followers believe that he had abandoned them?

Under an unusually vivid, clear blue sky, three people—two men and one woman—stood on the footpath in front of the White House. The thick coats they were wearing indicated the freezing conditions they were tolerating to get their message across to the people inside. The placards they were displaying had a simple message: "Free Daniel."

Peter, Caris, and Garry Foster wasted little time after their arrival from Australia in starting their protest in front of the world's greatest administration. Inside the White House grounds, a security guard spoke on his mobile phone as he walked adjacent to the three protestors. He joked as he highlighted a change in the number of people out on the path. "Sorry, Miss Gatton. I was wrong about the three; looks like they are being joined by a black American. He just hopped in behind them; maybe we should call out the National Guard." He laughed to himself as he terminated the call.

Miss Gatton turned her phone off as she made her way into the Oval Office for her daily briefing with her boss. "Good morning, Mr. President," she said to the smiling blonde man. "Still no rain or snow out there. Weird, isn't it, sir? Not a cloud in the sky. That's over a month now with no rain reported anywhere on our soil—as a matter of fact, anywhere in the world."

"Who are we to question God's will, Miss Gatton?" He eyes lingered on her beautiful figure. She was unusual, with obvious American Negro features, yet she had natural honey-blonde hair and beautiful hazel eyes.

"There are four protestors out front," she reported, feeling uncomfortable with the way he looked at her. "They are demanding the release of Daniel—guess that's the man John B. talked about on TV last night."

"Put them on the monitor." He pointed to the large flat screen on the wall in front of him. "Get the control room to zoom in on them for me, please, Miss Gatton."

An intrigued private secretary, wondering why the president would show any concern for such a minor matter, rang the control room, and before she could utter a word, she was asked to look out the window.

The president, with his advisers gathered around him, sat in silence as they watched the screen before them. The crowd grew larger by the minute, and within three hours of the start of their protest, the protestors numbered in the thousands. Television news crews were setting up their equipment, and food vendors catered to the crowd. News came that protests were being held in front of government buildings across the country.

Twenty-four hours later, the traffic in Washington had come to a standstill, with people sitting on roads, blocking all major thoroughfares leading to the White House. The same was happening in other major cities. The protest now involved millions of people. Military helicopters were constantly landing and taking off from the lawns of the White House as they shuttled hundreds of armed personnel to protect the president.

Not far away, a lone man more dead than alive floated in a steel tomb; his breathing was intermittent, and the hose attached to the mask over his face held him in one spot. The vague thoughts of the dying man were locked on the woman he loved. He saw her with tears in her eyes as she walked, holding something in her hands; next to her was another familiar face. Then he saw many more people were with her, and they were all calling his name. His mind's eye lifted skywards and soared up ever so high, and its imagination saw the millions of protestors demanding his freedom.

Daniel smiled internally; his message was getting through to the masses. He felt a new spirit emerging within him. The energy of millions of people descended into his mind, and as if an electric shock were going through his body, he started to spasm. The convulsions were so strong that his body stiffened into a solid mass. He ripped the oxygen mask off his face, and defying the lack of gravity, he stood erect with his feet on the floor. The personnel upstairs were perplexed with what they were witnessing; they rang their superior, Teasdale, to advise him of the situation.

"Stop the oxygen, and gas him. If he dies, he dies," he ordered, and they activated the gas pump.

Daniel could hear the invisible gas rushing into his enclosure, and as the room filled, he let out a scream that frightened the men watching him on the monitors. They watched in apprehension, knowing that he should already be asleep or dead. But he defied all human expectation; not only was he not getting any oxygen to breathe, but instead, he was inhaling chloroform gas.

Teasdale, still on the phone, was being kept informed. "Keep the gas going till he drops; don't turn it off until that bastard drops," he ranted.

The cell filled to full capacity, and the watchers could barely make out the form of Daniel in the densely clouded chamber. They watched his form completely vanish; now only the gas remained, along with the gas mask floating in the centre of the cell. A thin column of denser gas congregated around the mask and started to snake its way up the plastic hose. The chloroform gas cylinders on top of the roof of the chamber were suddenly tossed through the air, crashing onto the concrete floor of the warehouse; personnel scattered for their lives as they heard the gas escaping from the cylinders.

Gas started to seep from the broken hoses protruding through the roof of the chamber, merging with the gas from the cylinders, and the mass raised high up to the ceiling of the large building. The thick cloud hovered for a few seconds, and as it expanded, it touched the electric lights suspended from the ceiling. A flash of light ignited the whole mass into a massive fireball.

A small snow cloud appeared and hovered above the crowd, and they became excited at the sight above them. They had only seen the clear blue sky for the last month, and now they were watching with intrigue as the lone cloud started to grow in size. Within only a few minutes, it covered the entire sky above them.

With the sun gone, the overcast day had become dull; the protestors had a warm feeling of being embraced by the covering that hung low over them. Even with the threat of snow appearing imminent, they were not going to abandon their cause. A strange and wonderful event began to take place when the people below became engulfed in a bright glow that surrounded them; they looked up to see a magnificent sight. The vivid, inconspicuous white cloud was now a massive collage of bright rainbow colours that covered the sky as far as their awe-inspired eyes could see. Slowly, all the different colours radiated down on them as if multicoloured sunrays shone down to highlight each person there.

Within minutes, the silent crowd started to disperse; they had enjoyed the greatest experience of their life: a connection with the Creator. The food vendors and the television crews were the last to pack up and drive away, leaving three smiling people looking up into the sky.

The president instructed Miss Gatton to cancel his appointments for the day and to arrange a meeting with his vice president and the former president, John B.

An hour later, the president and his vice president sat across from each other in the Oval Office. They stared uncomfortably at one another, seemingly each waiting for the other to break the silence. After a few excruciating moments, the younger vice president could not endure the tension any further. "Chuck, you summoned me to come see you about something that Miss Gatton said was very urgent."

"I did?" the baffled president said vaguely.

"Yes, sir, you did."

"Yeah, Martin, come to think of it, I think I did. No, I don't just think I did; I'm sure I did, but I honestly can't remember why or what I needed to see you so urgently about."

The vice president, Martin Dade, was at a loss with the vagueness of his president; he, like many of his colleagues, didn't particularly like the president, but he hadn't hesitated in accepting the offer of running for the position of vice president in the recent elections.

Chuck Foreman needed him because Martin's principles were not as radical as his own, and he appealed to the younger voters.

"I think John B. was supposed to attend this meeting too," the president muttered in an indistinct manner.

Almost simultaneously, they both realised that they were not alone in the room.

Martin turned and looked behind him to see a man dressed in a white suit; he turned back to look at the president and saw a terrified face looking past him at the intruder.

"I summoned you both here." A quiet yet commanding voice came from the man.

"Daniel." The cowboy quivered and, slowly raising his voice in a squeaky, surprised tone, yelled, "You're dead! It's impossible, it can't be you." He tried to stand but found his legs too shaky to support him.

"Mr. President, who is this man, and how did he get in here?" the alarmed vice president asked in an insistent manner, but the president, completely fixated on the intruder, ignored him.

"You are the devil himself—I know you are. You are not human, are you, Daniel?" He wanted vindication for his actions.

"I'm calling security," Martin uttered as he headed for the door.

"Stay where you were," Daniel's soft voice commanded. The dark-haired man sat back in his seat.

"Chuck, why are you doing this? You have been told how important my mission is for the welfare of the whole world—so why?"

A thought from the president gave Daniel an answer he hadn't expected but an answer that showed an understanding for the aggression against him.

"Your fanatic belief in your Catholic faith is worse than any fanatical Muslim I have ever met. The pope was behind all this."

The president stood up, and his face became distorted and turned red as he started raving about the true faith. "The Roman Catholic religion is the one and only true religion. We must follow and obey the word of our God through our leader, the pope!"

Daniel became more irate the longer the ranting went on. The unnerved vice president saw the intensity showing on the stranger's face as he glared at the raving man. The tirade was cut short; the president collapsed and slumped back into the rear of his chair, rigid. His mouth gaped, and his seemingly lifeless eyes were open and staring up at the ceiling.

Daniel didn't hesitate in his next step; this man had taken too much precious time from him, and he wasn't going to lose any more. The president's mind was warped, and his religious fanaticism towards the Catholic faith made him a dangerous man in these times of religious tensions.

Dade was too scared to even look around at the man who had come and sat on the seat next to him. "Martin, like it or not, you are going to be the next president of the USA," Daniel told him.

A scared, timid voice whimpered, "Who are you? Is he dead?"

"He is in limbo at the moment; whether he dies or lives is entirely up to you."

"Up to me? Why up to me?"

"I'll explain that later; now I need you to listen to me, and listen well."

Daniel took his time and told the vice president every detail of his mission. He concluded with his imprisonment at the hands of the US president, who, to Daniel, was obviously unstable.

"Wow, that's quite a story," the vice president said. "Obviously, you are the Daniel that John B. Rose talked about on TV last night, and the demonstration out there was all about you." He hesitated and then keenly continued. "Those messages that the heads of state of most of the nations around the world are giving out to their people about a new prophet—that's you."

"It's not just about me; it's about saving the world, even though most people don't realise that."

"What do you want me to do?" the bewildered man asked.

"I want you to become the next president ASAP and to cooperate with John; he is fully committed to my mission, and I can tell that you do believe in me."

"Even if we could get Foreman committed, it would take months to prove he is insane; I can't see how I can become the full-time president in a hurry—unless he is dead."

Martin Dade grimaced as he realised what he had just said, and before he could rescind those words, he knew it was too late for Foreman. The president slumped face down on his desk, dead.

"What did you do? Did you kill him? I didn't mean to say what I said."

"He died of a stroke; he has taken five precious weeks out of my life—five weeks that the world could not spare. He is not taking one more second out of my mission." Daniel sounded cruel, but the new president understood. "My goal must prevail above all else."

Outside in the beautifully decorated hall, John B. Rose hurriedly made his way to the desk of Miss Gatton. "My apologies, Sarah. I have never seen so many people before; I had to walk the last mile or so." The old man puffed and gasped to get his breath. "It was hard work walking against that tide of people."

Miss Gatton poured out a glass of water from a pitcher on her desk, and she stood and handed it to her old boss. "The cowboy hasn't said anything, Mr. President, so I wouldn't worry too much, sir. Go straight in, President Rose—after all, he is expecting you," she said with a smile.

He opened the large mahogany door, and the first thing he saw was the back of the familiar white suit. "Daniel," he called out excitedly. Daniel stood up and walked towards John, and at the same time, he looked at the open door, which closed slowly.

"John, it's good to see you, my friend." The two men embraced in a genuine show of affection for each other.

"That explains the cloudy sky out there," the old man said in delight. "I believe it is going to snow."

Martin stood and greeted John B. Rose just as he noticed the president.

"What's with the cowboy? He seems to be dead," John said in bewilderment.

Daniel held his hands on the ex-president's shoulders and said, "John, you and I need to move on, so briefly, the cowboy is dead. Martin is to be the new president, and you are to help him—to help us with our mission. But right now, we need your limo to take my friends to their hotel, and after that, you and I are going visiting."

Pointing to the body of the dead president, Daniel morbidly said, "Martin, you'd better report his death, and, John, I will meet you out front." With that, the sound of rushing air filled the room, and as the two astonished men watched, Daniel melded into his surroundings. The door opened and shut again.

Garry was arguing with Peter and Caris; he could not understand why they were still waiting outside the front of the White House in the freezing conditions, especially now that it had started to lightly snow.

"They're just waiting for a ride." A comment from someone behind him made Garry turn around to the sight of a familiar man with a big smile. Caris gave out a scream of delight and leapt at Daniel; she cried uncontrollably as she tightened her embrace around him. Peter joined in and hugged the two of them as Garry uncomfortably watched for a moment and then happily decided to make it a foursome.

Peter, with teary eyes, mumbled, "I knew you were okay as soon as I saw that colourful cloud. I knew it had to be you; that's why we waited here, hoping you would come." He released Daniel from his hug. "Where have you been? We have been so worried about you; I even thought the very worst for a while." Peter was asking Daniel questions over the head of Caris, who still hugged him. The sound of a car horn brought them all back to reality, and they looked over to the road to see a long black limousine waiting.

The car took them to their hotel, and they watched the limo drive off with John B. Rose sitting in the back, waving goodbye. Daniel had sent him on another errand. The Grand hotel stood up to its name, from the grandeur of the lobby to the magnificent, large rooms. Caris grabbed Daniel's arm and eagerly pulled him through the hallway and into her room.

Half an hour later, a smiling Caris turned onto her elbow and looked at her man as she ran her fingers up and down his muscular chest.

"You disappearing like that got me really thinking," she said coyly. "I want your baby—no, I need to have your baby."

"It's not the right time," he cruelly replied.

Downtown in the CIA headquarters, Bill Baxter was in his office, having a heated discussion with his deputy, Terrence Teasdale. The overdue confrontation between the two men had only been in progress for a couple of minutes before a knock on the door interrupted them.

"Not now!" the frustrated man called out at the top of his voice.

"Sorry for the interruption, Bill," a smiling John B. Rose said as he opened the door and walked in, followed by three men. Gerald Waite, Howard Green, and the ex-director of the CIA, Bob Wilson, raised their hands in acknowledgement, mainly aimed at the director. Howie closed the door and quietly stood next to the others.

"Mr. President," exclaimed the still-unsmiling Bill Baxter as he came around his desk and extended his hand in greeting to a man he admired greatly. He released the hand of the president, and with his own hand still extended, he greeted his mentor, Bob Wilson, with a handshake and a hug. The director stepped back and looked at Bob in admiration; the last time he had seen him, he'd looked like death warmed over, but now he was looking better than ever.

"Mr. President," he said excitedly as he again turned to John. "This is an unexpected pleasure, sir—twice in one week. Come sit down; Teasdale and I will finish our conversation later."

"There is no reason for the deputy to leave, Bill," the former president suggested, but Teasdale, who certainly didn't want to be in the room, took the cue from his superior and made for the exit. He opened the door and shakily retreated backwards to the rear of the room. Daniel walked in and headed straight for John and his three companions; he greeted Howie and Gerald and smiled at the ex-director and the president before he looked across to the serious face of Bill Baxter.

"Director Baxter, very pleased to meet you in your official capacity as head of the CIA. The last time I saw you, you were assisting Bob Wilson in our little escapade at the White House library." Bill Baxter was impressed at being recognised and remembered by a man he held in awe.

Teasdale was finding it hard to put a sentence together as he pointed his outstretched finger at Daniel. "How … how did you … how did you get here?" he finally uttered.

"I wanted to be the first to tell you that I am no longer your prisoner and that the man you were taking orders from is dead."

"The president is dead?" A distraught gulp came from the deputy.

Bill Baxter looked over at John B. Rose and received a nod from him, confirming the news.

"Bill, Daniel would like you to reinstate these guys." John pointed to Howie and Gerald. "And then they are to be assigned over to him for a special project. They will be leaving for overseas within three days."

"Consider it done," the director quickly replied.

"That's undermining my authority," Teasdale protested.

"What authority?" A raised tone from Bill Baxter told Teasdale that his position as deputy director was over.

John B. Rose stood up and walked over to Bob Wilson, and putting his left arm around his shoulder, he turned to face Baxter. "Bill, we would like Bob to come back to the agency on a special assignment that we would like to explain to both of you later."

"Consider that done too." The director again made a quick decision as he came up for a closer look at Bob. He couldn't get his eyes off his hair; the comb-over that used to be the joke of the whole department no longer existed. Instead, a short crop of hair was growing thickly on his pate, and it appeared to have the shape of a hand, with the fingers running towards the back.

"Mr. Wilson"—the man was showing his respect for his old superior—"I have never seen you look so well in all the years I have known you. The last time I saw you, I thought I would be coming to your funeral, but now you look as fit as a fiddle. How?"

In answer, Bob placed his right hand on his scalp and covered the growing hair; he took the hand from his head, placed it on his chest, and looked at Daniel. No further comment needed to be made; Bill Baxter understood.

Late in the afternoon, four days later, on a warm summer day, five passengers alighted from their private jet and headed out of Rome's airport while the pilot tended to the plane in his charge. The overweight and balding manager of the exclusive Belvedere Hotel rushed out from his office and over to the reception counter to personally take Caris's hand and lead her, followed by the others, to the lift and up to their rooms. Daniel smiled at the nervous woman and winked at her as she looked across to him for help.

Later that evening, not far away from the Belvedere, at the Vatican, the elderly Pope Gregory XVII died in his sleep.

The world press outlets were inundated with news; a few days ago, they'd had the death of the American president, and today they had a new headline with the death of the pontiff.

The pope lay in state in St. Peter's Basilica, and the public was allowed to parade past his coffin for the next three days before his burial. The small number of cardinals who made up the sacred congregation of the papal administration closed a portion of the Vatican, including the doors to the Sistine Chapel, the greatest tourist attraction in Rome. They waited for the majority of their members, who were bishops of dioceses located throughout the world, to arrive.

Within two days, with their numbers complete, the College of Cardinals assumed supreme ecclesiastical authority. They gathered in front of the main altar in the basilica and prayed in unison for the soul of the father of the world's largest religion. They prayed to the rock of the Catholic Church, St. Peter, whose body they believed to be buried under the main altar. Their prayers to St. Peter were for guidance to the College of Cardinals in the conclave who would elect the successor of Pope Gregory XVII.

The second day of prayer had the attendance of the full contingent of 184 cardinals all praying for direction, and the haunting sounds of their never-ending prayers echoed throughout the great basilica. Even over this chatter, the cardinals could hear an unusual noise emanating from under the great altar. They continued praying while taking sly glances at each other as the noise, which sounded like rock sliding on rock, became louder.

The cardinals' attention was drawn to the main altar, and slowly, the humming noise from the prayers stopped as the intrigue of the grinding sound took over.

In the dim natural light filtering down from the leadlight windows, a multicoloured mist shone before the altar, and the sunrays that beamed down played with the swirling, thin cloud. A figure started to take shape in front of them, and the humming noise of the prayers commenced again, slowly and quietly at first and then louder and faster as the figure of the man became more distinct. The wide-eyed, kneeling cardinals crossed themselves several times in between running the rosary beads through their fingers.

A grey-bearded man in a white robe stood in front of the altar, looking down at the cardinals kneeling in front of him. In his left hand, he held a long staff with a cross at the top. A whisper went through the excited congregation: "St. Peter—it's St. Peter."

As they watched in amazement, the image before them changed to a man in an immaculate white suit. This new figure raised its hands and quelled the buzzing coming from the colourful group.

One of the cardinals tried gasping out words that the others around him found hard to understand. He fought to regain his composure. "Daniel, Daniel." His words fumbled out of his puffy mouth as he pointed to the man in front of the altar.

Cardinal Bradley remembered well the man who had visited him in his Melbourne jail cell and who had vanished before his eyes.

"Yes, Cardinal Bradley, I am Daniel," the man who was the centre of attention said in an authoritative voice. "All of you heed well what I have to say. I am the Prophet Daniel, whom you have discussed in depth. I have been sent by the universal Creator to guide you and your followers in this hour of need. The world requires the supreme head of the Catholic Church to be a visionary, a man of open-mindedness, and he must work towards the unification of all religions. I have chosen this man for you, and you will elect him unanimously. You will assemble in your normal private meeting for the election of the new pope, and you will keep your oath in maintaining the voting secret from the general public. There will be no debating my choice, and the elections are to take place tomorrow. I do not have time to waste, so be assured that I will not tolerate those who defy me. If you do, you will end up like the American president or your previous supreme leader. There is a reason for my haste, and I will tell you why we have no time to waste and why we must work together for the good of all in this world."

Daniel began to explain his task, and with this group, he held nothing back.

Daniel concluded, "The universe, or the natural force all around us, is an ever-encompassing energy that is within each one of us and within each living creature, be it animal or plant. This energy is also found in what we humans consider nonliving things, such as the very earth itself. There is a belief that all natural objects and even the universe itself possess a soul, and this belief is called animism. Basically, that is the creed of our new belief."

When Daniel finished, as had happened in the past, it took several minutes before someone broke the silence. One of the cardinals cleared his throat and nervously put up his hand. The tense man with his hand up in the air relaxed once he saw Daniel smile down at him. The big man was having trouble standing.

"Cardinal Bradley, this is certainly a better place to meet than the last one," Daniel joked as the large frame of the red-faced man finally was able to stand.

"You brought young Father Costa back to life, and you told me about your quest. Daniel, I have tried to pass on your words, but they would not believe me." He pointed to the men around him. "They have done nothing but ridicule me."

Daniel's stern voice intimidated the cardinals. "They may have done so in the past, but they will not do so in the future; they will not ridicule their supreme leader. Yes, Cardinal Bradley, you are to become the next pope, and you will take the name of Pope Innocent XIV, for I have searched your soul, and I know that you did not intend to hurt Andrew. I believe in your innocence due to temporary insanity brought on by the pressure you were under from the people here."

Not a murmur came from the religious leaders; they seemed at a complete loss.

"You will follow this man as your pontiff, and your priority will be to start dialogue with the non-Christian religions. The difficulty that faces you with the Muslim world is that there is no real living leader controlling Islam." The thoughts in the cardinals' minds went out to Daniel as they squirmed and shook their heads. They whispered to each other in disgust at the mere thought of the fat man being their new supreme leader, Pope Innocent XIV, the murderer.

"I hear what you are thinking, and though I may sympathise, my mind is set; Bradley will be pope, for I know he believes wholeheartedly in me, and at this time, I need men such as he. You will abide by your laws that state that anyone over the age of eighty cannot vote, so all those of you who are eligible, go now to your rooms, and by morning, I expect an announcement on the election of the new pope."

They rose and walked towards the rooms that surrounded the chapel, which were divided into small living quarters for each of the cardinals. They each had a secretary and a single servant who prepared food within the unit, as the cardinals might not leave their apartments or communicate with anyone from the outside until a pope was elected.

Normally, there could be several ballots taken each day in the Sistine Chapel until one candidate received at least two-thirds of the votes. On this occasion, only one vote had to be taken, and by early the next morning, a single cardinal left the conclave and announced the election of the first Australian pope, Cardinal Bradley, who would assume the name of Pope Innocent XIV.

The red-faced new pope sat on his throne as he and Daniel held a private session. Daniel would send advisers from many parts of the world, including Andrew Costa, to help the new pontiff and the cardinals in their major role as the unifiers of the world's religions.

CHAPTER 14

In the beginning of their summer, a Learjet landing amongst the various Ariana Afghan aircraft that were scattered off the only runway at the Khwaja Rawash Airport caused some excitement throughout the Kabul airport.

Kabul, the ancient capital of Afghanistan, set high in the mountains near the Khyber Pass, on the way to Pakistan, could easily be missed from the air, as it blended into its surrounding mountainous countryside. Two-thirds of its terrain consisted of steep ranges with natural passes, most as high as three thousand metres, winding their way around the peaks.

This was a war-torn country that had only known a relatively new peace. The United Nations with ten thousand troops under their control assisted the current Administration in keeping this often broken peace. The majority of the people resented these forces, but they had to tolerate them to keep the previously ruling Taliban fanatics at bay.

Peter and Caris stayed in Rome to assist the new pope and to arrange for Andrew and others, including world leaders, to come together and plan their programme for the unification of all religions. Daniel made his way to the terrorist centre of the world, Afghanistan. Along with him were Howie, Gerald, and Jamas, whom they picked up from Jordan on their way from Rome.

The CIA agents made their acquaintances with the ex-terrorist as they travelled the relatively short trip from Jordan to Kabul; they were friends by the time they landed at the capital.

Howie and Gerald's task had been to acquaint themselves with the latest information the CIA had on the terrorist front in Afghanistan. They gave details of what they had learned to Daniel and Jamas, and they planned their next move. The whole exercise was simple enough; Daniel wanted to find the unknown terrorist leader.

The CIA had great concerns over a rumour that a new rebel leader had emerged and might have nuclear weapons at his disposal. Death from terrorism was minor when compared with deaths from diseases such as the AIDS virus, but if nuclear weapons got in the wrong hands, the mass destruction that would follow would spell the certain end of the world. A nuclear attack on America or its allies would see retaliation unparalleled in the history of world warfare.

The CIA was adamant that the mountains of Afghanistan were still hiding the leadership of the Muslim terrorists. However, their efforts to find them, even with the technology at their disposal, had failed them.

Howie and Gerald had names of contacts in Kabul, and they had clearance from their head office to deal with these secret agents if they could be found. There was a great fear for these contacts' safety, as they had not been heard from for over two years.

As per usual, Garry was left at the airport to tend to the plane, while the other four men made their way through the airport with Daniel in the lead. The followers found it difficult to understand how, with just a smile from Daniel, the staff at the passport counters waved them through without looking at any papers.

A young man dressed in a dirty caftan gave a wide smile, showing his set of deteriorating blackish teeth, as he hurried to welcome them. "This way, sirs—this way. I have the best taxi in Kabul. Come—come see," he shouted at them in reasonable English as he tried to take the luggage off the travellers. "My name is Dost, and I am best taxi driver in all Kabul; you can ask anybody, and they tell you Dost best taxi driver in all of Afghanistan—you ask anybody."

Dost grabbed the pieces of luggage from his prospective passengers, tied them together with twine, threw the lot over his shoulders, and led the way out of the airport. The men followed the persistent young driver to an old multicoloured van. The colours were mainly made up of rust and dirt, with a smudge of yellow paint showing spasmodically. He gently put the luggage down and struggled to open one of the back doors of the vehicle, and as soon as he succeeded, he took a rag from under the seat and proceeded to wipe the dust off the seats.

Daniel had no objection to being given an unsolicited tour around the struggling city. The poverty was much worse than he had imagined, but he could see the pride and strength on the people's faces. This country was the world's largest producer of opium, and with the legalisation of illicit drugs and the removal of the big money from the industry, all the opium farms were now run by family concerns under the strict control of new government authorities with the aid of the United Nations.

The peacekeeping force assisted the elected government; they patrolled the country, trying to keep some sort of order after all the turmoil it had been through over the last fifty years or so. The countryside was still littered with unexploded bombs and minefields, and many of these soldiers were employed in clearing this menace.

Dost was proud of his city and eager to point out any place of interest. Outwardly, he showed the world he was a happy young man, but Daniel could sense a more sinister and worried person behind the big smile. Even with his powers, Daniel could not read the deep thoughts Dost hid from the world as well as himself.

Two hours later, the taxi drove out to the outskirts of the city. After struggling up a steep incline, it came to a halt at the top of the dirt road. On one side of the narrow laneway was a sloping mountainside that descended into a barren ravine, and on the other side stood an old single-story mud-brick accommodation with many old and run-down houses on either side of it. Curious peasants were outside watching and wondering who had stopped near their homes.

"This my uncle place; he give you good deal. This place best in all Kabul—you ask anybody, and they tell you this best place in all Kabul," he said enthusiastically and proudly.

Dost ushered them into what they assumed was the reception area, but it turned out to be the kitchen. A sweating, fat man sat in a dark corner, leering at them apprehensively. When he saw Dost enter following the four strangers, he gave a sigh of relief and stood up and greeted his nephew.

Once the guests settled into their respective accommodations, they met in Daniel's dingy room; they had ordered lunch from the fat man, and while they hesitantly ate the food, Daniel discussed their next move.

"Howie, Gerald, you two definitely stand out in a crowd here, and as Americans, your safety is a concern; your every move will be watched by Taliban supporters. Jamas is the only one who could mingle with the locals."

Daniel put his arm around Jamas's shoulders and, walking him to the door, assured him, "Do not worry, my friend; you will be okay. Find somewhere to stay, and settle in. I will be with you wherever you are, and when you feel it's safe, track down the people we are looking for and wait for me."

"Daniel, I do not know their language. How will I communicate with them?"

"Of course you can speak Pashtun."

"No, Daniel, I do not."

With a little smile and a wink, Daniel again reassured him, "When you speak, they will understand you, and when they speak, you will understand them." Daniel had confused Jamas even more. "Now go, my friend; the people here will always welcome a Palestinian." Daniel opened the door for him, and the perplexed man hesitated for a few seconds and then reluctantly raised his arm in farewell. He walked out into the street, and Dost immediately ran out of the motel and led him to his taxi.

"Why are you going to all this trouble?" Gerald queried. "Why send Jamas out to search for our agents? Couldn't you use your powers and track them down yourself?"

Daniel looked at Gerald. "Maybe I could scan the minds of millions of people until I find the right person who is thinking of our agents or the whereabouts of the leader of the terrorists." Daniel sounded annoyed. "There are no records whatsoever held by the number-one spy agency in the world on this new terrorist leader, and I am assuming that he is keeping his secret well hidden from most of the people of this city." Daniel felt ashamed of what he was to say next. "I believe that your agents have been discovered and are dead. Jamas will be out there amongst the people, asking questions about them as he tries to track them down, and undoubtedly, news of this will reach the terrorists. Hopefully, they will want to interrogate him, and again, hopefully, they will take him back to their lair."

Gerald was astounded. "You sent Jamas out there as bait? They'll simply kill him!"

"They will not kill him," Daniel assured Gerald.

Howie asked a question he had on his mind: "Why did you want us to come along with you, Daniel? Surely we are going to be of little help to you, if not a hindrance in your search."

"My friends, a deep instinct I have tells me that I must keep doing what I have done in the past—establish a network of people to carry on with the programmes that I start." A saddened look came over Daniel. "It will be people like you who must carry on the fight to save the world.

You two will be the contacts between the terrorist group here, the United States, and the United Nations, while Jamas, with his compatibility with the terrorists, will be the man who will help spread the peace in this land and the surrounding countries."

"Daniel, you sound as if you plan to leave this world," Howie said.

"I do not know what fate has in store for me; I have a feeling that my job is to instigate these programmes, and they will be completed by followers such as you."

Daniel motioned towards the door and said, "But you are right, Gerald; when Dost comes back, we will go out amongst the people."

When the three men stepped out from their door onto the hardened dirt road, Dost immediately greeted them. The taxi driver had lost the big smile he'd had when they had first met him a few hours ago, and his enthusiasm had deserted him. "You want me to take you everywhere you want to go?" he said nervously as he tried to grin.

Howie followed Gerald to the van parked on the other side of the road, and as he opened the back passenger door, it suddenly slipped out of his hand and slammed shut. A confounded Gerald tried the door again, but it would not open.

The car starter clicked over, and the engine roared to life, giving off a cloud of smoke from the exhaust. The two men looked inside the car, but there was nobody in it; they stood watching as the old vehicle placed itself in first gear, and turning its steering wheel towards the steep drop, it accelerated and disappeared over the edge into the ravine.

A frantic Dost ran to the other side of the narrow road and, along with the two CIA agents, watched his van career down towards the bottom of the gorge. The vehicle hit a large boulder on its way down, making it roll over and burst into flames. A massive explosion followed, which sent the blaze back up the incline, knocking the three men off their feet.

Dost lay where he had fallen, crying hysterically, while the other two laboriously rose up off the hard road.

"That wasn't a car exploding after catching fire," a traumatised Howie mumbled. "That was a bomb." He turned towards Daniel, and seeing the concentration on his face, he immediately comprehended what had happened. Howie reached down, grabbed the distraught young taxi driver, and lifted him to his feet. "You mangy bastard!" he shouted at him. "You were going to kill us."

Howie raised his closed-fisted hand and brought it down with all his might at Dost's face, but instead of connecting with the young man's jaw, he found his knuckles cradled in Daniel's hand.

"That won't help!" Daniel exclaimed. "Take him back to the room."

Dost, still too distraught to be interrogated, sat on an old chair in the middle of the room, with Howie and Gerald standing over him. This time, Daniel was able to obtain the full story from the young man's thoughts; the boy's tale ran over and over in his mind.

Daniel translated his thoughts into words for the other two men. "This young man is in a no-win situation; he either kills us, or he and all his family will be killed." Daniel shook his head in disgust. "The terrorists in this region take over young men's and women's lives by helping them to make a living; as in Dost's case, they gave him a taxi and also set up his uncle with this rooming house. They expect him to keep an eye out for any strangers that come through the airport and report to them. He has been trained as a suicide bomber, and that is the condition that he had to accept for the taxi and this house, which support the rest of his family financially. You have to appreciate that in this country, the average annual income is only about two hundred thirty US dollars, and the people have to work very hard just for that meagre wage. So accepting the terrorists' proposal is basically the only way of funding his family's survival, even if it means his own death. The poor beggar has committed himself by swearing to Allah that he would go all the way when called upon to do so, and if he fails to complete his mission, then he is killed, along with the rest of his family."

Daniel walked over to Dost and put his hands upon the young man's shoulders in a show of sympathy for him. He looked over at the two men, and he could see that their anger with Dost had subsided.

"He has been dreading this day, and he prayed very hard for it to never come, but it did when we arrived here. He knew deep down when he first saw us that his time had come, but he put it out of his mind until he was contacted by the terrorists, and in the end, Dost had no choice but to obey their orders to kill us as well as himself."

Howie had a sympathetic look on his face as he gazed down at the sobbing Dost; he knelt down beside him and spoke to him. "I understand why you had to do what you did, but now you need to help us so that we can help you." Howie waited for a reply, but nothing came forth from the boy.

Daniel took a deep breath and continued with more information. "He can't help us; he doesn't know anything of any value about the terrorists or even the name of his only contact. This man makes contact with Dost with instructions whenever they want him to do anything for them. The only thing I can learn from him that might be helpful is a name that he is scared stiff of: Shah. Just the Shah."

Daniel turned and looked deeply at Dost, who immediately stopped his hysterical sobbing and stood up. "Dost, go and gather your family and bring them here to your uncle's place." Daniel pointed to Howie and Gerald. "These two men will protect them; go quickly."

Without a word, the young man ran out of the room, leaving the two CIA agents agog and staring at each other. "He probably has over a hundred relatives. How are we going to protect them?" Howie asked.

"Just do your best. The Afghans are good fighting warriors, and they will no doubt bring arms; organise them. Hopefully, the bait will be taken soon and this whole situation with the terrorists will be over once and for all."

"Walk quicker, walk quicker. Can't you keep up with an old man?" An elderly man in tattered clothing, using a pair of home-made crutches, leapt along on one leg at such a pace that the younger man following had to run to keep up. Jamas felt embarrassed as people watched and laughed at the obvious game the one-legged man was playing with him as he paced himself amongst the mud-brick hovels and through the narrow dirt road.

"It will be dark soon, and I don't walk through these streets in the dark," the old man called out. "It is not safe in the dark here."

Jamas was not happy with the situation, and he didn't trust this man; trying to trace Amin Mullah, one of the contacts he had been given, had proven harder than he'd thought.

He had given up trying for the day and had been making his way to the modest room he had rented, when the one-legged man had approached him. "You are looking for a friend of mine. Why do you look for Amin?"

Jamas had explained that he was a Palestinian and Amin was a friend to his people; he needed to find him urgently, but unfortunately, he seemed to have disappeared. The lame man had taken off in a flash and asked Jamas to tag along if he wanted to see Amin Mullah.

The wiry man stopped in front of one of the houses and waited for the younger man to catch up. He knocked on the door, and it immediately opened to reveal a better-dressed man; the man quickly showed them both into his abode.

"This is Amin," the old man said as he put his hand out for payment. Jamas handed him a few notes, which he quickly shoved into his pocket.

Amin presented a small cup of coffee to Jamas before he even had spoken a word, and he sipped it eagerly as the host motioned for him to sit.

"My one-legged man here tells me you are looking for me. Who are you?"

"My name is Jamas; I have a message from friends who are trying to find you."

"Which friends are looking for me?"

"I would rather tell you privately," a yawning Jamas muttered as he tried to concentrate on his words, which he suddenly found hard to put together. He looked up with squinting eyes at the two men looking down on him, and he vaguely heard something about camels before he lapsed into unconsciousness.

Dawn broke when an uncomfortable and panicky Jamas awoke. The first thing he felt was the stifling heat, and he sensed that his clothes were wet through from perspiration. His struggling made him gasp for air, and he became aware that his hands were tied behind his back and his mouth was covered by strong tape. He was wrapped up in a thin blanket that reeked of a familiar odour, and the way his body was being thrown around made him realise that he was draped over a camel. The beast sauntered along a rough track, and Jamas made a muffled sound as he vainly struggled to free himself. A hand smashing across the blanket and slapping him hard on the head made Jamas conscious of the throbbing headache he had.

The slap was quickly followed by a stern voice, which he recognised as belonging to the man claiming to be Amin Mullah. "One murmur out of you and you will die very quickly."

Jamas could see shadows of people and camels all around him, and he listened to the many conversations of all the people travelling with them. He thought that at least he had one consolation to his current problem: he could still understand them, thanks to Daniel. *Ah! Daniel. Where is Daniel?* He certainly needed him now.

The journey seemed endless, and he wondered how long he had been travelling. His ribs were aching unbearably; he wanted to call out for mercy and was nearly at the point where he didn't care what fate lay before him as long as he was taken off this damned beast of burden. He opened his mouth to scream, but his own voice was drowned out by the loud shouts of the camel drivers as they halted the beasts in their charge.

Before all the noises of the camels and their drivers had time to subside, Jamas, still wrapped in the blanket, was dragged off his ride, lifted up, and quickly carried away. He heard the mob shout at their camels as they restarted their journey, and in moments, the noise from the large group dissipated into complete silence.

Both sides of his body were being smashed against rocks, and it wasn't hard for him to figure out that he was being carted through a long and narrow crevice. Jamas heard the sound of rocks rolling over and grinding against other rocks; he felt his body being hurled through the air, and as he landed heavily on the ground, he heard the sound of the rolling rocks again.

The hot sweat covering him instantly went chilly, and he started to shiver from the cold. Now in complete darkness and still wrapped in the blanket, he realised that he must be underground and that nobody was holding on to him. After a few moments in absolute silence, he rolled over a few times until he was able to shake the blanket from his face. Almost immediately, he could make out that he was in a narrow cave sloping steeply down towards a distant light.

He had just managed to get to his feet, when a shove from behind startled him; Jamas turned around to the darkened entry and saw the shadowy outlines of several men who began shoving him down the slope towards the light. Halfway down, two of the men grabbed him and threw him through the air, and he rolled down the rest of the incline, coming to an abrupt halt at the bottom.

With his hands still tied behind his back, he again struggled to his knees and managed to get to his feet to face several armed men who were pointing their rifles at him. When the others coming down the slope caught up with Jamas, he was completely surrounded by them.

He stared in wonder at how well lit and how large the cave was. He likened it to being in another city within the city of Kabul, and he surmised that they were not too far from the capital. Amin Mullah showed his authority by giving orders to the men around him, who recommenced shoving and dragging the hapless man deeper into the cavern.

They travelled at least another hour through various tunnels that wound downward before they came to a much bigger room, which had been fitted out for comfort. Here Jamas could see wooden furniture, carpets on the floor, and even curtains on some of the walls, giving the false impression that there were windows behind them. Many chairs with gold decoration dotted the large room, and there were women, clad in black from head to toe, sweeping, dusting, and carrying food into smaller caves that probably housed the chieftains of these underground inhabitants.

Constant humming sounds explained the lights that shone brightly from various points on the walls and ceilings—sounds coming from many generators insulated to muffle the noise. Jamas was dragged to a corner of the cave and forcefully pushed backwards against the rough wall. One of the men produced a knife and made a sudden move towards him. The man reached behind the unnerved Jamas and cut the twine that bound his hands. He then put iron clamps around his wrists, and the chains attached to them were fitted through iron rings inserted in the wall above the prisoner's head. Two men pulled the slack in the chain, lifting the prisoner until his toes barely touched the ground; next, they manacled his feet to the cave floor to make Jamas even more miserable. The one man in the room whom Jamas knew came towards him with a grin of contempt on his face, and almost in a whisper, he began to talk to him.

"Hope you are not too uncomfortable as our guest, but things will get a lot worse unless we have your full cooperation." Amin was close to Jamas's face, and the pitch in his voice rose higher. "For the moment, there are several things we already know about you, such as your name, which you have told me is Jamas Galli, and you have told us that you are a Palestinian." He was now screaming. "What we have found out for ourselves is that you are a spy for the Americans and that you are a traitor to your own people! Your greed for the infidels' dollar has made you betray them, and for such a thing, your death will be long and painful."

"No! You are wrong!" Jamas shouted in desperation. "I am not a traitor to my people; I have lived for the Palestinians, and by Allah, I will die for them."

"You lie, and you blaspheme freely!" shouted his accuser as he stepped forward and spat at him. "I am not the man you came to seek. I am not Amin Mullah; that pig died like one, as did all his family. You came to seek him to assist you and the infidels, and just knowing that man alone is proof enough that you are a traitor."

An even louder voice came from the back, and everyone in the room went completely silent and turned to face a tall man majestically covered in a golden robe and wearing a simple black mask covering his face.

"I have heard enough; I do not see why we are wasting our time talking with this man. Ask him a question, and if he doesn't answer it to my satisfaction, you"—he pointed at Jamas's accuser—"will shoot him—firstly in the left leg, and then if he still doesn't answer truthfully, shoot him in the right leg. Keep wounding him until he either dies or answers the question correctly. I would think that the pain would make him answer just so we can put him out of his misery."

The masked man sat on one of the beautifully engraved chairs, when suddenly, two agitated men came running into the room. They profusely pardoned themselves several times before daring to look up at their master for permission to speak. The eyes leering from the hidden face made their leader even more intimidating, but something else had scared these men even more. One of them could not contain his excitement any longer and started trying to stammer out some words. His weathered face frowned stressfully as he finally found his voice. "We saw a strange man outside on top of the mountain." The scared man pointed upward towards the cavern's roof. "All dressed in white in infidels' clothing. He stared at us as if he could see us through the rocks; I shot him several times at very close range."

The masked man became frustrated with the jabbering; he stood up and kicked the man in the crotch. Angrily, he turned to the other man and yelled at him, "If you fools shot someone on top of the mountain, then for the love of Allah, fetch the body and bring it inside the cave. We don't want any of the patrolling helicopters' pilots becoming suspicious of this area."

"No, Your Greatness, what Abdul was trying to say is that we saw the man from our peephole in the cave—the one at the very peak—and we both shot him at point-blank range. Your Greatness, we both shot him several times, but this man didn't die—or at least I don't think he died. He vanished right before our eyes. He was there in front of us one second and gone the next; it was as if he was consumed by the very air around him."

Jamas's spirits lifted on hearing about the man in white, knowing that his friend must be close by. The words that were about to come out of the agitated masked man were interrupted when a slight tremor shook the cavern. The whole mountain vibrated slightly, and a few pieces of rubble fell from the cave roof onto the middle of the room, scattering the people below to the shelter of the side walls.

The tremor ceased, and the rubble also stopped falling from above. A sigh of relief came from the man in the golden robe, who had maintained his position near his golden chair. On hearing another quiet rumble, he looked up to the roof and let out a piercing scream that horrified the others and made them cling to the walls even harder

The roof of the cave was falling; a massive portion of the roof collapsed down to the cavern floor with such violent force that it knocked everyone off his feet. The whole room was instantly covered in thick dust, and for a few horrifying seconds, the only sound they could hear was the crashing of rocks onto the floor. The people could not take breaths of clean air, and all were panic-stricken, as their lungs felt ready to explode.

To the bewilderment of the onlookers, all the dust raised skywards, and in an instant, the air in the cave became clear. The dust gathered like a cloud inside the big cavern, as if waiting for a storm to brew. The masked man looked up from his new seat in the dirt and saw the massive rock wall that surrounded him; he was astonished at how close he had come to death.

Shakily, he stood up to find his chin reached the top of the pile of rocks. He peered around him; at least a third of the floor area was taken up by fallen stones. He saw his people all agog and cowering against the cave walls, too frightened to move. They were looking at the cloud of dust above their heads; it had started to twirl around the cave roof, and some of the debris began to deliberately form into a distinct shape—the shape of a man. They watched the form descend towards their leader and settle behind him.

An opportunity had presented itself to the masked man—an opportunity to enhance his leadership and his bravery in the eyes of his people. Climbing up on top of a flat rock, he called out for order and calm.

"Allah is great; he has spared our lives. Should we not be celebrating such a fact instead of cowering like dogs?" The masked man in his dusty robe could see that he had all the people's attention—but why did they keep cowering and pointing at him? A little tap on his shoulder made the masked man's whole body become rigid. He slowly turned and peered into a pair of the bluest eyes he had ever seen.

"You could be right; Allah probably had something to do with it," a calm voice said. With a terrifying scream, the rebel leader ran backwards right off the rock and landed on his back on the hard dirt floor.

Daniel walked to the edge of the rock and sat with his feet dangling as he looked down at the surprised man lying on the floor. He looked over at the chained Jamas, and the manacles around his wrists and ankles opened and clanked against the wall and floor. A sneering Jamas walked over and stood looking down with hate in his eyes at the masked chieftain. He reached out and grabbed the mask, but Daniel stopped him from wrenching it off his face. "All in good time, Jamas—all in good time."

"I would take great pleasure in killing this man, if you would allow me," Jamas begged Daniel.

"We are not here for that, my friend." Daniel gave out a serene feeling as he talked to the people. "So far I have not harmed any one of you," Daniel warned. "I have not come here to make war; to the contrary, I have come to make peace with you and all the creatures of this world. I am here to make a peace that will last throughout the ages, and if I do not succeed in my endeavours, then there will be no ages left for any of the creatures of this world."

Daniel left them to ponder those words as he again concentrated on the masked man. "Come and sit next to me—up here." Daniel patted the rock next to him, and slowly, the body of the man in the mask rose off the ground, turned, and descended in a seated position next to him.

"Would you answer some simple questions? Who are you? Have you purchased nuclear weapons, and if so, how, when, and against whom were you going to use them?" He grinned at the nervous man. "Take your time; I do want correct answers."

Daniel waited a few moments, and he couldn't help smiling at the man next to him. "You have all the answers already? That is very good of you, my friend," Daniel said, playing with him.

"I will never answer any questions put to me by any infidel," the man, with newfound courage, retorted.

"But, my dear friend, you have already answered my questions and then some." Daniel nodded, and he sounded, especially to Jamas, sympathetic to the masked man.

"I remember you well; you do not need the mask of the Shah to hide your shame from the world or from your own people." Daniel reached out for the mask, but the Shah raised his left hand, and Daniel understood the gesture—he wanted that privilege himself.

Amidst the whispers coming from his people, he slowly removed the cover that had hidden his features from them. They murmured to each other as they peered at the dark-skinned middle-aged man with large brown eyes and a grey goatee. He looked over at Daniel and, almost in complete resignation, quietly said to him, "I remember you too, Mr. Leeder; from the first time I met you, I suspected that there was more to you than just an assistant to the Australian prime minister."

"Daniel, you know this man? This pig—you know him?" The hate still emanated from Jamas, and the look of surprise was plain to see on his face.

Daniel slid off his seat on the rock, and the Shah jumped down next to him; both faced Jamas.

"Jamas, the good in a human being can sometimes be whipped out from under him in an instant," Daniel counselled the Palestinian. "You of all people would know this."

He then turned to the object of the hatred. "Mr. Habib, when I first met you at the White House over dinner with John B. Rose and the Australian prime minister, you were certainly pro-American, and you genuinely were trying to bring peace to this area. It certainly is amazing how quickly things can change. I know everything that I need to know about you from your thoughts, but I want you to talk to us both, especially this man here." He touched Jamas on the shoulder. "I need for him to accept you."

Habib was astounded. Although he undoubtedly had come to the realisation that Daniel was indeed a great man, surely he could not listen to his thoughts.

"Why am I even bothering to tolerate all this humiliation from you?" Habib found another bout of courage. "I have hundreds of armed soldiers at my beck and call. Why do I not just have you both shot?"

Daniel gave him a nonchalant wink. "I would prefer if we left any further hostility until later."

As if by some unseen force deep within him, the Shah became compelled to do as he was commanded. "You want to know why I have become this animal? I will tell you why, and I will tell you in the language of the animal makers—English."

Daniel realised the Shah wanted to speak English so that his people wouldn't understand. He found it hard to talk about his past, and it took him some time to gather his thoughts.

"Mr. Leeder, when I first met you some two and a half years ago, we were dining in the majesty and the glory of the White House as guests of the president of the most powerful and richest country the world has ever known. Alas, here we are today, our second meeting, in a cave somewhere in one of the least powerful and poorest of all countries in the world, Afghanistan. How ironic, wouldn't you say, Mr. Leeder?" Habib shook his head from side to side as his eyes became teary.

"I was a man who wanted to help, and for years, I played the role of the neutral man; I belonged to no country, for that was the way it had to be. As you may recall from our past conversation, Mr. Leeder, I was born in Iran, spent my youth in Afghanistan, and lived my young adulthood in New York. You know, it was my idea to be a go-between man between Iran and America, between Palestine and America, between Afghanistan and America, and, most of all, between the terrorists of this region and America. Do you know how many times I came close to death when I came back here to talk to the so-called terrorists or to the Iranians?

"It was certainly touch and go for me with the Arafat people in Palestine. Can you imagine the fanatical Taliban regime here in Afghanistan, when I told them that I wanted to be the neutral man so that each entity could contact the other through me? It took years for me to convince each party to endorse the idea and to trust me completely with vital information. In the end, they did, and because of this ability to talk to all concerned, I saved hundreds, if not thousands, of lives. When I travelled between these countries, I took my entire family with me to prove that I was willing to put up their lives for their trust in me. My family went with the locals to the mosques to pray together. My three boys played with their young men and went to their houses, while my two beautiful daughters entertained the young ladies of these so-called terrorists. My wife was a vision that only I beheld; her beautiful face was reserved for only me, as my Muslim faith dictated.

"During the American invasion of Afghanistan, John B. Rose was a general. He and I became good friends, and we learned to respect each other when I helped with negotiations with the Taliban and the Northern Alliance. That was some thirty years ago, when they came here in their search of the terrorist Osama Bin Laden. Where has that time gone?" He mused about those days before he came back to reality and continued his story.

"Three days after I met you, Mr. Leeder—just three days after—my world collapsed from under me, and I didn't even know it." Tears fell freely from his face. "I remember you and the lady prime minister coming out of the president's Oval Office because he had another appointment. I was that appointment, Mr. Leeder—me. The president wanted to see me, which was why I was there that night. He asked me to come over here to Afghanistan to help with some negotiations with the army of the Northern Alliance—the ones who helped them overthrow the Taliban in the first place. They anticipated that I would be here only a few days, and as my children were at a critical phase of their schooling, I decided to leave them at home. I travelled all over these hills, talking to the many different tribes, and I was gone for over three weeks before I finally returned to Kabul. How does one put into words when someone is standing there looking you in the eyes, saying how sorry they are? Sorry that all my family had been murdered, with the exception of one, my youngest son, who was just clinging to life? Those words were not real then, and they don't sound real now, no matter how many times I think of them."

Habib cried uncontrollably as he crouched down with his head on his arms against the rock wall, as if to hide his weakness from his people.

"What happened to your family?" Jamas asked.

"I wanted for my family to live in a country where they did not have to be scared of expressing their thoughts, a country where they would be safe and not have to be worried about a landmine—a country such as America, where I thought they had a future. So we settled in a borough just outside of Manhattan; we had a beautiful house that had everything we needed, neighbours who outwardly welcomed us. The authorities told me that a group of youths broke into my home and were there for over two hours doing whatever they wanted with my wife and daughters. They bludgeoned two of my boys to death and beat my youngest so badly that he is no more than a blade of grass. When they finished with my wife and my beautiful girls, they killed them. The police told me that they died horrible deaths and that their screams were undoubtedly heard by our good neighbours, but they didn't report the disturbance, because it was none of their business. They didn't want to get involved with their strange neighbours. These people had been over to our place for dinner parties, and at times, my wife had driven their children to school. These people greeted us with a good morning or good evening, and they smiled at us, what we believed were genuine smiles.

"I went over to my house after I identified all the bodies at the morgue, and there were no more tears inside me; my feelings were now so completely numb that I thought it was not possible to feel any more hurt than I had already felt." He gave out a loud sigh as he took a deep breath before continuing. "I was leaving my house, which I knew I would never return to, when some of the neighbours walked towards me; I thought that my good neighbours were coming over to console me. But how wrong I was—no, that was not the case. They didn't come over to console me; they came over to abuse me and to tell me that I didn't belong in a country like America. They shouted at me to leave such a beautiful and tranquil setting and said that people like me and my family shouldn't have been there in the first place. One even called out that they had gotten what they deserved."

The Shah had to stop, as he couldn't talk over his sobbing; Daniel touched him, and he slowly regained his composure. "I looked up to see who could be so cruel as to say this. I could not believe it—it was the same woman who had run over to my house asking for help when her boy had broken his leg. I had driven her and her son over to the hospital and stayed with her until I drove them home again hours later. She had thanked me profusely, even kissed me on the cheek—she had been so grateful. Now she was saying my children deserved killing."

Jamas dragged one of the big chairs over for Habib to sit on and motioned to a dismayed young woman to fetch some water for her master. The Shah shook his head at Jamas as he tried to get him to sit.

"I have gotten this far; now I want to tell you more and how I plan to get revenge on these heartless people." There was venom in the words he emitted.

"They would not even let me take the bodies of my loved ones out of that country, and they would not even let me bury them. They wanted to keep them until maybe they found their murderers. They are still looking for the killers even to this day, so I brought my only living son here so that I would end his life in a country that at least has people who are honest with themselves and their lot and have so much higher value in their pride than the false and pampered Americans. On my way here, I thought of a way to use my riches—every American cent. I would devastate as much of that murderous country as I could. My brothers here welcomed me into their fold, and after I told them of my suicide mission that would overshadow their meagre Twin Tower attempt on the American foreshore by more than a thousand fold, believe me, they bent backwards to help me. I donned my mask to keep my identity secret from the prying eyes of the Americans so that I could still come and go as I pleased in and out of that country, which is proving invaluable to our cause. With the death of their leader, Bin Laden, I was the natural one in line. I am a negotiator, and that's what I did; I negotiated with the corrupt Russian army, and I am now in possession of one of their atomic bombs."

Nuclear bomb. Nuclear bomb. Nuclear bomb.

The words echoed loudly in Daniel's mind, and an eerie, empty sensation overtook his whole body. With his consciousness fading, he tried to find support against the rocks at his back, but the rocks were no longer solid. They were no more than the air that surrounded them, and Daniel fell backwards and disappeared from sight as the rocks enveloped him. They solidified again, and Daniel had become a part of them; he could see the people in the cave and the unbelieving eyes that looked in the direction of his disappearance.

Memories flooded back to the day he had become part of the air at Wilpena Pound and all those years he had lost as he'd traversed the planet at the whim of the air currents. Was this happening again? He had become part of the rocks but was still conscious of his own individuality within them.

Awareness came to him, and he looked up towards the cavern ceiling and saw the cloud of dust that he had guided there when the rocks had first broken away from the roof. The cloud began swirling in a circular motion, and it slowly descended as it did so; it accelerated faster and faster until the whole mass became one giant funnel. He felt his body being sucked up out of the rock, and he was swallowed up into the blackness of the swirling wind; his body melded into it, and he became part of it.

Although the speed had accelerated to a level where it became incomprehensible to him, Daniel felt motionless, and he witnessed a bizarre event happening in front of the rocks, which he now hovered over. The Shah stood next to Jamas, and they were so static that they appeared to be no more than photographs. Suddenly, there was movement as the images began to change.

Instead of the Shah and Jamas standing in front of the rocks, he now saw the Shah talking to his men, and in the corner, he saw the chained Jamas back where he had found him when he'd first entered the cavern. The next image upset Daniel, and he tried desperately to escape from his impenetrable gaol. He saw the slaughtered bodies of many people in front of Dost's uncle's accommodation house; the headless remains of his friends Howie and Gerald were in the foreground of this photographic vision.

The pictures kept changing, and in one brief moment, he saw men carrying a large object covered in a blanket on a litter and others wheeling out the dreaded bomb the Shah had mentioned. The next instant showed a plane landing in Mexico, and this vision quickly changed to a scene in Cuba. He saw his friend John B. Rose on a fishing boat, and alongside him, the Shah had his arms around his shoulders as they held up the catch of the day for a photographer.

The image that followed was one of bustling New York City; this changed instantly to a mushroom cloud hovering over the metropolis. Complete devastation was the scene in the next illustration, and Daniel felt himself shouting loudly, yet no sound came from his gaping mouth; all was silent.

Many other images came and went; some showed men and women hanging by their necks from trees, while others showed butchered bodies lying in streets. The areas he saw were definitely American, and the victims were obviously Muslims. Another scene showed Western men and women bent down on their knees while Arabs with swords raised in the air stood over them, ready to decapitate their captives.

There were men in uniforms marching and boarding warships; a full-scale war between the Christian and the Muslim countries had started. To Daniel, these visions meant only one thing, and it was out of his control: the end of the world was evident.

He looked beyond the photos flashing before his eyes and looked across the room, and there on the wall, he saw the remains of his friend Jamas; his body was nothing more than skin and bones, and Daniel could see that he had been dead for some months.

Daniel became aware that he had travelled through time, months into the future in a matter of only a few seconds, and his thoughts on the demise of Planet Earth were backed up by what appeared to be a black negative or maybe a black hole—the last vision that flashed before his eyes.

Blackness overtook Daniel, and he found himself being hurled through a black void, heading out somewhere in space, out amongst the brilliance of the never-ending universe. Heading towards him in the void was a round light with a streaking tail behind it, and this object headed straight for another large, bright sphere, which appeared familiar to him; he recognised it—Earth's moon. A comet was on a collision course with the moon.

He watched as the two hit, and he saw the surfaces of the moon and the comet become one in a blaze of shattered debris. The entangled mass went out of orbit like a ball being pitched in a baseball game, and his heart sank as he saw the direction it headed. The blue ball of Earth was the target it had been pitched at. He saw the jumbled mass hit Earth, and the whole agglomerate headed out through space towards a bright fireball thousands of times bigger than the orb heading towards it.

Daniel had no idea what the real time factor had been in the process of the world ending; all he knew was that men had finally brought to an end a species that the almighty Creator had envisaged as, in time, being the rulers of the entire universe.

In the void, Daniel closed his eyes, and he heard a voice within himself—a voice telling him that this was the future of the planet called Earth if a war were to break out amongst its two largest religions.

A smile came across his face as he opened his eyes to see Jamas and the Shah standing in front of him next to the fallen rocks in the cavern. The Shah was a little bemused by the smile that had appeared on Daniel's face; maybe this strange man was not believing the seriousness of the plan for his revenge against the Americans.

"I have worked out a route for the bomb to travel through Mexico and then to Cuba; there I will kill my son, and I will use parts of his body to conceal this bomb inside his coffin. By coincidence, at this time, I have already arranged to be on board the well-known luxury yacht the *First Lady* with our friend the ex-president of the USA. This yacht has a crew consisting of many unsuspecting Americans. I will get a call while I am on board and while sailing close to the Cuban coast to tell me that my son has died on that island. He, of course, was there being looked after by his caretakers while I cruised the Caribbean Sea with John. We will pick up his body and make for Miami, and from there, I will travel in a hearse all the way to New York. It will be up to me when to press the button that will destroy the Big Apple and propel the United States into war against the Muslims of the world."

Although Daniel was already aware of the Shah's plan, actually hearing it made it sound worse—and so feasible that it scared him. If a man like the Shah could plan and carry out such a scheme, what hope was there for the future of mankind? This man was indeed clever; even if the security guards opened the coffin, the chances were that John would stop them from desecrating the body of the only son his friend had left after the tragedy his family had suffered at American hands.

Daniel now realised that the Creator had taken a hand and propelled him into the future; time had moved ahead so quickly that the snippets he had been able to comprehend had appeared to be photographs. This was the primary aspect of his mission. If he had not been endowed with his powers, the Shah would have succeeded, and the world would have undoubtedly been destroyed. The Creator had given Daniel a warning that he must stop the Shah and men like him, and at the same time, Daniel was encouraged, as he realised that the universal force wanted Earth to be saved.

Had Earth already been destroyed sometime in the future, and had the Creator reversed time to give the humans another chance? Was he to be that chance by correcting the wrongs that had already happened in the future, whilst all along, he had envisaged that he had to correct the wrongs of the past?

The screaming of Habib as he snapped at his men to shoot the two infidels interrupted Daniel's thoughts. The men hesitated as if entranced; they were unsure of what they should do. Some of them considered this man to be a reincarnation of Muhammad. A few felt intimidated by their screaming master and reluctantly cocked their rifles, but they went no further.

The Shah shouted at them, and in frustration, he ran to the nearest man and grabbed his rifle; he quickly aimed it at Daniel. He stood with his hands on the trigger, looking at his target, but instead of firing, he started to sob loudly and uncontrollably. "Who are you? Why must you do this now—why now? My plan is set; it cannot fail. I must have my revenge; the death of my family must be avenged."

Daniel was not an overly sympathetic man—he had no time to be—but at that moment, he felt for this one human being. The first time he'd met Shahma Habib, although Habib had given the impression of being a braggart, he'd perceived him to be a genuine person, and he'd liked him. Now the feeling he had for him was one of pity—pity that such a good man had been turned into such a beast.

"Where is your youngest son?" Daniel asked.

"I have no son; he died with the rest of his family."

"Your son lives, Shahma—he lives."

"He is nothing more than an unseeing vegetable with no feelings and no thoughts; he is dead," the once-proud man sobbed.

"Go and bring him before me so that I may see him."

Habib looked up at Daniel, and a feeling of wonderment went through his body; he became inwardly excited. Anything was possible. He turned to one of the women, whose wide eyes peered through her burka, and told her to fetch his son. She motioned to several other females, and they followed her into a smaller cave whose entrance was sealed by a wooden door.

Several tense minutes later, the women reappeared in the large grotto, grasping a blanket from the corners and the sides and hauling an obese, screaming, grotesque form. More than ten women grasped a piece of the blanket as they struggled with the weight, and with sighs of relief, they placed the large hulk at the feet of Daniel. They squatted down on the blanket and firmly held the screaming, thrashing boy down.

Daniel looked at the obese form before him, and he saw that the eyes in the badly scarred and deformed face were rolled back into the boy's head, revealing only thin white lines.

"This is what remains of my son Ruhman," the dejected father said as he lowered his head in shame.

Daniel understood Habib. He was not ashamed of his son; he felt shame for not being there to protect his family when they had needed him; instead he had been out in the hills of Afghanistan, helping others to protect their families.

"Your son is in a bad way, Habib; I will try to bring him back to you," Daniel told him.

The intrigued yet guarded man asked, "Are you telling me that you are some kind of god?"

"I am not a god but a messenger from our Creator."

Whispers started to emanate from the people in the cave, and it took Habib some time to realise that his people were listening to their conversation.

"How can they understand what we are saying? None of my people speak English."

"I wanted your people to know what I was saying and especially what you were saying. They needed to know why you have such hatred for the Americans, and I want them to know how forgiving you are." Daniel put his hand on Habib's right shoulder. "For the moment, I mainly want them to see what I am doing. My reasons will become clearer to you as we talk further; right now, let me be with your son."

Daniel motioned for the women to release their firm hold on the boy, and as they reluctantly did so, the boy started to kick and flail his arms around in a mad frenzy. A stare from Daniel calmed him; the fury in the rapid movements of his whole body eased, and he became still

As he covered the boy's face with his hands, a deep concentration came over Daniel. Stillness overtook everything and everybody inside the cave. Although only a couple of minutes passed, to the people in the cavern, it seemed to take ages before Daniel made a slight movement. He ran his hands over the boy's face and closed his eyes with his fingers, and as Daniel stood up, he whispered to him, "Sleep well, Ruhman—sleep well."

Turning to the anxious father, Daniel said to him, "Your son will sleep for some time now. For the next few days, only give him water; he has enough fat on him to sustain him."

A reluctant and suspicious Habib came closer to his son and bent down to touch him, and as he did, Daniel smiled, and the boy slowly opened his dark brown eyes and smiled at his father.

"He looked at me! He looked at me!" the jubilant man cried out in sheer excitement. Habib looked down at his son again, but his eyes were closed.

"They were the eyes of my son; I could see my Ruhman in them," he said to Daniel as he grasped his shoulders with shaking hands.

Daniel sat the emotional man down in a chair and asked him and all the people who now gathered around him to listen to a story—a story that he had to make them believe so thoroughly that they would pass it on to many hundreds of thousands of Muslims who, in turn, must also believe and pass it on to others so that in the end, all would believe the one story.

He told them of the mission that the Creator of the universe had given Muhammad so many hundreds of years ago and revealed that he was the new messenger chosen to further the teaching of the Creator. "The word *creator,*" he told them, "can be interpreted to mean 'Allah,' as Allah is the Creator."

Two hours later, Daniel concluded his first session with these keen listeners. "The Afghan people are a proud and a resilient race. The ancient art of storytelling still flourishes amongst your people, and I am asking you to go forth and tell my story at the campfires of all in your country."

He asked if they had any questions that they wanted to ask, but there were none forthcoming. Daniel could sense that his message had gotten through to these awe-inspired people, but he needed to reinforce their belief in him once and for all. He would do this on another day, for today he would let them rest and let them deliberate further amongst themselves on his teachings.

An hour passed, and a shaking hand touched Daniel's shoulder.

"Daniel, Daniel!" an excited father whispered. "Look, Daniel—his face. The scarring has gone; the nose of the boxer is now the nose of my son." It had been a long time since Habib had felt tears of joy run down his cheeks.

"I can see my son's face again—my Ruhman; my Ruhman has come back to me. Daniel, you have given me back my son. What do you want of me, Daniel? What do you want me to do?"

"Shahma Habib, my friend, it is not I who needs you; it is the whole world that needs you desperately. What I have told your people is not the entire truth; these simple and innocent people might not be able to handle the complete truth, so you will be the only one amongst them who will know why the world needs you so badly."

Daniel told Habib about the threat to all the creatures of the world and explained that time was quickly running out for them all. He explained his plan for Habib to become the spokesman for the entire Muslim world and outlined how he and other religious leaders were to structure a forum to combine all the religions of the world into one.

Daniel had to laugh to himself at the irony; so far, the two largest religious groups were to be led by a murderer and a terrorist.

Shahma Habib found all this information daunting, but he only had to look across to the young man lying on the blanket a few metres away from him to realise that everything about Daniel was astounding. "Do I have any choice in this?" the intrigued man asked.

"You always have a choice, my friend, but I already know that you will do my bidding; it is in your old nature to help others, and that old urge seems to be coming back to you."

The misty-eyed look on Habib's face was all the answer Daniel needed.

"There is one more thing: I want you to start spreading the word amongst your people; tell them to leave these caves and return to their homes and families. The United Nations will agree to an amnesty for all of them. You must send messengers out to tell them that they must vacate these caverns within seven days or they will perish."

"Daniel, these caves are more like underground roadways; they are made up of natural caves and crevices as well as tunnels made by the many gold and silver miners. We have ways of travelling underground all the way to Iran or Pakistan. There are thousands of people hiding here."

The reluctant Shahma gathered his people and instructed them to do Daniel's bidding; without any questions, they headed into the many directions of the various smaller caves running off the main grotto.

Recalling something that Daniel had mentioned earlier, Shahma walked over to him; he was sitting, in deep contemplation, on one of the massive rocks. "Daniel, you mentioned that it was important that Jamas Galli respected me. Why is this?"

He waited for an answer, and his mind took several seconds to register that Daniel was no longer there; he had disappeared. To Shahma's amazement, he received an answer to his question in his own thoughts.

"He is to be the go-between between you and the Americans; there are two CIA agents here to also help you, and I have another—Bob Wilson—back in Washington who will be in charge of bringing a peaceful resolution to the terrorist activities all over the globe."

Women cowered over the many children who were crying and screaming in the rooms as a distraught Dost ran from window to window, shouting abuse at their attackers. Gerald and Howie had taken control of the situation and had positioned Dost's male relatives at various vantage points. Until now, with their old rifles, they had kept the mob outside at bay. They had plenty of weapons, but weapons were useless without ammunition, which they had all but exhausted.

The attackers sensed the situation and teased the men inside by running between the rocks they were sheltering behind and exposing themselves as targets.

Their leader's patience had run out; he stood up from behind one of the rocks, and with his rifle raised above his head, he charged towards the accommodation house, calling on his men to kill all inside.

Suddenly, a gust of wind came up from the steep slopes of the ravine, halting the run of the lean, scruffy man and his followers. At first, the strength of the gale and the dust it blew before it only slowed the attackers, but as the wind grew in power, it brought them to a complete halt. They tried hard to fight against it, but slowly, they tired, and the wind became so powerful that it knocked all the surprised attackers off their feet.

From where they lay, and above the noise of the wind, they heard an explosion from the ravine, and through the dust, they saw a fiery ball of flame coming up the side of the steep hill towards them. In what seemed an instant, they saw the blaze blast over the embankment and land with an enormous crash in the middle of the road only metres from where they lay.

The wind swirled around the fire, and with an upward thrust, it lifted the flame into the air, and the wind and the fire dissipated into nothingness. The fire and the wind had gone, and where the flame had been, between the petrified rebels and Dost's family, now sat the crumpled body of an unrecognisable, burned-out motor car.

The torn, crushed, and burned-out shell of the van began to slowly vibrate from side to side, moving of its own accord, and it started changing shape. The van started to stretch out in all directions, and in front of the amazed onlookers, the whole mass began getting the finer details of its original shape. The lump of metal started fusing together and altered from its jagged form to a cylindrical one, and at the same time, the charred grey exterior was turning into a bright, shining yellow colour. Within a few minutes, the crumbled, shapeless, and burned-out body was a new vehicle.

All who were witnessing this miracle were flabbergasted, and fearful cries went out amongst them as the back door of Dost's reconstituted van opened and a man dressed in an immaculate white suit glided out of it and onto the road. He stood in front of the petrified onlookers, pointed towards the mountains on the other side of Kabul, and spoke to the awestruck men who had attacked the accommodation house. "Go—the Shah wants words with you."

They didn't need prompting again; they ran down the steep road and were out of sight in seconds.

Dost, his kin, and the two CIA agents were outside the front of his uncle's house, watching what transpired, too scared to move. Although they were frightened, the curiosity of the people of the neighbourhood overcame their fear, and they too came out of their hovels and watched from a safe distance. This day was, without doubt, the best entertainment they had ever had.

Daniel looked up at Dost, who was partially hidden by the large frame of his uncle, and motioned for him to come forward; although petrified, he shuffled towards him, and when Daniel pointed to the van, Dost lost all fear and ran the last few steps to his new vehicle.

Gathering all the people around him, Daniel told them his story in simple terms, concluding with instructions that they were to follow the teaching of the Shah, who had repented from his world of terrorism and revenge and now promoted love for all humans and for all the creatures of the world.

Daniel had learned never to let an opportunity go by and had realised that witnesses to miracles he instigated were the best people to carry his word, especially throughout an ancient land such as Afghanistan.

A rumour spread that the new prophet would appear before the people of Kabul, and thousands made a pilgrimage to the surrounding hills across from the old accommodation house, which had a bright yellow van parked in front of it.

Daniel did not disappoint them; he came to the crowd out of the air in front of them and told his story of the expectations of the Creator. He passed on messages from the great Muhammad and, to a lesser degree, from the prophet Jesus. All the people heard the news echoing inside their own minds, as if the man talking stood next to them.

A proud Shahma Habib walked behind six men who were carrying his son on a litter, and they made their way out to where Daniel stood. The boy, although still overweight, had regained his faculties, and the happy smile his father saw on his young son's face made him impatient for his full recovery. News had spread throughout the country of the miracle Daniel had performed on the boy as reward for the redemption of the Shah's way of life. Shahma Habib himself pointed out that his son was proof that the messenger was just to all men, be they Christian or Muslim.

Ruhman's leg and arm muscles had seriously deteriorated since his attack, and the excess weight he was carrying made it impossible for him to walk at this early phase of his recovery. Shahma believed Daniel and had every confidence that his son would fully recover once he lost more weight. The boy, dressed in a striped caftan, sat on a blanket to listen to the sermon.

When Daniel finished talking to the people, he went over to the boy; kneeling down in front of him, he started to massage his feet and legs. He then took hold of Ruhman's arms, rolled up his sleeves, and massaged both upper limbs. Daniel stood in front of the boy and extended his hands to him; Ruhman reached out, grasped them, and slowly rose to his feet. With Daniel walking backwards holding his hands, the wary boy took a few steps forward and followed the man who exuded confidence into his mind. Daniel let the boy's hands go, and he walked on his own back to where his father stood teary eyed and watching with joy. They embraced, and together they walked through the bewildered crowd and over the hilly countryside back to the main road, leaving the people who had witnessed this miracle with no doubt as to the power of the messenger.

Daniel sat on a large, flat rock in the middle of the massive cavern that had once housed the Shah and his followers. He sat in a motionless stance, looking down on the rocky floor. Before him lay many weapons, piled high on top of each other. Next to the pile stood a solidly built wheelbarrow laden with a complex glass-topped box. It had a multitude of coloured buttons that were flashing intermittently and a complicated keypad with a green light at its side that blinked with a sense of urgency. On top of the keypad, a digital timer displaying a time of 510 seconds was counting down. The bright green light sent an eerie colour throughout the cavern, and it highlighted the man sitting on the rock with an armed nuclear bomb before him.

The midday sun beat down unmercifully on a herd of wild Bactrian camels foraging in the arid land beneath the mountain ranges close to the city of Kabul. Some stood with their heads hung down, sniffing the ground in the faint hope of finding food, while others lay down to rest in the limited shade of the only small tree for miles around. Their heads lifted in unison and turned towards the mountains; the ones lying down painstakingly stood as restlessness came over them. A loud bellow sounded from the lead bull, and they stampeded westward, away from the mountains and farther into the desert.

In the few days since Daniel had made his appearance in this harsh country, peace that its people had not known for scores of years had befallen them, and the population buzzed with excitement, knowing that the prophet walked amongst them. The people went about their daily business, trying to eke out their meagre existences, and in a land of few entertainment activities, one of their favourite pastimes was haggling at the market place.

Thousands of people all over the city stopped and listened to a faint rumble coming from the mountain ranges close by, and simultaneously, they felt a tremor beneath their feet.

Minutes earlier, inside the mountain, Daniel had been perched on his rock, still concentrating on the ground in front of him.

A pencil-line crack appeared in the floor before him, and it travelled across the width of the cave until the entire solid rock base was fractured. Nothing else happened for a full minute; all was quiet and still until the line began to widen, and the sides were now collapsing. As the fissure grew, it made the ground shake; the vibration was slight at first but soon grew more violent, and the noise became deafening. The crevice now began to widen more quickly, and its gaping mouth revealed an ever-growing inner space that kept on deepening until its bottom could no longer be seen.

Steam escaped from the deep hole and hissed its way up into the cavern, and as it touched the walls and roof, the coolness turned the hot vapour into raindrops. The weapons before Daniel were vibrating along with the ground, and they slowly tumbled into the bottomless pit. The wheelbarrow, with its deadly cargo, worked its way towards the crevice, and Daniel smiled as he watched it go over the edge into a fiery grave.

The citizens of Kabul feared the worst and ran out of their houses into the streets. Would Allah—or this so-called Creator—not give them rest from more disasters? An earthquake would surely devastate their old city. They heard a thunderous blast coming from deep down in the earth beneath them, and most of the crowd dropped to their knees, crying out to the Creator to have mercy on them.

They looked up at the mountains that overshadowed their city, and what they saw terrified them. The mountains were visibly shaking, as if something inside were forcing its way through them. It took a while for the people to realise that although the mountains were trembling, the ground they stood on was still.

In the mid afternoon sun, the people watched intently as hissing steam started to escape from the crevices of the hills around Kabul. The vapour formed clouds over the city, and a warm mist fell over the watchers as the day slowly turned into dusk. As the sun descended over the western hills, they could see a beautiful bright orange glow forming over the mountains and slowly moving in all directions.

Government sources informed citizens that the mountains had erupted internally and that a lava flow was moving through the myriad of tunnels that ran throughout Afghanistan's mountain range. The city was safe, they were told, and they had no reason to panic, as the lava flow appeared to be moving away from Kabul and heading towards the neighbouring country of Pakistan and could travel as far as Iran to their west.

The United Nations peacekeeping force sent up helicopters to monitor the extent of the danger this eruption posed to themselves and the surrounding settlements near the mountain ranges. The cameras on board beamed back video footage to their headquarters in Kabul of the scene below them. The pilot of one of the choppers called out excitedly over the radio to the other aircraft in the area, "There is a man down there just sitting amongst the flames coming out of the mountain just below me." He veered the craft for a closer inspection of the mountaintop. "He seems all right, but I can't get any lower; the heat is too intense. I can feel it from my position here, yet it does not seem to faze him." The pilot started to doubt his own eyes when he saw how casual the man appeared to be.

"Ground control, do you see it on your monitor, or am I seeing things?" He wanted confirmation from someone else.

"Copy, Chopper Three, copy; I see him too," headquarters quickly replied. "He seems to be dressed in a white suit, and he is now just walking around as if he is going on a Sunday stroll."

"No, he's gone; I've lost him," the pilot called out. "He was there one second ago, and the next second, he completely vanished."

Within the next few weeks, the majority of the people of Afghanistan were believers in the new creed put forward by the messenger. People came from afar to witness the miracle of the burning mountains and to listen to the reformed Shah, whom they hailed as the leader of the Muslim people. He would be the one to lead them in the interrelation of all the religions of the world, and he would sit with the Catholic Pope Innocent to represent the Muslims of the world. Word was that the headquarters for the new religion would be Jerusalem.

The peacekeepers had clear proof that Daniel was the man they had seen on the burning mountains, and it was not possible for him to be a mere mortal. No human could have survived the intense heat being generated by the lava flow that engulfed the empty spaces deep within the ranges. Another quandary puzzled them: Why did the head of the UN insist that copies of the pictures they had of Daniel up on the mountain be freely distributed to all the television stations and newspapers around the world?

The Hindu Kush mountain system in central Asia extends over eight hundred kilometres through Afghanistan, Pakistan, and Tajikistan, with over twenty peaks exceeding seven thousand metres above sea level. The highest of these snow-covered peaks is known as Tirich Mir, and it is raised 7,690 metres in the Islamic Republic of Pakistan.

To the east of Kabul, through the Khyber Pass, across the border in Pakistan, a lone army helicopter hovered over the mountains, assessing the danger that approached.

The pilot panicked as he grabbed the joystick with both hands, and with the sound of fear in his voice, he called out, "Allah, be with us; I have lost all control."

"What are you saying? What is happening?" the passenger next to him demanded with a voice that was frightened yet showed an air of authority.

"Mr. Sharif, I have absolutely no control over my craft, sir; it's flying by itself."

"What are you talking about? The helicopter is flying normally, isn't it?" the smaller man in the white caftan asked.

"Yes, it is, sir, but I am not flying it; it's going down by itself, sir." The pilot shifted the joystick in all directions without much effort. "A second ago, I could not move it; now it is not engaging. It is useless; this helicopter is moving by itself as if on autopilot, but there is no autopilot on this craft, sir."

The helicopter descended towards the bottom of the ranges, and as they neared the ground, a level area appeared below; they hovered for a few moments, and there beneath them, a man appeared. The amazed pair stared in disbelief as the chopper landed softly beside a man dressed in white.

Dust flew in all directions, and the ground around them was no longer visible, but they could clearly see the man outside; the debris splattering in all directions veered away from him, and not a speck of dust touched the apparition before them.

"I know him," the little man with the goatee and the narrow glasses covering his small dark eyes uttered. "That is that man Daniel; I know him."

He gestured for the pilot to open the door, and Mr. Sharif slid out and, to the pilot's surprise, strutted over with his hand extended to greet the man waiting for him.

"Mr. President, it is good to see you again," Daniel greeted the small man.

"It has been a long time since Malta, Daniel; I have been wondering when it would be my turn for a visit from you."

"It is indeed your turn." Daniel smiled. "I know you will need me to explain to your people about the natural Creator. The mountains in your country are some of the tallest in the world, and they have much snow on them. If this snow were to melt rapidly, it would devastate much of your country, and it would kill hundreds of thousands of your people."

"Daniel, surely you would not let that happen?" the concerned man asked.

"I would not like to see this happen, so rest easy for now, and use my threat as leverage to go forth to your countrymen and introduce the Creator and the concept of one religion to them. To prove the power of the messenger, the heat from the lava flow will not melt the snow on the peaks. Tell them that the lava will stay inside the ranges, and it will stay there until I am satisfied that the people of Pakistan believe in the words of the Creator. If this belief is not forthcoming in a reasonable time, the heat within the lava tubes inside the mountains will increase and will melt the snow. If they are heeding and embracing the teachings of the Creator, the lava will start to cool and seal off all the cavities of the ranges forever. Tell them that I will send a man they all know and respect as one of their heroes in the fight against the people you consider infidels. The Shah himself and his many followers will preach to them about the truth the messenger spreads."

The wide-eyed pilot watched as his president shook hands with the stranger and walked back to the helicopter; Daniel vanished in the same way he had first appeared. Without saying a word, the president gestured to his pilot to take off. The surprised man, realising that he now had full control of his craft, didn't need to be told twice to head for home.

The next day, after much advertising by the television stations, a message to the nation began with a recommendation that neighbouring Islamic countries should tune in to hear the president's speech. The small, obviously nervous Pakistani president started his talk negatively, with an apology to the Muslim watchers and listeners. He stressed that he should have been making this speech eighteen months earlier, but because of the strong beliefs of the Muslims in their faith, he had feared for his life.

He told them about Daniel and his mission to unify the religions of the world, and he pointed to the mountains and stressed the threat emanating from within. "We have a new messenger who will bring all religions of the world—not just the Muslim world but the entire world—to a modern understanding. There must only be one belief for all. If this does not begin to happen and spread quickly throughout the world, then we can expect devastation like we have never experienced before." He paused and was surprised that there was no reaction from the people in the studio.

"I will take this opportunity to warn the religious and political leaders of the surrounding countries. The messenger has a limited time to achieve his intended goals. Be warned that to oppose his teachings will mean death to you."

The president extended the talk to what the Creator expected of his people in their behaviour towards their fellow man and their attitude towards the other living things as well as the planet itself.

As he wound down his talk, two men, one masked, came onto the set, and the president welcomed them. He introduced them as Jamas Galli, a reformed Palestinian freedom fighter, and the Islamic representative for the unity of world religion, the greatest freedom fighter since Osama Bin Laden, the Shah himself. The camera locked onto the Shah, and he slowly removed his mask to reveal a kindly looking man.

When he began to speak, the nation listened.

The elderly Ayatollah Muhammad Assyria, the spiritual leader and supreme authority of Iran, watched the broadcast of the Pakistani president and immediately arranged for a rebuttal to the blasphemy committed. The government-controlled television station had its programmes interrupted without warning, and the ayatollah promptly commenced a speech to the nation.

"This farce that came out of Pakistan will not be tolerated by the Islamic countries, as without doubt, the Americans were behind this propaganda." His open mouth froze on the next word, and he stared at the camera without blinking.

It was several minutes before the intimidated show producer gathered the courage to approach him. He peered at him and whispered, "Your Eminence, are you all right?"

No answer came; the sweating producer reached out and touched the back of the holy man, whose limp body slumped forward and fell face down onto the desk he sat behind.

"Get a doctor; I think he is dead!" he shouted in a panic.

"He is dead." A voice came from behind the elderly man. He turned around, looked up, and, with a wild scream, stumbled backwards as he recognised the man he had seen on many foreign news reports. The stranger put his right hand on the right shoulder of the dead man, and as he lifted his arm up, the body rose as if glued to his palm. With the slightest of effort, Daniel cast the body aside and took the ayatollah's place in front of the camera.

He began to speak to the people of Iran. "This man did not heed my warning and has paid the penalty; his replacement must be a true believer in the Creator, and nobody in your current administration would qualify."

The producer, realising everything was still being televised, gestured to the cameraman to cut the transmission. Daniel looked at the frightened cameraman, and with a toothy grin, the man understood and ignored his superior.

"My suggestion is to leave the religious fanatics out of politics and let a man who was born in this land come back to help you. Shahma Habib, whom you know as the Shah, the leader of the freedom fighters in Afghanistan, is the man I want to lead you and the Islamic countries to the one religion. I, as the messenger of the natural Creator, decree this of the people of Iran."

As Daniel spoke, everyone who listened understood what he was saying, no matter what dialect he or she spoke.

"There is a lava flow making its way through the mountain ranges, and it will reach Iran in a few short weeks. If you have not resolved your leadership problem in that time and you, the people, are not listening to my teachings, then your country will be overrun by the molten rock."

With that, Daniel disappeared before all who were watching.

Kuhla Chatterjee looked down from the podium at her many ministers. The short, rotund woman was well respected by the Indian parliamentarians as their prime minister. This extraordinary meeting of her cabinet being held in the government buildings in the capital, New Delhi, was to be telecast on the television channels and broadcast to the hundreds of radio stations throughout her country.

Before she started her talk, she had the broadcasters play videos of the speech made by the Pakistani president, followed by the rebuttal made by the Iranian leader. She also telecast a previous national message she had given to her people some eighteen months ago—a message made by most leaders of the world, introducing the new prophet, Daniel.

Finally, she appeared on live television and started to tell her attentive people why she needed to talk to them again. Speaking in Hindi, the official language of India, she spoke about the concept of the Hindu religion, which was followed by over seven hundred million devotees. It was one of the oldest religions known to mankind, with its basic teaching defining and applauding what people did rather what they thought.

She mentioned that many Hindu followers worshipped the goddess Devi and that others worshipped hundreds of other deities, including solar and lunar gods.

"The Hindu religion has many facets to it and is a very complex religion," she said, "but the best part of its teaching is where it encompasses the meaning of existence and the nature of the universe.

"Now I must explain Daniel's mission. The man sent to us by the Creator of the universe is to bring this world towards a combination of all the religions into one. All Hindu worshippers should welcome this new religion, as it also encompasses much of our own beliefs." The prime minister wanted to continue, but a sudden unrest amongst her ministers distracted her, and she turned to see what had caused the disturbance.

"Daniel!" she exclaimed, and she quickly turned to the people. "This is the messenger who has been sent to us!" the excited leader shouted to her people. "He has come to talk to the people of India."

Daniel stood next to the short woman and spoke in English, but to the surprise of the Indian people all over the country, they understood every word in their own dialect. This alone convinced most of the watchers and listeners that he was indeed a man of exceptional powers. India had eighteen major languages, including Hindu, Bengali, Assamese, and Gandhi. Besides those, it had more than a thousand minor ones spoken by the 72 percent of Indians who lived in the rural areas of the twenty-eight different states.

Daniel had known all along that converting the mainstream of the Indians to this new religion would not be a difficult task, as the creeds of the majority of their religions were already halfway to the new teachings.

CHAPTER 15

Garry Foster had received instructions from Daniel to fly back to Rome to pick up Peter and Caris and bring them to India, where he would join them en route to China.

Peter became immediately aware of the anxiety that showed on Daniel's face as he greeted them at the hotel in New Delhi. Daniel hugged Peter and kissed Caris repeatedly as they made their way to their rooms.

"Anything wrong, Daniel?" Peter enquired.

"No, Peter, everything is okay; I'm just a bit tired."

That answer worried Peter, as he had never known Daniel to get tired.

The next morning, a smiling Caris hugged Daniel and drew him closer to her; she looked out the window and pointed at something down below. "The window of the world—we're going over Nepal, and that must be Mount Everest. Even from up here, you can see how majestic it is."

"We have a long way to go before we get to Beijing," Daniel mused in a bored tone as he tried to resettle in his seat. "China—now there is an amazing country, with a fifth of the world's population and probably the oldest civilisation known to men. I have to do something special here."

"Do something special? Like what?"

"You will see. Now let me think."

The first thing they noticed as they approached Beijing was the smog over the city, and in the distance, the peaks of the oddly shaped mountains protruded through it.

The People's Republic of China was paying a high price for becoming the world's greatest industrialised country.

On this overcast and hazy day, an assistant to the foreign minister welcomed them at the airport; he was apologetic that the minister himself could not be the one meeting such an illustrious person as Daniel. The premier wanted to keep their arrival quiet, for fear of mass hysteria by the Chinese. It would not be difficult for a huge crowd to gather in a city such as Beijing, which had a population much larger than most countries.

He escorted the three to the premier's residence close to the Great Hall of the People in the capital. Hu Enlai Ho humbly greeted Daniel and his friends; he bowed and apologised for not speaking English but said that he understood that Daniel spoke all languages. Premier Ho introduced Daniel to the second-most-powerful man in China, the secretary of the Communist Party, Deng Xiaoping Qing, a tiny, obnoxious man with only slits for eyes and a skeletal face sporting a grey moustache. His overlapped hands revealed scrawny digits with the manicured fingernails, and as he bowed to the Westerner, a slight snarl came out of his almost-nonexisting mouth. Daniel immediately saw an enemy to his plans to align China religiously with the rest of the world. It was obvious that the little man detested Westerners by the way he stared at them, but it was also obvious that he appreciated beauty by the way he leered at Caris.

The guests and their hosts sat at a large table in a magnificent dining room, surrounded by antiques from the many past dynasties, and they were served lunch as Daniel and Mr. Ho conversed.

"I have done as you asked and told my people of your mission; I have told them of the Creator, but the message is not really getting through to them. But please forgive my people for this ignorance; it is not their fault that they are not great believers in religion. You see, when the Communist Party gained control as far back as 1948 and eliminated organised religion, the Chinese people became mostly atheist and didn't believe in a higher being. Since the death of Moa, we now have followers in Confucianism, Daoism, and Buddhism, but in the main, they don't believe."

"I understand your predicament, Mr. Premier, and that is why I am here; I also realise that you are thinking that I have come at a bad time."

The sneering Qing interrupted Daniel. "Yes, Mr. Leeder, you have indeed come at a very bad time." Daniel almost laughed at the sound of his squeaky voice. "The National Congress of the Communist Party gathers in the Great Hall of the People only once every five years, and we meet in four days' time." He put his cup up to the little slit and sipped a drop of tea out of it before he snobbishly continued. "The premier has much to prepare, so maybe you should pick a better time to come again."

"No, Mr. Qing, I have come at the perfect time; my being here needed to coincide with your meeting in Beijing."

The little man didn't appreciate Daniel's answer and wanted to continue his protest, but before he could utter another word, he was mesmerised by the large greyish eyes that were looking at him. The mousy man recomposed himself only to find that he had another issue to contend with: he could not open his small mouth.

"Mr. Premier, I want you to break with protocol and televise the opening of the National Congress, not only to your people but also to the world. You are going to have some unexpected visitors."

Polluted water ran down the middle of the potholed streets, reflecting the bright moonlight that worked its way through the thick and hazy night air, giving the water an eerie, ghostly appearance. In the middle of the night, in the town of Xian, approximately 750 kilometres south-west of Beijing, strange occurrences were taking place in the three massive iron warehouses that sheltered the ongoing excavation of the findings made by a peasant.

In 1974, a farmer digging a well had discovered the tomb of Emperor Shi Huangdi of the Qin Dynasty, who had died in the year 210 BC. The normal practice of the day had been to bury all the emperor's guards with him upon his death, but an enterprising general had convinced the emperor's son that the soldiers were needed in this restless time and that if they replicated the soldiers in clay, the spirit of his father would be pleased.

Artists had painstakingly modelled the faces of all the emperor's men into clay, while apprentices had mass-produced the multicoloured armoured bodies. Once finished, the heads, which had long stems extending under the necks, were placed on the appropriate hollow bodies. Each stem fitted into a hole between the shoulders, and the charade was completed to the satisfaction of the new emperor. Six thousand figures depicting the actual individual soldiers—which consisted of a general, officers, archers, and cavalrymen as well as horses and chariots—were constructed from clay, and the legend of the terracotta warriors was born and hidden for over two thousand years until the relatively recent discovery.

Each of the warehouses had two guards watching over this valuable tourist attraction and historic national treasure. One guard walked around the grounds outside, while the other remained inside, looking down at the eerie terracotta figures in the excavations below the walkway that catered to the thousands of tourists who came every day of the year. The guard from outside the first warehouse opened a side door and made his way towards the kitchen.

"Eh! Lin, do you want a cuppa before we swap?" he called out to his workmate, but no reply came. He yelled louder; there was no one to wake there, so he kept calling out louder and louder, knowing full well that his fellow worker must be hearing him.

"You in the toilet, or have you found a whore you want to keep to yourself?" He laughed as he neared the bathroom. A noise came out of the shadows, and the guard tut-tutted and shook his head as he headed towards where the noise had come from.

"Is that you snoring, Lin? Come on—you'd better wake up and get outside; it's your turn." Having never experienced any trouble, he was unperturbed as he made his way to the only dark spot in the whole area. He pulled out a torch from a halter he had around his belt, and as he shone the light into the darkness, he gave out a frightening gasp that took his breath away.

It took him a few moments to recover and to realise what had frightened him. Up against the wall stood two of the warriors—an archer and a cavalryman—looking straight at him. He gave out a loud sigh of relief as he inhaled a lungful of polluted air.

"How did you two get out here? Lin, what are these warriors doing out of the hole?" he called out as he stood looking at them. Another sound came from his right; he spun around and directed the torch towards the noise. What he saw made his legs tremble, and he fell to his knees, too frightened to move.

Lin was up against the wall with a sword thrust at his throat—but the most terrifying part of the ordeal was who or what was holding the weapon. A craggy, stony hand was wrapped around the handle of the sword, and it took some time before the kneeling guard realised that the hand belonged to one of the warriors. From the corners of his rounded eyes, he became aware that he too had a sword to his throat; the archer and the cavalryman were standing over him.

The small local police station was manned by only one police officer during the night. A few minutes after one o'clock in the morning, the young constable was surprised and annoyed to be disturbed by another young man who burst into the station, babbling so badly that the police officer could not comprehend what he was attempting to say.

After calming the man down and again trying to decipher the rambling, the policeman grabbed him and dragged him into the only cell at the station. "Idiot," he mumbled to himself. "Knocked off his cycle by a terracotta warrior—hundreds of them, marching along the main road." The constable was still laughing at the thought of seeing warriors coming out of the excavations and marching away, when another two men burst into the station.

"They're coming, they're coming!" they shouted as they pointed to the door, indicating that he should follow them.

The constable walked out of the station, shouting abuse at the men in front of him. He was only gone a few seconds before he ran back into the station, trembling with fear. He gathered his wits, reached for the phone, and pressed a button on the quick dial. "Chief, chief!" That was the only word the young man could utter as he looked out the window and watched a horde of disciplined, marching grey warriors pass by under the reflection of the street lights. The young constable dropped to the floor, senseless, with the phone still in his hand and with his chief shouting at him on the other end.

The new sunrise welcomed a day like no other ever witnessed by the people of the region; the day was unusually calm for that time of the year, with not the slightest breeze blowing. On such a still day, one would have expected the smog to be at its worst, but not that day; the air was clean and crisp, and the sky was the bluest the people had ever seen, with not a cloud in sight. The multitude of people, most of them cycling on their way to work, stopped and gathered in amazement to watch the sight before them.

To some of the peasants, the spectacle they were witnessing was a show being put on by the local authorities. They marvelled at how authentic the costumes appeared and how well disciplined the thousands of actors were to stand so still for so long, but more astonishing were the horses and how they had been trained to stand so motionless.

Others wondered why the authorities had allowed this national treasure to be put on exhibition for all to see freely and out in the open; normally, the artefacts were so protected that visitors were not even allowed to take photographs, especially using a flash, for fear of causing damage. Here was one of the greatest icons in China—a replica of an army of long ago. The terracotta warriors were assembled together facing in a north-eastern direction, appearing as if they were ready to embark on a long march.

A few of the spectators insisted excitedly that these were the genuine warriors; they had escaped from their enclosures, marched through the town, and assembled there in that field outside the town.

People took advantage of the unguarded exhibits and walked amongst the figurines, knowing that this would be the closest they would ever get to them, and for once, they were able to touch the art of their early ancestors.

A strong gust of wind sprung up, picking up dust and debris and swirling it over the heads of the warriors and the people walking amongst them. The crowd watching the show was amused as the adventurous people ran out from among the warriors to shelter from the gale, and the onlookers could see that each figurine seemed to be individually touched by the air now rushing and whirling around each of them.

One skinny man who had stopped to admire the face of a warrior let out a wild scream and ran out into the crowd that surrounded them. "It's alive!" he cried out. "Its eyes came to life, and it looked at me!"

The crowd laughed loudly, but their laughter was curtailed; they too started to notice movement coming from the back lines of the mighty, rigid warriors. They watched in awe as one by one, starting from the rear, the soldiers came to life; most of the audience clapped, as they now believed that the warriors definitely were actors and that the show had begun.

Dust blew off the figurines as the wind passed them, and soon they were all stirring as if they had just awakened from a long sleep. The magnificent horse at the lead, with an obvious commander, probably a general, mounted on him, reared and moved forward a few steps. Two mounted officers took their positions on either side of him, and then the cavalry, with archers walking beside them, came next, followed by the horse-drawn chariots and the rest of the army.

The baffled police and councillors of Xian stood at the edge of the empty excavation sites; not only had all the complete and intact human figures, chariots, and horses disappeared, but the broken ones were also gone. Not one piece of terracotta could be found anywhere in the excavation.

An excited police officer came running up the ramp and straight to a scruffy-looking man; with his arms flailing in all directions, he tried hard to communicate with his superior. The officer's animations stopped, and he pointed in the direction he wanted his superior to follow. As soon as he was able to utter, "Terracotta warriors," the man in charge rushed out of the covered excavation site, followed by the other police officers and the councillors.

The great army had their bearings, and nothing stood in their way. They marched in a straight line, and whatever lay in front of them did not deter them. They knocked down fences and trod small trees, vegetable gardens, and smaller out buildings into the ground. They walked tirelessly, and their long strides were too quick for any of the people who had started to follow them. The onlookers stopped and watched the army disappear into the hills and forests.

The police chief in Xian was having great difficulty convincing the authorities in the capital of what had occurred in his town, and it wasn't until the next morning that finally the defence minister agreed for an army helicopter to be dispatched to the area to pick up the police chief and his men. The chopper had no difficulty following the trail of destruction left by some immense force, and it headed directly towards the township of Tsinan.

On the outskirts of the town lay another of China's great icons, the Great Wall. The locals had heard a massive commotion through the early hours of the morning, and now, in the daylight, they could see the cause of the turmoil. The terracotta warriors, nearly four hundred kilometres from where they had been the day before, had again assembled—this time, near a ramp that led up to the wall.

The majestic terracotta steed with the general mounted on his back reared and moved forward, reaching the top of the wall first; the two mounted officers quickly followed and took up their positions on either side of the general. The ground vibrated when the cavalry, the archers next to them, the horse-drawn chariots, and the rest of the marching army made their way behind their leader up the ramp and onto the Great Wall.

The chopper had finally come to the end of the trail, and the sight before the pilots and the passengers was difficult to accept as reality. The police chief from Xian finally had proof that the terracotta warriors had indeed come to life, and his superiors owed him many apologies. He had a smug expression as he turned to look at the other five police officers in his charge. The young constable who had first reported the incident was even more relieved.

News broke out of a phenomenon occurring over the Great Wall, and it was not long before the television stations had their helicopters hovering over the wall. They were observing an army that had not been seen for over two thousand years, and this army was now marching in a north-eastern direction along the walkway on top of the wall.

They were in time to witness the clay warriors urging their steeds up one of the many irregular stairways, and after unhitching the horses, the soldiers lifted the few chariots up to the top of the stairs. They then hitched the horses up again to continue their march. They made impressive footage for the news crews as they marched five abreast following the heroic figure of the general on his great steed.

Police, led by the scruffy-looking man and the young constable from the police station at Xian, kept the crowd away from the approaching warriors. The police chief, in his ill-fitting uniform, and the young constable broke rank from their men and stepped forward to meet the awesome sight as it drew closer. When the warriors were only a few metres from the two perspiring police officers, the mounted general raised his right arm, and instantly, in one swift movement, the whole parade of soldiers became motionless.

Overhead, the news cameras were still recording the sight below. Whether this was a hoax or whether it was something else didn't matter to them; this spectacle made a good story for a news-starved society, and for the authorities to allow them to film any event this freely was a great bonus.

The chief nervously motioned and yelled out an order for the man on the lead horse to step down. Not a sound or the slightest movement came from him or the other petrified statues, which were seemingly frozen in time. With perspiration running down his face, the officer slowly drew his old gun and aimed it at the general. Both motionless, they stared at each other for several minutes.

The statue of the general suddenly raised its right arm in such a swift motion that it startled the constable; he fell backwards onto the floor, jerking his firearm and squeezing the trigger. A shot rang out, and the sound it made echoed throughout the hills; the figure of the general shattered, almost as if in slow motion, into a hundred pieces, showering the two constables with debris. Immediately, from the line of soldiers, an archer drawing an arrow from his quiver jumped up onto the side wall of the walkway, and in an instant, an arrow flew through the air and hit the chief's loose-fitting shirtsleeve, knocking the gun out of his hand.

All who witnessed the event were petrified and glued to the spots where they stood; now there was no doubt that these soldiers were the terracotta warriors of Emperor Shi Huangdi.

The other police officers were at a loss as to what action they should take; they watched, transfixed, to the sight that unfolded before their eyes. The head of the general had landed close to the young constable, and it was mainly still intact except for a broken nose, while the body had scattered over a wide area.

A gust of wind sprang up, and grey dust formed into a small whirlwind that meandered around the broken fragments. The wind was powerful enough to gather the pieces spread on the wall and slowly place them in a pile close to where the head had fallen. The heaped pieces started to vibrate and move about, and each bit sorted itself into its appropriate position; slowly, the shape of the general's reclining body took form. The policemen who were close to the action could see the cracks between each splintered joint, and as they watched, they saw the cracks fuse together and the fine lines disappear, making the general's body whole again.

The headless body came to life, and to the amazement of all who saw, it sat up, rolled over onto its knees, and rose to its feet it, standing erect. The body turned, slowly shuffled forward, and stood in front of the petrified young constable; the statue bent slightly, stretched out its right arm, and pointed to the head that lay next to the young man. The police officer understood what was expected of him, but he was too scared to move.

The police chief, still lying close by, stuttered out a command. "Pick it up—pick up his head, and put it back on," he whispered to him.

All of China saw a brave man bend down and pick up the heavy head. They watched as he hesitantly lifted it above the general's body and put it in place between his shoulders. The general's eyes opened, and the boy noticed the missing piece that had broken off his nose. He looked down and saw it at the general's feet; he picked it up, and smiling confidently, he placed it on the commander's face, where it immediately fused back into place.

The general walked back to his steed, placed his left foot into one of the stirrups, and leapt onto his mount. He raised his arm, and the army started their deafening march forward as the young constable helped his superior out of the way. The line of policemen who had been in front of the approaching horde had deserted their posts the moment they'd seen their comrade put the general's head back in place.

The many news helicopters had to shuttle backwards and forward between their refuelling depot and the awe-inspiring events happening below them. The Chinese premier had ordered the television networks to telecast this phenomenon to the rest of the world. Billions of people watched as the grey warriors paraded on one of the great wonders of the world—the Great Wall that threaded its way through mountainous countryside for over 2,700 kilometres.

The untiring soldiers marched day and night, heading north-west towards the capital, stopping only to carry the chariots and sometimes to aid the horses up or down the many stairways that the Great wall consisted of.

On the morning of the third day, the warriors' advance was interrupted. A figure dressed in white appeared as if from the air itself; he stood two hundred metres in front of the warriors, who, in unison, came to an abrupt halt as soon as they saw the general's right hand rise. One of the officers riding alongside the general dismounted, and instantly, the dull-coloured steed reared up on its hind legs and galloped towards the man ahead.

The horse stopped next to the man in white and reared and, whilst doing so, turned to face the direction it had come. Nobody saw how the man ended up on the steed's back; one second he was standing next to the horse, and the next instant, he was mounted in its faded saddle, and it began to canter back to the waiting soldiers.

This new incident unfolding before the world's eyes was to get stranger; the horse's colour made a transition from dull green to a vivid white that matched the rider on its back. The saddle turned a satiny black and shone in the morning sun, and the grey blankets underneath the saddle were now made up of many bright colours befitting an emperor's steed's dressage. Even the bridle and the reins had changed to their original black tones.

The white steed pulled up when it met up with the other soldiers. It reared once more and majestically turned to take its position in between the general and the other officer. The world soon understood that Daniel, the messenger, was leading the terracotta warriors.

Overhead, the people in the hovering choppers recorded an unbelievable sight: the general and the first few rows of warriors were no longer a dull grey colour; their armour had changed to the bright colours it would have originally been before being ravaged by time. They could see that slowly, each line of soldiers changed to match the rows in front of it, and it took several hours for the thousand-plus warriors to transform to their original splendour.

In Beijing, the State Council had gathered at the Great Hall of the People to commence their meeting of the Communist National Party. The premier stood on the podium, closely watched by the thinly built secretary, who sat at the rear of the stage; rumour had it that the secretary had been unable to talk for several days, and the doctors had no answer as to what had caused his sudden and unusual affliction.

The meeting of the leaders of the most heavily populated country in the world was being telecast live worldwide for the first time.

"In the past, I have mentioned to the honourable state councillors the meeting that I attended on the island of Malta. I also enlightened the people of the republic in a special speech to the nation some eighteen months ago. Most of the world's leaders highlighted to their people the existence of the prophet, Daniel. You chose to ridicule me and wanted my resignation; I declined and assured you that proof was forthcoming. Today there is no jeering; you are listening to me because you have seen what is happening at our Great Wall. You know who is leading the warriors, I suspect, to this very place."

The premier's speech was interrupted by a thud on the massive wooden front door, followed by several other thumps coming from the entrance, which they could hear throughout the Great Hall. The guards on the inside of the double doors drew their guns as metal spikes protruded through the thick, old wooden planks. The premier indicated for them to open the doors, and they cautiously pried them apart. The people on the inside clambered over each other to see what was occurring outside.

On the grounds of the great Tiananmen Square, the symbol of China, with Chairman Mao's portrait looking down over them, the terracotta warriors were assembled in perfect rows before the Great Hall of the People. In the front line, the archers—some kneeling and others standing—had their bows drawn, awaiting further signals from their general, who was mounted on his black steed on their left flank. On the right flank, on a white steed, was a man most people of the world now knew: Daniel. There was no need for the authorities to control the crowds of people watching intently; they stood well away from the frightening army.

Simultaneously, as if by some mental signal, the man on the white steed and the general on the black one guided their mounts front and centre of the troops. The general and the civilian stopped when they came face-to-face, and the mighty horses reared and neighed as if to greet each other. The general and Daniel turned their mounts to face the Great Hall, and with a quick spurt, the white horse carried his rider up the few steps and into the Great Hall, causing all before them to scurry away.

In an instant, with one brief motion, the warriors resumed the stance that they had held for centuries, and they were once again no more than they had always been—lifeless terracotta warriors. The repaired and colourful warriors would become a present to the people of China from the messenger.

Daniel's charger cantered down the middle aisle and stopped at the podium, where the amused premier greeted him. As soon as Daniel had dismounted, the white steed cantered back to the outside of the Great Hall and took up his position amongst his peers, and the horse too became nothing but clay.

Daniel stepped onto the podium and smiled at the terrified secretary. The little man's thin lips parted, and he uttered some words that embarrassed the lady councillor at his side.

Daniel had an attentive audience to talk to, from the leaders of China and their people to all of the world's population who had access to a television set or a radio.

The whole planet focused on him, and there was little doubt in the majority of people's minds who this man was.

Professor Morey peered through the massive telescope for some time before he lifted his head and looked in bewilderment at his young assistant.

"I can't figure it out, Clara; you're right—it is going away. It seems to be heading on a collision course with the sun."

"You have to wonder, Professor, just what is happening here."

"What is happening?"

"Yes, I mean, we had a comet on a collision course with Earth. We told the world authorities, and they did and said nothing." Clara shrugged, emphasising her puzzlement. "It was as if they knew something we didn't know. What information did they have that we didn't?"

"I agree; I have an unscientific theory you will laugh at."

"Anything to do with that guy—you know, the prophet?"

A surprised look came over the older professor. "Yeah, I hate to say this, but I really believe he is for real. I have been reading about his teachings on the natural Creator, and let's face it—what else could make a comet change its course like that?" He walked over to a globe of the world and spun it around a few times. "All the many activities that have taken place on our small planet had me thinking that something big was happening. Just imagine getting the AIDS problem under control and the Middle East crises nearly solved; there hasn't been a suicide bomber over there for over a year. Now drug use has gone down dramatically, and the reforestation of the world is happening at an unbelievable rate. The threat of a holy war is all but over, and the march of the warriors in China has this new religion instigated by Daniel growing so fast that I would say that a quarter of the world's population is already following it. By the end of this decade, I predict that ninety percent of the people, including me, will be believers."

"You can count one more here, Professor," a smiling Clara added as she looked up at the night sky.

CHAPTER 16

A lone and despondent man looked down from the rooftop of the building across the road from the Beijing Hotel. He looked down on the many thousands of people chanting his name.

Daniel's prominence had become his greatest dilemma. Word had spread that he was staying at the hotel, and so many people had converged on it that Daniel had to avoid being seen, mainly for the safety of the people themselves.

He was pleased with what he and his team had accomplished in a relatively short period, but he missed his anonymity. His friends were greatly concerned that they had not heard from him for several days after the terracotta-warrior saga. The man on the rooftop melded with the air around him, and the air became a breeze that blew over the people and entered the hotel. It went up the stairs and glided underneath one of the doors on the top floor, and it materialised into the man the person in the room had been anxiously waiting for.

"Daniel, where have you been? My God, we have been beside ourselves."

"Peter, I am grateful for your concern, but I have to consider my next move; please arrange dinner for tonight in a private dining room at the hotel, and I will see you there."

"Aren't you seeing Caris?" Peter asked in a surprised tone.

"I'll see her tonight; the less she sees of me, the better." He seemed abrupt to Peter.

Caris waited anxiously along with Peter and the cheerful pilot, Garry Foster. The waiters serving dinner to them were puzzled as to why they were serving for four; they were assured that another person was expected.

When the two waiters were out of the room, a mist entered the room, and Daniel materialised sitting next to Caris, who excitedly grasped his left hand and squeezed it tightly. Garry, who sat silently across the table next to Peter, although dumbfounded, accepted that nothing was beyond the power of Daniel.

The waiters came back to finish serving the first course and were surprised to see one of their countrymen as a guest of the Westerners. The uninquisitive waiters welcomed him in their language, to which he replied in perfect Mandarin, and they smiled and bowed as they served him.

Daniel lifted his glass, which was filled with a local red wine, and toasted Peter and Caris and thanked their pilot for his good work. They discussed the world situation and what their next step should be. Daniel believed Indonesia would have to be the next port of call, although Peter was quick to point out that President Dachamer Islamiyah was having great success in convincing his people to follow the new teachings.

The group talked gaily into the night until a sudden silence came over Peter. The others noticed his sombre face and the way he stared intently at Daniel, who sat across from him. He gave out a little, hesitant laugh and pointed at the lapel of his friend's immaculate white suit.

"I don't believe it." He smirked. "You have a spot on your suit; you actually have a spot on your suit."

Daniel looked down at the lapel to see the dark mark left by a droplet from his wine glass, and instantly, almost panicky, he tried to brush it off with a cloth napkin. He stared at the stain in disbelief for some time. To the others around the table, Daniel's reaction to something as trivial as a spot of wine on his suit seemed unwarranted.

A grave-faced Daniel looked up at Garry and, in a subdued voice, asked, "Would you please prepare our flight back to Australia? Early tomorrow would be great, if you can arrange it. Now, if you will all excuse me, I am going upstairs."

Daniel pushed his chair back, stood up, and looked deeply at Peter and Caris, and without saying another word, he left the table.

An uncomprehending Caris looked anxiously at Peter, who gestured for her to follow Daniel. She frantically pushed her chair back and hurriedly ran after him.

Upstairs, Daniel, motionless and silent, lay on top of the bed, staring at the decorated ceiling. Caris, knowing that words would not suffice, slowly stripped off each article of her clothing and let it fall onto the floor.

She sidled up to Daniel and took off his white shoes, and then, resting on her knees, she straddled him as she slowly undid the buttons on his shirt and unbuckled the belt on his trousers. She stood at Daniel's knees and managed to pull his trousers off and then help him out of his coat and shirt.

Caris tried hard to help Daniel get over whatever was troubling him, but she found it difficult to get any reaction from him. She straddled his naked body again and rubbed herself over him until she felt the hardening between his loins that she was longing for. He grabbed her, pushed her over onto the bed, and fell on top of her. Daniel kissed her passionately as he thrust himself into her; he looked into her eyes and whispered, "Now is the right time."

Sometime in the middle of the night, Caris woke and reached out for Daniel, but as she had found so often in the past, he was not there. She sat up in bed and saw his shadow out on the fifteenth-story balcony, staring up at the full moon. She quickly went out to join him and started rubbing her nakedness against his bare body, and they looked deeply into each other's eyes. Daniel took her hand and said, "Caris, will you take me, Daniel Leeder, as your wedded husband?"

Caris did not hesitate. "Yes, I will, and will you, Daniel, take me, Caris Marie Garvey, as your wedded wife?"

Daniel was quick to reply, "Yes, I will; and now, by all the power that has been vested in me by the universal Creator, I pronounce us husband and wife." And with that, Daniel kissed his bride.

Coming home to a dim, cold Melbourne day only made Daniel's growing depression worse, and he hated the thought that in the future, he would have to keep out of the public's sight. Boarding a cab at the airport, Caris sat in the back, while Peter sat next to the young Indian driver, who emitted a loud sigh and shook his head in agitation as soon as Peter gave him their destination.

"I am sorry, mister, but that road has been closed off for the last few weeks; the police control all traffic, and there are detours bypassing most of it, so I will only be able to take you as close as I possibly can."

"What's the problem?" Caris enquired.

"It is some bullshit, missus, about a prophet who lives there; no one has seen him there, but thousands of people are waiting for his coming, and more and more people go there every day," the driver answered as he manoeuvred his cab out of the airport. He peered at Caris through the rear-vision mirror, and he envied the man in the white suit sitting next to her.

It took him several moments before he realised that there was a man sitting in the back seat next to her who had seemingly appeared out of nowhere; he was sure only two passengers had boarded his cab, but now there were three.

The cabbie did his best to get them as close as he could to the warehouse as he tooted the car horn and weaved through the meandering crowd. The area for a kilometre around the warehouse was inundated with people. The driver reluctantly gave up, and apologising, he stopped the cab.

Peter put the fare into the cabbie's outstretched hand, and he had to laugh as he saw that the young man's main priority was having another look at the pretty blonde in the back of the cab. He looked at her longingly through the rear-vision mirror, and it again took him a few moments to realise that the man next to her was gone. The driver looked around the vehicle, but only the passenger who had sat next to him and the beautiful woman were there. The mystified man looked at Peter inquisitively, and the wink he got back answered his question.

"Was that him—was that the prophet? Now I remember; the man with the terracotta army—that was him," he raved excitedly as he watched the two walk away and disappear in the mass of people.

Young David Chan sat working on his computer. He had mastered the art of share trading and enjoyed what he did tremendously. His thoughts were with his mentor, when a tap on his right shoulder startled him. He quickly turned around to see a familiar although somewhat older face smiling at him.

"Daniel!" he called out as he jumped from his seat and hugged him.

David eagerly brought Daniel up to date on what had been happening at the warehouse. Their headquarters, now no longer a secret, had crowds of people endlessly walking past or stopping to pray in front of it. Scores of reporters had knocked on their door, trying to get information about the prophet. A group of worshippers had started a vigil a couple months before, and it grew larger each day. There were peddlers out in the crowd selling portraits and statues of the new Messiah, and David chuckled as he described the white-suited statuettes and portraits that were replacing or standing next to images of Jesus in most Australian homes. Across the road in front of the warehouse, newspaper and television reporters had taken over the shops and offices, and active cameras protruded out of the upstairs windows.

The curious crowd outside watched as a pretty blonde woman wearing a skirt that showed off her shapely, long legs battled her way through to the warehouse door with a handsome fair-haired male companion. Recognising the two on their monitors, the security guards automatically opened the front door and let them in. The burly men at the main door had to push back the few onlookers who tried to follow Peter and Caris inside.

The Indian taxi driver showed up at the door just as it slammed shut, and he excitedly yelled, "The prophet—he is here! I brought him here in my taxi."

Peter interrupted David's update and escorted Daniel to his room and insisted that he rest for a while. He rang the kitchen and ordered a cup of tea and a sandwich for him and then sat down and looked inquisitively at his friend. Daniel gave him a reassuring smile.

"I am so sorry for being so selfish," he told his friend.

"Selfish? When have you been selfish?" an intrigued Peter asked.

"Back in Beijing, when I realised that my powers may have reached their peak, I became very dismayed; I wanted them to keep growing. I realised I liked my powers for the wrong reason; I should have been elated that we were turning the corner for the better, but I wasn't." Daniel, disappointed with himself, spoke quietly. "Now I realise that my mission, the reason I am here, has been a success—at least for now. Peter, the planet has been saved, and we have to ensure it stays safe."

Daniel reached out and held his friend's hand, and although he tried to sound happy, the sadness came through the charade.

"My time with you is limited; it is much shorter than I had envisaged, yet there is so much more to do. The world seems to be safe for now, but for how long it remains safe, I don't dare to speculate."

Daniel fell into a calming silence, and Peter knew his friend well enough to know that he was contemplating something new to alleviate his concern. Caris walked into the room after having freshened up. "I'm not disturbing anything, am I?" she said sarcastically as she saw the two men holding hands.

"As a matter of fact, yes, you are. Peter was about to tuck me into bed," Daniel said with a smile that made both his companions feel better that at least he still had a sense of humour. "But in truth, I do need some rest,

Caris, if you don't mind staying in another room for tonight, and, Peter, thank you for the tea, my friend. Now I would ask you both to leave me be; I will retire early, and I will see you tomorrow sometime."

The next morning, young David knocked urgently on Peter's bedroom door, and when the response to his rapping didn't come quickly enough, he started yelling out.

"Peter, Peter, come quick! Come and see what's happening!"

"What's so damn urgent that it can't wait till daylight?" the yawning and jetlagged man said, berating David as soon as he opened the door.

"That's just it, Peter—it is daylight. It's after nine in the morning."

Peter looked back into his room and at the bedside clock and realised that although he had put the lights on, the room was still dark—not pitch black but dark and murky enough that he couldn't see the clock face. He looked out over David's head into the corridor, and all he could see was an eerie darkness. The atmosphere had a strange feeling about it.

"What is going on—is there a fire?" Peter was now wide awake.

"No, it's not a fire or anything like that; it seems to be some kind of shadow," David said as he screwed up his face, highlighting his Asian appearance even more than usual.

Peter went to the window and looked out into the street and up to the sky, but all he could see was the murkiness. It didn't look like any type of fog he had seen before, and he reasoned that with a fog, one would still be able to see a reasonable distance around him or her. And fog would not be inside one's home. This darkness was all around, giving the appearance of sunset—the moment just before the sun fell over the horizon—only it had a dense feel and look about it.

"It's all over the place," David told Peter. "Mum rang me from the capital, and Canberra is covered in this black shadow too. And one more thing that I found very strange: Mum said that she had a very vivid dream last night about Daniel and his mission. The strange thing about it is that I had the same dream she described to me."

Peter looked at David and shook his head. "Even stranger then, I had a similar dream too." His mind suddenly came to a realisation. "Daniel—where is Daniel?"

David shrugged. "I knocked on his door first, but there was no answer; I thought he may have been with you."

Peter ran to Daniel's room, knocked loudly, and, not hearing any sound, tried to open the door; the handle turned, and Peter realised that although the door was not locked, he could not push it open.

Frantically, he called out, but to no avail, and he knew that to persist would be fruitless; he had no doubt Daniel was the cause of the blackness around them.

They heard Caris calling out to them from the lounge room. "Come and listen to this."

The ruckus Peter and David were making had awakened her, and she was intrigued by the mysterious fog around her. Caris was listening to the radio, and the two men joined her in time to hear the excited voice of the broadcaster repeat the announcement he'd previously made.

"The world has been engulfed in a shadow. Scientists have no explanation as to the cause of this phenomenon, but we do know that this darkness originated in eastern Australia and has worked its way rapidly westwards, seemingly following the night. The darkness is persisting even after the sun rises; so far, the half of Earth's surface that should now be in daytime is in darkness. Scientists are predicting that the rest of the world, which is currently in its night period, will awake also engulfed in this shadow. Just as a side note, which may or not be related to this phenomenon, the people from this station have come to the realisation that we all had a very deep sleep last night and had the same vivid dream. We received a message from the prophet, Daniel, warning us of an imminent danger facing our world unless we change our way. I, for one, am not into religion, but we have received hundreds of calls from viewers stating the same, and our investigations indicate that this is happening worldwide. I will leave you to contemplate that while we take a break."

"I'm making myself some breakfast," Peter announced. "I think we have a long wait before this is over."

Peter could not remember a day as unusual as this one or one that had passed so slowly; it was a Claytons day—the day that wasn't a day. The shadow lingered, and the people in the warehouse spent most of the time meditating; foremost on their minds was the message they had dreamed about the previous night. The well-being of the planet and all its inhabitants had been the essence of the dream. The environment was not separate but intermingled within each and everything on Earth.

The day climaxed slowly, and the persistent shadow had now amalgamated with the actual darkness that came with the night. Awareness was something that was missing from the group at the warehouse in their lethargic mood, so it was not too surprising that it took some time before they realised that the darkness of the night had actually taken over from the shadow.

Caris gave a yelp in excitement. "The television screen—I can see the TV."

Peter instantly leapt from his seat and ran down the hallway to Daniel's room; he cautiously pushed the door, and it slowly opened. The dark room lit up as he flicked the light switch, and his heart skipped a beat as he saw Daniel lying on the floor beside the bed.

"Daniel, Daniel!" he called to his friend as he picked him up with surprising ease and laid him on the bed. Caris and David ran into the room, and Peter held them back. "Leave him be for a few minutes. I think he is okay." Peter tearfully looked at them. "He weighs nothing; he's as light as a feather."

"I'll call an ambulance," David told them as he quickly headed for the open door, but the door suddenly slammed shut and would not open to let him out.

"It's stuck—the bloody thing won't open." He cursed as he pulled on the handle. He stopped his struggling and sheepishly walked to Daniel's side. "You don't want me to get help for you. But, Daniel, you are sick; we have to take you to the hospital. Please, Daniel, you have to get better." David cried openly. His tears subsided when he saw the feeble smile coming from his mentor.

Daniel slowly opened his mouth, and a weak voice came forth from between the stained teeth. "I will be all right, my young friend—just need a little rest."

The other two gathered over David and peered down over his shoulders at the once-magnificent large blue eyes that had now faded to a dull, darkened, indistinguishable colour.

"Why—why do this to yourself?" Peter asked. "Why put yourself through all this when you are not well? You have overexerted your powers again, Daniel; you could have killed yourself."

Daniel gave Peter a little smile of reassurance. "This was the only way I could ensure that everyone on this planet received my message." Daniel struggled to talk, and as Caris reached down and touched his lips in an endeavour to stop him from wasting his strength, he shook his head. "Do not worry, Caris; my time is not quite yet. Let me talk." He smiled at her, and her mind went back to only a few days ago, when a handsome, strong man had told her that it was the right time and had made her his wife.

"All the people of this world now know of our mission, and they have been warned. The twenty-four-hour shadow cast all over the world has now started to lift, and it will be another twelve hours before it completely vanishes from the face of the world. The whole planet went into a dreamtime and is still partly so; all have now been warned, but only the very soul-of-the-earth people—the free spirits of the old world who still live in the forests and the deserts—will understand and follow the dream that came to them. They will understand, for they are the ones who do not hold those high college degrees that so many of today's people have. These highly educated people are too smart, and they think they know all there is to understand. They are not smart enough to appreciate that they know very little of what matters most. They are the logical people who do not comprehend that the universe is not logical and is in itself a being that houses all that we have and all that we see and all that we can imagine."

Daniel gave out a long sigh and looked at his three friends. "I need to rest to prepare myself for the guests who are on their way here." And with that, he closed his eyes and fell into a deep sleep.

They sat around the large table in the boardroom, waiting for Daniel to open discussions. The long-and-stringy-haired man in tatters at the head of the table stood up and officially welcomed the many guests from all over the world. "You are wondering why I now look like a shadow of the man I used to be. Well, rejoice, my friends—rejoice, for what you see in front of you is the sign that I—or should I say we—have been waiting for. My demeanour is the Creator's barometer of the state of our world, and the condition of my clothes is the first indication that my powers are waning. My friends, my time is near, but yours has just begun."

The ailing man sat and rested as he sipped some water, while Peter comforted Caris, who was in tears as she listened to the man she loved talk about his demise. Daniel stood up again and gathered his strength to enthusiastically utter, "You and many more have all been pivotal one way or another in our mission, and all the hard work you have done has paid off. The world is now safe—at least for the present."

"Daniel, how can you be so sure that all is safe?" Paula Chan asked.

"Paula, the comet that was approaching Earth has veered from its course and is now heading towards a self-destruct rendezvous with the sun. Such is the power of the natural Creator."

John B. Rose said, "Surely that would mean that our planet is safe, but you just mentioned that it was safe for the present."

"John, all it means is that we have set in motion enough programmes to start the reversal of the damage that we have caused to Earth. If you"—Daniel feebly pointed to the many disciples before him—"slacken in your endeavours and we go back onto the wrong path, a new comet—or something else—will destroy our planet. You must make your mission in life the beautification of our world and all that is in it. All the peoples of the many lands must be made aware of how close we came to utter destruction because of the ill treatment of our planet. The extent of the power of the Creator must be taught to all from childhood so that our children will grow up knowing that they are not just a creation but a part of the Creator, which loves every part of its body. All the Creator asks of us as his chosen caretakers of this part of his body is to look after it. That is all the gratitude it asks of us for our existence."

Daniel faltered, and a worried attitude came over him. "In my effort to help you and the people of this planet, to make it easier for all to follow the teachings of the Creator, I did something that may yet backfire. You, my friends, have a tremendous responsibility; you must remind the population of the world—and remind them constantly—of the dream that came with the shadow, for if they do not follow its warning, they will perish. For now, the people of the world have been left with part of the shadow contained deeply within each of them, acting like a gauge, and if they stray too far from what is expected of each of them, this gauge will activate and kill them—no different from the gauge the Creator has placed inside me.

"My friends, if too many people die because they ignore the warnings or go back to the old ways, then surely this in itself may make matters worse for the world. The Creator may yet destroy this planet because of my impulsiveness."

The listeners could sense that Daniel doubted himself and the success of his mission. Silence overtook the room, and in turn, Daniel also sensed their doubt in their ability to continue the mission without him. He gathered all his strength, stood up, and enthusiastically smiled as he picked up a wine glass, and looking over all his companions, he called out, "A toast to you all, for you are the leaders of this world, and I have no doubt whatsoever that you will complete the mission I was put on Earth to instigate." Daniel drank to them, and when he finished, he again called out, even louder than before. "Again I say to you, rejoice, as you have all done me proud; let us enjoy this supper together and drink heartily for a job well done."

Dinner was served, and they all smiled back at Daniel as they realised that for now, the impossible had become possible and the major task that they had undertaken had succeeded.

The meeting adjourned, and Daniel spent the next few days talking to the attendants individually to instruct and help them in their own special tasks. On the first day, he initially met with Paula Chan, Boris Zabloski, and Phillip Azage. They ruled their countries and, therefore, needed to return to their duties.

Paula stayed after the other two dignitaries had left, and Daniel embraced her and thanked her for the great effort she had personally put into their quest. She tried hard to keep her composure, but the thought of Daniel not being somewhere in her life made her burst out in tears, and she hugged him one more time, turned, and, still sobbing, quickly hurried out of the room.

Throughout the day, he met the others one at a time until he only had four more to go. Jimmy came into the room, followed by Henry, whose face showed the sorrow he was feeling, yet the young Aboriginal had his usual large smile. Henry wondered how Jimmy could be so happy, knowing that Daniel's time was near and that soon they would have to face the fate of the world on their own.

"I have looked into your mind, my friend, and I can answer that question for you. You still have not grasped what death really is, and you believe that I will be lost forever, but Jimmy knows that death does not mean it's the end. He knows that death is but the next step of the evolutionary process. Henry, you have just proven the point I was making a few days ago—an educated man such as you would not understand, whilst an uneducated man such as Jimmy would understand the simplicity of death."

Daniel had purposely avoided any contact with Caris since the group meetings had begun. There was a knock on his bedroom door, and he watched from his seat as it opened slowly and Caris entered.

"Why are you avoiding me? What terrible thing have I done to warrant this treatment from you?" she pleaded.

"You have done nothing wrong, Caris; you know that I love you as much as ever," Daniel told her passionately. He raised his arms outwardly to his sides. "Take a good look at me; I am an old man."

Caris ran to him and dropped onto her knees in front of him, and as she grabbed his hands and put them to her face, she sobbed out loud. "Daniel, do you think that matters in the least? It's you I love! No matter what you look like, it's you I love." She kissed both his hands repeatedly, and then she stood and tried to kiss him on the lips, but Daniel turned his face away from her so that she could not see the pain he felt.

"Caris, please remember me as I was; remember the passionate kisses we shared when we made love—love that was so beautiful and lasting. Remember how we longed to be in each other's arms." Tears cascaded down her face, and he too had tears in his eyes as he pleaded with her. "That's how you are to remember me." Daniel was insistent. "Our time was then; it is not now or anytime in the future. You are a young, beautiful woman, and you have a long life ahead of you. You will have a lot of responsibilities to face in the near future, and you will need someone at your side to help you. More importantly, he will need you as much as I have needed you, for the safety of this world will fall into his hands."

Caris was trying to follow what Daniel was saying, and it suddenly dawned on her; now she understood.

"Now is the right time." She smiled as she remembered what he had said to her the last time they had made love. "Now is the right time," she repeated as she touched her stomach, and looking up at Daniel, she saw his large smile beaming back at her.

"Peter loves you, and he always has," he told her. "Help him as you have helped me."

The night of the seventh day was an eerie one; the dark clouds blanketed the night sky in pitch-blackness, a deep darkness never witnessed before. An air of the supernatural surrounded all things, and all earthly creatures experienced a haunting feeling. Complete stillness filled the night, and not the slightness movement could be felt or seen. The humidity was so thick that it was a burden to breathe. It was as though the small blue planet had been deserted and left meandering meaninglessly through the universe.

Thousands of people kept their nightly vigil and huddled together beside the many fires outside the warehouse, which was now considered a divine shrine. The lights over the city of Melbourne and its suburbs had dimmed beyond the control of the power companies.

In the faint glow of the candlelit boardroom, Peter sat across from Daniel, and the two talked of the last few years together and their achievements. Peter, distraught and bewildered, fought back the tears that had built up within him. The sight of his friend aging before him was hard to bear.

A voice that made Peter leap to his feet boomed inside his whole being; he looked across at Daniel and realised it was not him talking. Daniel appeared lifeless and stared in front of him.

"You were the person chosen to see me in my incarnation as a human, and I want you to be the last to see me when I leave again." The booming voice faded, and Daniel's voice came to the fore. Peter could see his lips moving. "Peter, you have been a loyal friend, and I beg your forgiveness for what I have done and for leaving you."

"Daniel, you can't go anywhere—the world needs you. Caris needs you. I need you. Without you, we are nothing; you have made us what we are. Please fight, Daniel—fight whatever is doing this to you. Fight hard, and stay with us."

"I know that you realise that this is not of my doing. My time here has passed; it had passed once before, and it has passed again."

"Daniel, I do not understand what you mean by it 'passed once before.' How could your time have passed before?" the puzzled man enquired.

The booming voice echoed inside Peter once again. "I am the embodiment of all creation condensed into the body of one human body." Daniel's voice then continued. "I am the man who murdered his wife. I am Daniel Leeder, and I killed her in a murderous rage when I discovered she was having an affair with my best friend. My love for her was so great that I would have died for her, but in an instant, this love turned to hate, and I took her life. I drove away and somehow ended up at the Flinders Ranges. I wandered through the bush for several days, mostly in a daze, not knowing what to do, but mostly I wanted to die.

"Somehow I found myself back at my car, and I desperately tried to find something to kill myself with. What I found were a cigarette lighter and a plastic water bottle, and I siphoned petrol from the car into it. I piled a heap of dry branches, sat on them, and poured the petrol over me, and with no hesitation, I set myself alight. I remember the excruciating pain as the flames engulfed me and the sheer panic as I tried to stand, but in an instant, as everything went black, I felt a heavy mist covering me as if a blanket were being wrapped around me—and I dissolved into it." Daniel stopped talking, and Peter could see the pain on his face—a pain that he was reliving.

"The rest you know." He let out a long, deep sigh. "My mission was not to save the world on my own; my mission was to find the right people to lead the rest of the world on the right path. The irony here, my friend, is that I have turned out no different from the ones who came before me. Peter, in my mind, I wanted so much to be different, but now I know that I basically imitated the messengers who proceeded me. I preached and performed miracles, and now I leave you with the inauguration of yet another religion. The only difference between my predecessors and me was that I didn't rely on faith; the majority of the populace of this world witnessed my miracles with their own eyes, thanks to modern technology. The future generations will have visions of my deeds, and they too will not have to rely on faith, so maybe it will be easier for them to believe.

"I wonder—if my predecessors had had the same advantages I had, would the world be different today? Would they have achieved what I have in such a short time? Peter, my friend, only time will tell, and time is the most precious commodity we humans have. Time passes swiftly. People forget the past, and they tend to go back to the easier way of life. Do not let this happen, as I do not believe the Creator will be as tolerant in the future by giving humanity another chance. You, my friend, must be the one to keep my followers together and lead them, for the world's future is in your hands. You must keep them focused on their own individual tasks and help them to achieve their goals. This will be your life and your mission, Peter: save the world, and keep it safe."

Daniel's voice faded for a moment, and Peter heard the sadness that came from deep inside him.

"I will be leaving you, and I will be leaving the way all creatures on this world do; we come with nothing, and we leave with nothing. Tell the world that I am and I was the last hope for this planet, for I am to be the last warning, the last messenger. One personal thing I ask of you, my dearest friend: please look after my Caris and my children."

Peter was intrigued by this request, but only for a moment, as the voice of the figure in front of him faded even more, and Peter could tell that Daniel's time had come. In the dim room, Peter stood up and walked closer to his friend, but he was lifted off his feet by a bright light that emanated from Daniel's body, and the force of the light carried Peter through the air and pinned him gently to the back wall. He watched as a man in a tattered white suit stood with his hands extended before him, and Peter noticed that the man had three fingers missing from his left hand.

Suddenly, a wall of fire erupted and engulfed the man totally, and almost as quickly, the flames turned into a fine mist that hid Daniel from sight. Peter's face showed fear—not only at what he saw before him but also for the unknown fate of his friend. In the now-well-lit room, the hazy mist expelled all the colours of the rainbow from within it, and he saw a grotesque shape emerge from it. A mess of burned flesh all meshed together hung down from a horribly scorched body.

Peter saw the outstretched limbs reaching out towards him, grasping at the air. The hazy mist, with all its glorious colours, became denser; it engulfed the shapeless body like a blanket, and instantly, the whole mass became one. Only two large blue eyes remained, vividly visible amongst the brightness of the mist, and Peter wept openly as he saw the teardrops of sadness falling freely from the eyes.

A new brightness emanated from the glow that swirled around the odd shape that had changed from a lumpy mess to an illumination as bright as the sun itself. The room glittered with a brilliance that blinded Peter to the extent that he could no longer distinguish anything else before him except for a rising light.

A voice he knew well—and a voice that had new strength within it—called out to him, "Peter, nothing can ever be utterly destroyed."

The light vanished through the roof of the warehouse and out into the world outside.

The bewildered people out in the street were on their feet; they had just witnessed a light so bright that the inside of the whole building in front of them had become visible. They too were blinded, and they too could see only the concentrated light, which their eyes had followed from the ground to where it had reached a few metres above the warehouse. The light hovered for a few moments, and in the excitement, the people did not notice the strong wind that had sprung up. The light started to move and started to spread over the dark sky, and as quick as a flash, the sky was not dark anymore; it took on a brightness of all the colours of the rainbow. The brilliance lasted only a few seconds before it dissipated. Then the clouds suddenly disappeared, and they could see the stars again.

The light that had come out of the warehouse had spread throughout the sky before them, and it had become a part of the brightness that now was there. The brightness that emanated from the holy shrine was now indistinguishable from the rest of the glow given off by the full moon and the stars that made up this part of the universe.

When one looked forward at the time to come, it moved ever so slowly, but when one looked back at the time that had gone, it passed in a flash.

Another year had lapsed quickly, and people still gathered at the old warehouse, awaiting another miracle—or maybe the reappearance of Daniel. For now, they would have to be satisfied with watching the people who lived there go about their business.

They often saw the prime minister being escorted to this holy place as she came to visit, and she spent hours in consultation with the people who were the leaders of the new belief that the people of the world were quickly embracing. The masses held the occupants of the warehouse in revered awe and had learned to respect their privacy, for the fate of the world depended on them and their teaching. The world's population was now indeed a universal-Creator-fearing people, and they knew that to wander back to the path of wanton destruction of the planet meant the utter destruction of the world.

The outside watchers' favourite twosome was the handsome fair-haired man and the shapely blonde whom he often escorted. They pushed a large pram out of the warehouse and along the tree-lined footpath as they headed towards the new parklands that had been established close by.

On this particular day, a short, balding man approached them, and he kissed the woman on the cheek and shook hands with and hugged the man. "Henry, how are you, my friend?" the smiling fair-haired man said in greeting.

"Peter, it's terrific to see you and Caris again; it has been far too long. My work in the Middle East has kept me very busy for the last twelve months." He looked across at the pram and was hesitant, almost reluctant to satisfy his curiosity.

"This is them?" he asked Caris in a serious manner. "These are the twins?"

"Henry, they won't bite; they are only babies," Caris reassured him.

He sighed loudly and nervously as he went over to the pram; leaning down, he looked at the two babies for a long time, as if trying to take in every detail of their facial features. One baby was dressed in blue, and the other wore pink.

Henry stood up, bright eyed and almost in tears. "They are absolutely beautiful. Twins—one of each—and they have the biggest blue eyes I have ever seen." He hesitated for a moment, and as a sad afterthought, he muttered, "With one exception."

The leaves of the tree they were adjacent to rustled as a slight breeze sprung up and swirled around them. Not the slightest iota of dust or debris embraced the gentle wind, and they simultaneously felt as if a hand had touched their faces. They raised their hands to their cheeks and stroked the spots the breeze had touched, and they looked at each other in amazed wonderment with smiles of acknowledgement.

The two men looked up to the heavens and wondered, while Caris looked down at her babies, and tears of happiness came over her at the sight of the happily smiling twins.